RAEFORD'S
MVP

Rick DeStefanis

ISBN: 1519199260
ISBN 13: 9781519199263

Author's Note: For my readers unfamiliar with military jargon, there is a glossary at the back of this book. I strongly suggest you glance over it prior to beginning the story. Military acronyms, jargon and terminology are a reality of the world in which soldiers live. For this reason I use them in the same manner as those soldiers would. I also wish to express my sincere appreciation to all those who have assisted me in bringing this story to print. Thank you, Ellen Morris Prewitt, Chris Davis, Carol Carlson, Brian Patterson, Stacey Keene, Margaret Yates, Laura Stevens and Melody Bock. You all have been a key part of the creative process, and have made this a better story.

This book is dedicated to military veterans and the women who have stood with them during the worst of times.

1

PUT A CANDLE IN THE WINDOW

Central Highlands, Republic of Vietnam, 1970

Billy Coker sat on a sandbag, smoking a cigarette and staring out at the fog-shrouded mountains of Vietnam. It was another dripping wet afternoon—quiet, except for the muffled voices of his men, playing cards in the bunker below. The rain had passed, and somewhere on the firebase behind him a radio played Credence Clearwater Revival. John Fogerty's plaintive voice came from the outside world, "Put a candle in the window." It was Billy's invitation to become human again, because in less than thirty days the freedom bird was taking him home. He'd have a real bath, sleep in a real bed and no longer worry about dying or watching others die. He was happy to be leaving Vietnam alive and unscathed, but without a clue as to why. It was as if somewhere along the way his life had ended, and he didn't even know when it happened.

He dropped the cigarette into a puddle, and fished another from the pack in his pocket. Other than escaping his current predicament, a total lack of anticipation had him teetering on the finest edge between happiness and despair. Those years in high school when he thought he was on top of the world now came back to haunt him with guilt and regret. And the strangest part of it all—he wasn't even thinking about the last eleven months in Nam. His thoughts weren't about the futility of the war or any of the recent events that should have culminated as the defining experiences of his life. He wasn't thinking about the man he'd become, or the men he'd seen die in the mud and rain—men like Butch and Danny, men closer to him than his own brother.

He absentmindedly rubbed his thumb over the Saint Sebastian medal hanging around his neck. He rubbed it as he had a thousand times in the last eleven months. He had clung to the silly medal like a raft in a storm. It was a gift from Bonnie Jo Parker. He smiled at the thought.

Were she given the chance, Bonnie Jo probably could have charmed the pants off of most men, but she wasn't that kind of girl. She was one of the fat girls at Raeford High who wore glasses and laughed too much. She laughed, not because she was silly, but because she was happy. Billy had spent time talking to her when he could—just to be nice—but Bonnie Jo wasn't his type. Perhaps, this was why he thought about her so much. Seems the fat girls never got a break, and he sure as hell never gave Bonnie Jo one.

Of course, they hadn't been *close* friends—only buddies of a sort—but he'd seen her almost every day. He ran cross-country track, and he was good at it. Back then he was skinny as a rail, and he liked the running. It was a way to clear his mind, not that there was much to clear. But cross-country track was the only thing he did well, besides chasing girls. Billy lit another cigarette as he thought about his after school runs. Crossing the pasture behind the school, he took the same course every day, down the hill to the creek and up through the woods. Skirting the back of town, he went behind the drive-in and around the old gravel pits, making a six-mile circuit. And Bonnie Jo was almost always there sitting at the tables behind the Dairy Queen with a couple other girls. When he passed on the trail in the woods, they waved, but he seldom did more than raise a finger in acknowledgment.

They had been in school together since their freshman year. He'd passed her in the halls almost every day, but the first time they spoke more than two words was at the beginning of their senior year. It was a Saturday in September when she walked out of the dollar store in Raeford. Billy was staring at the sale sign in the window, "Women's Summer Clothes 50% Off", thinking of—what else?—a girl with half her clothes off.

"Hey, Billy."

Bonnie Jo stopped and smiled, but he was daydreaming his way into Sissy Conroy's pants, and several seconds passed before he realized she had spoken. She started to turn away, but he snapped out of his trance.

"Oh, hey, Bonnie Jo."

She turned back. "What's up?"

He cast another glance back at the sale sign and lingered a moment before giving up on his daydream.

"Oh, nothing. Just trying to figure out how I'm gonna pass natural science this year. I failed the first test."

Billy began walking toward his truck. It was parked down by the Laundromat. Bonnie Jo tagged along.

"The way the football players talk, I thought you helped them with their studies."

"I only help those assholes with English," he said. "Grammar and comp are easy, but I'm not worth a crap with math and science. I missed all the test questions on population statistics."

"Why do you call them assholes?"

" 'Cause they are—and so are most of the cheerleaders and the rest of their cliquey friends."

"Hmmm," she said. "I thought you were part of their group."

"Not really. I just run cross-country and try to survive in their world. All I want to do is graduate and get the hell out of here."

"I can probably help you if you want."

"You think?"

"Sure."

Climbing in, he cranked the truck and rolled down the window.

"Need a ride?"

"You don't mind?"

He glanced over his shoulder to see if anyone was around. Giving a fat girl a ride in Raeford, Mississippi got you permanently stigmatized by the Lizards. The name was his personal invention—one he was proud of. They all wore shirts with little Alligators on them—but he figured they were more like lizards.

"Get in," he said.

"My house is out that way, off the highway." She pointed up the street then glanced down at the schoolbooks on the seat. "So, let's start with what you know."

She picked up the science book and opened it.

"That won't be hard. I don't know shit about natural science."

Bonnie Jo giggled but stared straight ahead down the road.

"What's so funny?" he asked.

"Nothing," she said, "except that's not what I've heard."

"Huh?"

"Never mind. I was just kidding."

It finally dawned on him what she was implying.

"You can't believe the crap you hear," he said.

It was better to lie than to be like the jocks who bragged about their sexual conquests, most of which Billy was pretty sure were with their hands and not with the girls they claimed. He continued driving past the traffic light, and headed east out the highway. The roadway narrowed just outside of town passing a pasture ripe with the odor of cattle manure. White cattle egrets roosted on the backs of Black Angus that grazed in scattered groups all the way to a distant tree line.

"Oh, well, I'm glad it's not true," she said.

The tone of her voice was patronizing, but he let it pass as she thumbed through the first chapter.

"So, tell me," she said. "What do you consider the best relationship for humans to have with their environment?"

"What the hell does that have to do with anything?" he asked.

"It's the first chapter, dummy—Humans and Their Relationship with the Environment."

"You mean like what's my idea of a perfect world?"

"Okay, what's your idea of a perfect world?"

"Are you sure you want to know?"

"Sure," she said. "Tell me about your Utopia."

It was time to give goody-two-shoes a dose of reality—show her what really matters.

"Okay," he said. "In a perfect world there's a high school called Beaver Valley High, and all the girls have perfect bodies and wear cheerleader outfits year round. And on weekends they're barrel riders in the local rodeo, crouching low on their quarter-horses with their perfect little butts bouncing high in the air as they whip around the barrels with auburn, blond and chestnut hair flowing from beneath their lady Stetsons."

She laughed. "Like I said, I've heard this about you, Coker."

"Heard what?"

"That you have a one-track mind."

She seemed so self-assured. It was time to turn up the heat.

"Hell," he replied, "You just don't know what *really* makes the world go 'round. Do you have a clue about the power women have over men?"

"Power?" she said.

"Yeah. If women could find a way to make men mainline that stuff, they could rule the world with a syringe. I mean they practically own it anyway, but they can't disengage their hearts long enough to really take charge."

She rolled her eyes. "You're confusing 'means' with 'motivation'."

"Means and motivation?"

"Yeah, most girls just don't think that way."

He turned and looked at her. "You think I'm crazy, don't you?"

Bonnie Jo pointed to a blacktop road up ahead. "Turn up there on that road," she said. "No, you're not crazy. Your hormonal overload isn't any worse than most guys your age. That house down there on the right."

"So you think it's only the guys that are crazy, huh?"

He slowed his old truck and turned into her drive. A long gentle curve of pavement took them through mature oak trees and up to the house. One of the nicer places around Raeford, the house had large gables and a big front porch.

"You want to come in?" she asked.

He shook his head. "I can't. I gotta get home to check on Mom."

"Is she sick?"

"No, not really—I mean, I don't know. It's just—she hasn't been doing so well since dad got killed last winter. Too much nerve medicine, I reckon."

Bonnie Jo looked off to the side and squinted. "I read about it in the paper," she said. "I mean, when your dad died."

"What's done is done," Billy said. "So, when do we have our first tutoring session?"

She gave him a sad smile and shrugged. "What's a good time for you?"

"How about Monday after I run?"

"Where?"

This was something he hadn't considered. The tables behind the Dairy Queen came to mind, but if he was seen hanging around town with her, the Lizards would harass the hell out of him, and it would definitely cost him some popularity points. He noticed a wooden swing hanging from a huge oak in her front yard.

"How about over there?" he said.

She shrugged.

"Weather permitting, it works for me."

"Sergeant Coker!"

Jarred back to reality—such as it was in Nam—Billy realized someone was calling him from somewhere in the warren of sandbagged bunkers encircling the firebase. Firebase Echo had been home as of late for his airborne infantry battalion. They'd been holed-up there for a month overlooking a road crossing near the A Shau Valley—'interdiction and pacification' they called it. George Custer tried the same thing with the Sioux. Billy almost laughed at the thought.

The surrounding mountains were crawling with North Vietnamese regulars, and the battalion had been whittled down to the equivalent of three lean companies of men. This was bad-guy territory, and the enemy called most of the shots. They even had anti-aircraft guns somewhere in the surrounding hills, which made re-supply choppers few and far between.

Again, someone call his name. Martin, one of Billy's men, stuck his head out of the bunker below. "It's one of the cherries," he said. "You want me to go get him, Sarge?"

"Yeah, if you don't mind. Go get him before a sniper takes his dumb-ass head off. And stay down."

They'd made him squad leader, probably by default, because had there been any competition, Billy was pretty sure he'd still be a buck private. Instead he'd spent the last three months trying to keep his men all in one piece. He figured that was the most important thing, because nothing else about this war made sense. He remembered how Bonnie Jo always said he was too cynical—especially when he called the Lizards egotistical jerks. If only she could see him now. He'd perfected cynicism in Nam. It was his forte, and he'd raised it to its highest form.

Martin crouched as he trotted back down to the bunker with the cherry. "Cherry here says Bugsy wants you up at the CP. Says it's real important."

Billy turned to the cherry. Dumb-ass nodded earnestly as if his role as messenger gave him some kind of authority. "If you don't stop wandering around in the wide-ass open, you ain't gonna live long enough to really enjoy this war."

"But, Sarge."

"No 'but' to it, dumb-ass. If you want to stay alive, start thinking like a soldier. These goddamn hills are crawling with NVA snipers, and they *will* put a round through that thick head of yours if you don't start using it for something besides a helmet holder."

Lieutenant Busby—or 'Bugsy' as the men called him—was the platoon leader. Billy decided to finish his cigarette. Sitting back down on the sandbag, he looked out across the mountains, wondering who he had become and where he was going when he left this godforsaken place. Other than eight weeks of Basic, nine weeks of Advanced Infantry Training and Airborne school, his resume before getting to Nam would say he'd read a few books and did a focused study on female anatomy. It was a damned shame. Here he was just nineteen years old and CMFIC of a combat infantry squad.

The CMFIC—that's who they ask for when they want to talk to the person in charge. People often thought it was an official military acronym, an understandable assumption, but an incorrect one. Billy exhaled a cloud of smoke into the stagnant afternoon air. CMFIC was an *unofficial* military acronym, that stood for Chief Mother Fucker In Charge. The real kicker was that his men actually thought he knew what he was doing. He was their squad leader, and they watched his every move, hoping he could show them something that would keep them alive just one more day. It would have been laughable had it not been so serious.

It was simply a matter of the one who'd been here longest leading the ones who'd just shown up. If it wasn't for the war, most of them, himself included, would have been down at a McDonalds by nightfall, trying to pick up chicks, drinking Old Milwaukee talls and listening to Hendrix or Steppenwolf. Instead, they were here on this godforsaken firebase, and Billy only hoped he could make a difference whenever the shit hit the fan.

Actually, he'd been fairly successful as a squad leader. He thought about it. Perhaps it was his ability to use their vices to motivate people. God knows, he had a few. And, the cherry was just a big dumb oaf—kind of reminded him of Raymond Hokes, another old Raeford

High classmate. Like Ray, the cherry wasn't too bright, and Billy realized he had to find a way to motivate him— give him something to think about beside the rain, rats and mosquitoes. He figured the best way was to find something he desired, perhaps tell him about the whores in Phu Bai, or the navy nurses on R&R down at China Beach. And if his experience with Raymond Hokes had any relevance, the theory might just work.

Sex was always his prime choice as a motivator, and it was with Ray that he first tested the theory. The way Billy had it figured, there wasn't a red-blooded boy anywhere in Raeford who wouldn't sell his soul for a few hours with the right woman—his reasoning being based on his own experiences since puberty. Women ruled the world, and he, Billy Coker was their slave. Albeit a willing one, he wasn't the only one enslaved by feminine charms, and his strategy for dealing with Ray Hokes greatly depend- ed on that assumption.

Ray always liked to start shit with anyone he found hanging around in the halls after school. Problem was he was a man amongst boys. Having failed the fourth grade twice, he was nineteen years old and the star line- man for the Raeford High Wildcats. Ray was a sum total six-foot-four and two hundred and eighty-nine pounds of pot-bellied redneck. And for some reason, he had de- cided to make Billy his whipping boy that year.

It was only the third week of school, and Billy had no intention of spending his entire senior year get- ting his ass kicked by Ray. Problem was a head-to-head confrontation with him was tantamount to suicide. Normal-sized humans had to rely on wit and guile to survive run-ins with Ray. That's how Billy came up with the plan he hoped would, as the guidance counselor might put it, 're-align Ray's priorities' or to put it in simpler terms, 'get him off his ass.'

School let out that day as the final bell rang and the student body burst through the doors like a covey of quail, leaving the ancient hallways all but empty. Billy was on his way to the locker room, his footsteps echoing in the silence, when he spotted Ray going into the boy's restroom. It was risky, but it was time to face his nemesis. It was time to try his new theory. And if it blew up in his face there'd be no witnesses. He would die and be buried on the schoolyard battlefield like thousands of nerd-warriors before him, but at least his annihilation wouldn't include public humiliation.

The way Billy had it figured, Ray was going to pound his head every day until he got creative and found a way to distract him. That's why he decided to ask him if he'd ever had any pussy—an exceptionally stupid question to ask Ray of all people, if he really meant it. One look at Ray and you knew he hadn't been near one since the day he was born—at least not one belonging to a human. Knowing his "agricultural" background, though, there may have been an unlucky farm animal somewhere along the way.

Billy slipped into the restroom behind Ray. Ray glanced over his shoulder and shuffled closer against the urinal. He was probably one of those delivered by a midwife in the country and never circumcised. You could always tell, because they often hid themselves, even in the locker room. Billy walked over beside him to take a quick pee.

"What the hell are you doin' in here, Coker?"

"Oh, hey, Ray. I saw you and was going to tell you something."

Ray finished and zipped up before backing away from the urinal.

"What?"

"Well…" Billy hesitated. He should have rehearsed. "Have you ever had any? You know?"

"Any what?"

Ray always seemed angry for no reason, and Billy found himself unable to muster a pee, so he zipped up and turned to face him.

"You know, pussy."

Priming Ray first hadn't occurred to him, but it was too late. The fuse was lit. Ray began stuttering, then turned and charged like a rodeo bull. Grabbing Billy's throat, he lifted him off the floor and pinned him against the wall between the urinals. This wasn't the way it was supposed to happen. Bad timing he figured, but he had to come up with plan 'B' quick or die.

"Wait a minute, Ray!" Billy said breathlessly. "Hold on a second. I need to tell you something, something important."

Ray hesitated with his fist drawn back as he held Billy there against the cold tile wall.

"What?"

His moronic little eyes came together like a pair of B-B's in the middle of his country ham face.

"What if I told you I know a girl who likes to mess around—you know? And she kind of likes you, too."

Ray's eyes narrowed even more until his brows nearly touched as he fought to focus on some shadow of a thought deep within. With this mask of total concentration covering his face, it seemed certain the cognitive overload was about to melt one of his two brain cells. Deep down in his heart Ray must have thought making love to a real girl was beyond the realm of possibility in his lifetime.

"Who?" he said.

Billy froze again. It wasn't that he didn't have in mind several of the finest specimens of female anatomy at Raeford High, but for some reason, he had a forevermore-unbreakable radar-lock on Sissy Conroy's most magnificent buns. This would never work. The mere idea was a desecration. Letting Ray have the misguided thought that he could dip into that little honey pot was totally repulsive. Death would be a better option, and for the moment, that possibility seemed imminent.

Skydiving couldn't have given Billy the adrenaline rush he had dangling there, his back against the wall and Ray's sledgehammer fist staring him in the face. He had to think. The toes of his tennis shoes barely touched the puddles of water on the floor, and Billy tried with all his might to come up with a name other than Sissy's. That was the one part of the plan he'd neglected. He needed a name—a believable one.

"Bonnie Jo Parker," he blurted.

The words no sooner left his mouth than Billy felt sickened by what he'd done. He was a loathsome jerk. He had just betrayed the girl who was going to help him graduate high school. Ray would trail her everywhere she went.

"I wouldn't touch that little pig," he snarled.

Guilt-ridden or not, it was too late to start over.

"Ray, I can't believe you would say that about Bonnie Jo. She's a little on the chubby side, but she's really a sweet person, and I think she likes you."

Billy's heart raced as he fought to catch his breath. Again, Ray's face became masked with concentration. Beyond the odor of Ray's bologna and mustard breath, Billy could almost smell his two brain cells smoking from the overload. Then slowly—so very slowly—Ray loosened his grip from around Billy's throat. His tennis shoes settle back onto the tile floor, and the smell of the urinal was like that of life itself, almost invigorating.

"What makes you think she likes me?"

It was think-fast-or-die-time again.

"I heard her say your name the other day while she was talking with some girls in the cafeteria."

Ray didn't say anything. That a female mentioned his name in conversation seemed an incomprehensible concept to him.

"I saw her looking at you in the hall, too."

Billy laid it on thick, and after a few moments the hormonal influence must have been too much for Ray's teenincy brain to overcome. He walked over to the mirror and gazed into the biggest section that wasn't cracked. With the heel of his hand he pushed his larded locks into place. Billy was frozen in place, pinned by his own fear, unable to move. Damn, Ray was ugly, and this lummox could go either way at any moment. Sucking down a deep breath, Billy took the first tentative step toward the door. Ray didn't seem to notice as he turned his head and studied his profile in the mirror. Billy bolted and didn't look back.

Sissy Conroy, the most glorious hunk of teenage womanhood in the school, owed him a big one. He had saved her from Ray, but since she was the heartthrob of most of the football team, crossing paths with her would probably never happen, at least in any significant way, such as undressing her and engaging in mad and passionate love making. She would never know how he had made Bonnie Jo her stand-in human sacrifice.

Taking another hard drag on the cigarette, Billy watched as the cherry stumbled down into the bunker. He was just another Ray Hokes. All he needed was the right motivation.

2

THE LAST PATROL

fter a while it dawned on Billy that Lieutenant Busby might be calling him to the CP to send him back to Camp Eagle for out-processing— a little early, but it *was* less than thirty days until his DEROS. They called it the date of estimated return from overseas service, but he was almost too burned-out to care. Flipping the cigarette butt into a puddle, he headed up the hill toward the command post. As he made his way up the muddy path, he spotted the young lieutenant coming down past the latrines. He was such an antsy fucker everyone called him 'Bugsy.' The lanky platoon leader must have grown impatient and come looking for him.

With his helmet on crooked and a couple days growth of beard, Bugsy looked a little ragged as he wove his way through the shell holes pock-marking the ground. The NVA had just about decimated the officer ranks, and Bugsy was both covering as a platoon leader and acting as company executive officer. The two men met and crouched together in a mortar pit. Billy glanced up to make sure they were below the edge of the sandbags.

Canvas tarps were draped over the mortar tubes to protect them from the rain, and wooden crates of ninety-millimeter rounds were stacked all around. The two men were sitting on enough explosives to blast them into a fine mist and eternity, something Billy would hardly have noticed until now. Now, with less than thirty days left on his tour, he was seeing danger everywhere, but the only way to escape it was to already be dead.

Incoming mortars and rockets were almost as common as the rain, but the thing he hated most was the sniper fire. The NVA would crawl through the high grass to within five hundred meters of the perimeter. There, they lay in wait, sometimes for days, waiting for someone to get careless and stand in the wrong place for too long. A whispering crack of a round would break the silence, punctuated by the screams of the poor fucker who'd been hit—unless, of course, he got it through the head. When that happened, there were only the screams of his buddies calling for a medic, a futile gesture since medics weren't much needed when someone got the third eye.

There was a hill directly behind the firebase—Hill 819. It rose up out of the ground over a klick away, a huge monolith. The firebase sat on a plateau overlooking the highway, but behind it was this mountain of jumbled ravines and broken timber towering above all else. Billy and his men watched day after day as everything from artillery, to helicopter gunships, Puff the Magic Dragon and F-4 Phantoms pounded 819. They dropped napalm, HE and every kind of human exterminator available, and what wasn't destroyed was pretty much vegematic'd, but the NVA still came out of the ground every night and showered the firebase with rockets and mortars.

Straddling a wooden crate of mortar rounds, Billy sat with his M-16 across his lap while Bugsy squatted against some sandbags and lit a Chesterfield. He shook another one from the little C-ration pack and gave it to Billy.

"So, wassup?" Billy asked.

"CO says we have to send a patrol up 819 to poke around," he said.

Billy laughed. "No shit?"

"No shit," Bugsy said.

Bugsy was always pulling practical jokes or saying some off-the-wall-bullshit until no one believed anything he said. Still, he was better than most of the officers. He never took himself too seriously. Unlike some of the gung-ho, John Wayne types, he wasn't here to get his ticket punched. Like Billy, Bugsy took care of his men, but his jokes got old after a while.

Billy shook his head. "Try again, LT, 'cause if it was April, I'd tell you that's the dumbest April Fools joke I ever heard."

Bugsy pooched out his lips and looked back toward the CP, as if he thought the CO might come down and participate in the joke.

"It'd take a reinforced battalion to recon that hill," Billy said.

The lieutenant still didn't smile, so Billy tried to humor him. "Lighten up, man. You should try that shit on one of the cherries. They'd take it hook, line and sinker."

"I'm not kidding, Billy."

Billy felt his face stuck on smile as he stopped laughing.

"What do you mean?"

"I'm not kidding. The old man says we have to send a reinforced squad over there to take a look around."

"No way."

Billy still didn't believe him. Bugsy always carried his jokes past funny.

"Look, Billy. Just get your men together for a briefing. I'm putting Curtis Teague and his gun crew with you, along with a couple extra riflemen. That'll give you two sixties and a total of fourteen men counting yourself."

"You're not going?"

Bugsy looked down at the ground.

"Why no officer on this one?" Billy asked.

"Look. You know me well enough that I'd go if the CO would let me."

"Why won't he?"

"I'm the only experienced officer left in the company besides the CO. He was going to get one of the platoon leaders from Alpha Company, but I talked him out of it. They're all brand new officers fresh out of OCS at Benning, and I think you'll do a better job."

"It's still bullshit! One hundred percent unadulter-ated bullshit! You and the goddam old man are out of your fucking minds. No, Sir. No way. Never happen, Sir. Court-martial my ass if you want, but I'm not taking my boys up in those woods, not now, not ever."

"Calm down, Billy."

"Calm down my ass, LT. We go up there, and some of us ain't coming back, and you know it."

"Look, just shut the hell up, and get your ass up to the CP, *now*! The men don't need to hear this crap."

Billy followed him up the hill to the CP and was about to tear into him again when the old man rounded the corner. The captain was pushing thirty, a real ass-kicker who was on his second tour. Billy respected him. Bugsy shook his head, and the CO nodded then turned to Billy.

"I figured you'd balk on this one."

"More like all-out revolt," Bugsy said.

"Sir, you can't be serious. No one in his right mind would go up that mountain, at least not without some serious manpower and a lot of TAC air on standby."

The CO pulled his helmet off and tucked it under his arm. He looked down at the ground for several sec-onds, then up at Billy. This wouldn't have meant much, except it was out of character for him. He was always 'fist-on-the-hip, stare-you-in-the-eye' honest. This sud-den change of demeanor said more than words ever could express.

"We don't have a choice," he said. "The orders are coming from people with a lot more brass than you and me, Billy. Yeah, it could get a little rough, but we're going to cover your butts. I'll have tactical air cover and arty on standby, and we'll put a big hurt on the little bastards if they fuck with you."

It was the tone of his voice that gave him away, and he called him "Billy" instead of "Sergeant Coker." It was a done-deal, one he'd probably already argued against himself, but it was out of his hands.

"Look, Billy," the Captain said. "All you have to do is make your way across to the hill and ease up to that first ridge. Try to spot any gun emplacements or signs of them digging in. With all the shit we've dropped up there, I don't expect you'll find much, but while you're up there we're going to bring in some gunships. If the enemy opens up with those anti-aircraft guns, you can try to pinpoint them."

Billy bit his lip as he fought to remain calm. "Sir, we've been cultivating that goddamn hill with everything we've got, and every night they show up again. They're up there all right. Hell, that whole goddamn mountain is full of tunnels and bunkers. The only thing that'll fix it is an Arc Light strike. You know it, and I know it, so let's not play games. If they get after us, we're fucked."

"How about let's stop the bitching and try to make the best of this?" the captain said.

"You think all I'm doing is bitching?"

The captain's face reddened. "Okay, Sargent Coker, I only wanted you, because you're my best NCO, but if you're scared, I'll get someone else."

Billy laughed. "Scared? Scared of what, sir, the heat, the mosquitoes, rats, rain, leeches—dying? Hell, why don't you just order us to do an all-out frontal assault on that damned hill?"

The CO turned purple as the veins bulged on his temples. Bugsy held up his hand to hold him in check. "Wait a minute, sir. Let me say something."

He turned to Billy, and put his hand on his shoulder. "Okay, Billy, you've made your point. It's a risky patrol, no doubt. Now, listen to me. Do you want someone else to take your men up there? I mean, we can tell them you aren't going because your DEROS is coming up, and you're going to start out-processing in a week or two."

Bugsy acted goofy at times, but he was slick.

"Are you saying my squad is going, with or without me?"

"Top to bottom, they're the best and most experienced squad in the battalion. We can put one of the new second lieutenants from Alpha Company with them, but one way or another, they're going."

Billy prided himself for taking care of his men, and he had played right into Bugsy's hand.

"Goddamit, Bugsy, you know damned good and well…." Billy paused. He didn't know what to say, and the two officers simply stood staring back at him. He was boxed in. Unless he wanted his boys going up that mountain with an inexperienced officer he had no choice. "Okay, goddamit. Show me what you have, and give me another one of those cigarettes."

Bugsy fished the wrinkled pack from his shirt pocket, and winked at the captain, but Billy caught him in the act, fixing him with a steady glare.

"Okay, Billy," the CO said. Billy slowly turned away from Bugsy to face the captain. "Here's what we're gonna do."

Spreading the topo map on an ammo crate, the CO exhaled and the bulged veins on his temples receded as he laid out the plan. The patrol was to depart the next morning, going through the wire at first light. This became the next point of contention. It made better sense to depart before dawn, and avoid crossing over a kilometer of relatively open ground between the firebase and the mountain in broad daylight. It was better to keep the enemy guessing, but Billy was overruled.

They were going to cross the open area after daylight so a forward observer could watch them through binoculars and coordinate air and artillery support if it was needed. The CO was right to some extent. The enemy always seemed to know when patrols were coming, anyway—probably the result of one of the Kit Carsons still switch-hitting. Billy didn't trust any of the turncoat VC they used as interpreters and guides, especially when his men were at stake. He won that small concession: no Kit Carson scout on this patrol, but it was a hollow victory. The scout wasn't needed anyway.

The next step was to take the plan to his men. He had to make them think the patrol was something necessary and worthwhile. Laying on the bullshit was going to be tough with this one. With their experience, his men wouldn't buy it, unless he spread it thick and wide. His jungle boots sank into the mud as he took his time walking back down the hill. Overhead the clouds were growing thicker, a precursor to more afternoon rain. He was in no hurry to face the guys and stopped to light another cigarette. If the enemy didn't kill him, the unfiltered Camels probably would, but it no longer mattered. Everyone dies eventually.

Leaning against a hooch, he thought how he had to bullshit his men the same way he had Bonnie Jo. The weather held the day he met her for the first tutoring session. He sat on one end of the swing, while she sat crossways with her sandals resting on his leg. It was still hot, and the September cicadas were buzzing in the leaves of the giant oak tree while she thumbed through the science book. Turned out she was pretty good at tutoring, and it didn't take her long to get him prepared for the next test. They finished, and she sat gazing up at the sky.

"There's a fall talent show coming in October," she said.

It was obviously something she wanted to talk about, but Billy couldn't imagine her having much talent. He figured she would do one of those numbers where she danced around in a sequined body suit with a string of feathers—a feathered boa, or whatever it was they called it.

"A talent show?" he said.

"Yeah. I'm thinking of singing in it."

Bonnie Jo was sweet, but singing in the talent show was probably a pipe dream—at least for her. She just didn't look like a singer—too quiet, a little too mousy and a little too chubby.

"Go for it," he said. "Maybe you can get discovered, like Elvis or something."

She laughed. "You're *so* full of crap, Billy."

"Sorry," he said, and he was sincere.

"I just like to sing," she said. "I sang a cappella at midnight Mass last year, Silent Night."

"That's right. You're Catholic, aren't you?"

"What does that have to do with being in the talent show?"

Being sincere didn't necessarily mean being stupid, but Billy had just mixed both, and Bonnie Jo stared hard at him with big green eyes. Being a Catholic had everything to do with it in Raeford, but it was better to simply leave it alone.

"Hell, I don't know why I said that. I didn't mean nothing by it."

She laughed. "No problem. I was just trying to figure out why you said it."

"I was mumbling incoherently, you know? You really should go for it. Go sing. Hell, you could win it all."

It was something Billy had never truly understood, but if you were black or Catholic, people around Raeford called you a nigger or a papist. At least he didn't have those problems to deal with, but he figured if Bonnie Jo insisted on entering the talent show, the "Catholic" thing put her in the hole right off. Even if she was a great singer she probably didn't have a chance.

Bonnie Jo grasped the chain and sat up in the swing as she gazed to the west where a storm front was building. Barely audible thunder rumbled in the distance as lightening flashed and skittered across a purple horizon.

"What do you want to do when you graduate?" she asked.

Billy shrugged. "Haven't thought about it much."

A sudden breeze came up with the approaching storm, scattering her hair across her face. Billy grabbed his ball cap to keep it from blowing away.

"Someday, I want to sing," she said, "in a rock band, maybe. You know?"

He raised his eyebrows and nodded. "If you have the voice, you should try it," he said, attempting to make his bullshit more palatable.

She smiled. Bonnie Jo's satisfaction with life was Pollyannaish, and her twaddle about being a rock singer was silly, but it wasn't his place to crush her dream. He didn't want to hurt her feelings like the Lizard crowd did almost every day. They made shitty little remarks about her size, but there wasn't much he could do about it. It wasn't his fight.

He decided not to attend the talent show. Anything would be better than sitting in the school auditorium for two and half hours watching students make fools of themselves, but Bonnie Jo carried on about it for the next several weeks, until he promised to go.

It was October, and the talent show was about to begin, but the weather was still warm and the air conditioning was running in the school auditorium that evening. The towering burgundy curtains were drawn back, and the stage was awash with light. Down in front, several gray-haired women, all teachers, sat at a table with the football coach, Coach Roper. They were the judges.

It actually became a fairly entertaining evening as various students made fools of themselves, dancing, playing guitars and twirling batons. Bonnie Jo's was one of the last acts, but just before her, they announced the "Rock Jocks", a band made up of some of the football players.

Billy had seen a GM&O freight train derail on the overpass in Raeford one time, and the sounds were frightening. There came the roaring impact of freight cars crashing into one another, the squealing of rending metal and the thundering impact of loaded hopper cars slamming down onto the highway below. He thought he would never again hear anything so horrifying, but this night at the talent show was proving him wrong. Broken glass, banging metal and cats screaming in the night, even the big derailment couldn't have made a worse sound than The Rock Jocks.

The drummer, a big ape named Hank Bowers, overpowered the rest of the band, except for one out-of-tune guitar. Then there was the constant squeal of feedback, punctuated by popping static, but the worst of it was the vocals. These were especially frightening—not that the lyrics incited fear, but that the jocks actually believed they were giving an acceptable display of talent.

When they finished, Billy pulled his fingers from his ears as everyone including parents and teachers stared at one another in disbelief. A brief but sparse applause tittered across the auditorium. That's when Coach Roper rose to his feet, clapping. His big clumsy hands thudded together for nearly a half-minute of solo applause before he sat back down and turned to the other judges. Nodding his head, he held his finger in the air as if to say his jocks were number one. The other teachers seemed to ignore him.

By the time Bonnie Jo appeared, the audience was bordering on exhaustion and nearly comatose. She was the last contestant. The lights went down low, and a single spotlight drenched her. She wasn't wearing her glasses, and her green eyes sparkled. Talk about guts. She started singing a cappella. It was a Mamas and Papas song called *Dream A Little Dream Of Me.*

As her voice rose it was difficult to believe it was coming from one girl standing alone at the center of the stage. It filled every corner of the auditorium with a resonance that seemed to echo from a chorus of non-existent backup singers. Not so much as a cough came from the entire auditorium as people began sitting up, mesmerized by this voice coming from somewhere, anywhere other than this chubby little kid from Raeford.

Mama Cass Elliot herself would have been proud, and when she finished, Bonnie Jo bowed her head. For a moment the auditorium remained as quiet as a church at midnight, before suddenly exploding with applause. Several people rose to their feet, followed by the rest of the audience as people cheered and whistled their approval. Bonnie Jo was undoubtedly the hands-down winner of the show.

Twenty minutes later the air conditioning was beginning to fail, and the crowd was restless, as the judges were obviously embroiled in an argument that had gone beyond mere votes. Red-faced, Coach Roper was alternately popping the table with his middle finger and pointing into the faces of the gray-haired women on the judges' panel. They were shaking their heads, but after a while they shrugged and seemed resigned to reaching a decision. Coach Roper stood to address the audience.

"Ladies and gentlemen, may I have your attention please." The audience fell silent. "Ladies and gentlemen, the judge's panel has reached a decision. The two finalists for this year's talent contest are Miss Bonnie Jo Parker and the fine group of young athletes from the Raeford High football team called The Rock Jocks. It was a tough decision, but because it was a team effort, and understanding that rock music is something new, the winner is...The Rock Jocks!"

Roper all but screamed the announcement, but other than a row of cheerleaders shrieking and clapping down in front, the auditorium remained strangely quiet.

The silence said it all. No one agreed, but no one wanted to stand up and tell the judges they were full of shit. Billy saw Bonnie Jo the next Monday at school, but she simply shrugged and smiled when he said she'd been robbed.

"It really doesn't matter," she said. "As long as I have friends like you, Billy, I'm happy."

Billy smiled back at her. If the meek were really going to inherit the earth, she was well on her way. As for him, it was probably his fault for having encouraged her. He should have warned her. He should have told her about the Catholic thing and the Lizards. She never had a chance, no matter how good she was. She'd been slapped in the face by reality, and he'd set her up for it.

"You mean we're gonna walk out there across the wide-ass open in broad daylight?" Curtis asked.

Curtis Teague was six-foot-four, and had the typical hardened glare of an angry black man, but it didn't mean shit to Billy, because everyone carried M-16's. Still, Curtis stared back at him like he thought he might be pimping his sister.

The mission briefing wasn't going well. Billy had convinced Bugsy and the CO to let him take the word to the men. This he hoped would at least prevent any insubordination when they heard the plan. Crammed inside a musty hooch to get out of the afternoon rains, they were six feet underground with a two-foot thick wall of sandbags stacked around and overhead. The hooch was built like a bunker into the side of the hill. Empty wooden ammo crates stacked in rows doubled as bunks and chairs.

Outside, the rain poured like a waterfall over the doorway, while inside they sat enveloped in a swirling fog of cigarette smoke, working out their plans for the next day. Casey had his transistor radio tuned to the AFVN where the disk jockey had just predicted rain nine out of ten days for the next ten years—a pretty safe bet in this soggy hellhole. Johnny Rivers was singing *Mountain of Love* as the signal scratched and popped to the lightening outside. Billy remained patient as he listened to the men voice their objections, waiting until everyone had their say. When they were done, he responded.

"Curtis, if you don't like the plan go up there and tell those assholes yourself, but you won't be telling them anything they haven't already heard from me."

Curtis drew hard on his cigarette and flipped the butt into the corner. "Motherfuckers are crazy," he said. He cut his eyes back at Billy.

"You just now figuring that out?" Billy asked.

Curtis wasn't a regular member of the squad, but he was one paratrooper the others respected.

"Personally, if it was up to me, the NVA could keep that goddam pile of dirt, but the colonel says we've got to go up there and take a look around."

RICK DESTEFANIS

"I don't like it," Curtis said.

It was working. He was coming in off the ledge. If Billy got him, the rest of the men would follow.

"I don't like it either, but it's something we can handle. Like Bugsy said, a bigger patrol might get a bunch of people fucked up on booby traps, and he's right."

"Yeah, but how come we ain't leavin' out before daylight?" Curtis said. "Can't we be smart about this shit?"

Like Billy, he knew the enemy would be watching when the patrol left the firebase, and they'd probably let them walk all the way across to the base of the mountain before opening up. If they tried to fall back, there was over a thousand meters of open ground to cross back to the firebase.

"That's exactly what I intend to do," Billy replied. "We're going to be smart."

He paused and lit another cigarette. The flare of the lighter shone on the men's faces and sent shadows dancing across the sandbagged walls of the hooch. Not one squad member was over twenty-one, but every man had the eyes of a fifty-year old.

"Sure, it'll be daylight, but I figure it'll be foggy as hell in the morning, like it's been the last few days. The gooks won't be able to see us at all."

Curtis nodded, "Yeah. That makes sense."

"And if we do get hit," Billy said. "We won't do anything stupid like running back this way. They'll have their big guns zeroed on the open ground, and we'll be like ducks on a pond if we run out there. If we get hit, we'll just hunker down and call in arty on their ass. We'll also have some Cobras on hand, for close support."

A couple of the old heads glanced up at him, but Billy avoided their stares. If they hadn't been so burned-out they might have laughed, because they'd all heard it before. They knew, like him, no matter how sound the strategy, when the shit hit the fan, battle plans and Murphy's Law became inseparable. All of his men had experienced the 'fog of battle,' a term describing the point where communications break down, men become separated from their units, confusion reigns, and every-thing goes to hell. For a small unit like his, it could spell doom in the face of a larger NVA force.

They were only fourteen men making a patrol that was supposed to be strictly recon, but if they made con-tact it could get ugly in a hurry. No amount of artillery or air cover would help if the enemy got on top of them too fast. The NVA would close quickly, and each man in his squad would face the beast toe-to-toe and eye-to-eye. It often came down to this, and nothing helped except maybe a rabbit's foot or some good-luck charm dangling with your dog tags. Billy's was the Saint Sebastian medal Bonnie Jo had given him. He caught himself subcon-sciously thumbing it once again.

After the briefing he inspected each man's gear and told them to lay low the remainder of the eve-ning. Inside the hooch, Billy rested a flashlight on his shoulder, while reading the last of a mildewed Louis L 'Amour paperback. Casey's radio was still tuned to the AFVN. The hooch, dank and reeking of tobacco and body odor, had been home for Billy and nine other men for several weeks. He was actually going to miss this place in the morning when they crossed through the wire.

Outside, the distant thunder of artillery rolled through the mountains and the gentle sough of the wind sifted around the blanket hanging over the doorway. Inside, Strawberry Alarm Clock was doing a distant and scratchy version of *Incense and Peppermint* on the radio, and somewhere back in west Texas, L 'Amour's rugged hero was trapped in a rocky arroyo surrounded by a half-dozen bad guys.

The flashlight was growing dim, but it didn't matter. Billy had picked up the book at the USO in Vung Tau while on R & R, and it was missing the last few pages. He tossed it in the corner and lit a cigarette. It was probably a better ending that way, like waking up before the end of a bad nightmare. Maybe, he could wake up from this one, too. Not that he had anything to do when he got back home, but dying in this rat-infested hellhole surely wasn't the way he wanted to go.

Somewhere in the distance the rumble of the artillery continued as Billy turned out the flashlight. The glow of his cigarette was the only light other than the dim reflection of another illumination round falling outside the perimeter. He wondered what was happening back home. It seemed like a place he'd left many years ago, a place that was destined to become a distant memory, a place never to be seen again.

3

DANCING ON HO CHI MINH'S GRAVE

They say once you become an adult, the nickel-dime crap from high school is forgotten. They say it no longer compares to things in the adult world. And that may be true for the unconscious bastards who were at the top of the heap back then, but Billy had come halfway around the world and watched men die, and he still couldn't escape his adolescent experiences. They, too, had defined the man he had become. They affected everything in his life—the way he thought, the way he acted and the way he lived. Not that Vietnam wasn't serving the larger part, because it did in a big way, drop-forging the final imprint on his psyche. It had also marked him with the scarlet letter of a genuine combat neurotic—the thousand yard stare.

He tried to put the war out of his mind, and perhaps this was why he always thought about high school.

Besides, before Nam there hadn't been much else. Lying awake that night, he was wrapped in a poncho liner and smoking another cigarette as he stared into the darkness. Around him the men in the hooch all slept as he wondered if he'd done everything possible to talk the CO out of a useless and risky patrol. Probably not, but every time he stuck his neck out for someone, he got into a world of shit. It was a repetitive pattern that began in high school, the first time being in a phys-ed class.

If you were an athlete, phys-ed wasn't required, but Coach Roper thought running cross-country track wasn't a manly enough sport and refused to remove Billy's name from the class roster. Of course, refusing his invitation to play split-end for the varsity football squad didn't help either. The big, helmet-haired moron thought of himself as another Bear Bryant. He even wore a hounds-tooth hat like The Bear's. Except Billy was certain in Roper's case, he was The Bear without a brain.

Most of the guys in the class decided Roper was an ex-Nazi, because every day he made them do pushups and run around the gym till someone started puking. And he always brought in a couple of his glory boys from the varsity football team to assist with the verbal abuse. They were like him, except younger and dumber, *if that were possible.*

The worst was Hank Bowers. The humungous bastard played tight-end only marginally better than he did the drums for the Rock Jocks. A Roper clone, Bowers was dumb as a brick, and with the same mean streak that caused him to push and curse the scrawny boys in the class. Every day he worked tirelessly punishing them with verbal abuse for their failure to have proper muscle mass. He bullied everyone except Billy. Bowers seemed to sense he should leave him alone. It may have been because the running never bothered Billy, and he ran the wind sprints and laps effortlessly, until the tormentors grew bored and went off to watch game films in the coach's office.

Billy endured their shit and said nothing until one day when an overweight boy who had tits bigger than Mary Lou Baker's fell out with an asthma attack. That was it. They took him away in an ambulance, and Billy went to another teacher. He told her how Coach Roper and his pig, Bowers, had taunted the boy, pushing him around the gym until he collapsed. He thought that would be the end of Roper, but failed to understand that a coach who took them to the regional championship every year was allowed certain indiscretions. Nothing happened until a week later when Earline Simmons came up pregnant.

Roper thought the baby was his and freaked out. He disappeared from school, and they said he was about to fly to Mexico when Earline miscarried. Afterward, a half-dozen of the football players admitted they'd been poking her too. Roper quit or got fired, and the last Billy heard he was selling life insurance somewhere in Florida.

Word got out later that Billy was the one who narced on Roper and Bowers, and the football players blamed him for the loss of their hero coach. "Made things out worse than they really were," they said, "and it put too much pressure on Coach." Having brought it on himself with his "crusader for the downtrodden" mentality, Billy began to believe they were right. Maybe the world was just this way, one where people like the Lizards, the ones who depended on cliques and letter jackets to prove their worth, wrote the rules and got their way.

Billy tried to avoid the conflicts, but it seemed inevitable that he found himself sticking up for someone in the middle of a controversy. It was simple fate, he figured. Yet it was something driven by his irrational inability to butt-out, and the result was never predictable. Earline getting pregnant was the stroke of luck that saved him from Roper, and that was when he began understanding fate could take you down whatever path it chose.

The Raeford High Homecoming Dance was another time the theory was proven. He avoided Bonnie Jo that night by staying on the opposite side of the gym. Sweet kid that she was, he didn't need her doing something stupid, like asking him to dance. That would really give the Lizards something to feed on, and his acceptance by them was already tenuous at best. Bonnie Jo sat at a table with the other chubby girls, giggling and talking while Billy danced with several of the hot chicks.

Dancing with Mary Lou Baker was like dancing with Dolly Parton. He pulled her close and his chest felt like it had died and gone to heaven, but it was watching Sissy Conroy that left him totally distracted. Most of the students were doing their best to make this little mating ritual seem natural, but they were all nervous, all except Sissy. Billy watched her as she sauntered out on the dance floor hand-in-hand with a different jock for each new song. Her hips moved with an ease and fluidity that belied the pent-up tension within. Sissy was the homecoming queen, and each time she passed by his nostrils flared as he inhaled the intoxicating scent of her perfumed body.

He was a coyote watching a lamb on a rope, but resigned himself to admiring her from afar. There wasn't a chance in hell of ever getting to dance with her. It was beyond the pale of his imagination. He could only watch as she fell into the arms of the star quarterback, Jake Tupperman. Life was a screwed-up proposition when you weren't one of the big dogs, or in this case, one of the Lizards. It just wasn't right, and if he had the opportunity, Billy would show her he was deserving of her affections.

The thought ate at him until it became a sudden catalyst for a growing flood of anger. Why shouldn't he dance with her? Envy and anger rose from deep within as he found himself riding the crest of an emotional Tsunami. It overwhelmed all rational thought as he was suddenly driven by a suicidal impulse. No doubt overcome by a pheromone-induced mental incapacitation, he decided to do it. He was going to dance with Sissy Conroy the homecoming queen.

Strutting bravely out on the dance floor to where Sissy was wrapped in the arms of Jake Tupperman, Billy

resolutely tapped him on the shoulder and stepped
back. He waited for Jake to respectfully pass Sissy into
his arms, but it didn't work that way. Jake, the bellwether
of the Lizards, looked over his shoulder and laughed.
"Fuck-off," he said.

Billy did as he was told, and the flaming anger that
had so boldly motivated him, subsided to a cold ember of
regret. He was a fool. He'd embarrassed himself in front
of Sissy. Later, as he skulked along the back wall toward
the concession stand, he came face to face with her. She
looked at him, and he looked into her eyes, knowing she
was about to break into uncontrollable laughter, but she
smiled instead.

"I'm sorry about what happened," she said. "Would
you like to dance now?"

It was an epiphany that left him dizzy with euphoria
as he came to understand how fate was not only random
as a bolt of lightning, but could be as good as it was bad.
He, Billy Coker, was about to dance with the sexiest girl
in the senior class, the freaking homecoming queen.
The lights went down low, and the band's lead vocalist
sounded like a clone of Tony Williams as he began a
Platters song, *Smoke Gets in Your Eyes.*

Sissy's perfume was an aphrodisiac, and Billy imagined such a wonderful scent could emanate from only
the most intimate parts of her body. His mind roamed
over the possibilities, and his head spun from the effects
of a hormonal high. They walked out onto the dance
floor, and he pulled her close. The burning warmth of

her breasts sent him teetering to the brink of hormonal overload as he became lost in a surreal world of blind lust.

Clutching one another, they drifted across the darkened gymnasium, until something happened. Billy dropped his hand down and grabbed her butt, pulling her even closer. She gasped, and realizing what he'd done, he tried to let go, but it was as if a five-hundred-volt electrical current had welded his hand in place. He was certain it was all about to end with a slap to the face, until she looked up at him and smiled. Quickly, she spun away from the crowd, putting her back toward the band. Billy was in heaven.

A few days after the homecoming dance, Barbara Barnes saw him talking with Bonnie Joe and asked why he was so self-destructive. Barbara was one of the groupies who bounced around like a little Chihuahua, eagerly sucking up to the Lizards. He asked her what she meant, and she explained how he could probably be "*really* popular" if only he made the right friends. Billy wanted their acceptance, but he hated them for the 'unworthy' status they cast upon everyone outside their clique.

"That's why they call you Weird Billy," she said. "Moping around reading books and hanging out with creepy people isn't good for your reputation."

"In that case," Billy replied, "I'll try to avoid you."

"You're *such* an asshole, Coker!" she said.

Melvin Henderson, though, was the catalyst for most of Billy's high school troubles. Melvin was the second and last person Billy ever stuck up for in high school. The epitome of his caste, Melvin was too tall, too skinny and too studious. To make matters worse, he carried all his books between classes, along with a slide rule, mechanical pencils and various other accoutrements of the trade. This made him a prime target for the jocks who would sneak up behind him in the hallway and pull a book from under his arm. Inevitably the entire stack would explode across the floor while the jocks walked away high-fiving one another.

Billy stopped to help him one day and saw tears in his eyes. Melvin tried to blame it on allergies, but he was lying. Poor old Melvin lived through hell, and that must have been what was going through Billy's mind the day Marty Macklin pushed past him in the hallway. Melvin was up ahead, and Marty was homed in on him like a killer shark.

Billy bumped Marty, causing him to look back. "Why don't you leave him alone? He hasn't done anything to you."

Melvin glanced over his shoulder, and, realizing what was about to happen, scurried away. Marty missed his mark. Exploding with anger, he shoved Billy against a row of gray wall lockers, rattling the doors and locks as he jabbed his finger in his face. "Why don't you mind your own business, jerk wad?" he shouted.

Twenty or thirty students stood watching as Billy felt his popularity meter dropping to zero, but he didn't need to get his butt whipped right there in the hall. He wrenched himself free of Marty's grasp and turned to walk away, but it was too late.

"Okay, Coker," Marty shouted. "You think you're such a bad ass. Out back, after school. Your ass is mine, and don't make me have to come looking for you."

Everyone in the hallway stood in silence, staring as if they'd just witnessed someone being sentenced to the gallows. And it was coming, as certain as final exams. There was no way to avoid it. Billy was going to be pummeled, bloodied and humiliated before the entire student body. By the time the last bell rang, the murmurs rolled like the buzzing of summertime cicadas through the classrooms.

"Macklin's gonna stomp Coker's ass."

"Macklin's gonna stomp Coker's ass."

"Macklin's gonna stomp Coker's ass."

The Christians must have felt the same way when they were escorted into the Roman Coliseum. He was about to be eaten alive by Marty, another of the chosen ones, a stocky linebacker with a nasty redneck disposition. Billy's interference had cost him a two-dollar bet, and Macklin was going to take all two dollars' worth out of his ass. When he came out of the classroom last period, there was no escape. The legions were there to escort him to the arena, a corner pocket hidden between the utilities building and the field house.

"Macklin's gonna whip your ass," someone said.

Probably so, Billy thought. It was funny how acute one's senses became during moments of crisis, the flow of adrenaline sharpening every nerve to a razor keenness. He smelled the layers of wax on the floor, and the click of a hundred shoes sounded a death knell as they walked down the hallway toward the door. From somewhere in the ancient building came the distant roar of a toilet flushing. Built just after World War II, the school had plaster walls with thick coats of paint, faded and yellowed, and everything above arm's reach was coated with a permanent layer of grime.

The student body seemed drawn and tense as they made their way to the exits. One of their own was about to be sacrificed to the Lizards, the gods and rulers of Raeford High. Outside, the grass, dead from the winter frost, smelled like straw, and the air was pregnant with a stillness that precipitates a storm. By the time Billy arrived, the scene had taken on the appearance of a pep-rally. Letter jackets, cheerleaders and a mob of students spilled out from behind the building. An electric tension precipitated by the coming execution filled the air.

This was insane. All over a stupid book. Some girl had her transistor radio turned up to a staticy full-blast with The Regents singing *Barbara Ann*. "*Ba-Ba-Ba, Ba-Ba Barbara Ann....*"

It was a circus, and Billy wanted to scream at her, telling her to shut the damned thing off, but he thought better of it. Best to keep the sympathy of the crowd in case this thing got out of hand. Their cries of 'mercy' might save him from permanent disfigurement.

He glanced around hoping a teacher would notice as he made his way through the milling hoard, but there was no such luck. It was as if the faculty and staff were a part of the plot. The big mob assassination was about to occur in the prison yard, and all the guards had mysteriously disappeared.

The jocks acted as ushers, clearing the crowd away as Macklin appeared and walked over to the wall of the building. Tight-faced with the grim continence of a ruler forced to punish a peon, he held his hand at shoulder level and motioned Billy with a single finger to follow. Billy obeyed and walked toward him. Macklin turned, and his grimace changed to a smile as he began unbuttoning his black and gold letter jacket. He had morphed from the reluctant ruler to just another one of the Lizards about to experience a little sadistic pleasure.

"I'm gonna teach you something about minding your own business, Coker," he said.

Marty's lip had that Elvis upward curl, and Billy stood mesmerized by the surrounding spectacle. As Marty pulled open his varsity letter jacket, Billy glanced around. He was meekly going to slaughter without so much as a protest, and Marty was dictating how this ritual killing would play out. That was it, but it didn't have to be that way. Macklin didn't have to be the one in charge.

It was one of those moments when Billy felt his creative genius peak as he stepped forward. Marty's arms were still tangled in the sleeves of the jacket when Billy came with an overhand right to his face. Putting his shoulder behind it, he caught Macklin flush on the chin with the best punch he'd ever thrown. Marty's head bounced against the brick wall, and Billy was about to come with a left hook, but it wasn't necessary. Marty's eyes rolled back in his head as he slid slowly down the wall, landing in a motionless heap.

Billy froze in disbelief. He had just KO'ed Macklin with one shot. And for a moment he worried that Macklin had some kind of serious injury, but the cries of amazement quickly brought him back to his senses. From all around came expressions of "Holy shit!" and "Coker just stomped Macklin's Ass!"

There was no sense of pride, but more that of relief as Billy turned away. He didn't look left or right as he pushed his way through the stunned crowd. Making good his getaway, he broke clear of the mob and was feeling pretty good until he heard someone say, "Coach ain't gonna like this."

Marty missed football practice that afternoon, and Billy became a marked man. Word was the new coach said no one sucker-punched one of his boys and got away with it. It wasn't long before it got around that the jocks were planning to take care of Billy, but that wonderfully random thing called fate intervened once again. The principal got wind of things, and it seemed Roper's legacy was still stuck in his craw. They said he told Coach King that if Billy so much as stubbed his toe he'd find himself looking for a new job.

Billy skipped his tutoring session with Bonnie Jo that week, and by the time they met the following Monday there was no doubt she had heard about the fight. Despite being a cold gray day, they sat out on the swing again, and she wore a green windbreaker with a white knit cap. A cold breeze kept blowing her reddish blond hair into her face, and she kept pulling it back. Bonnie Jo was actually very pretty, and she had better hair than most of the good-looking chicks at school, even Sissy's. And she was a hell of a lot nicer person. Too bad she couldn't find someone other than Ray who liked her.

"Hello. Are you listening?" Bonnie Jo asked.

"Sorry," Billy said. "I was daydreaming."

She closed the science book and set it aside.

"What's wrong? When I saw you running the other day you didn't look like yourself. You didn't even look up."

"What do you mean? How do I usually look?"

Rubbing her hands together she pushed them between her legs as she gazed down the hill at the pasture across the road. The cattle, white-faced Herefords, had their backs to the wind as they grazed on the opposite hillside.

"When you run, you always look so, I don't know, focused maybe, and yet, at ease, like it's the most natural thing in the world. I love it when you come by up there behind the Dairy Queen, because no matter how much we try to distract you, those blue eyes never leave the trail and your expression never changes. You just keep that same look of calm determination."

"You have to pay attention when you're running so you don't step in a hole or trip on a tree root."

Bonnie Jo always took his smart-ass remarks in stride.

"So what were you thinking about when I saw you stumble last week? You looked distracted."

"You know what it was, my fight with Macklin."

She raised her eyebrows. "I heard it wasn't much of a fight."

"The jerk deserved it."

"I know. I heard he was picking on Melvin again, and you said something to him."

Billy shrugged.

"Well, I think you're great, Billy Boy. Nobody else has the nerve to stand up for poor Melvin. He's lucky to have a friend like you."

"He's not my friend."

She bowed her head and pressed her lips together.

"It's okay, Billy. I mean, it's okay if you like people like him—or me."

His face was burning, and Billy tried to make out like he didn't know what she meant.

"What's that supposed to mean?" he asked.

"I mean—well, I know it's kind of embarrassing for you to hang around with a fat girl like me, or to take up for someone like Melvin, but you always do—"

"Aren't you cold?" Billy asked.

She pursed her lips, and dropped her eyes again as she stared down at nothing in particular.

"Yeah, I'm freezing," she said in a low voice.

"Let's go over there and sit in my truck. I'll crank it up and turn on the heater."

After opening the door on the passenger side, he made out like he was moving his books and placing them under the seat, but he was really making sure there was no evidence of his front-seat frolics with Sissy. Only the week before his stupid older brother, Eddie, had found a pair of her underpants and carried them into the house to show his mother. Since Eddie was already a hoodlum of sorts, Billy figured on being his mom's only hope for a decent son. She cried.

The next day would be a long one, but Billy slept little that night as he fought to think about something besides the war. High school or anything was better than the last eleven months, but it was useless. The war was his life now. He thought about a vow he'd made only a month after arriving in Nam. They were down to the last day of a mission that had lasted nearly a month. He scarcely thought he would survive at times, but after weeks of humping steep hills, cutting through thick jungle and experiencing a nearly continuous stretch of battle that lasted ten days, he was exhausted and well on his way to becoming a first-class combat neurotic.

Eating c-rations, humping up steep ridges, slapping mosquitoes and catching sleep in restless snatches wasn't the worst of it. It was the firefights, too many to count, up close and personal encounters, with entrenched units of NVA regulars. It was a baptism of blood and fear. By the time they fought their way up one mountain called Dong Ap Bia the 101st had seventy-two men killed and another 372 wounded, but Billy was unscathed. It was because of his friends Butch and Danny, two old heads who had kept him from making 'dumb-cherry' mistakes.

They'd made it, too, and the company was less than a half-klick from the LZ. Everyone was looking forward to the chopper ride back to Eagle for their first hot meal, shower and full night's sleep since leaving almost four weeks ago.

They humped through heavy jungle down off a ridge onto a flat hilltop. A light mist was falling, and despite their general debilitation, everyone was damned near giddy about getting the hell out of the A Shau. The firebase was less than an hour away. Perhaps that was why Lieutenant Leatherman sent Butch and Danny across the open hilltop to the other side. After all, the entire area had been prepped with 105's earlier that morning. Maybe that was what was on the platoon sergeant's mind too, when he didn't question the Lieutenant's order. After all, the real bad-guy country was up in the hills behind them. They were damned near home-free.

The Company was moving in platoon columns as they approached the LZ. Billy, who was exhausted, had just been replaced on point by Butch who had Danny walking slack for him. They probably should have done the smart thing and skirted the hilltop, avoiding the open terrain, but they didn't. They did the stupidly predictable GI thing. They walked straight across the center of the hill to set up security on the other side. It was the perfect joining of bad decisions.

Perhaps if Butch hadn't been so exhausted, or maybe if he hadn't been thinking about that nurse he met down at Vung Tau, just maybe, he would have spotted the ambush. The enemy detonated a booby-trap blowing Butch and Danny backward, and within seconds more explosions sent everyone sprawling as mortar and RPG rounds landed in their midst. The NVA had caught them in the open. A devastating crossfire between a machine gun near the tree line on the right and an ambush line on the backside of the hill, shredded the vegetation, but Billy knew what he had to do.

Geysers of water spewed from old shell holes as clumps of dirt showered down all around and shards of shrapnel skittered through the grass. Butch and Danny always said, "Gain fire superiority and don't let it go."

Billy emptied his first magazine within seconds, slapped in the second and charged to the far side of the hill, directly at the enemy. It worked as the enemy fell back into the darkness of the jungle below, but by the time the other platoons moved in, it was too late for Butch. The initial explosion had torn him apart, and Danny was badly wounded. Four others were also hit, and the drizzle became a steady rain, delaying the medevac choppers.

The next afternoon they held a memorial service for the men from their battalion that had been killed in the last twenty-one days. Thirty-six pairs of empty jump boots lined the volleyball court. An M-16 was stuck up in the ground by its bayonet behind each pair and a helmet was placed on each rifle. Billy wondered which ones belonged to Butch and Danny.

It was a dreary day, and the flags hung limp with rain as the Colonel arrived to address the troops. They were in formation around the volleyball court, trying to stay dry beneath their ponchos while the chaplain said his piece then stepped aside. After climbing atop the makeshift stage of empty ammo crates, the colonel looked out over them. Rain-soaked ponchos hid all but their eyes— sunken eyes that were tired and unfocused.

With his new starched fatigues and spit-shined jump boots, the colonel was a figure of envy, not so much for the way he looked as much as his socks were no doubt dry, and he'd probably slept on a real mattress the night before. Probably hadn't had crotch rot since basic. He put his hands on his hips, and his rock-hard chin jutted outward, as he stared out over the formation, while waiting on an aide to hook up the microphone. The drizzle slackened as the microphone screeched with feedback. The sound carried across the firebase and down the hillside, echoing in the distant hills.

The Colonel began his speech, "Troopers of the One Hundred and First Airborne..."

He explained how their buddies hadn't died in vain, as he justified the dead and wounded with a litany of accomplishments, including hills already relinquished, numbers of enemy killed, weapons captured and whatever ratios made them the victors. He talked, and the weeks of sleepless nights caught up with Billy as he nodded off, replaying those events in a half dream, half memory. It was a living nightmare—enemy soldiers suddenly appearing from nowhere in their midst, a shower of grenades seeming to fall from the sky without warning, jammed rifles in the middle of a firefight and men dying, for what?

And despite his drowsiness he heard the colonel speak. He listened with his eyes closed, and it wasn't simply a declaration of victory based on "they-had-more-bodies-to-bury-than-us." There was something more, something that made Billy open his eyes and tilt his head up to take notice as the Colonel held his fist high in the air and shouted into the microphone. It was the emotion in his voice that carried the righteousness and fervor of a true believer.

"Victory is within our grasp," the colonel shouted.

Beneath his poncho, Billy opened a pack of cigarettes. The Colonel continued his speech, standing there over the rows of empty boots, as he said without so much as a blink of an eye, that the next operation would be even more successful. And as Billy wondered by what measurement "success" might become failure, the colonel's next words stripped away the last remnants of reality.

"Someday," he said, "we're going to kick the enemy's ass all the way back to Hanoi. And when we get there, we're gonna kill that sonofabitch Ho Chi Minh, and we're gonna dance on his grave."

The nightmare was now bordering on nonsensical. Surely this colonel didn't believe his men were stupid enough to buy the drivel he was serving up. If he was that blind, there was truly no hope. Billy had been there barely thirty days, and even he knew better than that. They might dance in hell, but they would never dance in North Vietnam.

He made a vow that day, and that was to fight for one thing, his buddies. And if he ever became a squad leader, no one's poor judgment would needlessly endanger his men. If the colonel wanted to dance on Uncle Ho's grave, he wasn't going to step over the mangled bodies of Billy's men to do it.

It had been ten months since he'd made that promise. And when he became a squad leader he kept it. His men had done their job, and they'd taken casualties, but not once was it because of something stupid. His men trusted him to keep them out of trouble, but things had changed. Bugsy and the CO had talked him into this recon patrol. The patrol was risky beyond reason. One misstep could put them all in body bags. Billy's only hope was to get through it alive, get his men back to the firebase and go home.

4

SAINT SEBASTIAN

Sometime in the night the distant rumble of the artillery tapered off and the rains stopped. The memories faded as Billy dozed off, but there came the sounds of someone retching outside the hooch. He sat up and shone his flashlight around inside. Jack Jorgensen's rack was empty. Life in Nam was generally shitty. Bullets and shrapnel aside, someone was always getting sick, snake bit, rat bit or something even less romantic, like the crabs, diarrhea or jungle rot. Billy couldn't believe his own thoughts. 'Romantic' was a word he didn't vaguely equivocate with anything in Nam. He fished another cigarette from his shirt pocket.

If it could be contracted in Nam, Jack had gotten it, everything from dysentery to malaria. He had also been awarded a Purple Heart, courtesy of some shrapnel from a Chi-Com grenade. Billy eased outside where the stale night air hung dank and heavy. Jack was leaning with his head against the sandbagged wall. The air reeked with the odor of vomit, and sweat poured from Jorgensen's face in the pale moonlight. Trembling, he clutched his stomach.

"You gonna live?" Billy asked.

Jack didn't respond. Billy offered him his cigarette, but Jack waved him off, shaking his head.

"Okay, take your ass up to the CP at daylight. Tell Bugsy to medevac you out of here."

"No," Jack said. "I'm making the patrol. I'll be okay."

He was drooling like a distempered dog.

"Look hardass, you've got more goddam medals than anybody in this outfit. You don't have to prove shit."

Billy put his hand on Jack's shoulder, but Jack pushed it away. "Goddamit, Billy, leave me the fuck alone."

Jack was a big blonde-headed guy from Minnesota, but the rest of the squad came from the South and Southwest. The men had ragged him unmercifully about being a 'damned Yankee,' and Jack was always trying to prove himself, but enough was enough. He was one of Billy's best men, and Billy wasn't letting him go on the patrol just to prove himself for the umpteenth time.

"Jack, I don't need you out there in that condition. You'll get fucked up or get somebody else fucked up. If I come off patrol tonight and you're still here, you're getting an Article 15 for disobeying an order. You understand?"

"Yeah, sure, whatever." He began dry-heaving again.

Bugsy and the CO wouldn't question Billy on this one. If one of his men wasn't carrying his load, Billy always dealt with it. They also knew Jack was a man of character who never shied away from duty. Billy went back inside and laid down. Somewhere he had read how a person develops character by enduring deprivation or bad times. That being so, probably explained both Jack's and Bonnie Jo's personalities. They were two people who never made excuses.

Bonnie Jo got more than her share of character-building courtesy of the Lizards. And when she wasn't putting up with their crap, she was dodging Raymond Hokes, who was still trailing her like a buck in rut. Billy shook his head as he thought about what he'd done to her. It wasn't that he intentionally tried to hurt her. It just always seemed he was trapped in situations that left him with no good choices.

One day before Christmas Bonnie Jo showed up where he was sitting in the school cafeteria. She obviously wanted to talk about something, but he was at the Lizards' table. Bonnie Jo stood behind him while the girls at the table pretended not to notice her. Not exactly an outcast like Bonnie Jo, he figured his popularity ranking was probably more that of a second-tier hanger-on, which meant he was allowed to grace their presence on occasion, attend their parties and more or less fulfill their need for court jesters, servants and miscellaneous groupies.

He also fulfilled their need for a tutor at test time, taking up where their Cliffs Notes left off. Despite his ongoing feud with Marty Macklin, most of the jocks tolerated him because he ran track, and most of the girls enjoyed his undying devotion to their gender, especially now that he'd hit it off with Sissy Conroy. It wasn't a bad life, but his popularity ranking was something which Barbara Barnes continually reminded him wouldn't last. Perhaps, he was destined to be an outlier, never to be fully accepted and perhaps someday eaten in a fit of rage by the Lizards.

He sat at the table, reading his book, pretending he hadn't noticed Bonnie Jo standing behind him. That's when Jake Tupperman leaned across the table to Marty Macklin, cupping his hand against the side of his mouth as if to deflect his voice. "Hey, Marty, there's a big ol' babe waiting for your leftovers—better save her some."

Had he whispered, it wouldn't have been so cruel, but he said it loud enough for everyone at the table to hear. Billy already had enough troubles with Marty, and it just wasn't his fight. He said nothing.

Marty looked over his shoulder and wrapped his arms around his tray as if to protect it. Everyone began laughing. One of the girls made grunting sounds like a pig, and even after the others stopped, Barbara Barnes continued cackling as if it was the funniest thing she'd ever heard. Billy pretended to read his book while Bonnie Jo seemed oblivious as she hummed along with a tune coming from someone's transistor radio at the next table. It was another old Platters song called *The Great Pretender*.

Tupperman nudged the back of Billy's book to get his attention, then nodded toward Bonnie Jo. Glancing over his shoulder, Billy's eyes met hers, but he quickly turned away. The smell of greasy spaghetti and bologna sandwiches filled the air, making him feel sick. He looked across the table at Jake, gave him a quick smile and shrugged.

"She's been tutoring me with my math and science," Billy said.

He hoped the clatter of food trays and the screech of the metal chairs on the tile floor had masked Jake's comments, but Bonnie Jo's eyes were a dead giveaway. She could remain as poker-faced as the best gambler ever, but Billy saw her green eyes had softened just enough to show her feelings were hurt. Casually closing his book, he picked up his tray and told the Lizards he had to go. After turning in his tray at the window, Billy headed for the hallway. Bonnie Jo followed at a safe distance.

He didn't turn around until they were safely down the hall and out of sight. She smiled, giving him that look that said 'It's okay. I accept whatever tidbit of friendship you toss my way.'

He pretended nothing had happened.

"What's up?" he asked.

"I just wanted to tell you that my dad's company is transferring him to California."

"You're kidding. Does that mean you have to go, too?"

She rolled her eyes. "That's what I like about you, Billy Boy. You're really quick."

Sometimes he felt like a dumbass around her, but it always seemed that the chubby girls were smarter than everyone else—probably because they had to survive in a social jungle full of hyenas.

"That's really a bummer," he said. "And right in the middle of your senior year, too."

"Yeah, I know. I'm leaving all my friends behind."

As they walked down the hall, he glanced down at her to see if she was serious. Bonnie Jo was a sweet girl, but her only friends were a couple of the other girls, and of course, Ray.

"Ray Hokes will be broken hearted, too," Billy said.

She pursed her lips and nodded. "Yeah, I feel sorry for him."

"You what?"

Bonnie Jo looked up. "Well, I mean, I'll be glad to get away from him, and I still don't know if my sanity has survived, but he *is* human, and the poor thing follows me around like a lovesick puppy. Do you know that someone actually told him I had a crush on him?"

"No," Billy said, knowing he was turning Benedict Arnold-red.

"I wish I could get him interested in Roberta Ann," Bonnie Jo said. "She really *does* have a crush on him."

"Roberta Ann Hoefstra?"

"Yeah, she's been making passes at him, but he's too infatuated with me to notice."

"Maybe, I can drop a bug in his ear."

Talking with Ray wasn't as bad as the possibility that Roberta Ann would learn of Billy's involvement and come after him. She was a female version of Ray, except Ray wasn't quite as temperamental. If this new scheme backfired, he could find himself in deep shit again, but there was no good alternative. He owed it to Bonnie Jo.

"How are you going to do that?" she asked.

"Hell, I don't know, but I'll come up with something to get him off your ass."

"You know, if I ever find out who told Ray I had a crush on him, I'll probably...."

She didn't finish.

"You'll what?"

She just smiled, shook her head and looked down the hall past the rows of gray wall lockers.

"Oh, nothing. I probably wouldn't do anything. They probably thought they were helping someone."

"Helping someone?" he said.

She looked over at Billy and smiled.

"Yes. They probably thought they were helping one of us."

That was vintage Bonnie Jo. She had a kind heart and a way with words that made Billy feel like the worm he was.

A few days later, Billy slipped a note to Ray. When he finished reading it, Ray's lumpy face glowed with new-found love. He looked at Billy, smiled and nodded. The plan worked, and it was the final day of school before the holiday break when Bonnie Jo came to him and said she was forever indebted. At least he'd ended that one on a positive note, and Billy smiled as they said their good-byes. He thought it would be the last time he would see her.

Billy's affair with Sissy had gone sideways as well. After nearly two months of sexual experimenting down at the gravel pit she was a bit jaded, and since they'd been skinny dipping half the time, Billy figured he was lucky she hadn't come up pregnant. It was mostly her idea, but they made a mutual agreement to give the front seat of his truck a rest for the Christmas holidays. All in all, he was pretty lucky, because he didn't have to buy Christmas gifts for Sissy or Bonnie Jo. That left him with only one gift to worry about.

Two days before Christmas he drove his old pickup over to K-Mart in Tupelo to look for a Christmas present for his mom. He bought her a scarf and gloves and a rhinestone pendant. Leaving the store that night, Billy hurried across the frigid parking lot to his truck, but when he turned the key the engine only grunted—dead battery. It was almost thirty miles back to Raeford. With it cold as hell and nearing closing time, Billy kicked at the frozen asphalt as he trudged back inside to find a pay-phone. Fishing some change from his pocket, he dropped the coins into the slots and waited for the dial tone. The music of *The First Noel* jolted to a stop, and a voice came over the intercom announcing the store's closing in five minutes.

"Hey, Billy. What's up?"

He turned to find Bonnie Jo standing behind him with a large shopping bag.

"Hey!" he said. "What are you doing here?"

She gave him the grin he always got when he said something stupid.

"Just finishing the last of my Christmas shopping," she said.

"The battery's dead on my truck. I was calling somebody for a ride."

"I've got my daddy's car. I can carry you home if you'd like."

He took her shopping bag and walked with her across the parking lot.

"I can get somebody to bring me back tomorrow with some jumper cables to get the truck," he said.

She nodded. "It's really good to see you. You know, we're leaving for California right after Christmas."

Her breath vaporized in the cold night air and her cheeks reddened. He put his free arm across her shoulders. She just needed someone to be nice to her.

"I'm so glad we ran into one another," she said. "This is probably the last time I'll see you."

She seemed so much more affected by this final "good-bye."

"Yeah," Billy said. "I suppose it is."

"Can I write you sometime?"

He shrugged. "I guess so."

She smiled as he put the bag in the trunk. Her daddy's car was a new Lincoln.

"Nice car," he said.

"Daddy's company pays for it."

There was a paper bag and a stack of eight-track tapes on the seat.

"Are these yours?"

"No, they're Daddy's. All I have are my records at home."

Billy shuffled through the tapes then picked up the paper bag.

"What's in the sack?"

Bonnie Jo shrugged as he opened the bag. Inside were several small bottles of liquor. Billy held one up to the dashboard lights to read the label.

"Oh, those were left over from Daddy's going away party at this office."

"It says it's peach schnapps, and there's a bunch of other stuff here, too," Billy said. "Can we try some?"

"I don't know. Daddy doesn't drink much, so I don't suppose he'll miss it, but—"

Billy uncapped the half-pint bottle and took a tentative sip.

"This is good. Tastes like peaches and sugar."

He took another sip.

"Here, try some." He handed the bottle to Bonnie Jo.

"Can we try out the stereo?" he asked.

"I suppose, but his tapes are mostly old stuff like Eddie Arnold and Floyd Cramer.

"Yeah, I know, but I just want to hear the stereo."

Bonnie Jo took a sip from the bottle and licked her lips. The big Lincoln glided silently down the darkened highway, as Billy pushed a Floyd Cramer tape into the player. The first ivory notes of the piano blended gently with the bass rhythm as the already famous recording *Last Date* began playing. The stereo speakers filled the car with the sound of Cramer's piano, the notes cascading like diamonds into a golden urn, and Billy felt a sudden and deep sympathy for Bonnie Jo. It was Christmas, and her life was changing with an inevitability she had no choice but to accept. They passed the schnapps back and forth and listened to the music while she drove back to Raeford. The tape ended by the time they passed beneath the railroad overpass going into town.

"Turn down that road there," Billy said.

It was nearly ten o'clock, and there was no traffic.

"I was going to call you to say good-bye," she said.

He pointed to the house. "There."

Without even a bulb burning on the front porch, it was completely dark. She pulled into the drive and put the car into park as he grasped the door handle.

"Wait," she said. "I have something for you."

Using the dim light from the dashboard she fumbled for something in her purse. Billy took another drink of schnapps. They had nearly emptied the bottle. After a moment or two she switched on the dome light and came out with a small box and a folded piece of paper. Opening the box, she closed her fist around whatever was inside. After glancing downward, she slowly raised her head and looked up at Billy.

"Before I give this to you, I want to ask you—well, I want to ask you for a favor. I mean, if it's okay. I know it's going to sound silly, and if you say 'no,' I'll understand."

She paused and looked down again, and at the same moment Billy felt both embarrassed and sorry for her.

"It's okay," he said. "It doesn't hurt to ask."

He handed her the bottle again and she took another drink. She probably wanted a good-bye kiss, and after giving him a ride all the way home from Tupelo, she'd earned it. She looked up, her pudgy little cheeks aglow and her lips glistening from the schnapps.

"You sure?"

"Just say it, for Pete's sake!"

"Okay. On the way over here, while the stereo was playing, I was thinking....Look, I know girls aren't supposed to do this, but if I play that first song again, will you dance with me, just this once?"

"Are you kidding?" Billy said. "Where?"

"Right here. I mean, beside the car, on the drive... maybe...." Her voice trailed off as she looked down again. Billy looked straight ahead and sat in silence. "Never mind," she said. "I think I've had too much to drink. It was a stupid idea."

"I know," Billy said.

He opened the car door and got out. The cold December air bit at him as he momentarily swayed side to side, then walked around the front of the car to her side. She rolled down her window.

"You women come up with some of the sappiest ideas," he said. "Shut the engine off, and put the tape in. And for god's sake, please turn-off those headlights."

"You mean it?"

"Just don't turn it up too loud, I don't want the neighbors to see me doing this."

As he held her close, they swayed to the flowing rhythm of *Last Date*. Bonnie Jo lay her head on his shoulder, and Billy felt strangely attracted to her. She definitely wasn't Sissy Conroy. She was a person he respected much more deeply. Besides, this dance seemed to mean a lot to her. Billy figured it was the least he could do. She pressed against him, and the warmth of her body in the cold night was like nothing he'd experienced with other girls. He suddenly began wondering what it would be like with her. She might be more fun than even Sissy. But, no. She was too much of a sweet person, and a real friend. Billy couldn't believe his own thoughts. He was a mindless jackal.

When the music ended he wanted to push her away, but if he was too abrupt she wouldn't understand. It would hurt her feelings. He gave her a gentle pat on the back and smiled, but then he pulled her even closer. He held her like he'd never held Sissy or any girl. Momentary insanity, he figured as he quickly recovered and stepped back. Looking up at him, she smiled and held out her hand to give him whatever had been in the box.

"What's this?" he asked.

"It's a Saint Sebastian medal."

"Saint...?"

"Sebastian," she repeated.

Opening the car door, he held the silver medal and chain under the dim yellow dome light. Saint Sebastian was tied to a tree and sprouting several arrows.

"He's the patron saint of athletes," she said. "I tried to find one specially for runners, but I don't think there is one."

Billy nodded. "Looks like old Saint Sebastian is having a bad day—with all those arrows in him."

"You know, it actually happened that way. The Roman Emperor tried to kill him, but he lived through it."

"No shit?"

"It's true."

She took the medal and chain and hung it around his neck.

"Anyway, I thought it could be a kind of keepsake, for you."

Billy thought of the rhinestone pendant he'd bought for his mom, but Bonnie Jo was too smart for that move. He had no choice but to tell the truth.

"I don't have anything for you," he said.

She reached out and touched his arm. "You've already given me too much, Billy."

"Huh?"

She smiled. "Your friendship is something no gift can ever match."

Feeling like a heel, he gazed off into the darkness at nothing in particular. He'd done little more than tolerate her, while she'd helped him with science and math, and almost everything else that mattered.

"Look, Bonnie Jo..."

She put her finger across his lips. "No, you look, Billy." She dropped her head again and looked down at her feet. "I know I'm not...well...like Sissy and the other girls you date, but you've always made time for me, like after the talent show when you said I would succeed no matter what the judges said. You've always affirmed that I was...well, okay, I guess."

Bonnie Jo seemed to always find the silver lining in every situation. She handed him a piece of folded blue stationary.

"This is a poem, I wrote for you. You know how I've always told you to try to see the bright side of things? Well, it's a little reminder."

Without warning she stood on tiptoes and planted a quick kiss on his cheek. Billy flinched.

"I'm sorry," she said. "I probably shouldn't have done that, but you've always been so sweet to me.

"It's okay, Bonnie Jo." He wanted to tell her she deserved so much more, but words were inadequate. He pulled her close and their lips met. It was only meant to be a truly sincere kiss of affection, but Billy felt his hands running almost involuntarily up her back inside her blouse. Finding her bra strap, he freed it. It was as if a raging inferno had suddenly exploded inside of him. He was consumed. The sweet taste of the peach schnapps mingled with her hot breath and she clung to him while he found her breasts. She gasped ever so slightly as he gently turned with her and lay her back on the big car seat.

"Are you sure?" she said panting softly.

Billy nodded as he unbuttoned her slacks and pushed his hand down between her legs. The hair there was already moist, and his fingers probed even deeper. The eight-track tapes clattered into the floor as he carefully cleared the seat and pulled her pants from around her ankles. After lowering his jeans, he probed softly until he felt the right spot and let himself sink inside of her. She let out a soft cry, and he hesitated.

"Are you okay?"

"It hurt for a second," she said, "but I'm okay."

Their lips met again, and Billy felt himself explode inside of her. Bonnie Jo moaned and quivered beneath him. It happened all too quickly, and he suddenly became aware that they were still in his front yard on the seat of her dad's car. He slowly pulled away and glanced about. All remained quiet. They were a clumsy mess, and a deep regret was growing as rapidly as his passion was receding.

After pulling her upright, Billy caressed Bonnie Jo's hair, kissed her again on the cheek and slid off the seat. Standing in the drive he buttoned his jeans, then fumbled with Bonnie Jo's slacks and underpants, turning them right side out. She stood, and he helped her dress. A shivering guilt wracked his body. He couldn't believe it. All she had wanted was a reaffirmation of his friendship, but he had totally lost control. He hated himself.

After dressing, she looked up into his eyes. He again pulled her close.

"Bonnie Jo…" She too was shaking, and he was again at a loss for the right words.

She smiled. "Don't worry, Billy-Boy. Everything will be okay. You'll see."

"It's getting late," he said.

She got into the car and started the engine. When she looked up her eyes were moist, something that perhaps called for another heartfelt hug or another kiss, but he gave her a cheap wink instead.

She smiled and winked back, saying, "No matter how far I go, Billy, I'll always remember you. You're the greatest."

It was as if she saw his weakness and his struggle to make sense of life. If he could have put Bonnie Jo in Sissy Conroy's body, she'd have damned near been the perfect woman.

Later, sitting on his bed in his underwear, Billy unfolded the piece of stationary and lay back on his pillow.

Dear Billy,
I wrote this for you. It's called
Islands in the Sky. I hope you like it.

When we're lonely, cold and blue,
There are places for people like me and
you,
We only need to search the skies above,
And our hearts will find our one true love.

So, go, find your love, your dreams,
Leave the hurt behind.
Free yourself and fly,
To the islands in the sky.

Soar amongst the clouds,
And there your dreams you'll find.
Soar amongst the clouds,
And leave the pain behind.
Soar amongst the clouds,
To the islands in the sky.

Islands in the sky,
They take our hearts and souls.
Islands in the sky,
They hold our hopes and dreams.

Islands in the sky,
Islands in the sky,

Free your heart and see,
There are islands in the sky.

Love Always,
Bonnie Jo

After she moved to California, Billy didn't think about her much until a letter came in the mail around Valentine's Day. He was at a loss for anything truly meaningful to say, but wrote her a letter anyway. He put it in the glove box of his pickup, and never got around to mailing it. The bleach-blond, fun-in-the-sun people were probably a lot like the Lizards, and living in Southern California had to be ten times worse for Bonnie Jo than living in Mississippi. She was again no doubt having her nose rubbed in the grim reality of human nature. He hoped she would find someone nice out there, but he no longer worried. They would probably never meet again.

5

THE WET RAT TEST

Billy never fully appreciated clean socks until after his first firefight. The cracks of AK-47 rounds snapping past followed by the screams of the ones who had been hit was a surreal experience. The firefight was over in minutes, and he spent the entire time face down in a rice paddy with geysers of water shooting up all around. He never fired a round. There was nothing to shoot at, but it was the most terrifying few minutes of his life up to then. It instantly altered his perspective on almost everything in life.

After one buries his face in the buffalo dung at the bottom of the rice paddy, knowing not to look up, because if he does, the smoking gray mass of his brains may end up floating in the muck with the rest of the crap, he begins developing appreciation for simple things. Billy found that sleep, even a short nap in a twenty-four hour day was something sweet, a sponge bath over a helmet full of cold water was heaven when your ass was red as a monkey's butt, even dry socks were a pleasure when your feet had been submerged in muck for a week. And a day without the psychosis of dripping rain became an almost celebratory experience.

Now, there was this patrol he was about to lead up the mountain. He'd been up all night thinking about it, and all he wanted was a few minutes sleep, a thirty-minute nap. That would be enough. He pointed his flashlight at his watch. It was 04:30 hours, time to roust the men. There would be no small pleasures for now. After getting the men started, he shouldered his rucksack and M-16, and walked up the hill to the CP in the predawn darkness. Bugsy was there and merely nodded as he shoved a canteen cup full of hot black coffee at Billy. Bugsy was clairvoyant that way.

A clammy fog had settled over the firebase, but above it, the mountain was still visible in the predawn darkness, a hard black shadow against a bruised sky. The men began arriving at the CP, appearing as shadowy ghosts in the stagnant mist, moving silently, checking their equipment. Everyone murmured in low tones as if gathered at a gravesite, probably in preparation for the silence that was required once they crossed through the wire. Billy had them shed everything nonessential then load up with extra frags and belts of ammo for the sixties. He and Bugsy checked each man's rucksack—four fragmentation grenades, one willy-peter for the tunnels, one smoke, one claymore, signal flares, an extra box of c-rations, extra magazines, ammo, iodine tablets, poncho, socks, and a few other essentials. Every one topped off their canteens, then locked and loaded. It was show time.

"Strict silence," Billy whispered. "Absolutely no noise. Cough, and I'll kill you myself." He turned to Bugsy. "Wish us luck, sir. We're gonna need it."

Their eyes met in the dim reflection of a flashlight, and after several seconds Bugsy nodded. Billy tossed him the empty canteen cup.

"G'luck," the CO said.

Billy nodded and motioned for the men to follow. They made their way down toward the gate. He had always heard how good soldiers focus on their mission, but before becoming a squad leader he seldom focused on much of anything—at least anything important. It was this same bad habit that caused him to end up in Nam, and when he thought about it he realized if his squandered past floated to the top and washed downstream, the flotsam would be a trash heap of consequential decisions based on hormones.

After spring break his relationship with Sissy rekindled, and he became too distracted to think about such trivial issues as the future. For a while he even thought he and Sissy might someday find eternal bliss together. At least, such were his thoughts the day they embarked on their senior class trip to the new swimming pool over in Tupelo. It was May, 1968, a time that became one of infamy for him, because that was when he first experienced the wet-rat test.

RICK DESTEFANIS

The wet-rat test, the ultimate litmus test for feminine beauty from the neck up, occurred when a girl's cosmetic facade was washed away in the pool. The unvarnished woman in her natural state was there for the whole world to see, as her hair was slicked tight against her skull, and the eye-shadow, rouge and mascara were floating with the rest of the chemicals in the pool. Only then was the *true* picture of a woman's face visible with no alterations. Of course, one had to maintain concentration from the neck up, and with several of them that was difficult. He'd never seen any of them without makeup.

The first time Sissy bobbed to the top of the water that afternoon, Billy never again saw women quite the same. It was as if Toto had pulled back the curtain, revealing the true wizardry of cosmetic beauty. Sissy pushed her hair back and smiled, and she wasn't exactly ugly, but with her paint gone, she wasn't the same person. And she wasn't the only one who had morphed into this homely little-boy look.

Several of the cheerleaders looked the same way, except for one, Rosemary Norvesi. Billy had never noticed Rosemary didn't wear makeup. Unlike the other girls in the pool, Rosemary still had full lips, rosy cheeks and long eyelashes. Of course, it took more than that for him to really notice her for the first time.

That came while he was sitting on the side of the pool near the high-dive when she walked out on the board and waved. He gave her a thumbs-up. None of the other girls would go near the high board, but Rosemary was fearless as she bounced into her first graceful dive. With long raven hair flowing behind her, she plummeted perfectly into the water, and when she bobbed back to the top in front of Billy, she was gasping and smiling with success. But, it was the two things floating in front of her that held his attention.

It was Billy's firm belief that when you're a teenager, tits are like beer in as much as the worst of either is damned near fantastic. And he was looking at two of the most beautiful breasts he'd ever seen, nipples erect, floating like two white water lilies against her tanned skin. Only after shrieks from several of the other girls did Rosemary realize the top to her swimsuit was around her waist. She quickly wrestled it back in place, then swam over to the ladder beside Billy. As she climbed out of the pool, she glanced over at him, sharp-eyed and tight-lipped.

"I hope you got your eyes full, Coker," she said.

"What did you want me to do?"

"You could have told me."

"I'm sorry. I mean, I was going to. I just got caught up in the moment. I mean, you really look good, and I was going to say something, but, oh, never mind. Like I said, I'm sorry."

Her anger slowly melted, and Billy handed her the towel from around his neck.

"Thanks," she said.

"Want to go get a Coke and sit over there in the shade?"

She nodded, and Sissy became a girl of the past.

Rosemary probably had the personality that came closest to Bonnie Jo's, but it was Billy's distraction with her fabulous tits that occupied most of the summer. That fall he got a notice from the draft board saying he was classified 1-A. That was when it dawned on him that nineteen-sixty-eight was not a good year to screw around, metaphorically speaking or otherwise. With most of the hay baled and the fences mended, his summer job at the farm petered out, and Billy realized he had a hard decision to make.

After stopping at the army recruiter's office in Tupelo that afternoon, he went home bursting with pride to tell his mother the news. The recruiter had said if he wanted to really attract women he should become a paratrooper. The Airborne troops were the only ones who wore their spit-shined jump boots with the army dress uniform. And when he pinned those silver jump wings on his chest, he would be a real man. He bought the whole spiel and signed up. His physical was scheduled for the following Monday.

When he got home Billy found his mother lying on the couch. She hadn't been well since his father had died a year and a half ago. Her blood pressure was too high, probably because she always worried about Eddie. Billy's older brother constantly stayed in trouble, and every time she tried to talk to him, he told her he was an adult now. She always told Billy that she was proud of him for staying out of trouble and passing in school. He figured becoming a paratrooper would really make her happy.

"What's this?" she asked, sitting upright on the couch.

Her hair had turned a dull gray and she had the faint odor of liniment. Billy never imagined his mother could look so old. Hopefully, the news of his enlistment would cheer her up.

"Read it," he said, smiling.

She reached for her reading glasses on the end table and turned on the lamp. He waited for her to smile, but after a few seconds her face grew pale and her lip quivered. She pulled the glasses from her face and set them on the paper in her lap.

"Billy, is this final? I mean, have you officially signed up?"

"What's wrong?" he asked, sitting down beside her.

Tears filled her eyes.

"Oh, son, what have you done? Don't you know there's a war going on?"

"Well, yeah, but the recruiter said that I might not even go there, 'cause they have people stationed in Germany, Korea and a lot of other places."

His mother rubbed her temples with her fingers.

"Bring me a glass of water, so I can take my medicine."

The first gray light of dawn was breaking as Billy led his men through the wire that morning, and he again caught himself unconsciously rubbing the medal hanging around his neck. He remembered Bonnie Jo' words that night when she said, "Don't worry, Billy Boy. Everything will be okay." He hoped she was right, because if she wasn't, he'd likely end up like Saint Sebastian, shot full of holes.

He put the men in column formation with a ten-meter separation between each to cross the open ground. This kept them from bunching up and hopefully, far enough apart that they wouldn't all end up in the kill-zone of an enemy ambush at the same time. Tim Casey was on point with Red Willis walking slack. Tim and Red were two of his best men, both already had Bronze Stars with oak leaf clusters. Billy walked behind them with Chris Rutledge, the RTO. He secured Chris's radio antenna down the side of his rucksack. A protruding radio antenna was like painting a sign on your ass that said, "SHOOT ME."

The patrol moved across the open ground, finding several trails along the way that were evidence of the enemy crawling close to the firebase at night. The mountain was a thousand meters away and still lost in the morning fog. Billy used a compass to stay on course. Somewhere behind them the firebase disappeared in the mist, but there came the distant clap of a latrine door. The troops back inside the firebase were beginning to stir. A feeling of separation was setting in, and the men looked spooked. They were scared, and with good reason. Regardless of what the CO said,

Billy was leading them into a situation where contact with the enemy could easily spell disaster.

The fog was their friend, hiding the patrol from the enemy, but it seemed almost alive, crawling across the wet grass, slithering its cold tentacles around their legs. Billy shivered as goose bumps ran up his arms, more from the tension than the cold morning air, but it did seem deathly cold, and he felt terribly alone.

It was that way at times. A deep loneliness gripped him, even with his men all around. Friendships here were thicker than blood relationships, because everyone depended on the guy beside him, but that's when Billy also first realized he didn't have one true friend back home. In high school, he never had the guts to accept friendship from the people he cared for the most, people like Melvin and Bonnie Jo. He was Peter after Gethsemane denying his true friends when the Lizards came around. He had burned those bridges, but Nam was different. He had a second chance here, because every man you fought beside was someone you depended on.

When he first arrived, Butch and Danny took him under their wings. Unlike most of the old heads, it didn't matter to them that Billy was a cherry. They took care of him, and they became his friends. But that was early in his tour. Now that they were gone, Billy avoided getting too close to anyone, especially the new guys. It was safer that way. He couldn't lose something he didn't have. At least this was the lie he told himself.

By the time the patrol reached the foot of the mountain the sun was peeking over the firebase back in the east. A fine mist shrouded the jungle, leaving the vegetation dripping, but the fog had worked in their favor. Billy was pretty sure they had crossed the open ground hidden from the watchful eyes of the enemy. He studied the foggy slope with binoculars that were on special loan from the CO for this patrol. Billy focused them on the objective, a ridge about a quarter of the way up the mountain. It ran perpendicular to the slope and made an ideal defensive position. Artillery and air strikes had pulverized it until only bare dirt remained. Scanning the mountain, Billy visually picked apart every hump, bump and anomaly in the terrain.

After a minute or two, he whispered to Casey, "Let's move out."

Casey, son of an Irish father and Mexican mother, couldn't have grown a decent beard if you gave him a month, but he was from south Texas, and hunting deer and javelina made him unequaled as a point-man. Billy trusted him. Tim seldom missed anything, especially trip-wires. He was the guy every other squad wished they had on point.

Billy put his finger over his lips signaling silence as they began the ascent. Crawling over a jumble of broken timber, they quietly made their way up the steep grade. With any luck, he hoped to reach the top of the ridge in an hour or two. Taking it slow and easy, he stopped several times to investigate possible booby-traps, and it was nearly midmorning when they crawled to within sixty meters of the ridge top. Billy studied the terrain through the binoculars for at least ten minutes. There were no signs of bunkers, spider holes or anything except dirt and ashes. The ground looked as if it had been wrecked by a mad road grader. Directing the rest of the squad to spread out and stay down, he tapped Casey on the shoulder, and the two of them crawled to the crest.

The morning sun was shining brightly now, and most of the fog had burned away. They were terribly exposed as they reached the bald hilltop. Billy's only comfort was that the sun was at his back. If the little bastards were looking his way, they were facing it—probably that silver lining Bonnie Jo had always talked about.

Scanning the draw below and the remaining slope to the top of the mountain, Billy searched for signs of the enemy with the binoculars. The one thing he hadn't noticed from the firebase was how the mountain was somewhat "L" shaped, and the ridge where he and Casey sat was inside the "L." The mountain rose ominously, not only to their front, but on the left as well. They were in a fish bowl.

"You see anything?" Casey asked.

"Nah. You?"

"Nothing," he replied.

Billy pulled the map from his fatigues and marked a couple of likely spots where the anti-aircraft guns might be hidden. These were outcroppings and knolls that had

RICK DESTEFANIS

a better view of the surrounding terrain. He wrote down their coordinates.

"What now?" Casey asked.

"You stay here," Billy said. "Keep your eyes open. I'm going back down and get on the horn. We'll see what Bugsy says."

"You mean, stay up here alone?" Casey hissed.

"If you see anything, just haul ass back down to us."

Casey was wide-eyed as Billy left him behind and crawled back down the hill. The rest of the men were spread across the slope in a small perimeter. A couple had broken out c-rations, but most were drawn up tight, bug-eyed and sitting on hair triggers. Billy felt the same raw-nerved edginess.

"Contact the CP," he told Rutledge. "Tell them we've reached our objective, and it looks quiet right now."

He keyed the handset on the PRC-25. "Six-shooter one-one, this is Six-shooter three-three, over."

Bugsy must have been sitting there by the radio. He came back instantly. "Six-shooter three-three, this is one-one. Go ahead, over."

The CO must have been there, too, because Bugsy hesitated before coming back and telling them to sit tight. According to plan, the gunships were due to arrive any moment. Billy smoked a cigarette then motioned for Rutledge to follow as he crawled back up to the crest of the ridge. When they got there, Casey was acting antsy, looking first at Billy then at Rutledge.

"What's the problem?" Billy asked.

"Nothing," he said. "Nothing at all. Why should there be a problem? We're only out here in the middle of fucking nowhere on this bald-ass hill like sitting ducks. What are we going to do next, start waving a red flag to get their attention?"

"Stop whining. We're going to sit tight and wait for the gunships."

"Goddamit, Billy. I don't like it," he said. "This is spooky as hell. If those bastards don't know we're here by now, they must be blind or something."

"We might have crept up on them in that fog this morning," Billy said. "Besides, they probably think nobody's stupid enough to come up here with just a squad of men."

"Damned right, and I don't like it," Casey said. "Sitting out here in the open on this ridge is just asking for it. What the fuck are we supposed to do if—"

"Just calm the hell down, Casey. Ain't nothing happened yet. When those gunships get here, we're gonna try to spot the enemy positions that open up on them. We'll call in some arty. After that, we're getting our asses out of here. We'll di di mau right on back down this hill and be back at the firebase before dark."

"I still don't like it..." His voice trailed away as he mumbled under his breath.

Casey was right, but there was no sense getting everyone spooked. "Ssh—quiet," Billy said.

Somewhere in the distance came the rhythmic thump-thump-thump of choppers approaching through the mountains. As the sound grew louder, Billy hunkered down with the binoculars.

"Come up on their frequency," he told Rutledge. "Make sure they know where we are before they start blasting away."

The three gunships made several sweeps across the mountain, trying to draw enemy fire, but it was as if the enemy knew what they were doing. Nothing happened. Not a single shot was fired. The chopper pilots were about to drop back and spray some random shots into the mountainside when Billy suggested they fire at the likely spots he'd recorded earlier. He gave them the coordinates, and a few moments later the first gunship cut-loose with a salvo of rockets at a particularly strange looking mass of brush on the far ridge.

They hit pay-dirt as several secondary explosions thundered and echoed across the slopes and a cloud of dust and black smoke blossomed skyward. Far across the way little men scattered like ants fleeing the impact area. Almost immediately, the mountain became a beehive of anti-aircraft fire. Fifty calibers were chugging from at least three different locations. The first chopper flared and dove away down the mountain as a second came in low and fast. The second chopper fired his rockets at another target and pulled out to the north. Billy turned to watch the third chopper's approach. By now he had spotted the three enemy gun emplacements and recorded them on the map.

The third chopper was still well over a quarter-mile out when debris tumbled from beneath its tail boom and it stopped firing. A thin stream of black smoke marked its path as it turned back toward the firebase. For a moment it seemed the helicopter might make it as the crew fought to maintain control, but part of the tail rotor fell away, and the chopper began a slow spiral into the jungle below. The pilot still had partial control and was calmly calling "Mayday" over the radio as he disappeared into the trees several hundred meters down the mountain. Definitely a survivable crash.

Billy turned to Rutledge. "We'll pick them up on the way back. First, we're going to put some arty on those gun emplacements. Contact the other choppers and tell them what we're doing, then switch to the command frequency."

Several minutes passed. The choppers had pulled back, and Billy talked with the artillery officer at Fire Support Base Fargo while the first shells whispered overhead. The explosions echoed and thundered across the mountain as he called in corrections and walked the artillery rounds toward the target. Things were going well until Casey suddenly slapped Billy on the back.

"Holy Mother of God!" he shouted. "Look up there."

Casey was a Catholic boy, and like Billy he also wore a medal around his neck, but his was the Virgin Mary. He was also nervous as a cat, so Billy wasn't overly concerned when he pulled the medal from inside his flak jacket, kissed it and made the sign of the cross. Billy re-focused the binoculars to where Casey had pointed.

"Holy shit," he whispered.

There was good reason for Casey's hysteria. Seven hundred meters up the mountain to their left, the NVA were spilling out of the ground like hornets. They'd already begun streaming through the trees down the slope. Having seen the chopper go down, they were coming down the mountain in force, and Billy and his men were directly in their path. If they simply turned and ran, the enemy would overtake them in a matter of minutes. They'd be surrounded and chopped to pieces. There was only one solution. Someone had to stay behind and try to delay them while the rest of the squad made a dash for the firebase.

6

A GOOD DAY TO DIE

Billy focused the binoculars on the hoard of enemy soldiers weaving their way down the mountain. He had resigned himself to getting killed or wounded after the first few months in Vietnam. That first month it was Hamburger Hill, and for months afterward men got hit so often it seemed the odds of going home unscathed were slim. It was a life of tracers, illumination rounds and mosquitoes by night—heat, body bags and flies by day, all in a never-ending state of fear and tension. Billy had found it easier to resign himself to the odds, not exactly in a fatalistic way, but as a means of making peace with the madness.

Some men carried good-luck charms—a rabbit's foot, a spent round, a girlfriend's photo—whatever talisman that might put a magical spell on an enemy bullet or chunk of shrapnel, deflecting it midair. Butch had carried one, a peace symbol he wore with his dog tags. A lifer's daughter who lived in a trailer park near Fayetteville, North Carolina had given it to him. A chrome-plated piece of pot-metal she bought at a head shop on Hay Street, it was his going away present when he left for Nam. It was still around his neck the day Billy pushed his bloody corpse into the chopper.

With less than thirty days left on his tour, a vague hope of survival had rekindled in Billy's heart. And with the hope, also returned the old fear and paranoia. He was becoming human again. Life after Nam again seemed possible. At least it had until now. As he sat with Rutledge and Casey, watching scores of NVA soldiers weaving their way down the mountain, he realized that his hope had been a fool's gold. It was time to get back to the business of war.

Billy thumbed the St. Sebastian medal as he looked around at his men. "Rutledge," he said, "leave the radio here. You and Casey head back down to the rest of the guys. Tell Curtis to get up here with his sixty and as much ammo as he can carry. We'll try to slow the little bastards down, while you guys work your way down to where the chopper went into the trees. Tell Red he's in charge. Pick up the chopper crew, and head back to the firebase."

"What if they're dead?" Casey asked.

"Carry the bodies in. We don't want these bastards to get them."

They turned to run down the hill.

"Wait!" Billy yelled.

The two of them froze, bug-eyed and about to hyperventilate.

"Both of you guys calm down, and listen to me. Slow down. Don't get in such a big rush that you blunder into an ambush or trip a booby-trap. Use your heads. Keep your eyes open, and keep the point man well out in front. If they saw us come up here this morning, there's a good chance they've flanked us. They might be waiting for you between here and the firebase. Me and Curtis will try to hold them as long as we can. Now, git."

They scrambled down the slope. Casey passed Rutledge in the first ten steps, and Billy shook his head as he watched them go. They were scared shitless. Turning back to the radio, he stopped the artillery and switched frequencies, giving the choppers the coordinates of the advancing enemy hoard. The anti-aircraft fire was intense as the constant *wump-wump-wump* of the enemy's fifty calibers echoed across the slopes. The chopper pilots, knowing the patrol was about to be overrun, flew directly into the hail of fire, cutting loose with everything they had. Their mini-guns buzzed as nearly solid lines of tracers streamed into the ridge above, bouncing and scattering like fiery confetti.

The enemy advance stalled. The Cobras emptied their rocket pods as well, but they took more damage as another one limped off to the east trailing a stream of black smoke. The anti-aircraft guns were simply too much for them. Having guts was one thing, but it was suicide to continue flying across the face of the mountain, and Billy didn't want matters complicated further with another downed chopper. He told the remaining chopper to pull out and circle back toward the firebase to search for the crash site. The pilot wished him luck and dropped away down the mountain.

A few moments later Curtis came lumbering over the crest of the ridge. He was draped with at least eight belts of ammo, along with the one in the gun. Big-Boy was loaded for bear.

Curtis crawled up behind a burned log, while Billy returned to the command frequency, called in a new fire-mission and adjusted the artillery in front of the enemy troops. Realizing the choppers had broken off their attack, the enemy was again advancing down the mountain. Curtis opened up with the sixty.

Curtis Teague was a black guy from somewhere south of New Orleans, and he handled an M-60 machinegun the way some people dance—smooth, easy and natural. He dropped his tracers right on target as the first attackers disappeared in geysers of dust. He had already picked up and moved to a new position, when the enemy began chewing up his last position with their machineguns. Curtis raised up some fifty meters away and gave them another sustained burst from the Sixty. Curtis was good. Burning through four belts of ammo, he slowed the enemy advance.

Billy continued adjusting the artillery fire from Fargo, but the enemy troops closed to within four hundred meters. Just after calling in another artillery adjustment, he was forced to duck as the surrounding ridge erupted with explosions. The NVA had zeroed in with mortars. Explosions shook the ground, as the dust-filled air cracked and whirred with shrapnel.

"Curtis," he yelled. "We gotta get out of here."

Curtis rose to a crouch and began backing over the hill. Billy caught up, and they dropped behind the crest of the ridge.

"Come on. We need to move fast."

The jumble of fallen timber slowed their progress, and Billy grew winded as he leaped over logs and down ravines toward the jungle below. Curtis passed him bounding down the hillside like a gazelle, almost effortlessly. He was six-foot-three, weighed at least two-thirty-five, and carried the twenty-six-pound M-60 like it was a Red Rider BB gun. They said he'd played linebacker for Mississippi Valley State and had been destined to play professional football when the draft board got him. Despite Billy's four years running cross-country, he could barely keep up. His breath was coming in ragged gulps by the time they reached the tree line.

"You gonna make it, Sarge?" Curtis asked.

Except for his steel pot and flak jacket, Curtis was naked from the waist up, and a lather of sweat drenched his body, but he was barely winded. Billy's lungs ached as he fought to catch his breath. He still had all his gear, including the radio. Something had to go.

"Gimme that damned thing," Curtis said.

He reached up and pulled the radio from Billy's arms. "No. You need to be able to shoot the sixty."

Curtis ignored him and threw the PRC-25 on his back. Billy was too exhausted to argue. Reaching inside his rucksack, he pulled out the claymore and several extra frags, then shoved the pack under a log. He dropped the grenades in his pockets along with the wire and a detonator for the claymore.

"Let's go," he said.

Enemy gunfire splattered around them as they scrambled through the trees and down the ravines until they reached the last rise at the base of the mountain. There, Billy spotted the tail-end of the patrol. They were crossing the open ground toward the firebase. The two helicopter crewmen were with them. The pilots were lucky to be alive, but one was limping. This slowed the column as they slogged through grass and ankle deep water. It was up to Curtis and Billy. They had to delay the enemy until the patrol reached the firebase.

He turned to Curtis. "We need to set up here," he said.

"You go on, Sarge," Curtis replied. "Catch up with the others. I'll hold them up as long as I can."

"No. We stay together," Billy shouted.

Curtis shook his head. "You're the dumbest white boy I know. How come you're arguing with me?"

"Cause I'm in charge, dumb-butt."

Curtis looked up the ridge as the sweat streamed down his face. "Well, Sarge, since you're in charge, why don't you tell me how we gonna get away from all them little fuckers up yonder—crawl in a hole and hide like rabbits?"

"Find some cover." I'm going back up to that little rise and set out this claymore. Don't shoot me."

"You're one crazy motherfucker. I'm trying to give you a get-out-of-jail-free card, and you won't even take it."

Billy ran back up the trail. Curtis was right. He was crazy. They were in a hornet's nest, and the hornets were plenty pissed off. Stringing the wire for the claymore as he went, Billy stopped just over the crest of the rise. This was where the enemy would take cover when Curtis opened up with the machinegun.

From further up the mountainside came the voices of the enemy calling to one another. Billy hurriedly positioned the claymore so it would rake the backside of the knoll. After camouflaging it with loose grass, he glanced around. When it detonated, the mine would spray over seven hundred ball-bearing-size pellets across the slope, making Swiss cheese out of everything within seventy-five feet. Hopefully, it would buy him and Curtis the time they needed to escape.

With the sounds of men running above, Billy hurriedly retraced his steps, making his way back to the pile of logs where Curtis was hidden. He had shed the radio and laid out the remaining belts of ammo. Picking up the radio handset, Billy checked his map to call in artillery support. With the enemy closing in, artillery was their only hope for escape. They needed the cover-fire and smoke to make good their retreat. Enemy rifle rounds again ricocheted through the trees. They'd been spotted.

Down below, the patrol was already halfway across the open ground and trotting steadily toward the firebase. Curtis opened up with the sixty while Billy crouched behind him and keyed the radio handset—nothing. It wouldn't break squelch. He began pounding the radio with his fist until he noticed a gaping hole on the back-side. Shrapnel had struck it while Curtis carried it on his back. By the looks of the damage, it had saved his life, but it was useless now. With their only hope for a getaway shot to hell, Billy crawled up beside Curtis.

"The radio is dead," he shouted. "We're going to have to make a run for it."

Curtis didn't reply as he continued firing, but the ammo belt in the sixty was nearly gone. He paused for a moment while Billy clipped another belt to the one in the gun. This gave the enemy the advantage, and their fire intensified. Several RPG explosions sent shrapnel and wood chunks flying everywhere. Curtis opened up again. More enemy soldiers joined their comrades on the backside of the rise. There had to be at least a dozen of them. Billy detonated the claymore.

The explosion sent up a cloud of smoke and dust. The enemy gunfire ceased abruptly as screams and moans rose from behind the knoll. Billy slapped Curtis on the shoulder, and they scrambled further down the mountain. They had to keep moving, keep the enemy guessing. If they got pinned down, it would be over in seconds.

As they zigzagged down the hill, Billy spotted several enemy soldiers running down a ravine to his right. They were trying to flank them. Scrambling to an open spot he pulled the pins on two grenades and threw them into the ravine. The ones who weren't stunned or wounded by the explosions retreated back up the mountain.

Another RPG exploded, knocking Billy to the ground. Dazed, he shook his head, trying to stop the spinning sensation. He suddenly realized the machine-gun was no longer firing. Through the smoke and dust he saw Curtis lying spread-eagle on his back with his mouth open. AK-47 rounds cracked incessantly as Billy crawled to him. Curtis's face was ashen, but there was no blood, and he was still breathing. The explosion had knocked him unconscious.

Picking up the Sixty, Billy pulled the sling over his head and glanced toward the firebase. The patrol was nearly across the open ground. It was time to break and run, but Curtis wasn't going anywhere. The last belt of ammo dangled from the machine gun, and Billy tossed it over his shoulder. His only hope, now, was to try to hold off the enemy and work his way down the slope. Grabbing the back of Curtis's flak jacket, Billy pulled him down the hill, firing short bursts as he went.

The machine gun climbed and bucked out of control, scattering rounds across the mountainside, but it was enough to hold the enemy at bay. Billy backed down the hill, but with Curtis in tow he made little progress. Stopping, he grabbed the gun with both hands, zeroed in on the enemy and emptied the sixty. Tossing the machinegun aside, he pulled Curtis across his shoulders and started across the open ground toward the firebase.

Red tracers zipped overhead as the troops in the bunkers opened up on the enemy. At the same moment, artillery rounds began exploding along the slope behind him. Adrenaline pumping through his body, Billy labored across the open ground with Curtis on his back. At first he scarcely felt the weight, but the further he ran, the heavier Curtis became. After a while Billy slowed to a walk, but he refused to look back. He and Curtis were the only ducks left in this carnival's shooting gallery, and every sonofabitch on the mountain was shooting at them. All around the bullets cracked incessantly as Billy plodded toward the firebase.

A spray of muddy water showered him as yet another rocket propelled grenade exploded. It shook him, but he didn't stop. Dull thuds vibrated the ground at his feet, the impact of bullets missing by inches. Behind him rifles and machine guns chattered and popped relentlessly. Halfway across the open ground a glimmer of hope arose as Billy made out the forms of the men on the perimeter. Only a few hundred meters remained to the gate.

With his oxygen deprived lungs about to explode, he was growing delirious from the heat and exhaustion.

102

He became disoriented and found himself angling parallel to the bunkers. Stopping, Billy regained his wits and once again spotted the gate to the compound. It was only a couple-hundred meters away. He began taking slow deliberate steps toward it, but spotted another rocket trail coming his way.

Billy dropped Curtis to the ground, but before he could take cover the RPG exploded behind him. A strange, almost surreal sensation gripped him as Billy felt himself pushed skyward by some powerful force. When he awakened he was lying on the soggy ground, but he felt nothing. Barely conscious, he realized he had been hit and was too stunned to move.

The side of his face was half submerged in muddy water. It had seeped in, filling his mouth. He tried to raise his head, but nothing happened. With the one eye that was above the water, he saw Curtis on the ground. He was stirring back to consciousness. Shaking his head, Curtis looked around, and after a few seconds, he rolled over and looked at Billy. His eyes said what Billy already suspected.

There was something, an intestine perhaps, protruding through a hole in Billy's side, and he was drenched with blood from the waist down. His fatigue pants were shredded, and his legs were grotesquely bent and crumpled. This was it. This was where it would end. The explosion had riddled his body with shrapnel. Spitting out the muddy water, he took a shallow breath and exhaled. Curtis crawled to his side.

Tears and blood streamed down Curtis's face as he carefully slid his arms under Billy. He hesitated several seconds before carefully lifting him, then turning toward the firebase. Carrying Billy in his arms, Curtis walked up the hill, oblivious to the enemy fire. He didn't run. He simply walked, making his way the last two hundred meters to the gate.

Billy looked up past billowing white clouds floating like islands in the deep blue sky. He looked into the ocean of eternity extending far above as he no longer heard anything, not even the sound of Curtis' pounding heart or his heaving lungs as he cradled him in his arms. Rockets exploded silently and mortar rounds made not a sound as chunks of mud and grass rained down on them, and Billy felt his life rushing away. The sun was shining, and he was lost in serene silence. It was a beautiful blue-sky day, a good day to die.

SECTION II

7

THE GATES OF HELL

A head shone above him, bald and glistening in an aura of burning white light. What wasn't naturally hairless was closely shaven and infested with a web of purple veins. A hatchet nose hung long and sharp from his face with nostrils that flared open from the side. His skin was sallow and slick like wet leather, but seemed otherwise colorless. His lips were thick and turned down at the corners, and although darker, they were afflicted with the same deep translucence. A large mole protruded from the right side of his chin, and his tiny pale blue eyes were sunk deep under cavernous brows of sparse and grotesquely long red hairs. The brows were the only hair on his entire head, perhaps even his body.

It was the ugliest thing Billy had ever seen, the devil himself, no doubt. He was in hell, and his body was burning with a kind of pain he didn't think possible.

The odor of fetid flesh and strange chemicals surrounded him. A pool of hazy consciousness held him prisoner as he stared up at the head. Now slowly licking its lips with a tongue that appeared rough as sandpaper the creature seemed to realize he was awake. Billy heard a voice, deep and resonate, yet seemingly disembodied as it came from nowhere and everywhere at once.

"Can you hear me?"

The eyelids moved almost ponderously as the devil slowly blinked, and the sound of the monster's slow but heavy breathing filled Billy's ears. It was the beast, the personification of death staring him in the eye. If it wasn't, it was a nightmare beyond the pale of imagination. A blinding light filled Billy's eyes. This was it. They say there comes a white light when you are about to die, the warm, blinding, but all-comforting light of the Great Spirit coming to take you as your mind fades into eternity.

But this light burned, and it jumped from eye to eye, and back again. His eyes hurt and he tried to close them, but something held them open. A hand rested on his forehead while the fingers held Billy's eyelids apart. After a moment or two, he saw a small chrome flashlight.

"Can you hear me?" the voice said again.

It had to be the creature hovering above him, but its lips scarcely moved. Billy tried to answer, but nothing happened. Was he paralyzed? He tried to nod, but again nothing happened. His body would not respond, but the voice came again.

"Good," it said.

It was as if God himself were speaking, except Billy was pretty sure God wasn't this ugly. It made no sense. And the more he tried to understand the more he began to realize it was just a dream, a nonsensical illusion. He tried to force himself awake, but it didn't work. He tried to sit up, but it was as if he no longer had a body. He was in a disembodied state, floating in a sea of pain. Was this hell?

The light went out, and the creature's head reappeared from out of the haze, but this time Billy noticed something more. He wore a green surgeon's shirt and had a stethoscope around his neck. A doctor, a damned doctor! Everything tumbled back into his mind at once as he relived those final moments before losing consciousness. He'd been wounded and certain that he was dying, but he hadn't. The surgeon was at once the ugliest and the most beautiful sonofabitch he'd ever seen.

He was in a hospital and still alive, except there was nothing happening. He tried to look around, but couldn't move his head. It was quiet, too quiet. Nurses should have been running everywhere, carrying bottles of plasma and shouting at orderlies. They should have been giving terse commands as they prepped him for surgery. Instead, there was only the cold silence of inactivity. His elation sank into the bitter realization that they were doing nothing to revive him.

The distant beep of a heart monitor echoed somewhere back in the void of silence. He was one of those they had wheeled to the side. He'd seen it before when they went down to the MASH unit to check on some of the wounded. The ones shot up so badly that they couldn't be saved were wheeled to the back while the medical teams worked on those who had a chance. When they finished with the others, the doctors and nurses returned, and if the unlucky ones were still alive, they did what they could to make them comfortable, but it was usually a death vigil.

The morphine drugged him out of his mind, but Billy's body shrieked with pain. If they kept him breathing, he was doomed to a life of misery in a mangled body. Please God, just let me go back to sleep. Let it be over. He was ready to die. He had to die.

The doctor hovered above him for several minutes, and after a while Billy managed to look down at his body. Tubes were running from his mouth and nose, and plastic bags hung at the side of the bed, with more tubes running into his side. He was naked except for a sheet across his waist. His legs were swollen and purple, but they were both still there. Long tracks of black stitches crisscrossed his abdomen, and he looked like a grotesque Raggedy Anne Doll, stitched together from patches of red and purple vinyl.

It finally came to him. He'd already been through surgery, and by the look of the wounds, it had been some time ago. He tried to move, but nothing happened. Was he paralyzed, doomed to a life of drooling on himself and shitting in bedpans? His eyes found the surgeon's, and Billy tried to talk, but nothing happened.

He heard the voice again. "Just rest. You've got a long way to go."

For the first time in months the rhythmic thumping of helicopters had stopped. The distant rumble of artillery from back in the mountains had suddenly ceased. It was quiet, graveyard quiet, no shouts, no screams, no ear-ringing explosions, no bullets cracking in the air, no scythes of shrapnel whirring past. The air no longer lay over him like a wet blanket, and it no longer smelled like cordite and mildewed canvas.

He listened. He strained to hear, but there was nothing. There would be no more months of nonstop rains, no more leech bites, no clouds of incessantly buzzing mosquitoes, rats running over him in the darkness, rotted feet or days on end without sleep. It had all ended. He was no longer in Vietnam.

8

DREAMS AND NIGHTMARES

U.S. Army Hospital, Camp Zama, Japan

Billy was feeling it. He had his second wind, and three miles into his daily run he quickened the pace, stretching his stride. It felt good as he pushed himself. Today he wanted to improve his time, and the good burn came as his muscles found new limits. But the burn worsened, and he suddenly struggled to see the trail ahead. Everything was lost in shadow. He rubbed his eyes, and reality came crashing back once again. He had been dreaming of something no longer possible. He licked his lips and willed his numb legs to move, but there came only the nothingness of a totally unresponsive body. He was trapped, and his heart screamed in despair.

As for the place they call the hereafter, he must have gone there and rung the bell a half-dozen times the first month after he was wounded. He was certain, because every time he awakened they told him he had just come through another surgery. Most days were clouded by drug-induced nightmares that fed ravenously on his wrecked psyche. It became difficult to separate the nightmares from reality as he found himself tumbling earthward, tangled in the shroud lines of his parachute, fighting in dense jungle at point blank range as the enemy over ran his position or awakening at a Graves Registration Unit with a dog tag stuck between his teeth. At times he awoke with an exploding rocket again shredding his body, but the oddest nightmare was the one about Bonnie Jo Parker.

The Lizards had somehow driven her to her death, and they held a memorial service in the Raeford High auditorium. The entire student body was there. On the stage, Bonnie Jo's corpse lay in a silk-lined casket, a grim smile cosmetically stretched across her face. The auditorium's ancient burgundy curtains were pulled back, and tiers of flowers served as a backdrop. Around her coffin, Coach Roper, Marty Macklin and the rest of the jocks sat in folding metal chairs under the gleaming kliegs. They stared grim-faced out at the crowd, as if to dare anyone who wasn't a member of the Lizards to walk up the aisle.

One by one the entire cheerleading squad filed past the coffin, wearing their shortest skirts. As each girl passed she tossed a Twinkie into the coffin. They came, and they heaped their insults on her, until Bonnie Jo's corpse was buried beneath a mountain of snack food.

Marty eyed Billy from the stage as if daring him to speak, and Billy was bound by an invisible straightjacket of fear, fear that he would forever be ostracized from the people he most detested, and he didn't know why. He didn't know why he cared, but he did. He wanted their approval, their acceptance. It had to be a definition of one of the levels of hell. His voice was frozen deep inside, and there came only the desperate grunts and moans of a coward.

Some of the dreams weren't so bad, because Bonnie Jo would be there quietly holding his hand and reassuring him that everything was going to be okay. She had never asked for anything from him, except that one dance. She didn't act as if she expected anything in return for her friendship. It was a gift with no strings attached, but he had taken advantage of her.

Poor Bonnie Jo probably ended up with some tattooed Hispanic dude who sold weed in south LA, or with an Okie up in Fresno who drove a '59 Chevy he claimed was just as good as a '57. She probably had a couple of snotty-nosed kids by now, wearing diapers and crawling around in the dust of a trailer park on the outskirts of LA. She was out there with no hope, no dream and no place left to go, lost in the ocean of houses and people that sprawled across the brushy hills of Southern California.

After a couple months, Billy still felt like a distempered dog, but he was stable enough to return to the states. As the orderlies pushed him on board the gray hospital plane in Japan, a faint glimmer of hope crept into his heart. He was finally escaping. He was going home to the real world, a place with real people, a place where life had value and people didn't arbitrarily shoot the shit out of one another.

When the hospital plane landed at Pope Air Force Base in North Carolina, an Army field ambulance carried him and the other men to Womack Army Hospital at Fort Bragg. They arrived in the middle of the morning shift-change, eight wounded vets delivered like luggage, signed for and pushed to the side while clerks and orderlies changed shifts.

The men lay on gurneys waiting as the hospital grew quiet again. Billy had nearly nodded off when he heard a soft voice. A young nurse ran her hand over his forehead. Her blonde hair was pinned beneath her cap, but with dimpled cheeks and deep blue eyes, she seemed sorely out of place in an Army hospital. She picked up the Saint Sebastian medal lying on his chest, and examined it.

"Someone has a special sense of humor," she said.

Billy said nothing. There was no longer an ember left in the ashes of his burned-out soul. He was toast, just another human patched up project for this army nurse to handle.

"Let me go see where they have you assigned," she said. "I'll be right back."

With his medication wearing off, the pain increased. A few minutes later the nurse returned with a male orderly. The orderly looked at him as if he were a museum piece, but the nurse caressed the side of his face.

"Well, we didn't know who we had on our hands. I just discovered that the Vice President is coming down next month to award you a medal—The Distinguished Service Cross."

Billy already knew about the medal, but he was too far gone to care. Feverish and racked with nausea, he was more excited about his next dose of pain medication. The orderly pushed his gurney down the hallway to the elevator, while the nurse walked along side reading his chart. Everyone they passed spoke, but she was all business as she studied the chart. The color began rising in her cheeks.

"They used a stitch by the numbers kit to put me back together," he said.

She looked down and tried to smile, but it came off as a tightlipped grimace.

"Have you had any breakfast?" she asked.

. "No, but I'd rather have something for pain. I'm hurtin' pretty bad right now."

"I'll check with the doctor to see what kind of pain medication he wants you to have, and let's see if we can get you something to eat, too."

She returned several minutes later with a tray, and after giving him a couple pills, began feeding him a bowl of soupy baby cereal.

"I'm Janie Stafford," she said.

"Do nurses always spoon feed their patients around here?"

She laughed. "No. Just this one time."

Cereal dripped on his chin, and she wiped it away with her finger. "Here, lick," she said as she wiped her finger across his lips. "Your chart says you have shrapnel wounds and trauma to your kidneys and intestinal tract as well as your legs and hips, but you've been improving. The most important thing is that we get your plumbing fixed so you can get back on solid food. You're a little too skinny right now."

The nurse picked up the Saint Sebastian medal again and studied it. "Your dog tags say non-denominational."

"The medal was a gift from a Catholic friend."

"Your friend is a very thoughtful person. I suppose it's his way of telling you that you're a survivor."

"Yeah, except she gave it to me long before I thought about going to Nam."

"Really?" Laying the medal back on his chest, she spooned the last of the cereal from the bowl. "So, is she your girlfriend?"

"We never dated. She was just a friend."

"She seemed to know you pretty well."

He shrugged. "Female intuition, I suppose."

"You're scheduled for therapy twice a day. Are you ready to get started?"

He shrugged, but she took his indifference in stride. The more he thought about Bonnie Jo and the Saint Sebastian Medal, the more Billy believed there was something beyond the physical at work in his life. Perhaps it was that higher power people talked about, but so far he was still undecided.

Nurse Janie oversaw the orderlies as they lifted him into a wheelchair and pushed him down the hall to therapy.

"The Distinguished Service Cross is quite an honor," she said.

"Just got my ass shot off, helping a buddy."

She nodded but said nothing more.

After several weeks in the whirlpool, the feeling in Billy's hips and legs began returning. It came as a tingling sensation that alternated with lightning bolts of pain and a constant soreness. Janie said the pain and soreness were actually good things, signs the nerves were regenerating, but she was still worried about his internal injuries. With infection and multiple problems with his kidneys and intestines, Billy continued losing weight.

"We'll have you good as new in no time," Janie said as she checked the new antibiotic IV.

Billy glanced up at her, and she met his stare with a broad smile, one obviously meant to appear genuine, but the worry and doubt in her eyes betrayed her.

"Have you always had this problem dealing with reality?" Billy asked. "Look at me. It's been four months since I got hit, and I'm not getting better. I'm shriveling up."

Janie's eyes moistened, but she turned away. Walking over to a window, she gazed out at Fort Bragg and the Carolina landscape. A string of Hueys clattered almost silently by in the distance. After a while, she walked back over and sat on the bed beside him.

"We're doing everything we can," she said, "but you've got to stay positive, and most of all, you've got to put the war behind you. You've got to let it go."

"Let it go?" he replied. "Hell, I have nightmares about it every night, and how am I ever going to have a normal life with a wife and kids? My guts are like scrambled eggs."

She stared at him, her crystal blue eyes still glistening with tears.

"The doctor said that other than the bits of shrapnel, your reproductive organs are fine. Besides, there are ways to get pregnant even if you can't have sex."

"You've got to be kidding. Who the hell wants a life without sex?"

"You know, Billy, you are a very handsome man. And, because you're a fighter, I believe you will eventually pull through this, but you have to do the rest yourself. You've been through hell, but you have to decide what you want out of life."

Billy looked away. "All I want right now is to be left alone."

Several more weeks passed, and Janie was smiling that morning as she shook the thermometer and prepared to take Billy's temperature.

"You know what's happening next week, don't you?"

Billy folded the *Stars and Stripes* he was reading and looked up.

"You don't remember?" she said.

"Oh, yeah, the medal thing."

"Well, try not to act so excited."

"It's just a medal."

Janie pursed her lips as she shook her head. "Billy, that medal represents a lot more than even the citation can say. It represents the core of who you are. It also represents all the men you served with."

"Okay," he said. "Sorry."

She stuck the thermometer in his mouth. Although they were bland, he was beginning to look forward to meals. After the doctor had returned him to a normal diet he began gaining weight, and his prognosis was actually looking up. Janie pulled the thermometer from his mouth, but she hesitated and looked closer, frowning.

"How do you feel?"

"I've been feeling a little shittier than normal this morning. Why?"

"Something's not right. Let me call the doctor."

"Shit," Billy muttered.

Before leaving the room, Janie shook the thermometer down again and stuck it back in his mouth. When she returned, an orderly followed with a gurney. She pulled the thermometer from his mouth and looked at it again.

"We're taking you back down to X-ray," she said.

They were pushing him down the hallway when the nausea struck. An hour later the doctor appeared at the foot of the bed. After studying Billy's chart, he gently nudged and poked his abdomen, until his finger found a tender spot. Billy grunted and tried to draw back.

"Sergeant Coker, we're going to have to do another surgery," he said.

"What, now?"

"You've got dozens of very small particles of shrapnel in your body, too many to find at once. They move around, and occasionally a sharp one gets in the wrong place. I'm guessing this one has penetrated the wall of your small intestine, causing an infection. Don't worry, we should be able to get it out without much trouble."

Coming out of surgery was always a muddle of nightmares and reality, and Billy found himself looking up at Bugsy. He closed his eyes. Why Bugsy?

"Billy?"

He was even hearing his voice. After a few moments, he opened his eyes again. Lieutenant Busby, his old platoon leader was still there, except he wore captain's bars on his uniform, and on his left shoulder was the red and blue "AA" patch of the 82nd Airborne.

"Bugsy?" Billy said. "Is that you?"

"It's me, Billy."

"Damn, I thought I was having another dream."

"At least you're calling it a dream and not a nightmare."

"Shit, sorry, sir. I didn't realize it was really you."

"Save the "sirs" for when other people are around."

"What are you doing wearing captain's bars and an 82nd patch?"

"When I left Nam last month, I was promoted and reassigned to the 82nd here at Bragg. I've actually been assigned in my original MOS to the JAG office here."

Billy smiled. Bugsy deserved it.

"I was going to surprise you at the award ceremony next week, but you went and got sick again."

Billy closed his eyes, and he must have dozed for a moment, because Bugsy was now sitting in a chair beside the bed. Apparently seeing Billy's eyes open, the captain stood up.

"You back with us?" he asked.

Billy nodded.

"I have to go now, but there's something I want to say. I am more proud to have served with you than any soldier I've ever known. And if you ever need anything, any time, any place, you call me. I'll be there."

Billy raised his arm taped with an IV and heart monitor cord, and gave his old platoon leader a feeble but heartfelt salute. The captain popped his heels together and returned a sharp salute.

"As you were, Sergeant Coker."

With that Bugsy bent over and kissed Billy's forehead.

"Hang in there, trooper. You're going to be okay."

9

HAND GRENADES AND ROCK STARS

VA Hospital, Memphis, Tennessee

They say what doesn't kill you, makes you stronger, but that person never got his ass shot off in Vietnam. Of this, Billy was certain. Several months had passed, and he was being discharged at Womack Army Hospital. They were moving him to a special rehabilitation unit at the VA hospital in Memphis. The orderlies were preparing to take him by ambulance over to Pope Air Force Base, when Janie came in for a farewell visit.

"Who do you know in Memphis?" she asked.

Billy shrugged. "No one, I reckon."

"How far is it from where you lived in Mississippi?"

"Not far. Couple hours."

"Then your brother—what did you say his name was, Ed?"

Billy nodded.

"He can keep you company, right?"

Billy didn't bother to reply. He hadn't told her everything about Eddie, who like his mother's brother, Uncle Travis, was a slug. Uncle Travis had bartended at every joint up and down the Mississippi-Tennessee state line. Every few months he showed up broke and looking for a place to flop. Sleeping on the living room couch, he hung around sometimes for weeks, telling Billy and Eddie stories about fights and drag races out on the highway, or how Conway Twitty knew all about women. Eddie loved to run his finger over the naked lady tattooed on Uncle Travis' bicep.

Uncle Travis left his mark, and the first time the sheriff picked up Eddie, his mother cried. With their father gone, Eddie began acting like he was head of the family. Billy sided with his mother as she tried to set his brother straight, but she had a stroke, and her health failed. Billy looked after her, but she died the month before he left for Nam. Going into a war, it was something he had shoved to the back of his mind, and only with time had he come to accept her parting. And only now, like so many of the other lost opportunities in his early years, did he come to realize the mourning he never experienced. She was gone, and he'd done little more than toss a flower on her grave. It had all passed like another bad nightmare.

Janie sat on the bed beside him, staring out the window where the nimbus clouds billowed upward in preparation for another summer storm. There was no sense telling her the truth about Eddie. He didn't want to upset her. The orderlies stacked his few belongings on a cart, and Janie bent over and kissed him good-bye. She remained clear-eyed as they lifted him onto the gurney and pushed him away down the hall.

At the veteran's hospital in Memphis, Billy burrowed into a protective shelter of internal isolation. Avoiding televisions, newspapers and anything with news about the war, he became a mental hermit as he sought to keep the memories and nightmares at bay. This included avoiding his peers, wounded vets like himself. After physical therapy sessions, when he was most exhausted, he tried to sleep, but the nightmares came, and the orderlies always pushed him in his wheelchair into the rec room leaving him in front of the television. It was impossible to avoid everything, and Billy found himself watching a news report about anti-war demonstrations happening around the country. Americans, long ago recognizing the futility of the Vietnam War, continued their protests.

He tried to sleep, but the sound of the TV was unavoidable as the peace demonstrators shouted at the cameras. The vets gathered around the television watching as events unfolded, but they soon became divided.

Roger Frierson called the demonstrators longhaired troublemakers who hated their country. Roger lost a leg and a lung when his LRRP team was chopped up by an NVA platoon in the Ruong Ruong Valley.

"The police ought to club those freaks and throw their asses in jail," he said. "They don't have any respect for America."

Billy's wheelchair was in the semi-circle around the TV. He was directly across from Frierson, who began arguing with the others. Boo Fordyce, sat beside Frierson and nodded. A "pretty-boy" as the others called him, Boo was from Little Rock, Arkansas, and his real name was Beau. He was missing an arm and part of his skull. Boo stood and walked over to the television.

"That's right, Boo, shut that damned thing off," Frierson said.

"Wait a minute. Just hold on a second." It was Jackie Harmon, the ward clown. Jackie, had it not been for the stress creases around his eyes, would have looked like a typical childhood pal—the one that hid behind the fence, drinking beer and shooting bottle rockets at the bedroom window of the girl next door. Jackie wobbled on a cane to the center of the group where he stood wheezing and fighting to catch his breath.

"Don't you get it?" He paused, taking another breath. "Those damned people are heroes. They recognize the war for what it is, and they're doing something about it."

"Sit down, Harmon," Frierson said. "You don't know shit."

"How many patrols did you make, Roger?" Billy asked.

The room grew suddenly quiet. Every eye locked on Billy. He hadn't said a single word in the two weeks since arriving.

"Hell, I don't know," Roger said, his voice suddenly subdued. "Goddamned dozens. Why?"

Boo turned the TV down low.

"How often did you see enemy units, say platoon-size or larger?"

"Shit, damned near every time we were inserted. So, what's your fucking point?"

"That *is* my point," Billy said. "Our LRRPs with the Hundred and First said the same thing. Hell, we got reports constantly of columns of flashlights moving down roads and trails at night, columns with flashlights that kept coming and going as far as the eye could see, thousands of them. That was in the A Shau, and they practically owned the place. See my point?"

"And we blew them to hell with our air and artillery," Roger said. "We kicked their asses."

"Yeah, we did, but no matter how many we killed, more came down the Ho Chi Min Trail. We had our fingers crammed into a dike with a thousand holes."

"It's the damned politicians that won't let us win," Roger said.

"So, you're saying we could have stopped them?"

Roger's eyes reddened. "You think you've got all the answers, don't you, Coker?"

Jackie Harmon nodded, but Roger ignored him. Billy looked around at the other men. They had all given parts of their lives to a cause that defied reason. They were all trapped in the same nightmare, and Billy wanted them to see it. He felt his anger boiling inside.

"No," Billy shouted. He had never been short-tempered, but he lost it. "I don't have all the answers, and I'm mad as hell, too, but the people on that damned television are a hell of a lot smarter than you are." He pointed his finger at Roger. "They know our men are being wasted, and now, it's become a war we aren't even trying win."

Tears streamed from Roger's eyes as he rolled his wheelchair over to Billy. Swinging wildly he missed as Billy cocked his head to one side. Jackie and Boo grabbed Roger's chair and pulled him back while the others began cursing and yelling.

"Stop!"

Charging amongst them, the ward nurse pulled their wheelchairs further apart, and snatched away a squirt gun Jackie had pulled from his pocket.

"I'll have you all sedated and put in straight-jackets. Stop this fighting."

She turned and stared at Billy with her fists balled on her hips.

"If you men don't stop acting like hoodlums, you're all going to end up in trouble."

Nurse Riker, although only a few years older than them, was touted by the younger vets as the queen bitch of all ward nurses. They claimed she ruled with an iron fist. With her hair pulled back in a severe bun and stone brown eyes, the otherwise petite Margaret Riker watched over them like a prison warden. So said Jackie, who was one of her favorite antagonists, and now she was staring hard at Billy.

"Harmon, you take Coker and push his chair back to the ward. Man hasn't said a word in two weeks. Now, he starts a fight."

Hobbling on his cane, Jackie pushed Billy's wheelchair with his free arm as they left the room.

"We're winning every battle, but losing the war," Jackie said.

Billy looked over his shoulder. "I got news for you, bud. We didn't win that battle back there."

"I didn't expect the flank attack from Riker."

"Is she always that way?"

"Na," Jackie said. "Only when we mess with her. She's not really that bad."

They talked for hours afterward as Jackie explained how he had been wounded in the hip, and had even worse damage to his lungs, caused by napalm—and it wasn't an accident. The NVA learned early on that the best way to counter the American air and artillery superiority was to close quickly with ground units, move in as close as they could, overrunning them when possible.

Jackie, like Billy, had been with the Hundred and First, but he was in another battalion, and his platoon was overrun one day up in the A Shau Valley. With the enemy everywhere in the jungle around them and chopping them to pieces, his CO ordered his men to cover up with ponchos as he called in napalm air strikes within a few meters of their positions.

When it was over the pilots had done a magnificent job, but the roiling mass of flames took their toll. Thirteen men died, and dozens more were wounded. Jackie was one of them. Shot in the hip at the first contact, the napalm nearly finished him when it sucked the oxygen from the air, replacing it with lung-searing superheated gases. He now had a raspy voice, scarred lungs and a rebuilt pelvis full of titanium pins.

"So what the hell else is there around here for entertainment?" Billy asked.

"Not much. There's some pretty sexy Candy Stripe girls who come around once in a while, but some of them are jail bait. Screwing around with Riker and the rest of the staff is the only really fun entertainment. I've messed with her so much, I think she hates me."

"With the shape I'm in, I don't need any enemies," Billy said.

"Awe hell, they really don't mind that much. You need to get with the program, Coker. Have some fun."

Another week passed, and Billy found the nightmares closing in on his psyche, but it was the unexplainable anger that bothered him most. All the vets were required to attend sessions with Doctor Kleingold, the resident shrink, and Billy was in his office for his weekly visit. Kleingold wore a lab coat with his name embroidered in gold script over the pocket. Despite his ego, the little psychiatrist was a likable person, but he was an easy target. According to Jackie, Kleingold's very personae demanded abuse, and he dared Billy to come up with something to mess with him during the visit.

The doctor was beginning a new counseling session on 'dark thoughts,' something Billy read in the notes on Kleingold's desk that morning before he arrived. It was one-on-one therapy, and the way he figured, Kleingold was trying to make sure he wasn't going to blow up the world in a fit of rage. The young doctor sat behind his desk and beat around the bush for a while with the usual innocuous questions, before asking him how he felt about violence. Billy decided this was his opportunity to take Jackie's dare, because he sure as hell wasn't going to admit to the anger that ate at him. Better a little humor to remedy the good doctor's worries.

"I don't suppose I would ever do anything crazy," he said. "I mean—you know? Is that why you're asking me all these questions? You're afraid I'll do something crazy, like kill somebody or blow something up?"

"You have been through a very trying time in your life, Billy. It's my job to work with you and help you re-assimilate your thought processes."

"Is this about the hand grenades?" Billy asked.

Kleingold's eyebrows rose ever so slightly, but he did his best to appear nonchalant. The situation reminded Billy of when he was a kid, casting a big top-water plug out on the water at the gravel pit. When the initial splash from the lure settled and the ripples faded away, he would wait several seconds, then twitch the bait ever so slightly. The silence between the two men did the work as Kleingold's eyes narrowed. He was a relatively intelligent man, so it was surprising when, like a big bass charging from beneath the willows, Kleingold went for the bait.

"Yes, the grenades have raised some concern," he said. "We'd like to know more about them."

Billy set the hook.

"I don't think there's more than a couple left, and since we don't keep them on the ward anymore, there's really no danger of blowing ourselves up. Besides, I'm not crazy like some of the guys. The hand-grenades are really more like souvenirs to me."

Kleingold's face grew pale as he bent closer to his pad and scribbled a note.

"So, they're no longer in the hospital?"

"No, I didn't say that. I think they just moved them."

"Why did they move them?"

"Maybe I better let Jackie explain all that to you. You see, I really don't know anything first hand. It's just stuff someone else told him."

"What did they tell him?" Kleingold asked.

"Like I said, I don't know the exact story, but he said one of the guys was in the empty ward one day when nurse Riker and that new surgeon came in and laid on a bed. They didn't see him because it was dark and—well. Maybe, I better let Jackie tell you about it."

A fat bead of sweat rolled from beneath Kleingold's pre-maturely gray sideburn, and the odor of his cologne became more noticeable.

"Where are the grenades now?" he asked.

Billy was no expert on men's cologne, but he figured Kleingold was a British Sterling kind of guy. He rubbed his chin as he stared past the doctor at the rows of psychiatry books on the shelves behind him.

"Look, I've already said too much. I'm not sure they're around anymore. At least that's what I heard. I mean most of them aren't. I think maybe they threw them in a Dumpster out back. Jackie said old crazy Pete Calesari kept one under his pillow for a few weeks, thinking he was back in Korea, but I think the guys took it away from him."

After a few moments nervously tapping his pen on his notepad, Kleingold stood and walked across the hall to the nurse's station. He told them to bring Jackie up from physical therapy then picked up the telephone. A few minutes later Jackie hobbled into the office with his cane while Kleingold remained on the phone at the nurse's station.

Jackie walked behind the desk and sat in Kleingold's big leather chair, while Billy filled him in on the details.

"Coker, are you out of your mind?" he hissed. "That sonofabitch is probably on the phone with the FBI right now."

Billy laughed. "You said you wanted a practical joke."
"Yeah, but—"
Kleingold walked back into the office.
"I told him you know about the grenades," Billy said.
Kleingold cut his eyes over at Jackie, then back at Billy. He seemed to mull something over in his mind. Suddenly he turned to Jackie. "So, Mr. Harmon, tell me why you moved the grenades."
"I told you," Billy said. "They moved them because—"
"No!" Kleingold shouted.
He paused and immediately drew a breath as if to regain his composure. "No," he said, calmly now. "I want Harmon to tell me. You remain silent, Mr. Coker."
Jackie came in right on cue, "Well, I never actually saw anything. The guys said they were afraid with Riker and that doctor getting it on in the empty ward she might stumble over the grenades."
"And where did they hide the grenades after they moved them?"
Billy had covered that as well and effected a wide-eyed look of innocence as Jackie didn't miss a beat.
"Like I said, I never saw anything myself. I really think it was all just a big bullshit story, but someone said Pete was keeping one under his pillow for a while." Jackie scratched his head. "Are we in some kind of trouble?"
When the FBI agents arrived, Billy and Jackie told them it was just a rumor they'd heard, but the agents still questioned Riker about her "affair" with the nonexistent doctor. She reminded Billy of a nun, except she was

all business and smiled no more than once a week. He
couldn't imagine Riker having sex with anyone, but that
made it all the better as the rumor ran rampant through
the hospital. The FBI agents decided it was a misunder-
standing, but threatened them with Leavenworth, saying
it could have been considered a bomb hoax. The mission was a success, in as much as everyone on the ward
rolled with laughter for days.

Laughter, it seemed, was the only therapy that helped.
With the random specter of mutilation and death never
allowing him a full night's sleep, Billy had to laugh—
laugh like hell. To do anything else was to give up, and
he was also beginning to feel more fortunate after seeing
the plight of some of the other men. Some would never
leave the VA—at least not while they were alive. He visited
them regularly, talking and doing anything that might
help, but what do you say to men without arms, legs, faces,
genitals, minds? He often sat beside their beds reading to
them, but his own prognosis wasn't that good, either. His
intestinal tract had been perforated, and he had muscle
and nerve damage in his hips and legs. With the recurring infections Billy was miserable much of the time, but
given the initial prognosis of a twenty-percent chance of
survival, he figured he was beating the odds.

The doctors said he had to work harder. "If only you
would try," Riker said, "you could achieve a seventy or
eighty-percent recovery."

Life was a yo-yo of emotion, but Billy's psyche mostly
hung limp at the end of the string. He'd fallen from the

razor's edge into a world of despair with no care about the future. Sitting in his wheelchair staring at the wall, he contemplated the rest of his life as a "seventy-percent man." The one thing that interested him was an upcoming veterans' demonstration in Washington DC. Jackie said it would be great to go to Washington and tell the fat cats they were sending men to a dead-end war. Billy mentioned the demonstration to the doctors but they were adamant when they said he wasn't fit for travel.

This didn't stop him and Jackie from making preparations, but the Tuesday before the big event Nurse Riker discovered their overnight bags already packed under the beds. She told the doctors, and the shit hit the fan. Because of his recurring infections and other problems, they said the trip to D.C. was out of the question. Billy was again trapped in despair. Didn't they understand he had to do something? He was down to a hundred and twenty pounds. He was shriveling up and dying, both physically and mentally, right here in the VA hospital.

Jackie tried to humor him, and even Riker seemed apologetic, but Billy ignored them as he reverted to a self-imposed isolation, reading old books and speaking to no one. A couple of days before the big peace rally, Jackie offered to take him out for a push around the courtyard, but Billy refused. Most of the men were eating supper as he sat alone in the rec room watching an old Errol Flynn movie. Jackie walked in and changed the channel. The smoldering knot of ever present anger in Billy's gut exploded.

"Turn that damned thing back to my movie."

Jackie refused and walked over to the couch. Billy seethed in silence while a female rock singer performed a bluesy piece about missing her man. Jackie was screwing with him because he'd given him the silent treatment for the last two days. The woman on the TV finished her song and bowed as Dave Clark said her name. Had another rocket propelled grenade blown him into the sky, Billy couldn't have been more surprised. He rolled his wheelchair closer to the TV.

"That BJ Parker is the sexiest damned woman I ever saw," Jackie said. "And she's a helluva singer, too."

Billy studied the close-up of the female rocker on the TV.

"What's wrong with you?" Jackie asked.

"Who did you say she was?"

"My god, Coker, don't tell me you haven't heard of BJ Parker?"

"Hell, if she's who I think she is, we went to high school together."

"Yeah, right."

"No, really. We were friends."

Jackie waited several seconds as if Billy were going to add a punch line, but Billy simply nodded.

"Really?" Jackie said.

"Really. We even danced together one time."

Billy looked away as he thought of what else had happened that night.

"No shit? Damned, Coker. She's fucking famous."

The statement struck him like a brick in the face. And it wasn't that Bonnie Jo was living her dream, but the realization that he was sitting here in a wheelchair at the VA, a zero on the scale of life. Billy wheeled his chair out of the rec-room.

"Hey, hold up," Jackie said.

Billy kept going.

"Wait a damned minute," Jackie shouted.

Billy's mind was a swirling vortex of confusion. Angered and frustrated that his own fate was so starkly contrasted by Bonnie Jo's success, he wanted only to be left alone to sort it all out. He wheeled himself rapidly down the hallway as he sought to escape.

"Stop," Jackie shouted again as he struggled to catch up.

Jackie shoved his cane through the spokes of the wheelchair, sending it careening into the wall. It stopped with a jarring thump.

"There," he said. "That stopped your ass."

"Get your goddamned cane out of my wheel," Billy said. "I'm going back to the ward."

"I know, and then we're going to take a stroll out in front of the hospital."

Billy began rolling himself back to his bed. "I don't want to go."

"I'm taking you anyway. You need the fresh air."

"What part of 'I-don't-want-to-go' do you not understand?"

"What part of 'I'm-taking-your-ass-out-of-here' don't you understand?"

"Look," Billy said. "If you don't go away and leave me alone, I'm going to take that cane and break your other leg."

"Just shut the fuck up," Jackie whispered. He began gathering Billy's clothes and toilet articles, throwing them into a bag.

"What the hell are you doing with my stuff?"

"Keep it down, before Riker hears you. You got any money stashed around here?"

"What the hell for?"

"Bus tickets," Jackie whispered, glancing nervously at the nurse's station.

"Bus tickets?"

"Yeah. You said you wanted to go to DC, didn't you?"

10

STOP, HEY WHAT'S THAT SOUND

Billy found an article in an old Rolling Stone Magazine that said BJ Parker was an exceptional vocal talent and a kick-ass business woman as well. While he had been mired in the muck of his own inertia, Bonnie Jo had made something of herself—she'd achieved her dream. He closed the magazine and stared out the cab window at nothing in particular. Perhaps this was that "special power" telling him again to get off his ass and do something. And what better place to begin than at the big veterans' peace march in Washington?

He and Jackie had managed to sneak past Riker that afternoon and were in a cab on the way to the Greyhound Bus terminal. It was a short drive, and after paying the cabby, Jackie lifted Billy into his wheelchair and stacked the overnight bags in his lap. The sun had set, and neon lights were flickering to life up and down the street as the man with the golden voice came

RICK DESTEFANIS

over the intercom announcing the litany of cities on their route: "Nashville, Knoxville, Kingsport, Roanoke, Charlottesville, Richmond and Washington D.C. now boarding at Gate 3."

The attendants stowed the wheelchair in the luggage compartment, and Jackie insisted on carrying Billy in his arms as they boarded the bus. Even in his emaciated condition, Billy wasn't sure Jackie could carry him up the steps. They wobbled precariously.

"Are we gonna make it?" Billy asked.

Jackie was leaning against the rail inside the stairwell, when the driver leapt to their aid.

"Thanks," Jackie muttered as the driver helped them up the steps.

"Damned, Harmon, you're a thrill a minute."

"I know," Jackie said. "Sorry."

It wasn't a typical response for him. "Quit worrying," Billy said. "We got his thing beat, now."

"I just hope I haven't gotten you into something—"

"Harmon!" Billy shouted. "Freaking out isn't your MO. It's okay, right?"

Jackie grinned. "Okay."

Within minutes the bus door hissed shut, and they were headed east on I-40. Billy gazed out into the veil of darkness, and Jackie seemed lost in thought as lights, distant and soundless, flashed by in the night. What could possibly go wrong? Billy smiled at the thought of Riker going nuts looking for them. Somewhere between Memphis and Nashville his excitement faded and the whine of the bus motor drove him into an exhausted sleep.

Jerking awake, Billy faced a brilliant morning sun splintering through the bus window. The bus motor whined relentlessly, and he realized he'd been hearing it all night. Squinting, he gazed out at the distant hills where a blue haze hung on the distant horizon. According to the highway signs they were somewhere in the Blue Ridge Mountains of Virginia.

Stiff and sore, Billy pushed his hands down on each side, as he tried to stretch and relieve the pain, but he felt something strange. The seat was wet. Raising his hand, he sniffed his fingers, and the odor struck him full force. Urine. His jeans were soaked. Quietly, he nudged Jackie who was still sleeping. After a moment or two, he opened his eyes.

Billy said nothing, but it took only a moment for Jackie to realize what had happened. He slowly closed his eyes as if to gather strength, then opened them again and stared straight ahead. Billy wanted to say something, but there was nothing that would help. He was a fool. The futility of hoping for a real future was again gnawing at his insides. A life of pissing in his pants and depending on others was all he faced. Like the Midnight Cowboy's buddy, Rat Rizzo, he wished he could die on the bus.

Sitting in silence, Billy pressed his face against the window and watched another green interstate sign float past: ROANOKE NEXT EXIT. The scratch of static came from an overhead speaker as the bus driver announced they were stopping for breakfast in five minutes. Jackie cut his eyes over at him, but said nothing, and when the bus came to a stop they waited while the rest of the passengers filed past. When the bus was empty Jackie stood, and without a word lifted Billy from the seat.

"Damned, Coker, if you don't start eating something we're gonna have to put rocks in your pockets to hold you down."

The driver waited outside with the wheelchair. After struggling down the steps, Jackie carefully lowered Billy into the chair.

"I need his bag, too," Jackie said to the driver.

Billy shivered in the crisp morning air as Jackie pushed him across the parking lot toward a restroom on the side of the building. It was another brilliant blue day, just like the one when he was wounded, and for a moment he again felt those final moments in Curtis' arms. It seemed someone was always carrying him. The clean mountain air and the distant hills made him feel on the brink of eternity, the same as he had been that day outside the firebase. Jackie turned to back through the dented steel door of the restroom. It banged loudly as he kicked it open and pulled Billy inside.

"Oh, holy shit," Billy said. The putrid stench made his eyes water.

Jackie jerked open a stall to find the walls covered with graffiti, including a giant spray-painted peace symbol. The restroom's heater magnified the stench, leaving Billy nauseated as a feverish sweat formed on his face. Jackie was drawn up like he'd swallowed a bug as he worked the wet jeans from around Billy's hips.

"How the hell did you pee in your pants?" he asked.

"How should I know?"

"Well, you need to get some plastic pants or something."

"Fuck you, asshole."

"Oh, hell," Jackie said, his voice softening. "I was just trying to be funny. I'm sure it'll get better eventually."

Once Billy buttoned the dry jeans, Jackie seemed to relax.

"What do you want me to do with these wet jeans?" he asked.

"Put them in a plastic bag and save them," Billy said. "I might want to join Hell's Angels when we get back."

Jackie grinned for the first time that morning. "I just can't quite picture you riding a Harley and wearing a Nazi helmet," he said.

After eating an egg sandwich with coffee, Jackie pushed Billy back out to the bus. The morning air was still cold, and Billy felt a sudden chill as he shivered uncontrollably and zipped his jacket.

"What's wrong, now?" Jackie asked.

Billy closed his eyes and clenched his teeth as he fought back the shakes.

"Nothing," he said. "I'm fine. It's just cold out here."

It was later that afternoon when the bus finally rolled into DC. Billy looked out the window in awe as they crossed the sparkling Potomac River and the gleaming white dome of the Jefferson Memorial came into view. He was here, in the nation's capital. All around preparations for the big demonstration were underway. Hundreds of veterans in fatigue jackets milled about on the sidewalks, some wearing boonie hats and jungle boots, while others were in full dress uniforms with Bronze and Silver Stars, Combat Infantry Badges and Purple Hearts. The vets mingled with hippies and long-haired protestors, some already carrying makeshift signs with huge peace symbols.

Later, Jackie pushed Billy slowly up the crowded sidewalk past knots of people who glanced about and talked in low voices. They seemed gripped by an uneasy anticipation. Even the traffic cop's whistle sounded louder and shriller as he directed traffic with a grim intensity. And there were the ones in the trench coats, men who cast about furtive glances and covertly mumbled to one another while their eyes remained fixed on the protestors. A sullen determination amongst the vets had the bureaucrats worried. The betrayed had come for answers.

Back to the east, on the hill at the far end of the mall, the Capitol dome glowed with a tarnished amber in the evening sun. Down on the other end, the Washington Monument jutted skyward through the trees. They were in the middle of it all, and Billy felt that something of monumental consequence was about to unfold. Someone was going to have to answer to these men. They were here to make a statement, and for the first time since leaving Vietnam he was part of something important. It was one of those rare moments when even Jackie seemed at a loss for words. Perhaps, he too felt it. All the vets felt it, because they'd been there. They had seen the Vietnam war from the inside out, and they had credibility. This event was going to draw the attention of the entire nation.

"Do you want to camp on the mall with the rest of the vets?" Jackie asked.

"No way in hell," Billy answered. "I did all the camping I ever want to do back in Nam. Let's find us a room somewhere."

After getting a room at an ancient hotel near Union Station, the two men found their way to the nearest watering hole, a loud, smoky place filled with vets trading war stories. A day of "firsts" Billy was able to get liquor for the first time in months. As the warm buzz of the alcohol filled his head, he popped some pain pills to help with the fever. The last thing he remembered was sitting at a table with Jackie and couple of other vets.

It was after midnight when he awoke in the hotel room to find a blanket thrown over him. Jackie was on the other bed snoring. Soaked with sweat, Billy was still in his clothes, including his jacket and shoes. He sat up on the edge of the bed, removed the shoes and jacket, then fell back, too exhausted to bother with the rest.

Sometime in the night, Jackie shook him awake.

"It's okay, buddy. It's okay. You're back home, now."

"What?" Billy said, struggling to sit up.

"Man, you've been back in Nam all night, and you were getting really loud." Jackie helped him sit up. "It's almost time to get up, anyway, unless you want to stay here and rest."

Billy was exhausted. He trembled and mopped the sweat from his face with the sheet. Quitting now wasn't an option. For the first time in his life he was driven by something other than hormones or the will to survive. He was determined to be heard even if Jackie had to push his corpse in the wheelchair down Pennsylvania Avenue.

"Damn, Coker. You look like death eating a cracker. Are you sure you're up to this?"

"Damned right, I am. Help me into the wheelchair."

After throwing back several more pain pills, he chased them with a glass of stale water from the bed-side table. Between pains, Billy pinned his Bronze and Silver Stars to his old fatigue jacket, along with his Purple Heart. Beneath them he put his Vietnam Service Medal and his Good Conduct Medal, but he dropped the Distinguished Service Cross in his pocket.

Jackie turned and looked him up and down. "Dammit Coker! You look like a Russian Czar."

Billy smiled, and for a moment, he felt better. "So, you don't think I need my Boy Scout merit badges?"

"I didn't know you were a Boy Scout."

Billy again mopped his forehead with the bed sheet, as he managed another weak smile.

"Hell, I was a decorated Star Scout before I got booted out," he said.

"Booted out for what?"

"They said it was for water-front safety violations at summer camp, but that was just a cover-up."

Jackie grinned. "Cover-up, huh?"

"The real story," Billy said, "was me and Ronny Givens borrowed a canoe one night and paddled down the river to the Girl Scout camp."

"The Girl Scout camp, no shit?" Jackie pulled on a clean t-shirt.

"No shit, and they caught us playing strip-poker in a cabin with some of the girls."

"Now, that just figures," Jackie said.

"Hell, it was their idea."

"Yeah, right." Sure it was."

"No, I swear. They even supplied the cards. Hell, we had them down to their bras and panties, before some old heifer with a flashlight showed up. We hid under the bunks, but Givens laid his arm across a jump rope and thought it was snake. He damned near knocked the old lady on her ass, going out the door. Of course the Girl

Scout leaders kind of freaked out and wanted us summarily executed, but the scoutmaster just kicked us out of the troop."

Jackie laughed.

"Gee," he said. "And I always thought you were such a straight-laced kind of guy. Is that where you met BJ Parker?"

"No, I didn't really get to know her until the last year of high school."

"Good."

"What do you mean 'good'?"

"Well, if you'd told me you played strip-poker with BJ Parker, I'd have known for sure you were lying."

"You've got a real problem with me knowing her, don't you?"

"No. I believe you, but did you really dance with her? I mean was it a fast dance or a slow dance?"

"First of all, BJ must be some kind of stage name, 'cause her real name is Bonnie Jo, and it was a slow dance, but it wasn't like you're thinking."

"Huh?"

"Bonnie Jo was just a friend of sorts. We weren't even at a regular dance or nothing."

"What do you mean? Where'd y'all dance?"

"She gave me a ride home one night, and we played the car stereo and danced in my yard. That was the night she gave me this."

Billy pulled the Saint Sebastian medal from inside his shirt.

"Holy shit, Coker! You really *did* have something going with her."

"Look, it's not what you think. We were just friends. Now, I'm tired of talking about it. Okay?"

Jackie stared back at him. "You're not telling me everyth—"

Billy held up his hand. "Just let it drop, before you piss me off, okay?"

As they rode the elevator down to the lobby, Billy noticed the old black man running the elevator watching them from the corner of his eye. Wearing a double-breasted burgundy overcoat with brass buttons and enough scrambled eggs on his hat to make him look like an admiral, he stood regally at the control panel like he was at the helm of the fleet's flagship. The elevator moved at the speed of cold syrup, but no one made a sound until it clumped to a stop. As he opened the doors, the admiral's baritone voice boomed, "First Floor Lobby." Billy flinched. You'd have thought the man was making an announcement to a packed auditorium.

By the time the elevator door opened Billy was about to jump out of his skin.

"Have a good day, gentlemen," the old man added.

"Damned right," Billy said.

The admiral didn't changed expression as Jackie pushed Billy out of the elevator. They were two men on a mission. Jackie hobbled along, pushing the wheelchair through the lobby and out the front door of the hotel where he hailed a cab. By the time they reached the mall, it was packed with an ocean of people stretching all the way down to the Lincoln Memorial.

Vets, hippies, cops and just about every kind of person in between mingled as the Park Police rode their horses, clopping noisily across sidewalks and along the edge of the crowd. It was almost a carnival atmosphere, except for the crew-cut idiots wearing sunglasses and trench coats. They mingled about, their chins high in the air, as if they truly believed they were being inconspicuous.

Speakers down near the Lincoln Memorial echoed, but it was difficult to hear what was being said. After several false starts to penetrate the huge crowd, Jackie stopped and stared out toward the podium, several hundred yards away.

"I suppose we'll have to watch from here," Billy said.

"No we won't, Coker. Just hang tight a minute."

Billy waited for him to explain, while Jackie opened a pack of chewing gum and gave him couple pieces.

"Start chewing that," he said.

Jackie began carefully folding the foil gum wrappers. After a minute or two he had fashioned a set of silver captain's bars with the wrappers.

"There," he said with satisfaction. "Now, give me the gum.

"I'm chewing it," Billy said.

"Gimme the goddam gum, Coker."

Billy spit it into his hand, and Jackie snatched Billy's fatigue cap from his head. Carefully he pressed the two foil bars with the gum to the front of the cap then put it back on Billy's head. Smiling at his handiwork, Jackie popped his heels together, came to attention and gave a rigid salute. Billy rolled his eyes.

"Now, Captain Coker," Jackie said. "Let's see if we can get these people to step aside and let an officer pass."

Wheeling the chair about, Jackie pushed forward into the crowd and began shouting, "Make way for the Captain, men."

The crowd magically parted as he pushed Billy across the mall down toward the podium. The sight of a long-haired captain drew not only curiosity but respect as vets straightened and saluted. Billy returned the snappiest salute he could muster, but as they drew closer, the speakers echoed loudly. The man at the podium was recalling how he'd been ordered to call in air strikes on villages along the Mekong and how innocent women and children were murdered all over Vietnam. Billy grabbed the wheel of the chair.

"Stop! Stop!"

"What's wrong?" Jackie asked.

"Listen to that stupid fucker. I never killed any women and children, and nobody in our outfit ever did."

Jackie shrugged.

"Who the fuck does he think he is?" Billy said.

"Well, you know, it *did* happen in places."

"Maybe it did, but he can't speak for all of us. Nobody went over there just to murder people."

"Dammit, Coker, you know it's a fucked up war, and just 'cause that shithead is spilling his guts about killing civilians doesn't mean we're all bad."

Billy looked up at the podium. "Fuck you, you baby killing bastard! I didn't kill any babies."

The man at the podium didn't seem to hear, but people all around looked his way. Jackie spun the wheelchair around, and began pushing it back through the crowd. "You're going to get our asses stomped if you don't shut the fuck up," he said.

"I don't care. Just because that asshole killed civilians—"

"It doesn't matter."

"What doesn't matter?"

"Goddamit, Coker. You're such a fucking Pollyanna."

"A Pollyanna?" Billy grasp the armrests, raising himself and turning in his wheelchair. "What the fuck is that supposed to mean? We did our fucking job, and lot of guys got killed doing it. That pussy doesn't have any right smearing their names."

Jackie jerked the wheelchair to a stop, and Billy fell out on the ground. He immediately began crawling across the grass toward the podium. "I'm gonna kill that sonofabitch," Billy said.

Jackie grabbed his shirt, and with the help of several bystanders restrained him and lifted him back into the chair. As his anger receded, a mild delirium had Billy's head spinning, and later, his fever worsened as they rolled down Pennsylvania Avenue toward the White

House. The plan was to throw their medals over the fence, but Billy was having second thoughts.

This protest wasn't about the war or wasting soldiers' lives. It was some lame mea culpa by a bunch of guilt-ridden murderers. He had no guilt for what he had done, and his medals represented the only accomplishments in his life. He was proud of his service, but on both sides of him vets began throwing their medals over the fence in protest. He had done everything asked of him as a soldier, and now it seemed he was being asked to give even more.

Television cameras rolled as Billy snatched the decorations from his fatigue jacket and looked down at them. He was throwing away the only remnants of pride that remained in his life. He flashed a smile toward the TV cameras and sent the entire lot sailing over the fence. He smiled, but tears streamed down his face. Jackie turned toward him and their eyes met, but neither of them spoke. Billy pulled The Distinguished Service Cross from his pocket, and for several seconds they both stared down at the medal lying in the palm of his hand.

Before him stood Butch and Danny, along with Val, Doc Mazlosky, Tom Stoner, Reggie Washington, Sergeant Bentley, Roger Frierson, Curtis Teague and all those who never gave up, those who refused to accept the legacy of a lost cause. They would never throw their medals away. He looked up at Jackie.

"Put it back in your pocket," Jackie said.

Billy closed his fist around the medal as a reporter stuck a microphone in his face. "Sir, can you tell me what message you hope to send to the American people by your protest here today?"

Billy's head spun with feverish delirium, but his sadness again erupted into anger. "If I have to explain it to you," he said, "there is no hope. We have become a nation of idiots."

Jackie waved the reporter aside. "The Major doesn't feel like talking right now."

He pushed the wheelchair up the street, and the noise from the demonstrations faded behind them. "Dammit, Coker, can you believe that shit. They had a TV camera aimed at us. Everybody back at the VA is gonna know we were here."

"Yeah, including Riker," Billy muttered.

By the time they arrived back at the hotel, Jackie had promoted him to a full-bird colonel, but the fun was over. Billy was gripped with nausea as they caught the next bus back home. When they arrived in Memphis the next morning Jackie called an ambulance. They rushed Billy to the emergency room at the VA, and the doctor there said he was going back under the knife again. Jackie apologized for taking him to Washington, but Riker said it wasn't his fault. It could have happened anywhere.

Billy lost track of time. Uncertain of his whereabouts, it seemed he may have actually died on the operating table and awakened in hell. At least, he couldn't imagine hell being much worse. It was a flashback to his first waking hours at the hospital in Japan. Every cell in his body screamed with pain. Wired with a morphine drip, a piss bag and more tubes, Billy was again lost in the nightmare. Had he been able, he would have turned the morphine wide-open and ended it all.

The days were lost in a foggy haze, as everyone came by the intensive care unit to see him. After a few days he was released back to the ward. It was good to be back with the other men, but Billy remained pretty much drugged out of his mind as he lay in the bed. Jackie, like a faithful dog, sat cross-legged on the bed next to him reading a magazine. There came a gentle voice, and Billy opened his eyes. It was Riker.

"Billy," she said. "You have two very attractive visitors. Can you say hello?"

Appearing on the evening news must have made him a celebrity of sorts. The girls were old Raeford High classmates, Cindy and Judy. Ex-cheerleaders, they were bona fide members of the old Lizard crowd. Dressed fit to kill, with dangling earrings and red spiked heels, their miniskirts barely covered their butts. They had the attention of the entire ward. Jackie sat on his bunk, taking it all in, while, groggy with medication, Billy lay looking up at them. He opened his mouth to speak but nothing happened. He simply grinned.

"Well, I'll just leave you girls here to visit," Riker said.

She left, and they stood at the foot of the bed, staring wide-eyed at Billy laying half-naked and sprouting plastic tubes everywhere. They gawked in silence, and try as he might Billy couldn't rid himself of the stupid smile. He was feeling like a carnival freak as the girls simply stood and stared. Jackie watched too, but he remained silent. After a minute or so, Cindy put her hand over her mouth and whispered something to Judy. She shrugged and turned to Jackie.

"Can he talk?" Judy asked.

"No, not real good," Jackie said. "He had surgery a few days ago, and they've got him on the hi-test stuff right now. Premium blend, you know? He's out there in la-la land. Don't give a shit about nothing."

Cindy must have assumed Billy couldn't hear either, because she turned to Judy and mumbled how she thought they were coming to see a big war hero.

Judy played with a string of pearls around her neck. "Yeah. He does look sort of pathetic."

With his mind floating near the edge of reality, Billy wanted to laugh and cry at the same moment. Then the anger flared. This one-dimensional bitch had the gall to come here and say he looked pathetic. If only he could make his tongue work, he'd tell them both to kiss his purple-scarred ass.

"So, you were expecting John Wayne, maybe?" Jackie said.

Billy cut his eyes over to the next bed. He should have seen it coming. Jackie was about to handle matters with his usual diplomatic aplomb.

Cindy began stuttering. "Oh, no, I mean—it's just that—well, someone told us he was on TV the other day and in Washington and all, and we thought he was—like making speeches, or healthier or something. You know?"

"Sorry to disappoint you ladies," Jackie said. "If we'd known you were coming, we'd have unplugged a few of his tubes and put him in his dress blues for you." Jackie's voice grew progressively louder. "You two babes don't have a fucking clue, do you?"

Their eyes widened in unison.

"Well, let me enlighten you. This is reality, and this 'pathetic' man, as you called him is a fucking hero. He got this way because he put his life on the line for you. He got his ass blown off, so you can have the freedom to get your pretty little asses laid on the weekend. So, the least you can do is show him some fucking respect!"

Glaring with steel-gray eyes, Jackie's face was red and the veins bulged on his neck as he stood up in the middle of his bed. By the time he finished he was panting with clenched fists. Judy got teary eyed, and Cindy began mumbling half-baked apologies. Riker came trotting down the ward to their rescue. She took the girls by the arms, fawning over them like a mother hen and whispering some bullshit about combat stress reaction, a new term Kleingold came up with to describe their lousy attitudes.

The girls nodded and gave Riker looks of concern—the type used-car salesmen give people when they say they don't have enough money. Riker escorted them off the ward while the vets with arms gave Jackie an ovation. As his anger subsided, he stood in the middle of the bed and took several bows. Afterward he pushed the hair out of his face and looked over at Billy. "So, how was that, Coker?"

Too stoned to answer, Billy gave him another half-ass grin and closed his eyes.

11

A NEW VISITOR

A few days after the visit from Cindy and Judy, Billy's pain medicine was reduced, and he was feeling better. He awakened to find Jackie gone, and it was quiet on the ward, except for a commotion up at the nurse's station. He quickly realized there was another visitor trying to get in to see him, but Riker wasn't allowing it. Jackie was arguing with her. The would-be visitor stood in silence, off to one side and out of sight, while Jackie gesticulated wildly in front of Riker.

"Goddamit Riker, if she wants to see Billy, let her go in. It ain't no skin off your nose."

"Mr. Harmon, this is none of your business, and I will thank you to take yourself back to your bed."

"You don't have to thank me for shit," Jackie said. "You can't stop us from having visitors, and you know it. The doctor said we need them."

"Until you two begin acting more civil, you'll have visitors only during visiting hours, and no other time."

"Goddamit, Riker, why do you have to be such a hard-ass?"

"Take yourself out of here *now*, Mr. Harmon, or I'll call security." Her decibels had doubled.

The visitor spoke up. "Please, there's no need for this. I apologize for creating a problem. I was simply in town today, and thought I might get in to see him. When are visiting hours?"

The tone of the woman's voice seemed to find a crack in Riker's evil facade. "I appreciate your understanding, ma'am. It's just that Mr. Coker had visitors earlier in the week, and it caused such a disturbance, well, I hope you understand."

"Oh, yes," the woman replied. "It's no problem, really."

"Because of the nature of the injuries on this ward, we normally have extended visiting hours. However, if Mr. Coker is well enough, he can visit with you down at the visitor's lounge between 4 and 6 p.m. this afternoon."

Jackie waved his cane in the air. "Goddamit Riker, you know Billy can't get out of bed."

"Please, please," the young woman begged. "There's no need for this. I can come back another time. Just tell him Bonnie Jo Parker came to see him."

A sudden ringing grew in Billy's ears. Bonnie Jo was the last person he thought he would ever see again. What was he going to say to her? He felt his heart bumping against his boney chest and reached down to grasp the Saint Sebastian medal. He rubbed the silver medal with his thumb as he had so many times in Vietnam. It had remained on his dog tag chain to this very day, and it had brought him home. At least he could thank her for that.

Riker's voice came again behind the din of his ringing ears, "Bonnie Jo Parker? Are you BJ Parker, the singer?"

"Yes, I am," she replied.

"How do you know Billy?"

"We went to high school together in Mississippi."

"You went to school in Mississippi?" Riker said. "I didn't know that."

They talked in muffled tones for several minutes before he heard Riker tell Jackie to swear he'd behave. Jackie swore on Ho Chi Minh's mother's grave, and a few moments later they came walking from the nurses' station.

Billy had trouble focusing his eyes, but even with blurred vision he realized this wasn't the same girl he'd known in high school. A strikingly beautiful woman, she was several inches taller and no longer wore glasses. Thin, and with a face God usually reserved for fashion models, Bonnie Jo still had that gorgeous strawberry blonde hair. Billy blinked and tried to focus.

"You've got another visitor, pretty boy," Jackie said.

An adrenaline rush cleared his head, and Billy found his voice. "Like I couldn't hear all the ruckus. I think you guys woke up the whole ward."

Bonnie Jo stepped forward. "Billy? It's me, Bonnie Jo."
He squinted.

"Bonnie Jo Parker from high school," she said. "Remember?"

He tried again, this time focusing on her eyes. That was the one thing he remembered about Bonnie Jo. She had the most beautiful ocean-green eyes he'd ever seen. His vision cleared.

"Billy?" she said.

"I remember you, Bonnie Jo, but you don't look anything like you did the last time I saw you."

She caught his zinger like a world-class shortstop. "You mean you miss that twenty pounds of baby fat and the glasses I used to wear?"

"Well hell, you gotta admit, you *do* look different."

She laughed and stepped closer to the bed. "Yeah, I grew several more inches, and they gave me a stage name, too, BJ. They said Bonnie Jo sounded too country."

She looked like a million dollars, but she talked like the same girl he'd known back at Raeford High. There was a moment of awkward silence.

"And you don't exactly look the same either, Billy Boy. Matter of fact, you look like you've been having a rough time."

"Yeah, life's been a real bitch lately," he said.

Riker grabbed Jackie by the sleeve and pulled him away.

"I'm glad Jackie was able to contact me," Bonnie Jo said.

She smiled and pushed the hair from her face. "You've got a heck of a friend. If he hadn't sent me that letter, I'd have never known you were here."

"Jackie wrote you a letter?"

"Yes, and he told me you guys went to Washington D.C., and how you got really sick on the way home. He also told me about this."

She picked up the Saint Sebastian medal from his chest. "I can't believe you still have it."

"Yeah, well, I guess it's been kind of a good luck charm."

She glanced down at his embarrassingly scrawny arms. A tear appeared in the corner of her eye, but she quickly wiped it away.

"Tell me about this rock-singer-thing you're doing. When did you start that?"

She gave way to a sniffle of emotion and tried to hide behind a big smile. "You know it's funny. They had a talent contest that spring after I got out to San Fernando, and I won. One thing led to another, and I cut a demo single that took off. Everything changed after that. I got an agent, and she helped me lose some weight, but mostly I got taller. I got contact lenses and a recording contract, and well, things have been, uh, good, I suppose."

She seemed suddenly self-conscious, as if she'd said too much. She was probably thinking he looked like the Ginsu Chef had used his ass for a demonstration. He wanted to tell her everything was okay, but another uncomfortable silence ensued. He was happy for her. A late growing spurt had turned her into a twenty-four karat hunk of woman, a classic Cinderella.

"Billy..." She hesitated as she wiped another creeping tear.

"What the hell are you crying for, Bonnie Jo?"

"Billy." She paused again. "Jackie told me you were in a wheelchair, and how—Do you think you will ever be able to walk again?"

Riker stuck her head around the corner. "If the lazy rascal would try, he could. He doesn't even go to physical therapy half the time." She jerked her head back, and he heard Jackie giving her hell behind the wall as they whispered and squabbled like a couple of pet squirrels.

"Why don't you two go somewhere else to argue," Billy shouted.

It grew quiet again.

"Maybe, I can help you with your therapy," Bonnie Jo said.

He saw pity in her eyes.

"I don't need help. Like, Riker said, all I have to do is try."

"So why aren't you trying?"

"Because it's not so damned easy as it sounds."

She looked hurt, but her response was classic Bonnie Jo as she masked her feelings. "Maybe so, but you've always had grit."

Billy thought back to the time at Raeford High, when he told her about his science grades. She said the same kind of things back then, never a lecture, just encouragement.

"Look, Billy, I have to be in New York City tomorrow morning. I have a business engagement there, but I'd like to come back to see you Sunday. Do you mind?"

"Do I mind what?"

"Do you mind if I come back and spend some time with you next week?"

"Hell, whatever turns your crank. Just don't expect any miracles like me walking or something."

She bent forward and kissed him on the cheek. "I don't think we'll need any miracles, just the right motivation. See you Sunday."

She smiled and winked as she turned to walk out. It was the same wink she'd given him the last time he had seen her. He remembered how she'd said everything would be okay, and only now was he growing to understand how much more clearly she had seen things in life than he had. She had recognized his confused thinking early on, and reassured him that he was going to be okay, that he would figure it all out. He wondered what more she might see even now, things about life and himself that he was only beginning to understand.

As she walked away, her perfume filled his head, and he felt something coming alive. It felt strange, almost like something he had never felt before. But he had, and he remembered what had happened that night after they danced. A year had passed since he was wounded, and not once had he felt even the hint of a sexual urge. Now, here it was, not exactly a classic woody, but definitely a stirring, and it was his thought of little Bonnie Jo Parker in his arms that night that had brought it on.

Billy inhaled deeply as Bonnie Jo sauntered back toward the nurse's station, looking as if she'd been poured into her jeans. She had the most perfect body he'd ever seen, and as she disappeared around the corner he said to no one in particular, "Damned, she's got a nice butt."

She reappeared, poking her head around the corner. He'd been overheard. Momentarily speechless, the words for a groveling apology eluded him, but a smile spread across her face. "At least I know that part of you is still working."

She again disappeared, and it was several minutes before Jackie returned. He and Riker had no doubt been talking with Bonnie Jo, probably telling her what a cynic he'd become, but Jackie was grinning from ear to ear.

"I still can't believe you and BJ Parker are friends."

"So what's the big deal? We went to high school together."

"The big deal is she's one of the hottest rock stars in America. Do you know why she's going to New York?"

"How the hell should I know?"

"She's doing a concert at Madison Square Garden."

"That's great," Billy said.

"Well, don't act so fucking excited," Jackie said. "What did you say in that letter you sent her?"

"What do you mean?"

"I mean what did you say that made her think she had to come see me?"

"Nothing, really. I just told her what you told me, and yeah, I mentioned that medal she gave you and the trip to D.C. Why? What's the problem?"

"The problem is you're sticking your nose in my business."

"You're kidding?"

"No, I'm not kidding. Why did you write her?"

"I did it to help *you*, asshole. Of course, if you'd rather mope around and feel sorry for yourself, I can tell her not to come back. All you ever do is listen to stuff like Steppenwolf and the Byrds. You're stuck in a time warp. You play those same albums over and over, and you never watch TV anymore, except for the old movies. You don't even watch the ball games. Hell, you needed a visit from someone like her."

"Her kind of music doesn't interest me," Billy said. "Music, television and sports are just distractions to pacify the mindless masses. They keep people preoccupied so they don't stop to think about the important things— things like that damned war."

"That's just it, Billy. The war and the past are all you think about."

"Save the lecture."

"You're nuts, Coker. I can't believe BJ Parker came all the way from California to see you, and you all but blew her off."

"What the fuck are you talking about?"

"If 'whatever turns your crank' isn't a blow-off, it comes pretty damned close."

"And exactly what the hell did you expect me say? 'Sure, Bonnie Jo, I'd love for you to hang around and feel sorry for me. I need all the pity I can get'."

Jackie shook his head and looked away.

"Go tell Riker my goddamn pain medicine is wearing off," Billy said.

"You're the one who has to prove you don't need anybody. Go tell her your-damned-self."

"Maybe I will."

Throwing the sheet aside, Billy rolled off the bed, as tubes separated and monitors began chirping alarms. Jackie dove toward him, catching him before he fell to the floor.

"Riker," he screamed. "Get your ass in here. This fucker's gone nuts."

He pushed Billy back on the bed, and when Riker came running, she slipped and busted her ass on the tile floor. Jackie got her an ice pack for her butt, while she helped the aides reconnect the monitors and plug the IV back into Billy's arm. Later, she brought him a sedative.

12

ISLANDS IN THE SKY

Late Sunday afternoon, the cicadas were buzzing in the river birches while Billy and Jackie made their rounds at the VA. Having heard nothing more from Bonnie Jo, Billy figured he had scared her away. It was probably for the best. Whatever redeeming moral character she'd seen in him back in high school was forever lost in Vietnam. Jackie pushed Billy in his wheelchair around the building to the Jefferson Avenue entrance. At the same time, a cab stopped out front. A lump of salvation rose in Billy's throat as the door opened and Bonnie Jo stepped out.

Leaving the driver and her bags behind, she trotted up the walkway, her breasts bouncing beautifully in the afternoon sun. It was hard to believe this was the same girl he knew in high school. Tall, slender and agile, she grasped his hand and dropped to her knees beside the wheelchair.

"Hey," she said. She pushed her sunglasses back on her head and cast a glance up at Jackie. "What are you guys up to?"

"We were planning our escape," Jackie said.

Bonnie Jo laughed. With every last bit of his strength, Billy tried not to look like a tail-wagging dog excited about its master's return. She wrapped her arms around his neck, hugging him like an old friend.

"I hope you're in a little better mood than when I left," she said.

He didn't answer, but returned the hug while glancing over her shoulder at the most beautiful hips God ever sculpted. It was nearly too much to comprehend as she stepped back and gazed into his eyes. With a slender finger and well-manicured nail, she pulled a wisp of hair from her face and glanced again at Jackie. "Can I take him for a stroll?"

"There's not much of any place to stroll around here," he said. "Other than the courtyard, we usually go up and down the sidewalk."

Bonnie Jo glanced about. "We'll make it work."

"Okay," Jackie said, "but promise you'll give me your autograph later, okay?"

As she pushed Billy in his wheelchair, Bonnie Jo looked back at Jackie. "I'll put it on the cover of the album I brought for you."

"Alright!" Jackie said.

Since the AK-47 round had wrecked his thigh, Jackie wasn't too nimble, but Billy noticed a little skip in his walk as he headed back into the hospital. Bonnie Jo carefully guided the wheelchair to a bus bench on Jefferson Avenue. After giving the cab driver directions to deliver her bags to the Peabody, she sat on the bench beside him. The aches in Billy's legs subsided in the warmth of the afternoon sun as Bonnie Jo told him about the concert in New York City and the music business.

"It's really a lot of fun," she said. "And I still have to pinch myself just to make sure it's not a dream."

"So why did you come back here?" he asked.

Her jaw flexed ever so slightly as she turned to face him. "I'm not sure what you mean."

"I mean, this place, this hospital, it's the pits. You must have a busy schedule. How can you take time off to hang around a veterans' hospital?"

"I'm not just hanging out at a veterans' hospital," she said. "I came here to spend time with an old friend, and hopefully give him a helping hand. Why would you say something like that, Billy?"

He shrugged and looked away. He would never have said something like that when they were in high school, but now it somehow seemed okay. After a while he turned to face her.

"Sorry," he said.

"It's okay. I suppose I wouldn't feel much different. What do you think about me asking the hospital staff if I can help with your physical therapy?"

Billy maintained his best poker-face. Surely she wasn't serious. Besides being downright personal at times, physical therapy was gut-wrenching work. She didn't have a clue. This was a VA hospital, and it smelled of wounded men, bedpans and medicines. Going from cross-country flights and fawning fans to the grinding reality of physical therapy wasn't something she could handle, no matter how well intentioned she may have been. He decided to try a little humor.

"Depends on what kind of physical therapy you have in mind."

She playfully touched the end of his nose with her finger. "Not the kind you're thinking of, I'm sure. You need to start walking again before you can chase women."

"Are you saying you wouldn't make love to a disabled vet?"

She laughed. "You're not drawing me into that trick bag, my friend."

"I don't know what you're talking about," Billy replied.

She bent over and squeezed his chin between her thumb and fingers, then kissed him on the lips. There was no longer the slightest hint of her high school shyness.

"Billy Boy, I went to school with you, remember? I know how you think."

"Well," he said. "You can't blame me for trying. It's been over a year, and I think I'm turning back into a virgin."

She laughed out loud. "That isn't so bad. I would still be one if it weren't for one night when I drank too much peach schnapps."

"You mean you haven't since you and me?"

Bonnie Jo slowly shook her head. "You act like that's weird or something."

"Oh, no, nothing like that. It's just that—well, you're so good looking, and living out in California and all. I mean, this *is* the 1970's."

"You seem to forget. I was raised in Mississippi—got a whole lot of that Bible belt training. You know? Besides, maybe I'm waiting for the right man to make up his mind."

She began humming a tune.

"One of your songs?" Billy asked.

"Do you remember the poem I wrote for you before I moved to California?"

He nodded.

"Well, it was the start for the lyrics on a demo that went to number one. It's called *Islands in the Sky*, just like the poem. A friend of mine re-wrote the lyrics and put them to music. The melody is pretty, isn't it? You want me to sing it for you?"

"Sure," he said.

Billy closed his eyes and listened. Bonnie Jo's voice needed no accompaniment. They sat—her on the bus bench and him in his wheelchair—until the afternoon sunshine gave way to dusk. The traffic thinned as the streetlights flickered to life. Their conversation had faded into silence, and she rested her head on his shoulder. For Billy it seemed a dream too good to be real.

A half-hour later someone shouted from up near the hospital entrance. It was Jackie. Bonnie Jo stood and turned Billy's wheelchair. The night air had grown cool as they made their way back up the walk. Billy glanced over his shoulder at her. It was hard to believe. Bonnie Jo Parker was a famous rock singer, and she still had the same charm and personality she'd had back in high school.

Problem was, other than his military experience, he had nothing to show for the three years since he'd graduated. He was still little Billy Coker from Raeford, Mississippi, jobless, homeless and pretty much a zero on the scale of life.

Pool therapy was Billy's favorite daily ritual. Although it was physical therapy and not without pain, it was ten times easier than the other torture. The therapist made him swim and walk about in the water for almost an hour every day. It was tough, but afterward the men were allowed free time to do whatever they wanted. He would sneak off with Jackie to one of the mechanical rooms, fire up a joint and return to the pool to float in euphoric neutral buoyancy until they were made to leave.

Today, though, was a special day. With Bonnie Jo's celebrity status and the potential morale boost for the men, the hospital agreed to let her help with physical therapy. Most of the administrative staff, the patients, therapists and several doctors had shown up that morning in anticipation of the famous rock star's arrival. Of course she was late, and most everyone was in the pool when she walked out. Bonnie Jo carried a beach bag and was wearing a white terry cloth robe.

"Holy shit," a therapist muttered. "It's really her."

A tall leggy woman, Bonnie Jo carried herself like a fashion model. The entire pool area was suddenly still, and no one moved as the last few sounds echoed against the tile walls and faded into silence. Several female therapists were present as well, but there wasn't a single person who didn't stop to watch Bonnie Jo walk to the pool's edge.

Billy inhaled deeply of the chlorine scented water and rubbed his eyes with his fists. Tossing her bag on a wooden bench, Bonnie Jo glanced toward the pool as she reached for the sash on her robe. She froze. It was quiet, so quiet the water dripping from someone's hair echoed against the tile walls. Everyone stared in anticipation, and an embarrassed smile slowly crossed her face.

"I'm not taking this robe off, until you guys stop staring like hungry wolves."

Everyone laughed, and went back to what they were doing while she turned and discreetly undressed. Physical therapy lasted nearly an hour longer that day, and several men reached individual milestones. The way Billy figured, it was just another example of his old motivational theory. There was no motivation like hormones, and Bonnie Jo was the catalyst that turned them all loose that day. She could have been Miss America in her swimsuit, and Billy's eyes took in every square inch of her gorgeous physique.

In the next three days Billy made more progress than he had in the last three months, and by week's end they were allowing Bonnie Jo to take him down for the free swim. Jackie accompanied them, and on the way, they stopped by the mechanical room to inspect the machinery. By the time they reached the pool they were all three light-headed and giggling.

As Bonnie Jo and Jackie helped him from the wheelchair, her terry-cloth robe fell open. She wore a red, white and blue one-piece swimsuit that was cut high at the hips and low across the front. It hugged her every curve, thin and tight. Billy stared shamelessly.

Tossing her strawberry blond hair aside, she gently poked his chin. "You're going to get eye-strain, mister."

"It'll be worth it," he replied.

She giggled as Jackie helped her guide him down the steps into the pool. They floated in peaceful solitude for nearly an hour before Jackie left, saying he had a chair reserved at the poker table in the rec room. Floating alone with Bonnie Jo, Billy suddenly felt self-conscious and out of place. He didn't understand it, but the feeling made him afraid that he would say or do something stupid.

"You ready to go?" he asked.

"I suppose, if you are," she replied.

Bonnie Jo pulled him along as they made their way to the side of the pool. There they rested for a moment. Wrapping his arm around her waist, he pulled her close, pushing a wet wisp of hair from her cheek. For a moment it seemed so right, but another jolt of self-doubt caused him to hesitate. He looked down at the scars on his legs and abdomen. Slowly, Billy pulled his arm from around her waist.

"You okay?" she asked.

"Thanks for coming," he said.

"Thanks for letting me stay."

Clumsily, he bent forward and kissed her cheek, and for a moment he thought she might draw back. After all, he was now an almost skeletal, battle-scarred wreck. But she didn't. Bonnie Jo smiled instead and ran her hand behind his head, gently pulling him forward again, this time kissing his lips. Hers were soft and warm, and for the first time since Vietnam he felt truly alive. After a moment, they parted and Billy swallowed hard as he gazed steadily into her eyes. They were moist, and she took a deep shivering breath. If for only a moment, they had touched one another's hearts.

"Maybe we better go," she said.

She was right. Despite his elation, his body was beginning to act somewhat normal, and he hoped she didn't notice the circus tent trying to erect itself in his lap.

13

GOING BACK TO RAEFORD

Bonnie Jo became a regular at the VA, making trips to Memphis at least once a week. Billy felt like a man again, and he was drawn to her as they shared both the strain of therapy and the quiet moments of intimacy together. Her visits sometimes lasted two or three days as she refused to stop pushing, enticing and cajoling, until Billy finally took those first tentative steps. They were steps into the future, and Bonnie Jo was ecstatic as their lips met again in what had become a strong mutual affection—if not the first threads of an even stronger bond.

Those first steps became a glorious occasion for everyone, as even Riker joined in the celebration, serving homemade chocolate chip cookies and Coke. Of course the Coke was spiked with Jack Daniels as soon as Riker left the room, and Billy got tipsy. He fell for the first time, or perhaps it was the umpteenth time, but this time Bonnie Jo wasn't close enough to catch him, and he hit the floor with a thud.

Despite the sting of a bloodied nose, he sat up and smiled while Bonnie Jo held a wet towel to his face. She refused to let him drink any more, but it didn't matter, he was actually moving forward for the first time since leaving Nam.

Within a few weeks Billy was using crutches instead of the wheelchair as he grew steadily stronger. And it wasn't long before he tossed the crutches aside and replaced them with a cane. The doctors were happy, and Billy was happy. He supposed everybody was happy, but when Riker told him it wouldn't be long before he was released from the hospital a twinge of fear shot through him.

He stood at the window staring down at the city below, the cars on the streets and the people on the sidewalks. He was starting over. He would have to find a job, a place to live, a life—all things that until now had no longer mattered. And the world outside had changed. Everyone had grown long hair, wore weird shirts and even the music was changing. Billy had no doubt he could handle these things, but there was one ominous challenge he feared—finding a purpose. After staring the beast in the eye in Nam, he never quite understood who had won. He hadn't blinked then, but now he faced this unexplainable psychological monster that stood in his path. He could hardly open his eyes to face an uncertain future.

Bonnie Jo suggested a day-trip outside the confines of the hospital to help him re-engage. Obtaining permission, she took him in her rental car and headed southeast into Mississippi. They were going to Raeford. Billy gazed out at deer feeding along the edges of distant tree lines and cattle grazing in green fields. The rural scenery lifted his heart as they drove up and down the hills on the two-lane Highway 72 then south on 45. It was his first homecoming since returning from Nam, and not without apprehension. He wondered if Bonnie Jo felt the same sense of trepidation. She hadn't been back to Raeford since leaving for California.

A few miles beyond Tupelo they turned onto a narrow state highway. The original concrete sections had never been repaved, and the wheels of the car thumped rhythmically as they drove several more miles, arriving just before noon. It seemed nothing had changed. Piles of kudzu still hung down the steep cut banks on either side of the highway, the leafy green vines snaking up the power poles and into the surrounding trees. Bonnie Jo slowed as they passed beneath the once silver but now mostly rusted GM&O Railroad Bridge.

As they stopped at the first traffic light, Billy smelled the aroma of burgers frying at the Dairy Queen. With it came the odor of cattle in a nearby pasture. He couldn't help but smile. Like it or not, this was home.

The light changed, and Bonnie Jo drove slowly up the main drag. It seemed as if they had driven through a time warp. The old red brick buildings and the sidewalks downtown looked the same. Billy almost expected to see his old classmates sitting on their cars as they passed the Dairy Queen. Bonnie Jo, too, gazed at the people there, but none of the construction workers sitting in their trucks looked familiar. There were a couple of teenagers sitting at one of the picnic tables.

"Looks like the new generation has taken over our old table," Bonnie Jo said.

Billy nodded as they continued up the road toward Raeford High. The same graffiti still marked the red brick wall of the gymnasium, except there was a recent addition: a huge peace symbol. Someone had tried to scrub it away, but the outline remained, a testament to a truth no one could face. It all felt so familiar yet so strange, as if they were looking into their own past. Billy gazed at the kids with books walking between classes. Bonnie Jo pointed across the road at the old water tower. For years it had "Jake loves Cindy" scrawled in ragged blue letters high above town, but that too had changed. The tower now wore a coat of pale green paint, with "RAEFORD" proudly emblazoned in block letters.

The school hadn't changed much with its high multi-paned windows still as clouded with dust as they were years ago. The same footpaths worn in the grass marked the old shortcuts, and a white wrought-iron sign out front seemed timeless, except for its inscription: Raeford High School, Class of 1952. Everything seemed familiar, yet, it was somehow so different. Billy drew a deep breath.

He and Bonnie Jo were no longer a part of these things. They were interlopers into their own past.

A strange silence came over them as they took in more of the sights, and Billy wondered what Bonnie Jo was thinking, but to ask meant he would have to reciprocate. She glanced back at the school, perhaps hoping one last look might prove they weren't forever separated from this place. She gave a gentle sigh.

They decided to drive by the house where she had lived. It was in a much nicer area where the homes sat back off the road under big oak trees. This was where the pharmacist and the town doctor lived, and the ones Billy once thought of as being gloriously rich. Bonnie Jo's family was by no means rich, but with her dad's job as a consultant on the Tombigbee project, they were always better off than most.

Further down the highway where black angus once grazed quietly in the early morning fog, there now stood a new shopping mall, a gleaming sprawl of vanilla stucco buildings, surrounded by a black-topped parking lot full of vehicles. Turning off the highway, Bonnie Jo drove another quarter mile before stopping in front of her old home.

She pointed up the hill at the wooden swing still hanging under the giant oak. "I can't believe that old swing is still there."

Billy nodded, and they gazed in silence until he heard her sniff. He looked over at her. She had become teary-eyed, but she forced a smile.

"It's strange coming back, isn't it?" Billy said.

She nodded. "Yeah, I was just thinking about all the dreams I had lying out there, looking up at the clouds."

"It looks like the ones about becoming a singer came true."

"Yes, they did, and the one about finding you again did, too."

Their eyes met, and she put her hand atop his. Billy turned and looked out at the swing again. "You should go see if the owner wants to sell that old thing. I think it's got some bigtime mojo."

"Let's go by your house," Bonnie Jo said. "I've never seen it in the light of day."

"Let's not," he replied.

She turned the car around, and drove back toward town.

"You know, sometimes you need to understand the past before you can escape it," she said.

"It's nothing like that," he replied. "It's just that my pot-head older brother still has the place, and I don't feel like seeing him right now."

"We don't have to stop. Besides, he's probably not there in the middle of the day, right?"

Billy shrugged. "Okay, whatever lights your fire, but don't expect much. There never were a lot of dreams around that place."

A few minutes later they stopped in front of the house. A breeze rustled the leaves as Billy stared at a freeze-frame flash from the past, his childhood home.

Bonnie Jo was right—no one was home. They sat in the middle of the road, and Billy rolled down his window. The house was a one-story ranch style place built with pinkish red bricks. At one time it was almost too fancy for the little neighborhood of clapboard houses and yards with old cars on concrete blocks. Now, the years had let it make its peace with the others, blending with a degree of neglect that surely left the neighbors feeling more comfortable.

"Mama always said the color of the bricks was Valley Mist Sunrise, but dad said they were just plain old pink. He let Mama pick them out because they were the cheapest ones."

"I think they're pretty," Bonnie Jo said. "There are a lot of houses like that in California."

"He never said it to Mama, but he told me they were the most awful color he ever saw, but the brick salesman from Holly Springs read the situation perfectly. The only person he had to please was Mama."

The wood fence along the side yard was rotted and leaning precariously.

"Since my brother more-or-less inherited the place, it's gone to seed," Billy said. "He went off to prison one time for a year or so, left his old snaggled-toothed girlfriend here to live."

The white shingled roof was streaked with black, and one of the window screens was lying in the knee-high grass in the front yard, but the brick was still as pink as a Mary Kay Cadillac. Billy smiled at the thought.

"So, your brother never went to Vietnam?" Bonnie Jo asked.

"You can't get drafted once you've been in prison."

Billy glanced at Bonnie Jo. She simply nodded.

The blast of a car horn jarred Billy back to the moment as someone revved a car engine behind them. Glancing into the rearview mirror, Bonnie Jo hastened to put the car in gear. The driver continued blowing his horn. Billy turned and looked over his shoulder.

"Aah shit."

"What?" she said.

"It's him."

A dingy red Mustang pulled around and stopped beside them. Eddie, wearing a devil-incarnate face of rage, leaned over and rolled down his car window. He seemed on the verge of cursing and shouting, but Bonnie Jo spoke first.

"I'm sorry," she said.

Her preemptive strike for civility seemed to work as a flash of recognition crossed Eddie's face.

"Well, I *will* be damned," he said. "If it ain't my baby brother, the big war hero. And who are you, miss chickie?"

"I'm Bonnie," she said.

Billy leaned forward on his side of the car. Looking past Bonnie Jo, he raised his hand in acknowledgement.

"Well, y'all might as well get out and come on in. I just picked up a fresh six-pack, and my soap opera doesn't start for another ten minutes."

Eddie pulled the dented Mustang into the drive while
Bonnie Jo parked on the side of the road and got out. Billy
pushed open his door. "Peace" and "harmony" weren't
words in Eddie's vocabulary, and this would probably not
end well, but they had no choice. Bonnie Jo walked beside
him as he hobbled up the drive with his cane.

"So what's the honor I owe on this visit?" Eddie asked.

"We just stopped by to say hello," Billy replied.

Eddie all but eye-fucked Bonnie Jo, but Billy figured
she was accustomed to it, living in California.

"Do I know you?" Eddie asked.

She gave Billy a nervous glance. "You should," Billy
said. "We went to high school together."

"Oh yeah. Yeah! Now, I remember. You were a cheerleader."

Bonnie Jo wagged her head, but Eddie didn't seem
to notice as he pulled a can of beer from the paper bag.
Snatching the ring, he tossed the tab in the grass and
handed her the can. The foam ran over her hand as she
held it at arm's length.

"I can't, really," she said. "I'm driving."

Eddie laughed. "One beer ain't gonna make you
drunk, is it?"

Billy took the beer, and Bonnie Jo shook the foam
from her hand. Eddie eyed him up and down.

"My god, boy, you're skinnier than a Ethiopian. Ain't
they feedin' you nothin' in that goddam army?"

"I've been a little sick from when I got wounded, but
I'm doing better, now."

Billy nervously tried to sip the still foaming beer. Eddie smirked.

"Are you allowed to operate that walking cane under the influence?" he asked.

"No. Here. Take this." Billy handed him the wet beer can. Eddie laughed and slurped the suds off the top. When he wiped his mouth with the back of his hand, Billy noticed the homemade prison tattoo on his arm, "Born to Boogie."

"So, you're here just to visit, huh?"

"Yeah, but we can't stay. Bonnie Jo has to get back."

"Oh, yeah, well, that's too bad. I thought maybe you were looking to move back in," he said.

"No. I'm staying at the VA in Memphis."

Eddie's Adam's apple bobbed as he guzzled the beer for several seconds before coming up for air.

"So what's up? You looking for some inheritance or something? I mean, you can see there ain't much left of this old place."

"Ed, like I said, we just stopped in to visit, but we've got to go now." Turning, Billy took Bonnie Jo by the hand and led her back to the car.

"Well, whatever lights your fire," Eddie called. "I mean, it wasn't much of a visit, but I enjoyed it."

"Yeah, likewise," Billy said, glancing back.

Eddie tossed his empty can into the front yard and waved as they drove away. It was several minutes and several miles up the highway before Bonnie Jo spoke.

"I'm sorry," she said.

Billy stared straight ahead. "Don't worry about it."

"I should have listened to you."

"Forget it. It's no big deal."

"When was the last time he came to visit you at the hospital?"

"He hasn't."

"You mean he hasn't come to see you since you got back from Vietnam?"

Billy shook his head. "No, but he did call one time while I was at Womack—the hospital at Fort Bragg."

"That was nice. At least he cared enough to call."

"Yeah," Billy said. "He wanted to send me some papers to sign. Said he needed everything signed over to him before I died."

"God! How crass can one person be? Did you sign the papers?"

"Slow down," Billy said. "You're driving like a bat out of hell."

She let off the accelerator. "Sorry."

"No, I didn't sign them. I told him not to count me as dead, yet. He got pissed and hung up, and I haven't spoken with him again until today."

Billy wanted desperately to change the subject. "Hey, do you want to drive down by the gravel pits?"

The words were barely out of his mouth before he regretted them. Bonnie Jo had seldom if ever gone down to the gravel pits. This was the old swimming hole, and she always stayed away because of the

Lizards—the two-legged ones. They hung out there during the summer, drinking beer, swimming and doing all the things teenagers do. Had she shown up, the merciless jerks would have told fat jokes or else shunned her.

"Sure," she said.

"Never mind," Billy replied.

She smiled, and he wondered if she was reading his mind. There had been some good times down at the pits, but never with her. She probably knew this. She also knew that he had once traded their friendship for the charms of Sissy and the others. Now, she accepted him and all his neurotic guilt without question. He shrugged, and they decided to forego the gravel pits as they headed back to Memphis.

More weeks passed, and Bonnie Jo was in town again for her weekly visit. Jackie had been released, and with his partner gone, Billy looked forward to Bonnie Jo's visits all the more. They walked down to their favorite bus bench in front of the hospital and sat watching the traffic on Jefferson Avenue. It was another quiet afternoon, and they basked in the sunshine while trading small talk.

"You haven't said a word about your plans after you leave the hospital," she said.

"That's because I don't have any."

"Where will you stay?"

"Jackie has an apartment over in mid-town, off McLean. He said I could stay with him if I wanted."

Bonnie Jo snuggled closer, and put her head on his shoulder.

"Have you ever thought about moving out to California?" she asked.

"What the hell for?"

"To live with me, dummy."

"You mean, like husband and wife or something?"

"That's up to you," she said. "There doesn't have to be any strings attached. I just want to be with you, and I can look after you till you gain some weight and get your health back."

It wasn't that sleeping in the same bed with Bonnie Jo for the rest of his life wouldn't be the next thing to heaven. After all they had become close, and it wasn't necessarily that living like one of the rich and famous wasn't also tempting. He imagined such a life where your only worries were the weeds in the yard and the chlorine level in the swimming pool. He could get used to that. But there was something bothering him, that shadow that remained in the back of his mind. Somewhere back up Jefferson Avenue a siren wailed as if to tell him to beware of such a domesticated world. He still couldn't deal with life's cruel illusion, the one that denied it could end instantly with a stroke of fate.

"I appreciate your help, but you don't have to take care of me. Besides, I'm not sure I'd fit in out there in California."

She lifted her head from his shoulder and looked him in the eyes. "This isn't about taking care of you. It's about needing you."

"You don't need me. You've got the world in the palm of your hand. You just feel sorry for me."

"Billy, I don't feel sorry for you. You've had a tough time, but you're a survivor. You'll make it no matter what happens. I want you, because I love you."

Her words left him stunned, and he remembered that night when they danced in the yard beside her daddy's car and their subsequent sexual encounter. He had felt it then, that deeper attraction. And he could have said it then. He could have told her that he really cared, but it was now lost in the complexity of guilt for not having said it when it would have meant the most. And now, it was even more difficult, because his life was complicated by another guilt, that of escaping Vietnam when the others didn't. There were too many things he had to reconcile in his mind before committing to a relationship. Besides, Bonnie Jo deserved better.

"When I can give you something in return, I'll come see you."

"You have given me something. You've given me everything. I wouldn't be where I am today if it hadn't been for the way you treated me back in high school. Do you know how lonely I was then? You gave me encourage-ment. You talked with me and made me feel worthwhile. You gave me hope."

"And now you want to return the favor, right?"

A car full of teenage boys drove by, honking and whistling. She ignored them as her cheeks reddened and her eyes hardened.

"Dammit, Billy Coker, you love me, too, and you know it. You're just too blasted stubborn to admit it."

She saw through him. For the first time in his life, Billy had come to know what genuine love really was, and he loved this woman for something other than her body. At least he hoped that was the case, because she certainly had a world class one, now. Like always, his mind was leading him into another circular argument of self-doubt.

"What makes you think I don't want you just for your body?" he asked.

"Stop playing games with me, Billy."

"Look, Bonnie, I need time to think. You're right. I do love you, but my mind is probably more of a wreck than my body. And you need to stop and think. Do you really want a crippled old vet, who can't even dance, hanging around with you for the rest of your life?"

"Nothing matters except that I want to be with you." With that she stood and pulled him up from the bus bench. "Let's go get cleaned up. I'm coming back to pick you up in an hour."

"What for?"

"You're taking me on a date tonight, a real date."

"Where?"

"I don't know. You'll have to suggest someplace."

Billy went up to the ward to clean up, while Bonnie Jo drove back to her hotel room to change. When she returned they went to a place Riker suggested called Alfred's at Overton Square. Finding a secluded table, they ordered drinks. Overton Square was the happening place in Memphis, a trendy urban renewal in midtown with nice restaurants and bars. Hoping to blend in, they wore sunglasses and dressed down with jeans and T-shirts. It worked through dinner, but a sharp-eyed fan eventually spotted her.

The young woman whispered to her friends, before walking over to the table where Billy and Bonnie Jo sat. This first autograph request became an avalanche as word spread throughout the restaurant and up and down Madison Avenue. People came in asking to take photos with her, talking and buying her drinks. Bonnie Jo tried to please them, signing autographs for nearly an hour, until Billy took her by the hand. They left Alfred's, and drove up Madison Avenue toward downtown.

"Is it that way most of the time?" he asked.

"Where would you like to go?" she asked.

"Someplace quiet where we won't get mobbed."

"They usually don't recognize me when I wear sunglasses, but it can happen anywhere."

Billy spotted a liquor store. "Pull in there."

There was a 7-11 market next door.

"Run over there and get a bag of ice while I get some bubbly stuff," he said. "We'll celebrate in private."

He was back in the car, waiting several minutes before Bonnie Jo finally came out of the convenience store.

"What took you so long?" he asked.

She laughed. "The old man inside saw you go into the liquor store. He asked if I was okay. I told him you were just an old wino I'd picked up, and he started lecturing me about hanging around with hippies. I think I'm going to give you a haircut."

Billy pulled a joint from his shirt pocket and fired it up. "Here," he said, passing it to her. "Now, tell me how you plan on cutting my hair."

"Well, I haven't really given it a lot of thought, but since your intent is to get me stoned out of my mind, maybe it would be safest if we did it in my hotel room. I have a razor and some scissors up there and lots of towels in case I accidentally cut your ear off."

14

IMPOTENCE UNDER FIRE

"Champagne and a haircut in the famous BJ Parker's hotel room—what did I do to deserve this?" Billy asked.

Bonnie Jo cocked her head to one side as he raised his glass. Setting the scissors aside, she picked up hers, and they toasted with a clink of the glasses.

"Here's to a classy lady," Billy said.

"And here's to you, Billy Boy," Bonnie Jo replied. "And for better times to come."

"Better times than this?"

"Sure. There can be."

"I can think of only one thing that would be any better."

She winked. "Like I've always said, you have a one track mind, boy."

"That's right. I am a man ruled by my hormones."

"That's not true," she replied. "You've got more character than any man I've ever known."

"Still doesn't mean I don't like sex."

She picked up the scissors and continued cutting.

"Don't you think men and women can be in love without having sex?" she asked.

"No way," he said. "If women didn't have vaginas, there'd be a bounty on them."

Bonnie Jo laughed. She was unflappable.

"It's a good thing I know you," she said. "Most women wouldn't tolerate that macho bullshit."

"I am serious."

"Yeah, right. So how do you explain the fact that you love me, and we haven't made love since high school?"

"You aren't the average woman. Besides, maybe I'm holding out for the possibility of a second chance."

She ran her comb through his hair. "Well, sorry to disappoint you, but I am the average woman, and maybe, I'm holding out for the possibility, too."

He tried to turn and look at her, but she pushed his head back around. "Be still before I cut that ear off."

After several more minutes of snipping and combing she set the scissors aside and picked up her champagne glass. With her free hand, she held a mirror in front of his face. Billy looked into the mirror, but not at himself. He found himself gazing at her. Her face glowed and her green eyes sparkled like a living portrait in the mirror. Their eyes met.

"So, what do you think?" she asked.

"You're beautiful," he said.

"Not me, Dummy, your haircut."

"Oh." Billy turned his head to the side as he looked into the mirror. "I look damned near respectable again. What do you think?"

"I think you're downright handsome. Now, go in there and take a shower while I clean up this mess."

After the shower, Billy toweled off and opened the bathroom door. Bonnie Jo was lying on the bed watching television. He wrapped the towel around his waist and walked into the room.

"What are you watching?"

She jumped up and turned off the television. The lights were turned down low, and Karen Carpenter was on the stereo.

"Nothing," she said. "Do you want some more champagne?"

She poured the last of it into the glasses while Billy sat on the bed beside her.

"What's with the Dodger's jersey?" he asked.

"Sorry, but this is the closest thing I have to a sexy gown."

She fingered the tail of the shirt self-consciously. "A baseball player gave it to me. Said he wanted me to model it for him sometime."

"Did you?"

"Yep, at my next concert. He called later and said that wasn't what he had in mind. I told him that was the best I could do, but he still didn't get the hint. He got so pushy until I finally told him to put it on ice."

"Poor guy," Billy said.

Bonnie Jo reached over and pulled the glass from his hand, setting it on the bedside table. She turned to face him, and their lips met. Carefully at first, they explored one another with soft touches and a gentle embraces. Billy held her close and kissed her tenderly, then passionately as he pushed her back on the bed.

She ran her fingertips cautiously through the sunken purple scars on his back and across the ones on his buttocks. She kissed the largest scar on his abdomen and he watched as she explored his ugly body. The situation was surreal and strange to him. It wasn't this ravishingly beautiful woman he loved, any more than his ugly scarred body was what she loved. This was something real—something that was much more than a teenage dream of making love with a beautiful woman.

This was the girl who'd talked him through the insanity of high school. This was the pudgy little girl he had thought about almost every day in Vietnam. He loved this girl for whom he'd done so little at a time when she needed him most. He loved the Bonnie Jo who had given him the Saint Sebastian medal, a good-luck charm that worked when all the others failed. It was her last words from so long ago that came back to him again and again: "Don't worry, Billy Boy. Everything will be okay." And it was.

After a while he began unbuttoning her shirt, and her breathing grew heavier. Her breasts, round and full, rose and fell with each breath. He pushed her panties down and pulled them from around her ankles. Slowly, he worked his way back up, kissing her body as he went. They held one another close, but after a few minutes Billy realized nothing was happening. He was as limp as a wet spaghetti noodle.

Bonnie Jo seemed to sense something was up, or perhaps that it *wasn't* up. Her hand dropped down to his abdomen, then a little further. She touched him, and instinctively, she did all the right things. She caressed him, and it felt good, really good, but still, nothing happened. Frightened and embarrassed at the same moment Billy didn't understand what was happening. And after a while, they both realized it wasn't working. He kissed her, squeezed his eyes tight shut and held her close.

"Does this have something to do with your wounds?" she asked.

"Hell no," he said. "This thing has been as hard as the Hope Diamond for the last month. I don't know what's going on."

She giggled nervously. "Stage fright, maybe? Happens to the best of us."

Billy didn't answer, and she cuddled closer.

"Let's get some sleep," she said. "Maybe, you'll, uh, feel better, later."

Sometime in the night Billy realized he couldn't sleep no matter how much he tried, and making love to Bonnie Jo seemed impossible. He glanced at the bedside clock, then at Bonnie Jo. She was lost in a blissful dream-world. He studied the contentment on her face. She was as beautiful as she was loving.

Billy carefully touched her hair, but to truly touch her in a meaningful way seemed impossible. He was drawn to her like no woman he had ever known, but the thing that caused his impotence stood in the way. And he knew that at precisely the wrong moment it would return, drowning the flame in a monsoon of psychological turmoil. If he stayed and failed again, she would think it was in some way her fault.

She slept peacefully as he slipped from the bed and pulled on his jeans. The desk clerk called a cab, and Billy rode back to the VA alone that night. A misty rain was falling and the windshield wipers beat a weary rhythm as silent neon lights reflected from the damp pavement. He tried to think about what was happening, but nothing made sense. He wanted her, but he didn't want to hurt her. He had to search for the answers, because he was screwing up by the numbers.

Later that morning he left the hospital and went over to Jackie's apartment in mid-town. Located off of a busy thoroughfare near a school and several small businesses, Jackie's third-floor apartment had a great view of the tree-lined streets and sidewalks. Billy spent his free time there when he could.

Jackie had a gotten a clerical job with the VA office downtown, and the apartment was quiet, except for the low rumble of thunder outside and the patter of a morning rain. Billy stared out the window at the people on the street below. Hidden beneath yellow raincoats and umbrellas, they hurried anonymously down wet sidewalks, but for what purpose? What was it they so urgently pursued on this rainy day that couldn't wait? What reasons could there be for doing anything?

He thought of Bonnie Jo, knowing she would be hurt, but the pain would have been worse had he stayed. Something was confounding his every motivation, and before he wrecked someone else's life, he had to fix his own. The thunder passed, and the rain fell straight and gray into dimpled puddles on the sidewalks. With the sky darkened by the clouds, the neon sign on the Chinese restaurant down the street was burning at mid-morning.

Bonnie Jo returned to the VA the next week. She smiled and they hugged, but they didn't talk about the night at the Peabody. Her reaction made him respect her all the more, because she never bitched, she never nagged. She was simply there for him, quiet and strong. He wanted to be a part of her life, but no matter how he tried, he was unable to get beyond the invisible divide of the past. The ghost of the little girl who he truly liked but who he had so totally denied still haunted him. And there were the ghosts of Butch, Danny and the others who would never have and opportunity to know a woman like Bonnie Jo. He couldn't simply turn his back on them. He needed someone to talk with about these things, someone who could understand.

Billy's release from the hospital came on a Friday in August. The VA was sending him out on his own. He was a free man, starting a new life. After saying his good-byes around the ward, he hit the door to catch a cab to Jackie's apartment. Bonnie Jo had wanted to be there, but she was doing a concert in Seattle and couldn't make it. Billy told her to call when she got back, but something happened.

15

FINDING CURTIS TEAGUE

A letter had come in the mail a few days before Billy's release from the hospital. It was from Curtis Teague. They hadn't heard from one another since the day they were wounded, but Curtis had somehow found him, and his letter said he was doing well. He was working at a refinery in Louisiana and wanted Billy to come down for a visit. This was the answer. Curtis was someone who would understand what he was going through. He was someone who had been there, seen the same men maimed and killed, someone who perhaps would understand the psychological shadow that ruled his life.

Billy thought about Bonnie Jo. She would have to understand that he had no choice. Curtis was closer than blood kin. They'd put their lives on the line for one another. Together on the mountain, they'd stared the beast in the eye. Together they'd felt the razor sting of shrapnel, and together they had watched friends die, and together they survived. Billy had no choice. His friend had called for him. He was going down to Louisiana.

After signing the last form at the hospital that afternoon, he went straight to Jackie's place and made preparations. Stuffing Jackie's things into paper grocery bags, Billy set them on the balcony outside the door. By the time Jackie got home from work that afternoon, Billy had thrown most of the bags from the third floor balcony. Problem was the impact had ruptured the bags, scattering clothes on the sidewalk below. Jackie stood in the parking lot staring up at Billy as he came out of the apartment with the final armload.

"Have you lost your mind, Coker?" he shouted. "What the fuck are you doing?"

Billy looked down at him from the balcony. "We're going down to Louisiana to see Curtis Teague," he shouted. "I got a letter from him. He said he'll buy us all the shrimp, crawfish and beer we want if we come see him."

Jackie began gathering his clothes from the sidewalk. Billy carried an armload of breakables down the stairs as Jackie stuffed the bags into the trunk of his car.

"How come you threw everything over the balcony?" he asked.

"Because it's three goddam floors up, and in case you haven't noticed, I *am* a disabled vet."

Jackie didn't say anything.

"Why in the hell did you get a third-floor apartment anyway?"

"The landlady gave me a cut-rate," he said.

"So, you're gonna kill yourself just to save a few bucks?"

Jackie threw another sack into the trunk and stood glaring at Billy. "The surgeon said the more I exercise my lungs, the stronger they'll get." His response was low, slow and metered as he worked his jaw back and forth.

"I think you inhaled too much napalm," Billy said. "It got your brain, too."

Jackie broke into laughter and shook his head. "So what's your excuse?"

"Don't have one. It just comes natural."

"Okay, nature boy, so how do you propose we get all the way to New Orleans and back by Monday morning?"

"Hell, we're going past New Orleans, down in the bayou country, and to hell with Monday. I figure we can—"

"Wait a minute," Jackie said. "You seem to forget I have a job."

"Screw a job. We paid our dues. Let's get the hell out of here and have some fun. Curtis is expecting us."

After a late supper they finished packing, and Jackie stopped griping by the time they reached Interstate 55 and headed south into Mississippi. It was well after midnight as the green interstate signs rolled by in the headlights, Grenada, Rolling Fork, Yazoo City. Sometime in the early morning hours they crossed the Pontchartrain Bridge and managed to get by New Orleans before the rush hour. Bleary-eyed, they made their way south on

Highway 90 as the sun crept above a shimmering sea of saw grass stretching all the way to the horizon.

When they reached Houma Jackie stopped beside a phone booth, and Billy called Curtis. He got directions, and they found his place somewhere down in Terrebonne Parish. Not exactly a Hilton, the house had weathered cypress siding with a rusted tin roof, and it stood on the only high ground around. A pair of huge live oaks strung with shrouds of Spanish moss were in the front yard. They provided much-needed shade as Billy and Jackie walked up a dirt path to the front porch.

"Shit, man, what do you do if the water comes up?" Billy asked as he hobbled up the steps with his cane.

Curtis grabbed him in a bear hug. "Swim. By damned, it's good to see you, Sarge."

"Won't the alligators eat you?" Jackie asked.

Curtis turned and looked at him. "Not if you eat them first."

He shoved an open hand at Jackie. "Curtis Teague's my name."

Billy stood proudly watching him shake hands with Jackie. Curtis was his friend, and he represented what he had wanted most in Nam, to bring his men home alive. Although not unscathed, Curtis wasn't wounded nearly as badly as Billy, but he still had the telltale white scars where the shrapnel had cut him.

Billy looked around. A flight of brown pelicans winged their way majestically across a sea of grass and water. Above, exotic little birds—indigo, yellow and crimson—chirped and warbled as they flitted amongst the limbs of the live oaks.

"Damned," Billy muttered. "This place is a jungle."

"Aww Sarge, it ain't that bad. You'll see. We're going down to Mama Cici's at the lake this evening. Her old man is still in Nam, and I told her how you were my sergeant while I was over there, and how you saved my life. She said supper is on the house. She's got beer, crawfish and shrimp, and there'll be a band playing later, too."

"Sounds good," Billy said.

"Damned right, it's good," Curtis said. "There'll be girls there, and we're gonna dance with every last one of them."

"I'm not sure how much dancing I can do with this thing," Billy said. He held up his government-issue cane.

"So how did you get out of the hospital so fast?" Curtis asked.

"So fast?" Billy said. "Hell, it's been a year."

"Yeah, but the last time I saw you, your butt was chewed up and smokin' like hamburger meat. I didn't even think you was gonna make it."

"I guess I was lucky," Billy said, "but I still can't walk very good."

Curtis paused, and his eyes moistened as they lost focus. A hollow moment of silence ensued, and Billy wanted to tell him it was okay. It was okay because they'd made it home. But it wasn't. He saw it in the big man's eyes. Curtis was experiencing the same sense of loss and guilt that had haunted him since returning from Nam.

Billy looked out beyond the shade of the oak trees to where the sun was shining brightly and a gentle breeze stirred the tall green grasses.

"Don't worry, Sarge," Curtis said. He paused then nodded as if he was thinking of something. "Yeah, don't you worry none at all. We can talk more later. Right now, y'all need to get some sleep. I got a bed fixed in the back. You can grab a nap, and after sunset when it cools off, we'll head down yonder to Mama Cici's Place."

16

NEW ORLEANS TO SOUTH GEORGIA

Mama Cici's red and blue neon sign stood out like a spaceship in the Louisiana night. Like most places in the bayou backcountry, the restaurant had a weathered gray exterior with a rust-orange metal roof, screened doors and a wooden porch. From inside came the sounds of music and laughter. When the three vets walked through the door, chairs scraped the wood floor as a mixed crowd of Cajuns, blacks and whites stood, holding their bottles, cans and glasses high in the air. They greeted the three of them with a loud cheer. Treated like royalty, Curtis, Billy and Jackie were led to a table at the center of the room.

A huge alligator, its toothy jaws agape, was mounted on a shelf that stretched nearly half the length of one wall. And neon signs behind the bar advertised RC Cola and Jax Beer. In a side room there stood a large black woman. Her brow was beaded with sweat, and she held a ladle over a bubbling cauldron of oil. She was wearing a white butcher's apron over a purple flower-print dress. It had to be Mama Cici.

Curtis threw his head back and inhaled the aroma. "My weary soul is comin' alive," he said. "Mama Cici's fryin' up some of her special kind of redfish."

"Smells good," Billy said.

"Smells more like fantastic," Jackie replied.

The crowd gathered around them, shaking hands and slapping their backs. Through a screened door in the rear, steam rose from another huge pot out on the porch. The aroma of shrimp boiling in red pepper, bay laurel and celery crept inside to challenge the fried fish. People shoved drinks into their hands, and the three men ate shrimp that night cooked more ways than they thought possible, and they peeled crawfish until their fingers were colored by the cayenne.

It became the homecoming celebration they never had. A band with no name played music ranging from Country and Western to Blues and Zydeco. And while Curtis and Jackie danced with every woman in the place, Billy got pleasantly inebriated. For once, life was good.

Sometime in the early morning hours the party ended, and the three men sat around the table talking about the future. The band had folded-up and gone home, and overhead a dusty black ceiling fan turned listlessly, barely stirring the warm night air. Steaming cups of black chicory coffee had replaced the beer, and sugared beignets had replaced the shrimp. Mama Cici was behind the bar cleaning glasses and humming along with an old Son House tune on the jukebox.

"Life has really been good since I got back from Nam," Curtis said. "Folks around here appreciate their vets." His voice dropped to a whisper. "Mama Cici's husband is still over there. He's a master sergeant and about to retire, but she says he's always writing her about the fighting. She knows how it is, and so does most everybody else around here. They helped me get a good job at the refinery and two or three of these gals are bent on making me their husband, except I ain't about to let that happen, leastwise, not yet. I got more important things to do before I get hitched."

Tired laughter circled the table.

"You're a wise man," Jackie said.

Curtis pursed his lips and stared out through the screen-door at the Louisiana night. Insects swarmed around a yellow bulb on the porch, and the low ground across the road was alive with the drone of insects and frogs.

"What is it you want to do?" Billy asked.

Curtis rubbed his chin and looked over at him. "I don't know. I mean, I *do* have this silly dream."

"Yeah?" Billy said. "So, what is it?"

"You know how I told you I played football in college before I got drafted?"

Billy nodded as Curtis turned and looked him directly in the eyes.

"Well, I figure life ain't got no guarantees, and I was wanting to do something besides just sittin' around and workin' till I die. I mean, the refinery's a good job, but I always wanted to play pro football, you know? I mean, the NFL was about to draft me when I got out of college, but the army got me first. You know?"

"Why don't you give it a shot?" Jackie asked.

"Been too long," Curtis said. "I'm out of shape, and I just don't know about leaving a good job."

"No, you don't know," Billy said. "And you never will, if you don't take a chance."

"Yeah, but I got a good job, and—"

"Curtis, if you don't try, you'll always regret it."

"Maybe so," he said. "But I just can't see how—"

"You have to make up your mind," Billy said.

Curtis looked first at Billy, then at Jackie. After a moment he looked away as he sipped his beer. He absentmindedly flicked a crawdad head off the table with his finger, and one of Mama Cici's cats crept from the corner to nose the shell.

"You ain't gonna find no meat in that one, kitty," Curtis said "These boys done sucked it dry."

"So what are you going to do?" Billy asked.

"Well, I ain't gonna run out and do nothin' *tonight*," Curtis said. "Tryouts won't be for a while yet. Besides, I need to think on it some."

"That's good," Billy said. "In the meantime, you can get in shape."

"It ain't that easy, Sarge."

"Nobody said it would be easy. You just have to make up your mind to keep getting up and coming back at them. You can't quit."

Curtis's eyes remained unfocused as he stared at something deep within.

"Have you got a track or a gym, someplace you can go to work out?" Billy asked.

"No. Ain't no place like that around here. Probably, the closest public gym is up in New Orleans."

"Oh, come on," Billy said. "You're just making excuses. There must be someplace you can go, a high school or a YMCA."

Billy was beginning to sense how this was more than a whim for Curtis. It was something he was seriously considering, and he really believed he had a shot at the pros.

"It doesn't have to be any place fancy," Billy said.

Curtis shrugged. "Well, I've been thinkin' about my Uncle Sookey's place. It's a gym, but it's way up yonder in Atlanta."

"Cut him a deal," Billy said. "Tell him if he'll put you up and let you use his gym, you'll pay him when you get signed on with a pro team."

"And if I don't?"

"Tell him that's part of the deal. If you don't, then he gets nothing. Tell him it's like a stock investment. If your stock goes up, he makes money. If it doesn't, he loses."

Curtis looked up at Billy, and his tired eyes brighten. "You know, old Sookey might just go for something like that. He always did like a good game of poker."

"If I can walk again, you can play football again," Billy said.

"I just hope I can play football better than you walk," Curtis replied. His face grew ashen. "Man, Sarge, I didn't mean that the way it sounded."

Billy laughed. "Do I look offended?"

"Well, I'm sorry anyway, I wouldn't say nothin' like—." Curtis stopped talking, and for a moment his eyes again lost focus.

"I'm telling you," Billy said. "It didn't bother me."

"No, no," Curtis said as he came out of his trance. "Look, I got this idea. Why don't you go with me? I bet Uncle Sookey can get your legs in shape. Besides, he's a helluva cook, and you could stand to gain some weight if you don't do nothing else."

The sounds of the swamp outside the screen door grew suddenly louder as Billy thought about going with Curtis to Atlanta. He already knew the answer, and it had nothing to do with getting in shape. He had to get Curtis to talk to him. He had to make him tell how he had gotten past it all.

"What about it?" Curtis asked.

Billy shrugged. "I don't have much else happening, but it took them nearly a year to get me walking with this cane. I wouldn't expect too much."

"Don't worry none," Curtis said. "You ain't met my Uncle Sookey. See, he was a boxer back years ago, one of the best Golden Glovers in Georgia. Leastwise, he won a lot more than he ever lost, but he just up and quit one day. The trainers called him a quitter, but he said he was gonna retire while he still had more than scrambled eggs for brains. Later, he trained some of the best fighters in the South. You just work with him. I guarantee you, he'll get you to walking better."

"Sounds like a plan," Billy said. "When do we leave?"

Curtis nodded. "I'll give him a call in the morning.

"What about Bonnie Jo?" Jackie asked.

"I'll call in a day or two and let her know what I'm doing. She'll understand."

A couple days later Jackie found his job was still waiting for him and returned to Memphis while Curtis and Billy planned their trip to Atlanta. Curtis said a visit to New Orleans was in order before beginning a tour of duty with Uncle Sookey. "You ain't lived till you ate some New Orleans Beignets, sipped Southern Comfort on Bourbon Street and walked the French Quarter," Curtis said.

A thunderstorm blew in from the gulf that afternoon before they departed, and it was nightfall by the time they threw their bags into the trunk of Curtis's Monte Carlo. As they pulled out onto the road, the headlights reflected against a warm foggy mist hanging over the saw grass swamps. Curtis had quit his job at the refinery, said good-bye to his favorite girl, and was striking out into the unknown. More sober now, Billy hoped he hadn't pushed him toward a fool's dream, because getting on with a pro team was a longshot at best.

The storm moved off in the distance, but spider-webs of lightning continued skittering across the night sky, and the roadway was puddled with water as they drove toward New Orleans. Curtis didn't have much to say, and for a while Billy's thoughts returned to Bonnie Jo. Her feelings were probably hurt, and he needed to call her, but telephones were scarce this time of night. Besides, there wasn't much he could say. He saw no future in the headlights ahead. Like the county road they were on, there were no signs telling him which way to go.

After getting a room just off Canal Street that evening, Billy and Curtis walked through the French Quarter. The dank muddy odor of the Mississippi drifted off the levee beyond Jackson Square. A muggy night, the neon lights on Bourbon Street reflected from the rain-glazed pavement as they made their way through the crowd. Tattooed men with greasy hair and cigarettes hanging from their mouths hustled passer-byes into the darkened portals of places with names like 'Babes' and 'Fat Catz.'

With strings of colored beads draped around their necks Billy and Curtis wandered from one "gentleman's club" to the next, taking in the sights and drinking. It was near midnight when they stopped in front of yet another club. A big woman wearing an orange floral print dress and a red wig sat on a bar stool in front of the open door. Her huge white breasts all but overflowed the dress, as she sat with a cigarette in an amber holder between her fingers.

"You boys come on in here, now, and check out our new girl, Sarah Ann. She's right good."

"Check it out," Curtis said. He motioned inside where yet another stripper was on a stage twirling her mostly naked body around a brass pole.

For whatever reason, Billy was struck by a sudden sadness.

"What's the matter, Sarge?"

"Nothing," Billy said.

They paid the woman at the door, found a table and ordered beer. The girl was young and beautiful, and despite her smile, there was a shadow of sadness in her eyes. Her golden blonde hair glowed beneath the klieg lights, and her body, was toned and supple, but there was something more, something Billy sensed more than saw. Had a tear slipped from her eye at that moment it wouldn't have surprised him. He stared down into his beer and once again thought of Bonnie Jo.

"How come you ain't watching the show?" Curtis asked.

Billy looked up at the girl on the stage. The young woman wasn't at all average with her looks or her craft, and she danced without the raunchy moves most strippers found necessary.

"You ever ask yourself how a person gets to where they are in life, I mean like that girl up there, or us in Vietnam?" Billy asked.

Curtis frowned. "Don't go getting all philosophical on me, Sarge. I got enough problems without worrying about Nam or some stripper."

Curtis tipped up his beer, and later they walked up Bourbon Street, crossing Bienville past The Old Absinthe House, and each night they visited a different club, talking, drinking and taking in the sights. It wasn't as good as Mama Cici's, but the music and time together allowed them to again get to know one another.

Their last evening on Bourbon Street, Curtis and Billy stopped on the sidewalk and stared through the open door of a place they'd visited earlier in the week, where the "new girl", Sarah Ann had danced. The patrons sitting at the tables were a cluster of sharply defined black silhouettes, surrounding the klieg-light glow on the elevated stage. The woman in the orange dress wasn't there, but the same girl, Sarah Ann, was still swinging around the brass pole. Billy stood, his hands buried deep his pockets as he watched.

"Your girl is still going strong," Curtis said.

"I suppose there are worse ways to make a living," Billy answered.

As they headed back to their hotel that evening Billy and Curtis fell in behind several young women sauntering toward Canal Street. For three days Billy had tried to get Curtis to talk about Nam, but only for an occasional moment it seemed he would catch him off guard and make him reminisce about a buddy or R&R, but

Curtis would quickly take the conversation in another direction.

"Since I got back from Nam," Billy said. "I've had a lot of time to think about things. It's really got me—"

"Sarge," Curtis interrupted, "you know, I ain't tryin' to be nosy, but we've been here three days, and you ain't hit on the first lady."

He was doing it again, steering him to a different conversation.

"You ain't sweet are you?"

Billy let him have his way and forced a laugh. "No, Curtis, I'm not sweet. Why, are you?"

Curtis, stopped mid-stride. "Man, what's wrong with you?"

Billy didn't look back as he continued walking. "I thought maybe you were making a pass at me."

"You're fixin' to make me kill a crippled white boy."

Billy laughed. "Go ahead. You can't win. If you whip my ass they'll say you beat up a cripple, and if I win, they'll say you got your ass whipped by a cripple."

Curtis caught up with him. "Give me a break, Sarge. Will you?"

"Okay," Billy said, "but let me ask you a question."

"What's that?"

"Do you think about Nam much?"

"You know what I think about?" Curtis said. "I think about women. You see those girls up there? The three women in front of them were almost to Canal Street. "Do you know how I can tell they're country girls?"

He was doing it again—changing the subject. Billy wagged his head. "No, how's that?"

"They sashay when they walk," Curtis said. "City women can't do that without everybody thinking they're hookers."

"You know something," Billy said. "You're right."

He gave up trying to talk about Nam with Curtis. It was obvious Curtis had put it behind him, and Billy wished he could do the same. And he realized now that he was wasn't going to Atlanta to get in shape. He was running away. He was running from the past. He was running from Bonnie Jo. He was running through a shadowed jungle away from his memories of the war and failures as a man.

They left New Orleans the next morning and headed across Mississippi, through Alabama and into Georgia. Curtis drove at a leisurely pace as they took their time and avoided the speed traps. By late afternoon they were on a two-lane state highway somewhere in the pine flats of South Georgia. Curtis had grown tired and finally let Billy drive the new Monte Carlo. Billy immediately rolled down the windows, found some Lynyrd Skynyrd on the radio and mashed the accelerator to the floor. The hot air blew through the car, and along with it came the odor of the turpentine and paper mills.

Curtis nodded off, and after a while Billy had grown thirsty when he passed a little roadhouse in the middle of nowhere. There hadn't been another building for miles, but there it was, with several cars and trucks parked out front, along with a couple of motorcycles. Billy hit the brakes and Curtis sat up, rubbing his eyes. After making a U-turn in the middle of the highway, Billy drove back to the gravel parking lot.

"Where the hell are we at?" Curtis asked.

"Hell, I don't know, but it's time for a cold beer," Billy said.

Towering pines shaded the little aluminum building, and though the sun was still above the trees, a red and white neon Budweiser sign burned inside the window. The aroma of frying hamburgers hung heavily in the warm afternoon air competing with the turpentine odor. The parking lot was covered with a layer of brown pine needles, but as he stepped from the car Billy heard the crunch of broken glass beneath his feet. The surrounding countryside was flat as a pool table, with nothing but pine trees as far as the eye could see.

"You go on in and get the beer." Curtis said. "I'll wait here."

"What the fuck's wrong with you?" Billy asked.

"This is Georgia, my man, and we don't know none of these people. Some of 'em might not want colored folks coming in their place."

"This is the '70's. Things have changed. Nobody's gonna mess with us."

Curtis rolled his eyes. "Yeah, right, Sarge. I think I'll wait out here for you."

"Goddamit Curtis, ain't nothing gonna happen. Now, get your ass out of the car, and let's go inside."

Curtis didn't seem the least bit comforted as Billy pushed the building's metal door open and looked inside. Except for the dim glow of a light near the bar, they saw little else in the blackness of the interior. A jukebox glowed on one wall with Merle Haggard singing something about fighting. Perhaps Curtis was right, the place did look a little rough. Billy gave him a quick wink, but Curtis cut his eyes left and right as they stepped inside. The door closed behind them.

The glare of the outside sunlight still burned in Billy's eyes, leaving him blinded. It was as if he had just jumped from a chopper into the shadows of a triple-canopied jungle. Carefully he began making his way toward the bar. He sensed more than saw that there were others seated in the room as he felt his way through the darkened interior. His eyes began adjusting, and he recognized the silhouettes of ball caps and the dull glow of cigarettes.

In a backroom two men stooped over a shuffleboard table, their faces lit by the overhead lamp. Billy tagged one as a Hells Angel wannabe because of his backwards baseball cap and sleeveless denim shirt. The man held his beer bottle by the neck. The other had a cigarette dangling precariously from his lips as he bent low over the shuffleboard. Somewhere in the darkness, a male voice muttered, "He's got a nigger with him."

Billy made out the forms of several men sitting around a table in the corner.

"I think we've stepped in shit," Curtis whispered.

"I'll see if I can get a six-pack to go," Billy replied.

"Make it fast. I'll wait here."

Curtis hung back while Billy walked up to the bar and asked the woman there for a six-pack of Miller High Life. She was bent over the cooler, when a man appeared beside Billy.

"What's up, partner?" the man asked.

"Just getting some beer," Billy said.

The man was short, five-foot-five at best, but he had arms bigger than most men's legs. The light at the bar lit the man's blue-gray eyes. They had the dead look of a man who could stomp a kitten's head or snuff a cigarette on a sleeping drunk's face, and feel no remorse.

"What are you doing with him in here?" The man motioned toward Curtis.

"Oh, him? He's my hired hand."

For a moment the man seemed to buy Billy's story.

"Hey," he shouted at Curtis. "You work for this man?"

"Sho do, boss. Yes suh, he's my boss man, sho 'nough."

Billy felt his face would explode as he fought to keep from laughing. Curtis was over-doing it. The man beside Billy wore a Treflan cap, and had "Love it or Leave it" tattooed beneath the Stars and Stripes on his forearm.

"Where y'all from?" he asked.

"Man, you sure do ask a lot of questions," Billy said.

The man set his beer bottle down hard on the bar. "You got a problem with that?" His short-man's complex oozed from every pore.

Billy felt it—a tiny twinge of the explosive anger he held deep inside. He stifled it, and gave the man a big smile. "Last I heard, this was still a free country, which means we can go where we please without being interrogated."

"You're kind of a smart-ass, for being such a skinny dude," he said.

Billy felt a roiling lava pushing its way to the surface.

The woman placed a paper bag with the six-pack on the bar.

"How much do I owe you?" Billy asked.

"Ten dollars."

He would have complained, but he was intent upon getting out the door before he lost control. Tossing a ten-dollar bill on the bar, he reached for the bag, but the man put his hand over the bag.

"Are you ignoring me?" he said.

That was it. There would be no easy way out of this one. This guy was hell bent on a fight, and despite his debilitated condition, Billy was going to give him one. The combat instructors always said, "The best way to overcome an attack or ambush is to quickly answer with a strong offense. He turned to the man, laughed and said, "Oh, hell no. I'm not ignoring you. Matter of fact I was just fixing to buy you a beer."

He turned to the woman behind the bar. "Have you got any quart bottles?"

She nodded.

"Give me a quart of whatever this man drinks."

"What if I don't want a long-hair buying beer for me?" he asked.

She set a quart of Budweiser on the bar.

"That's okay," Billy said. "but first I want you to look back at that man standing over there." He motioned toward Curtis.

"What for?" The man looked over his shoulder at Curtis.

Billy picked up the quart and swung it, hitting him up side the head. "So I can give it to you anyway, you sorry fuck."

Billy set the broken bottleneck on the bar as the man went rubber-legged and collapsed in a puddle of glass and beer. Grabbing the six-pack, he headed for the door, but it was too late. Someone flew at him from out of the shadows. Billy sidestepped and caught the attacker hard across the back of the head with his cane. The attacker hit the floor face-down and didn't move. Two others had gone at Curtis, but they, too, were already lying on the floor. Billy and Curtis backed toward the door as several others charged out of the darkness.

Curtis grabbed a chair, smashing the first one with it, while Billy butted another in the face with his cane. A beer bottle flashed as it flew out of the darkness and burst against Curtis's temple. He shook his head and laughed.

"You shouldn't ought to have done that," he said.

With that he waded into their midst, swinging his fists like sledgehammers. A man pulled a pistol, but before he could raise it, Billy swung his cane like a baseball bat. An audible crack sounded as the man's wrist splintered and he screamed. The gun went skittering across the floor and disappeared beneath the tables. The one man left standing cowered behind the jukebox.

Billy brandished his cane and went after him, but Curtis caught him by the back of the shirt. "I think we better go, Sarge."

"No!" Billy screamed. "I'm going to teach this white trash—"

"You already did, Sarge. Now let's go before the police come."

With that he grabbed Billy around the waist and carried him to the car. Curtis stared straight ahead, his jaw set like stone as he drove up the highway toward Atlanta. Billy felt his anger subsiding. Before Vietnam, he had never been a violent person, but it came to him that he had been about to kill those men back at the bar if Curtis hadn't carried him out. After a minute or two, he looked over at Curtis. "Sorry," he said. "I totally lost it back there."

"Those crackers didn't give you much choice, but you should of known better than to go in there, Sarge."

"Dammit Curtis, not everybody in the South is that way. Don't blame me for that bunch of assholes."

"Hell, no," he said. "I ain't gonna blame you, but what are you gonna tell them dudes up there?" He pointed up the highway.

They were entering a small town, and up ahead a squad car was sitting crossways at the first intersection, its lights flashing. The heat waves shimmered from the highway as Curtis slowed to a stop. A cop wearing dark glasses and a Smoky Bear hat sauntered their way. Walking nonchalantly up to the driver side window, he rapped it with a black nightstick. His partner remained beside the squad car brandishing a pump shotgun.

"You boys step out of the vehicle," the first cop said.

"You, boy," the policeman said, motioning Curtis to the back of the car. "Put your hands on the trunk and spread your legs."

"You, boy!" the other cop shouted motioning at Billy with the shotgun. "You come on up here."

Billy held up his hands as he walked toward the policeman with the shotgun. The blacktop pavement burned like an oven beneath his tennis shoes, and the Cicadas were buzzing in the live Oaks. Several bystanders stopped to watch as they were spread-eagled and frisked. A few minutes later their hands were cuffed, and they were pushed into the back of the squad car. Billy glanced at Curtis. Even that day on the mountain when things looked hopeless, Curtis hadn't shown the fear that was in his eyes, now.

17

THE BATTLE HYMN OF THE REPUBLIC

The South Georgia county jail was a sauna-like arrangement with a maze of bars and doors located at the rear of the police station. It had the eye-watering stench of urine mixed with that of turpentine, but it was the hard smell of the iron bars and concrete that cut deep into Billy's soul. Sweat dripped from his brow as he sat staring at an unpainted concrete wall. Water leaked from a plastic garden hose in the corner, trailing across the concrete floor to a drain at the center of their cell. Whenever the steel door opened, a momentary whiff of cool air from the police station teased his sweltering body. Curtis sat on the cot across from him, his back against the wall, staring up at a single incandescent bulb hanging on a wire. Later, sunset brought some relief from the heat, only to be replaced by hordes of hungry mosquitos.

Bleary-eyed after a sleepless night, Billy and Curtis were ordered to stand beside their bunks the next morning as an arraignment was held by a judge standing outside their cell. Wearing blue bib overalls and an oil-stained ball cap, the judge hurriedly read their indictment and asked how they pleaded. They both pleaded not guilty to all the charges.

"Well, you boys are too much of a flight risk. I won't be granting you bail, but we'll set the trial date for early next week. Do y'all need me to get you a lawyer?"

"Yes, sir," Billy said.

The judge nodded and walked out. Later that afternoon a jailer escorted the court-assigned public defender to their cell. The public defender stood with a wrinkled bottom lip staring at them in silence while the jailer fumbled with the keys. Billy watched from the corner of his eye. The lawyer, who appeared supremely tired and bored, wore a seedy, blue polyester suit and brown penny loafers, and the odor of his aftershave overcame even the turpentine.

What little hope Billy had held for a quick release began a backward slide into the depths of despair. They'd been assigned the Barney Fife of public defenders, and his demeanor said it all. He was here because he had to be. As the jailer admitted him to the cell, Billy looked over at Curtis. He had his head cradled between his hands, staring at the floor.

"Watch yourself with these two, Ray," the jailer said. "They busted them boys up pretty bad down at The Tonk."

As if announcing it to everyone in the building, the public defender said, "Don't worry, Wayne. If they ever want to see the light of day again outside this jail, they'll behave." His high-pitched voice echoed from the concrete walls as he began lecturing Billy and Curtis on the proper behavior expected of guests in someone else's fair city. Explaining how it was a violation of Southern hospitality to refuse to converse with someone when they spoke, he said Billy's rudeness and unprovoked attack on little Buddy Payne made the case all but impossible to defend.

"Anyway, the best you can hope for is maybe a year down on the farm, and that's if you can come up with the money to pay for those boys' medical bills and the damages to Mrs. Sledge's bar. We might sell the car to cover all that."

Billy looked up at him for the first time. "So that's it?"

The public defender nodded grimly.

"So, you're assuming we're guilty without hearing our side of it?"

"It's pretty much cut and dried," he said. "Let's see here now. This here police report says you entered The Tonk at 4:05 p.m. and—"

"We were there," Billy said. "What's the short version?"

The public defender stared back at Billy as if he'd been slapped.

"Okay. If that's the way you want it. Mrs. Sledge said little Buddy Payne tried to strike up a conversation with you, and you hit him upside the head with a beer bottle. That's a felony assault, and it sounds to me like you boys were looking for trouble when you went in there."

"You can't be serious," Billy said. "*Little* Buddy was built like a tree stump, and he was fixing to jump me. Mrs. what's-her-name knew it, too, and so did everyone else in that place."

"Sheer speculation," he said. "You don't know that, and you can't prove it neither. They said he was just trying to carry on a conversation with you, and you got all snippy with him. You boys best get your heads right and figure on spending the next year down at the county penal farm sloppin' hogs, choppin' brush and pickin' up beer cans off the right-a-way."

Billy shook his head in resignation. This guy made Barney Fife look like Einstein.

"That judge we saw this morning, is he the one hearing our case?" Billy asked.

"That's him, Thomas Blount. He's tough, and he ain't gonna cut you no slack"

"Is he a veteran?" Billy asked.

"Veteran of what?" the lawyer asked.

Billy bit his lip. *Be patient,* he thought. This may be as good as it gets. "The military."

"Oh, yeah. Matter of fact, I believe he is. Why?"

"Find out for sure, and let me know. When's our trial?"

The public defender shrugged. "It can be pretty quick, I reckon, maybe tomorrow if you waive your right to a jury and plead guilty. Why?"

"Okay, we'll waive the jury, but we're not pleading guilty."

"Cain't do that," he said. "At least, I don't think we can. I'll have to check with Judge Blount."

"Just find out and let me know," Billy said. "Now, I need to make a phone call."

"Who you gonna call?"

"A friend."

"Cain't nobody help you down here, partner. I suggest you go into that courtroom, plead guilty and keep your mouth shut. Let me beg the mercy of the court, and if Judge Blount is in a half-assed decent mood he might let you off with six months to a year."

"Forget the guilty plea," Billy said. "It ain't happening. Just find out when our trial date is, and get me permission to use the phone."

The public defender called for the jailer, then turned back to Billy. "Have it your way," he said. "But don't say I didn't try to help."

As he left, the public defender traded whispering comments with the jailer. Billy turned and sat down beside Curtis. "Sorry I got you into this."

"You didn't get me into nothing," Curtis said.

"It's my MO. Sooner or later, all my friends get screwed."

"What do you mean, 'It's your MO?'"

"Modus operandi," Billy said. "It means—"

"I know what MO means, Sarge. I ain't fucking stupid. What do you mean when you say 'your friends all get screwed'?"

"I don't know. It just seems every person I ever had as a friend got screwed some kind of way. You remember Butch Goddard and Danny McCaughey?"

"Yeah, I remember them. They both got killed walking point my first month in country."

"Well, I'd been walking point that morning before it happened."

Curtis stopped staring at the floor and looked up at Billy.

"I spotted a break in the trees. We were at the edge of the LZ, and I passed the word back to hold up until I checked it out. I eased up to scan the hilltop, and stood watching for any sign of the enemy. The hilltop was wide open, so I took my time studying every bush, log and ravine. It looked quiet, but I didn't want to hurry out into the open, so I waited, but I was so tired I fell dead-ass asleep while I was leaning there against a tree. The platoon sergeant came up to the point to find out what the delay was and saw me there nodding off on my feet. He told Butch to take my place, and brought Danny up to walk slack for him."

"And so you think it's your fault 'cause they walked y'all into that damned ambush?"

"If I'd have been up there I'd have spotted that ambush."

"No you wouldn't. You'd a walked your tired ass right into it just like they did, Sarge."

"Maybe so," Billy said. "And maybe I wouldn't have had to sit there and watch Danny die afterward, and maybe I wouldn't have been here to make you go into that damned bar."

"You know something, Sarge? You didn't *make* nobody do shit."

"Hey, that's it. I can tell them that I forced you to go in there."

Curtis shook his head. "You're wasting your time, Sarge. These crackers got us by the balls, and they know it. We're gonna be plain ol' dipped in shit, rolled in dust and set out in the hot sun to dry."

"Maybe not," Billy said. "If I can get hold of Bugsy, he might help us."

"Bugsy? What's that goofy fucker gonna do?"

"You never knew him like I did. Trust me, that goofball act of his was a cover. He was damned smart."

"Why don't you call that lady friend of yours, Bonnie Jo? She's famous. I bet if she came—."

"A female rock singer will go over with these yahoos about as well as a Jewish lawyer."

Calling Bugsy wasn't a great idea either, but it was the only one Billy had. Bugsy had talked him into things he never imagined he would do. Tim Casey put it best when he said, Bugsy could sell Agent Orange to a flower shop. Bugsy was their only hope.

Mister Polyester, as Curtis began calling the public defender, returned later that day. He said Judge Blount had gone fishing that morning and the trial wouldn't be until Tuesday of next week. He had also talked the jailers into letting Billy have the requested phone call. That evening Billy was taken to a pay phone where he dialed up the operator at Fort Bragg, North Carolina.

"Person-to-person, collect call from Billy Coker," he said, "for Captain Charles Busby."

It was the day of the trial and only an hour until the hearing was to begin. Billy hadn't heard from Bugsy since they'd spoken a few days earlier. The connection wasn't all that good, and the best he heard was Bugsy telling him everything would be okay. Curtis was still sullen, and Billy was becoming increasingly worried about his state of mind. If Bugsy didn't show up, they were looking at hard time. His hope was that Bugsy would be a character witness and buy them some sort of reprieve. Without him, they didn't have a chance.

The hour was gone in a flash and Bugsy had not shown up. Billy and Curtis traded looks of desperation as the jailer unlocked the cell and stood guard with a pump shotgun while another deputy came in and put them in shackles. They'd been forced to exchange their clothes for bright orange jump suits the first day, and the guards watched them as if they were on the FBI's Most Wanted list. Polyester stood outside the cell with his vinyl briefcase, his lips pressed firmly together in a flat line across his face. He stared off into space with an edifice of disgusted boredom.

A phalanx of crew-cut deputies marched on either side of them brandishing Winchester pump shotguns as they crossed the square to the courthouse. A row of pigeons lined the barrel of a green Civil War canon, and other than the buzzing cicadas, the town was eerily quiet. A man selling watermelons from the tailgate of a rusty pickup watched with a bored stare as they struggled to climb the courthouse steps in chains. Billy fell. Curtis lunged to help him, but the guards shoved him aside and jerked Billy back to his feet. Several deputies pointed their shotguns at Curtis as he struggled back to his feet.

"He was just trying to help me," Billy said.

"Shut up," a deputy answered.

Billy stared hard at him.

"You best get your skinny ass to movin'," the deputy said.

Billy looked away. He had no choice. He had reached bottom, and this was destined to be his life for at least the next year.

They entered the courthouse through huge oaken doors, and the cool air inside offered instant relief from the sultry summer heat. Polyester mopped his brow with a dingy white handkerchief. There was an ominous odor, one of musty file cabinets stuffed with ancient, moth-eaten documents. Billy figured the documents were the parole papers for prisoners long ago forgotten and growing old on the county penal farm. He and Curtis shuffled across a marble floor, the clinking of their chains echoing high overhead in a giant rotunda where huge murals depicted a raging Civil War battle.

Escorted through another set of oaken doors, they were met by a sea of faces turning to watch them as they hobbled into the courtroom. This explained why there were only a couple of people out on the town square. Billy and Curtis were headline entertainment, and the locals were all in here waiting and watching as if at any moment these wanton criminals might fly into another mad rage. Several women shielded their children with their bodies, while the older men stared curiously over the tops of wire-rimmed reading glasses. The deputies lined the walls, standing rigid and stern-faced, holding their Smoky Bear hats at waist level.

Across the front row sat nine of the most pitiful looking human beings Billy had ever seen. Two wore casts on their arms, one a neck brace and two had their heads wrapped in gauze. All had cuts, bruises and swollen faces. He and Curtis had put a world of hurt on them. Buddy Payne stared menacingly at them through blackened eyes. Billy grinned and winked at him, and Buddy's eyes widened as his mouth twitched. *Might as well enjoy the moment*, Billy thought, because Bugsy was nowhere in sight and this was certain to be a kangaroo court.

"All stand for the Honorable Thomas J. Blount."

The judge walked in and gaveled the room to order, and they were no sooner seated, than a commotion came from the back of the courtroom. The double doors at the back swung open, and Bugsy appeared. He walked through the doors in full military dress uniform, wearing bloused jump boots and all his ribbons and decorations. Billy felt his heart leap into his throat as he heard an alleluia choir singing in the back of his mind. With a rigid military bearing that would challenge the Buckingham Palace guards, Bugsy looked neither left nor right as he came down the aisle, a large attaché case under his arm.

People turned, looking his way as the courtroom buzzed with whispers of curiosity. Removing his hat and taking one of the few remaining seats, Bugsy acted as if he scarcely noticed. Even Billy was impressed by his old platoon leader's entry. He had timed it perfectly. Billy bent over and whispered in Polyester's ear. "That's him."

"That's who?" Polyester asked loudly.

"Never mind," Billy whispered.

Blount rapped his gavel, and it again grew quiet. Polyester was none too subtle as he turned and stared at Bugsy. Bugsy gave him a cursory smile and looked past him at the judge. The trial instantly went south as the prosecutor made his case, and Billy realized the charges were much more serious than he had imagined. He was being charged with assault with a deadly weapon, a charge that could result in a three to ten-year sentence. His VA-issue walking cane was presented as exhibit 'A'. It was the weapon that caused a broken wrist for one victim and a cracked skull for another.

By the time they finished parading the witnesses to the stand, Billy and Curtis were characterized as wanton criminals bent on murdering the entire town, but who had been overcome by these few brave citizens down at

The Tonk and driven away like rabid dogs. Then Billy's turn came, and Polyester asked him to tell his side.

Billy explained how he knew old Buddy was about to whip his ass, so he just took the first shot in self-defense. The prosecutor, who thought he was Hamilton Burger, Perry Mason's old adversary, ripped him pretty good for assuming little Buddy Payne would jump a man eight inches taller. Curtis didn't do much better with his testimony, but when he was done, Polyester called Bugsy to the stand, explaining to the judge that he was a character witness. Billy almost grinned as the prosecutor went berserk, knocking his briefs off the table when he jumped up to shout his objection.

"Oh for god's sake, Earl, relax," the judge said. "This isn't going to take long, and it sure isn't going to change the facts."

They swore him in, and Bugsy was introduced by Polyester who asked him to tell the court what he knew about Billy. Bugsy looked over at the judge.

"If it pleases the court, Your Honor, may I stand just outside the witness box? I have some items in my brief case I'd like to share with the court."

Judge Blount nodded, and Bugsy stepped down in front of the bench. He glanced at his watch and opened his brief case, laying out several small posters. He then turned to face the crowd, but he said nothing for several seconds as he gazed steadfastly over their heads. It had its intended effect as people squirmed nervously.

"First of all, Your Honor, I want to clarify that I am here not only as a character witness for both Mr. Coker and Mr. Teague, alike, but also to help clarify some of the statements and evidence presented against them today."

The judge wrinkled his brow but slowly nodded.

Bugsy picked up Billy's cane from the evidence table and turned again to face the judge. "Your Honor, if I may, I would like to ask that it be entered into the court record that this walking cane, Exhibit 'A', is one issued by a Veteran's Administration Hospital to Mr. Coker."

"I suppose we can do that," the judge said. He glanced toward the court reporter and nodded.

Bugsy continued. "Your Honor, are you familiar with an Army commendation medal called the Bronze Star?"

"Yes, I am," the judge answered. "Got one myself during World War II."

Billy nodded. Bugsy had done his homework.

"Good. Then I am certain Your Honor knows what it takes to earn one."

The judge nodded.

"Just out of curiosity, Your Honor, are you aware that these defendants are both combat veterans?"

"No. I didn't know that."

"Your Honor, both of these men served under me as members of the One Hundred and First Airborne Division, in the Republic of South Vietnam."

The judge raised his eyebrows.

"Yes, Sir, Your Honor, they are both former para-troopers, Screaming Eagles."

A murmur rippled through the crowd. The judge rapped his gavel, and silence returned.

"Continue, Captain Busby."

Bugsy set a little color poster on the evidence table beside the witness box, depicting the Screaming Eagle patch of the Hundred and First. He also set up one showing a Bronze Star Medal.

"Is Your Honor also familiar with the Silver Star Medal?"

"Yes, I am."

"So as not to belabor the point, I will assume Your Honor is also familiar with the Distinguished Service Cross and the Purple Heart Medal."

He set up more little posters as he spoke.

"You may," the judge answered.

The judge again furrowed his brow, looking first at the placard of the Distinguished Service Cross then over at Billy with his five-day old growth of beard, and then at Curtis, unshaven and wearing a dirty white T-shirt beneath his orange jump suit.

"Objection, Your Honor!" the prosecutor shouted. "This little dog and pony show is a waste of time, and I—"

"Overruled, counselor," the judge said. "Sit down."

Rubbing his chin, the judge turned back to Bugsy, "You may continue, Captain."

"Your Honor, the two men before you have both received Bronze Stars with V's for valor and Silver Stars for gallantry and bravery in combat. They have also both received Purple Hearts for wounds they received in battle. Yes, Your Honor, Mister Coker's cane was provided to him by a Veteran's Hospital where he spent over a year trying to regain the use of his legs. And both men received Silver Stars for saving their patrol and two helicopter pilots from certain annihilation by a much larger enemy force. They did so at great personal risk to themselves. Mister Coker here was also awarded our nation's second highest military honor, the Distinguished Service Cross, for risking his own life to save Mister Teague. If it pleases the court, I would like to read a copy of the letters of commendation, which accompanied those medals."

"Your Honor," the prosecutor shouted.

Judge Blount slammed his gavel. "Dammit, Earl, shut the hell up. I want to hear this."

The judge nodded at Bugsy, "Continue, Captain Busby."

Bugsy began reading the citations, and the more he read the louder and more emotional his voice became. Billy sat up straighter in his chair. A Philadelphia lawyer with red suspenders couldn't have performed any better than his old platoon leader at that moment. Strutting back and forth across the front of the courtroom, Bugsy cast his voice with the drama and animation of a Pentecostal preacher, spinning and pirouetting as he pointed his finger heavenward. He was nearly shouting as he reached an emotional crescendo of glorious patriotism. When he finished, Bugsy handed the citations to the judge who was looking damned near teary-eyed. Billy swore he could hear the Battle Hymn of the Republic playing somewhere in the background as Bugsy turned to face the prosecutor.

"Yes, Your Honor, this prosecutor would take from these men the freedom for which they so valiantly fought, the freedom they bought with their own blood for you and me, and for little bullies like Buddy Payne and his friends to spend their time harassing people in road houses. Yes, Your Honor, this prosecutor would have you believe these two highly decorated war heroes didn't get enough fighting in Vietnam. But I respectfully ask, Your Honor, 'Do you really believe that story?' Do you believe these two men walked into that roadhouse and intentionally started a brawl with nine men, better than four to one odds?

"No, Your Honor, I don't believe you do, and you can right this wrong. You can judge this situation as it really is. You can recognize these men for the heroes they are, and with true wisdom and honor, you can allow them to go free."

When he was done, the courtroom was graveyard quiet. Bugsy walked back to his seat, and Billy turned to Polyester, telling him he could rest his case, which he did. After several long seconds of silence, Judge Blount slammed his gavel down so hard that the sound ricocheted off the two oak doors in the back.

"There will be no closing arguments, gentlemen. This court finds the two accused innocent on all counts.

Bailiff, get those boys out of those shackles, and give that man back his cane."

All hell broke loose as the prosecutor charged to the front of the courtroom, and several of the walking wounded on the front row stood and began booing. Blount slammed his gavel down again, but the ruckus continued until he stood and bellowed like a bull. "Earl, if you and your friends don't shut the hell up, I'm going to have the bailiff put every last one of you in the jail."

It grew quite again.

The prosecutor started to whine, "But, Tom—"

"But, hell! I've seen you and this bunch of bullies in my courtroom for the last time. This is the third time in the last two years you've come in here with the same self-defense story, and this time, it looks like your boys got what they deserve. They got their butts whipped by a pair of real men. Count yourself lucky, because if it happens again, I'm sending every last one of them down to the penal farm and you with them. Now, get the hell out of my courtroom, before I have you charged with contempt."

He turned and looked directly at Curtis and Billy. "Gentlemen, I sincerely apologize for what we have put you through. You are free to go."

Bugsy put them in his green Army Ford LTD and drove around behind the jail to where Curtis's car was parked.

"I'll be back in a minute," he said.

RICK DESTEFANIS

A few minutes later Bugsy returned, and a jailer appeared at the back door with their personal items. After they signed for them and the jailer had gone, Bugsy broke out a pack of Chesterfields, passing cigarettes to Billy and Curtis. They lit up and inhaled deeply.

"So, tell me, just exactly what you two are doing down here in South Georgia?"

Curtis looked at Billy, and Billy looked at Bugsy then shrugged. "It's a long story," he said.

"I'll tell you what," Bugsy said. "I'm driving up to Columbus to stay the night at Fort Benning. Why don't you guys follow me there, and I'll put you up for the night. You can tell me about it later over drinks."

Toward afternoon, they were nearing Fort Benning when Bugsy turned off the highway. Curtis followed him in the Monte Carlo down a military reservation road. They seemed to be headed to the middle of nowhere. Billy sat up and looked back at a road sign that said the main gate to Benning was in the other direction. "Where is he going?"

Curtis shrugged. "Damned if I know."

A few minutes later the road came out of the pines into a huge open expanse of sand and grass. Billy recognized it immediately. It was a drop zone. Bugsy pulled over and got out. Curtis and Billy did the same. It was a quiet afternoon, mild with only a slight breeze. Far out on the DZ, perhaps three-quarters of a mile away, sat a cluster of army vehicles, and somewhere in the distance came the drone of approaching aircraft.

248

"Looks like we timed it just right," Bugsy said.

The sky overhead was bright blue with only a few cottony clouds. In the nearby pines a woodpecker hammered a tree trunk, while the three men stood watching the Pathfinders far out on the DZ. Within seconds the vehicles began moving as they drove clear of the drop zone and green smoke billowed from a smoke canister. Billy spotted the first C-130 approaching in the distance. Stair-stepped behind it, flying low and level, rumbled a half-dozen more.

The turbo-prop engines of the aircraft roared overhead as the sky filled with paratroopers hanging beneath shining OD green canopies. More C-130's flew over, streaming more rows of paratroopers above the first wave. Billy rubbed his whiskered face, and Curtis scratched at his 'fro. It was hard to believe they'd been here only three years earlier, clean-cut, proud paratroopers making their first jumps.

As the jumpers landed, they shed their parachutes, gathered their gear and trotted clear of the DZ, assembling in clusters around the distant vehicles. When the last of them were gone, Bugsy glanced over at Billy and Curtis. "I just wanted y'all to see that again."

That was it. It was vintage Bugsy. He said nothing more, nor did he ask how they'd gotten into trouble. Later that evening he took them to supper and they talked about Nam—nothing morose, just some of the people and some of the good times. There was no lecture, no sorrow. Somehow, Billy knew his old platoon leader was doing it again. Just as he had talked him into that last patrol, he was now talking him into finding his self-respect. And when they parted the next morning, Bugsy gave them each a hundred dollars. They told him they didn't need it, but he said it came from his unit's charity fund back at Bragg and insisted they take it.

Billy looked at Curtis, and knew he was thinking the same thing. Curtis had let his hair grow, and his para-trooper swagger was long gone. They had both surrendered to the headwinds of life. Billy made up his mind to shave and get cleaned-up when he got to Atlanta. He had to get out of this blue funk that controlled his every thought. He also had to call Bonnie Jo.

18

UNCLE SOOKEY'S LOVE

Billy and Curtis moved into vacant rooms at the back of Uncle Sookey's gym in Atlanta, and went to work. Billy had yet to call her, but Bonnie Jo was always there lingering in the shadows of his mind waiting for him to look back. When he did, she would step into the light and remind him she was somewhere waiting patiently. He was running from his memories of Nam, but he was at a loss what to tell her. To explain was impossible, but forgetting the past seemed his only hope, even if it meant staying a while with Curtis and his Uncle Sookey in Atlanta.

Sookey, a gray-headed old widower with wire-rimmed glasses and an attitude, wore khaki trousers and white dress shirts every day. Sole owner of the ancient red brick warehouse down in Southeast Atlanta, he depended on donations from local charities to provide equipment, a basketball court and a boxing ring.

The outside wall of the building along the street was cluttered with posters advertising *The Atlanta Soulistics*, *Willie K and the Rhythmists* and other local bands. They played the Friday night sock-hops to raise money for the gym. The rest of the week the gym was home to every street urchin within walking distance, along with a few of the local punks, but Sookey ran a tight ship. No one talked trash, smoked or drank at his place. Billy, of course, was granted special dispensation on the liquor clause as long as he kept it in his room.

Sitting on a wooden bench in their sweats, Curtis and Billy panted, trying to regain their breath after a workout. Uncle Sookey stood staring at them, and noticed as Billy absent-mindedly pulled a little cobweb from between the bench and the wall.

"I could've gotten a place up near Cascade Heights," he said, "but me and the preacher decided this was where we needed to be. The local churches help out with the money, plus I get a little from the city, and the Friday night dances help, too. This way we give the kids something to do besides hanging out on the street corners."

"Who's complaining?" Curtis said. "I'm just proud we could come here."

Billy nodded. "Me too."

"Well, you boys get your proud butts to the showers, and come back and help me clean out that back hallway. It's full of junk."

Curtis hadn't exaggerated when he said Uncle Sookey was tough. Pushing Billy more each day, Uncle Sookey put him through a special kind of torture. He also sent him down to the indoor swimming pool at the YMCA a couple times a week. The forced exercise program continued for a couple months, and as Billy predicted, his progress was slow.

Sookey quizzed him about the pain, often asking if he was really pushing himself. Billy assured the old man that he was doing all he could. Late one afternoon, while walking laps around the gym with his cane, Billy noticed Sookey watching him from across the floor. Billy gave him a wave, but Sookey simply stood frowning.

"You gotta push yourself," he shouted. "You ain't pushing."

It was getting late. Everyone was gone for the day, and Sookey had locked the front door.

"Yes, I am," Billy said.

Their voices echoed in the empty gymnasium as Billy finished his last lap. Bent over with one hand on his cane and the other on his knee, Billy caught his breath. Glancing up, he smiled as Sookey sauntered over. Since he was walking a little farther and a little faster each day, Billy figured Sookey was happy with his progress.

"Stand up straight, Billy."

The no-nonsense tone of the old man's voice reminded Billy of a drill instructor. He took most of his weight off the cane and stood straighter. Sookey smiled, before suddenly kicking the cane from under him. It went clattering across the gym floor. Laughing with glee, Sookey slapped his hip and turned to walk away.

"What the hell was that about?" Billy asked.

Sookey stopped and looked back. His smile was gone. "You don't need that thing anymore. I want you to leave it back there in your room from now on. You hear me?"

They were alone in the gym that evening, and the only sounds came from the plumbing moaning somewhere in the bowels of the building. Sookey stood eyeing him, and the longer he stood, the more apparent it became there'd be no apologies.

"But I—"

"Ain't no 'but' to it, Billy-boy. You ain't got no business carrying that cane around like an old man. Some folks get to depending too much on canes and such. You need to break free, and quit making excuses."

Sookey was telling him something that had nothing to do with his physical maladies. He could lie to himself, but he couldn't fool the old man.

For the first time in over a year Billy began gaining weight, and he no longer had the skeletal look of a starving refugee. His strength was returning. Uncle Sookey, apparently realizing this, came to him one Friday morning and insisted that Billy attend the dance at the gym that night. Up to now, Billy had avoided them, but Sookey was insistent.

The idea of dancing left Billy once again spinning in a vortex of bad memories as he heard the Colonel's speech that day at Butch and Danny's memorial. Billy couldn't dance. The idea of it made him sick. Sookey meant well, and Curtis said he was only trying to help. Billy tried to beg-off, but Sookey wasn't hearing it.

"You're going, boy. Now quit your arguing."

Billy was trapped, and later that night Sookey and Curtis showed up at his door, wardens walking him to the gallows. They escorted him out to the gym, where dozens of kids were gyrating with the music. Billy tried to relax as the Soulistics did Wilson Pickett's *Land of a Thousand Dances*. The lead singer could have been Wicked Wilson himself.

A huge banner hung down from the rafters above the bandstand, "No guns, no knives, no drinking, no smoking. Have fun." Scores of teenagers moved with the music, but Billy's mind was a scratched record, replaying the same groove over and over. It was the voice of the Colonel saying how they were going to dance on Ho Chi Minh's grave.

Billy began backing away from the crowd and was about to sneak away when Sookey stepped in front of him with a young woman. A lithe girl with huge brown eyes, she wore jeans and a white linen blouse. Sookey pushed her hand into Billy's and shoved them toward the dance floor.

"I want you to teach this white boy how to dance," he said to the girl.

She seemed embarrassed and looked up at Billy with a shy smile.

"Go on," Sookey said.

Billy walked with the young woman onto the crowded dance floor where she took his hands and began gyrating with the beat. Standing flatfooted, he watched her. She let go of his hands and motioned for him to dance. There was no more inspiration in his soul than a hot wind blowing from an alley, an alley that came from only one place—the past. Billy stood, unable to move, unable to dance. His mind was again tumbling into turmoil as he heard the colonel's screaming rant about dancing on Ho Chi Minh's grave.

"I'm sorry," he said. "It's not you, but I can't. I just can't…."

He turned and walked across the floor to the opposite side of the gym, away from where Sookey stood. Without looking back he slipped into the hallway and went to his room. The drums and electric guitars continued vibrating through the walls, and Billy realized he was sweating. There was something about the music and dancing that had set off a firestorm of anger deep inside. He was mad as hell, and didn't know why. He punched the brick wall until his knuckles were purple and bloody, then fell back on the bed. Lighting a cigarette, he stared at the ceiling.

Blowing the smoke upward, he saw there the rows of empty boots at the memorial service. He saw Butch and Danny again, their faces shadowed ghosts from the past, and he heard the Colonel's speech again and again. Billy's heart was again screaming in agony. Those men and their boots would never again dance, and neither would he. He lay awake for hours before drifting into a restless sleep sometime in the night. His brain hummed in a nether world of dreams and nightmares until a strange sound echoed loudly somewhere in his subconscious. He jerked awake, sitting bolt upright in the bed. His heart pounded in his throat, but there was only silence. It was late. The music had stopped and everyone had gone home. But he *had* heard something, something very real—or so he thought.

Perhaps it was a cat knocking a trash can over outside in the alley, or maybe someone had broken a bottle on the street. Billy strained to hear it again, but there came only the sound of a monotonous rain falling outside his window. It had been another nightmare, and the strangest part of it was an old song from back in 1963 had been running through his head, but now that he was awake he remembered only the year—1963.

Sitting there on the edge of the bed, Billy rubbed his eyes. The sound came again. It was the same one that had awakened him, except it was now muted and distant, the heavy, low rumble of thunder vibrating the windows and rolling through the hills somewhere outside of Atlanta. A shudder ran down his spine, and even though the room was cool, Billy felt the damp sweat on his back. It was happening again.

The thunder was the sound of the drums from President Kennedy's funeral procession, the boots on the pavement, the flag-draped caisson and a riderless horse clopping down Pennsylvania Avenue. The thunder was the sound of artillery echoing far away in the Central Highlands of Vietnam where men were still dying. The thunder was a thief sneaking in to steal his sanity, sending him back there. He was kneeling in the rain, his tears mixed with the raindrops. Butch was already dead, shredded by shrapnel before his eyes. Danny had been hit, too. Panting, Billy searched the jungle ahead, but the enemy had evaporated in the fog and smoke.

After swapping magazines in his M-16, he stood and went back to look for Danny. Men rushed past him, and an NCO called out for him to follow, but Billy ignored everything as he spotted Danny sitting in a shell hole, up to his waist in water. Danny had his back to him, and Billy thought he was okay.

"Hey, dude, you alright?"

Only then did he see the water was stained crimson. Billy stepped around him, and Danny looked up. The explosion from the booby-trap had ripped his flak jacket and fatigue shirt all to hell. Bobby Mazlosky, the company medic, came running to help as Billy pulled Danny from the water.

Some others rolled Butch's body into a poncho and carried it toward the trees, while Billy and Mazlosky used another as a makeshift litter for Danny. Mazlosky hooked up a plasma bag and they began carrying Danny toward the edge of the LZ. The rain increased, hard and cold, dimpling the puddles all around as the men stumbled and slipped in the mud. When they reached the tree line, they left Butch's body beneath the poncho, but the wind blew the poncho, and Danny saw what was left of him. After that he refused to lie down. He insisted on sitting with his back against a tree.

Mazlosky carefully pushed some protruding intestines back inside where they belonged and bandaged Danny's multiple wounds. At first Danny had an embarrassed look on his face, and mumbled apologies for getting hit. Mazlosky's voice trembled as he tried to get him to lie down.

The worst came after they bandaged him and hit him with surrets of morphine. That's when there was nothing left to do but sit and wait for the medevac to arrive, but the rain delayed the choppers. The entire squad surrounded Danny offering words of encouragement, watching and waiting, while he sat there, his eyes open, barely breathing.

Billy looked at Mazlosky. "Isn't there something we can do?"

The medic's fatigues were soaked with Danny's blood. He stood and walked out into the muddy clearing. Danny was dying, and there wasn't a damned thing anyone could do about it. Billy knelt there, wanting to say something, but what words could there possibly be that would make a difference? Billy held Danny's hand, and slowly Danny turned and look straight into his eyes. Billy realized at that moment he was holding the hand of the loneliest person on earth.

It began raining even harder, driving icy pellets of rain, and Billy held Danny's hand until his eyes no longer focused. Mazlosky returned and checked for a pulse. He thought he felt one, but after a few minutes Danny's lips turned blue.

For the next several days Billy stayed in his room. Burrowing beneath the blankets, he tried to hide, but Sookey would have none of it. He ordered him to re-engage, and after several days his drill instructor approach began working. It was a miracle of sorts, as Billy again began feeling better in both mind and body.

"Focus," Sookey shouted. "Focus on the good things. God gave you a life. Make the best of it."

Week after week the old man was relentless, and by spring Billy's hips and legs were strong enough that he was actually jogging around the gymnasium. Under Sookey's watchful eye, and with a combination of running, swimming and weightlifting, Billy had far exceeded the predictions of the VA doctors. He was becoming a new man.

Life was getting better for Curtis as well. He was going to a spring try-out with the Atlanta Falcons. It was his first real shot at the pros, and Billy wanted to be there, but more pressing matters demanded his attention. Several months had passed, and he had never called Bonnie Jo. He needed to hit the road and mend some fences, but before he departed, he had a surprise for Curtis that morning.

"What?" Curtis said.

"Just come with me," Billy said.

"Where? I gotta go to my work-out."

"This will take only a minute. Come with me to the cargo door in the back. I've got something to show you."

Curtis cast a quick glance at his watch. "Okay, Sarge, but just for a minute. They're expecting me over at the training complex."

They walked down the darkened hallway in the back, past their rooms to an area seldom used and cluttered with old tables, chairs and furniture. Dank and dark, the room smelled of things worn and forgotten. Billy reached up on the wall and felt for the light switch, and when the dim yellow bulbs came to life, it was there.

Curtis stood in silence.

"So what do you think?" Billy asked.

"Sarge," he hesitated.

"What?" Billy said.

Curtis slowly shook his head side to side.

"Sarge, we just spent over eight months getting' you back in shape. Now, what the fuck are you gonna do with that thing?"

Billy was proud of the Harley. Chopped and raked, with Z-bars and chromed pipes, its seat was tucked and rolled black leather. The dim warehouse lights glinted like diamonds on the midnight blue luster of the gas tank and fenders.

"I'm going to ride it out to California to see Bonnie Jo."

"You gonna get your ass permanently crippled is what you're gonna do."

"Listen to you. You sound like an old man. I'm gonna be like Easy Rider, man. I'm gonna get out and see this country."

"Easy Rider got his dope peddlin' ass shot by a couple rednecks….I mean, in case you don't remember. Besides, I think he was that bitch Jane Fonda's little brother, you know?

Billy laughed. "You are such a goob. Lighten up. I'll be fine."

Cutis continued shaking his head. "Sookey ain't gonna like this at all."

Billy had his duffle bag strapped to the back of the motorcycle that morning as he twisted the throttle on the big Harley. Sookey gave him a cursory wave and turned to walk back into the building.

"What's he mad about?" Billy asked.

Curtis shrugged. "He's worried about you."

"Tell him I appreciate everything he did, and not to worry. I'll be fine. Now, I better get going."

"Hey," Curtis said. "I want to say thanks."

Billy shrugged. "For what? This was all your idea, and your uncle's place. I'm the one saying thanks. Hell, look at me, no cane!"

Curtis grinned. "You're gonna be okay, Sarge. Just keep pluggin' away. You hear?"

"Call me some time," Billy said.

Billy reached Memphis late that afternoon and went straight to Jackie's apartment. Jackie's car was parked in the usual spot, and the old neighborhood looked the same. He still lived in the same third-floor apartment, but the walk up the stairs was now nearly effortless. Billy rang the doorbell, and a few moments later the door opened. Jackie stood staring at him for several seconds, but said nothing.

Billy shrugged. "Hey."

Jackie's hair was cut short, and he had shaved. "Who the hell are you?" he asked.

"Who the hell are *you*," Billy replied, "all cleaned up and looking like you must have a girlfriend or something?"

Jackie didn't answer as he turned and walked over to the coffee table. Picking up several letters from the table, he shoved them at Billy. "These are from Bonnie Jo. You need to call her. We've both been trying to reach you, and she's worried sick."

"I'm going to do better than that," Billy said. "I'm going to ride my Harley out to California and pay her a surprise visit."

"Your what?" Jackie said.

"My Harley," Billy said. "Come look. Billy opened the front door and motioned down to the parking lot."

Jackie gazed out over the railing at the motorcycle down below.

"It gave me some problems on the way from Atlanta," Billy said. "I'm going to take down the carburetors and fix them before I try to ride it out to California."

SECTION III

19

EVERYBODY'S A LITTLE CRAZY

hree weeks passed while Billy lounged around
Jackie's apartment. The carburetors from the
Harley were broken down and the parts spread
on a tarp in the middle of the living room floor. Jackie's
job with the Veteran's Administration kept him busy
during the day, and he went to school in the evenings.
Billy was lying on the couch watching TV when Jackie
came in from work that Friday afternoon. He'd gotten
the mail from the box downstairs, and after tossing an
envelope on the table beside Billy, he loosened his tie
and tossed his coat across the chair. Billy glanced at the
envelope then turned back to the TV. It was another letter from Bonnie Jo.

"Aren't you going to read it?"

"Sure," Billy said, "but I'm watching TV right now."

Jackie snatched up the envelope and ripped it open.
Unfolding the letter, he began reading.

"Do you always read other people's mail?" Billy asked.

It wasn't that he really cared. He and Jackie were closer than brothers. And Jackie didn't answer until he finished reading the letter.

"Do you want me to call her, and tell her that you're back and you're okay?" he asked.

"I was kind of thinking I might surprise her, you know? I want to go see her in California."

"When, for Chris' sakes?"

"Soon."

"Coker, I can't figure you out. You have this good looking chick, who oh-by-the-way is also rich and famous, and she's head over heels crazy about you, but you can't get off your ass and act like you care."

"Look, I just want to get my life back in order first. Is that so hard to understand?"

"Dammit, Billy! Your life will never be in order if you don't start living it. Can't you see that?"

Billy looked away. Jackie was right, but a psychological inertia ruled his every thought. He wanted to live again, but he couldn't. He saw nothing, no life that made him want to move ahead. "Future" had become just a word—a napalmed cauterized notion of something that no longer existed. He looked back at Jackie and shrugged.

Jackie threw the letter in his direction and walked out. From the kitchen came the sound of the refrigerator door opening, then the click and whoosh of a beer can opening. A moment later Jackie walked back into the room.

"I thought you had school tonight," Billy said.

"I do, but I thought I'd just start fucking up my life, too, so I can be like you."

"Look," Billy said. "You don't have to be a smart ass. I'll start packing my shit tonight. Okay?"

"You've been saying that for weeks. How about I take those carbs over to the Harley dealer and let them rebuild them?"

"I already bought the parts. I'll start putting them back together tonight. You just take your ass to school."

"Okay, so you're going to ride that Harley all the way to LA, which, by the way, is a really stupid idea, but that's okay. If a spring snowstorm doesn't come and freeze your ass to death you should be fine. So, give me a day. When are you leaving?"

"I'll put the carbs back on tomorrow, and if the bike runs okay, I'll leave day after tomorrow. How's that?"

Four days later Billy had departed Memphis and was past Albuquerque, heading up into the San Mateo Mountains when the Harley began sputtering and bogging. Nursing it along, he eventually found a greasy mechanic shop in the middle of nowhere. Rusty gas pumps and several old wrecks lying around a metal building didn't do much for his optimism as he parked the Harley out front.

The days had been hot, dry and dusty, the nights so cold he shivered until pulling over and dropping into an exhausted sleep beside the highway. Coated with a sandy road grime, he'd been sun burned until he blistered, but he hadn't experienced a bad memory the entire time. This journey seemed to be the solution. It was a life with no tomorrow and no past, only the here and now.

An hour later, a dirty man, bearded with blackened finger nails wiped his face with a greasy rag and looked at Billy. "She's a really nice looking ride, but you got yourself a compression problem, my friend. You need to rebuild the engine."

"Can you do that?" Billy asked.

"I can do most of it, but I'll have to take the heads to a machine shop in Albuquerque. Probably take me at least a week or two, not counting the time it takes to get the parts."

Billy looked around the dimly lit shop, then out through the open door, where the sun was blindingly bright. Across the road heat waves shimmered off the desert. No way he was going to sit around this place for a week.

"You in the market for a used Harley?" Billy asked.

The man shook his head. "No, not really. I mean, I probably couldn't give you what she's worth. Just don't have that kind of money laying around."

"Make me an offer," Billy said.

"Mister all I could afford would be something like eight-hundred bucks, but I know you can't—"

"You can have it for eight-hundred cash."

The man's eyes widened as he looked first at Billy then at the Harley.

"Mister, do you have a clear title on this bike?"

"It's in the duffle bag," Billy said.

The man looked down at the ground. "I don't want to take advantage of man who is down on his luck. Why don't you let me see if I can fix it?"

"If you give me the eight-hundred, I'll be on my way. If you can fix it and sell it over in Albuquerque, you can probably better than triple your money."

"Okay, but I want to call and check on your title first, if you don't mind. If it's clear, you got a deal."

Two days later, Billy was still sitting on I-40 somewhere in Arizona. The traffic had thinned that day, and he sat on his duffle bag with his thumb in the air. It was mid-afternoon and a hot dusty wind buffeted him as big trucks roared past. With the fine grit coating his face and neck, he was cotton-mouthed and his eyelids drooped with fatigue. No one was stopping.

At first it seemed he was dreaming when there came a sound somewhere in the sky above. Billy gazed upward, and the sun reflected from a silvery jet high overhead, its white vapor trail cutting an east to west path across the blue sky. For a moment, he wanted to be up there. For a moment life again seemed possible. He could buy a ticket and board a plane, but he realized he would be living a lie. He would be pretending everything was okay. The jet disappeared over the horizon, and Billy realized he could never forget the friends he had lost in Vietnam. He could never forget life's tenuous existence, one that existed on the razor-edged whim of fate.

A car finally pulled off the highway and stopped beside him. It was a dusty blue '63 Chevy. Standing, Billy picked up his duffel bag and peered inside the car. The driver, a skinny cowboy-looking character with a white straw hat, had a girl sitting beside him. She wore wrap-around sunglasses and a scowl. With the jet airliner long gone, it seemed stark reality had returned.

The driver had a can of beer cradled between his legs and an engaging smile on his face. The woman simply stared straight ahead, sweaty, red-faced and looking incredibly tired and bored. She was also very pregnant, at least eight and half months. The back seat was stacked to the roof with piles of loose clothing, a coffee maker and a portable TV.

"Want a ride?" the man asked.

After stuffing his duffel bag in with the rest of the rubble, Billy got in and glanced over at the driver. Kind of a devil-may-care pretty-boy with sad brown eyes, he introduced himself as Darrell and the woman as his girlfriend, Linda. She merely grunted and continued staring straight ahead. Darrell wore a western style plaid shirt unbuttoned to his waist and had tattoos on his arms and chest.

"Where you headed?" Darrell asked.

Unlike his girlfriend, Darrell was grinning wall-to-wall teeth. The tattoo on his chest was an impish little red devil holding a pitchfork. One on his arm was a homemade prison type, a heart with the name 'Marcie' crudely scratched inside.

"West," Billy said, "as far as you're going."

Thin as a rail, but muscular, Darrell wore old cowboy boots and faded jeans full of holes. Picking up a pair of gold Ray bans from the dash, he put them on and pulled back onto the highway. Billy sagged down in the seat, exhausted but thankful. It was a relief just to sit in the shade of a car and let the hot wind buffet him through the open window. After a few minutes Darrell began fishing around in the over-flowing ashtray until he found a butt. Lighting it, he squinted and sucked the last quarter inch into ash, then looked over at Billy.

"Been on the road long?" he asked.

"Yeah, nearly a week. Going out to LA to see my girlfriend."

Darrell nodded, but again said nothing as several more minutes passed. Overcome with exhaustion, Billy nearly dozed before jerking awake. He looked over at Darrell. He was still wearing the same toothy grin and had begun talking again.

"I was just saying, I'm taking Linda here to stay with her mother in LA for a few months, while I head back to Texas and look for work."

The girl sighed and rolled her eyes. Darrell ignored her.

"Problem is we're out of money. I was hoping you could help us out?"

He effected another shy grin and looked over the top of his Ray bans with his sad brown eyes. It was the same look Billy was certain had gotten him into Linda's drawers. He glanced down at Linda's distended abdomen then back at Darrell, a southwestern-redneck-edition of Eddie Haskell.

"Well, I don't have much," he lied, "but I'll help out."

"Reckon you can buy us a tank or two of gas?"

"Sure," Billy said.

Darrell grinned. "Yeah, I'm going to drop her off and head back to Texas, so I can get a job and rent us a little place to raise the kid."

"Yeah, right," the girl said. "He hasn't had a steady job since he got out of prison."

The veins bulged on Darrell's temple, and he white knuckled the steering wheel. "Linda's been kind of cranky since she got knocked—I mean, pregnant."

"I've been cranky since you lost our last nickel playing eight-ball, Mr. Professional Pool Hustler."

"I had that sonofabitch beat, and you know it."

"Do you ride in the rodeo?" Billy asked, hoping to change the subject.

With Darrell's western attire, including his well-worn snakeskin cowboy boots, Billy figured it was his best bet at taking the conversation in a different direction.

"Ha," Linda laughed. "The closest he ever got to a rodeo was the mechanical bull at a bar down in Lubbock, and it threw his skinny little ass in two seconds flat."

Up ahead Billy noticed a cluster of businesses, probably the outskirts of Flagstaff.

"Is that a gas station?" Billy said.

They studied the road ahead, and for the time being, the sight of civilization seemed to disarm the weary travelers. After they gassed up, Darrell sidled up to Billy and motioned to a restaurant across the highway. "Reckon you got enough for us to get a little something to eat? We haven't had a bite since yesterday."

"I think so," Billy said.

As Billy paid for the gas, Darrell tried to look into his wallet, but Billy was prepared. He'd gone to the restroom and hidden the bulk of his cash in another pocket. Darrell saw only a wrinkled twenty and three fives.

"Give us a pack of Marlboros, too," Darrell told the attendant.

Darrell looked at Billy and grinned. "You don't mind do you? I need a cigarette real bad."

"No problem," Billy said.

"Yeah, I'm probably crazy, 'cause those things are gonna kill me," Darrell said, "but I gotta have my smokes."

"Everybody's a little crazy," Billy said. "Besides, dying's not the worst thing that can happen to a man." The attendant pushed the pack of cigarettes and change across the counter, and Billy glanced at Darrell. Darrell's lips were parted slightly, and he stood gazing at him, his cocky arrogance suddenly gone. He reminded Billy of his brother Eddie. Darrell needed someone to kick his ass, or to maybe at least talk some sense into him.

After buying a bag of hamburgers and fries, they headed west again toward California. Seems Darrell had lived in Linda's house trailer just north of Lubbock until they were kicked out for not making rent. Now, they were jobless, homeless, broke and about to have a kid. The remainder of the trip to LA was a verbal slugfest as Billy dodged taking sides. Never had he imagined the smoggy hills of southern California would have looked so good as when they finally drove out of the desert.

A few hours later they were sitting beside a phone booth in East Los Angeles, while Linda called her mother. Billy wanted to ask them why they hadn't called before they left Texas, but nothing these two people did seemed rational. Besides, he hadn't called Bonnie Jo, so who was *he* to say what was rational? They waited for Linda to finish her call. It didn't take long.

She slammed the phone at the hook and it bounced out, dangling by the steel cord as she threw the phone booth door open. Clutching her basketball-size belly, she waddled back to the car, tears streaming from her eyes.

"What's wrong?" Darrell asked.

"That bitch says I can't come back home. Says she's locking all the doors."

"Fuck!" Darrell said.

Linda sat back in the car with her feet out on the pavement. They were swollen and bulging around the straps of her sandals. She held her head in her hands and sobbed.

"You don't have any other relatives around here?" Billy asked.

She didn't look up as she shook her head. Darrell lit a cigarette and threw his head back, staring up at the ceiling of the car. "I told you we should'a gone to Lufkin and stayed with my mama," he said.

"Where's that?" Billy asked.

"East Texas," Darrell replied.

Linda stopped sobbing and looked up. "Do you think she'll let us stay with her?"

"I told you last week she asked me to bring you home, but you said you wanted to stay with your mama. How in the hell are we gonna get there now?"

Linda had crazy little brown eyes that darted about. "You could rob another bank."

"No. I told you I ain't never doing that again. I ain't going back to prison."

"Sell another pint of blood," she said.

"Yeah, I reckon I can do that, but I've sold so much lately I'm startin' to feel sick."

The traffic on the nearby Santa Ana Freeway roared past as Billy glanced at the yellow gas pumps in the service station across the road.

"Pull the car over there," he said. "I'll pay to fill the tank."

Darrell cranked the engine and pulled up to the gas pumps. "Fill it up," he said to the attendant. Darrell, like him, had totally screwed up his life, but now seemed intent on doing the right thing. He simply needed some help.

"Come here," Billy said. He stepped out of the car and motioned to Darrell. Reaching into his pocket, he pulled out the wad of bills. "Here," he said.

Darrell's eyes widened as Billy counted out twenty-dollar bills one at a time, four hundred dollars in all, into his hands.

"That should be more than enough to get you back to Texas." He turned to the gas station attendant. "How do I get to Glendale from here?"

"Straight that way," the attendant said, pointing northwestward.

Billy pulled his duffel bag from the heap in the back seat.

"Hey, man," Darrell said. "Nobody has ever done nothing like this for me. Let me and Linda take you up there."

"No thanks," Billy said.

"You sure?"

"Positive. Just stay out of trouble and get yourself a job."

Billy turned and began walking.

"I promise, I'm going to get that job." Darrell called out. "Man, I can't thank you enough."

When Billy glanced back, Darrell was looking down at the wad of money in his hand.

"You already have."

20

A PLACE STRANGER THAN NAM

"Yes!" Billy shouted as he watched Darrell's smoky Chevy swerve back onto the freeway and disappeared into the river of traffic. The last few hundred miles had been a living soap opera, Texas trailer park edition, and despite his sympathy for them, his patience had evaporated somewhere in the Mojave Desert. A good dose of Vietnam would have helped either of them, but he wouldn't wish that on anyone. The one thing it had taught him was that he wasn't quite yet the most pathetic human being on earth. Billy breathed a sigh of relief and looked about.

He was surrounded by graffiti-covered buses, people, sirens and jack-hammers and all the things he expected in a big city, but there was one difference. An eerie red haze hung low across the skyline, reminding him of a firebase shrouded in smoke and red dust after a rocket attack. This precipitated an odd déjà vu. It was the same feeling he'd experienced when he first stepped off the military charter at Tan Son Nhut, a strange sense of foreboding. That first day as he gazed out past sandbagged watch towers and beyond the distant barbed wire fences at the misty Vietnamese countryside, it struck him that he was walking into a strange new world. Los Angeles had much the same effect. It was as if he had entered a foreign country.

Sticking out his thumb again, Billy began making his way through the streets of LA. His first ride came from a skinny black guy sporting sunglasses with oversized white plastic frames and an Afro the size of the Volkswagen Beetle he was driving. Billy slapped and bumped hands with him for the first quarter-mile while the man shucked and jived about how he knew Billy was somebody, but couldn't place him.

"I know you, dude," the man said.

Billy looked over at him. "Oh, really? What's your name?"

"*Angeles Wilson*, King of the Sunshine Car Wash commercials," he said. "You've seen me. I go, 'From Alfa Romeo's to Z-28's, Sunshine Car Wash is where the stars take their cars'..."

His mouth was full of big teeth that were as bleached white as his shades. He went on with his spiel, while Billy nodded like he gave a shit.

"Yeah," Billy said. "You sure are."

"Okay, dude. I've come clean with you. Now, tell me the truth. Who are you?"

"I'm Billy Coker," he said.

"Ech, ech." It sounded as if he was coughing up a feather.

Smiling with his mouth open, he pointed at Billy. "Don't bullshit me man. You can play that shit with somebody else. All that dust and shit, I can tell you've been on a set somewhere."

Billy shrugged, and the man pointed at him. "Yeeeeaah. I know, now. You was in that movie, ugh, wait a minute. That ain't it." He pointed over the steering wheel with the same long bony finger at nothing in particular. His nails were painted enamel white like his sunglasses. They drove on for several minutes before Angeles suddenly jerked upright and smiled.

"I know! It was...shit, muthafucka! I know the name. Come on, help me out. I got some dynamite weed here. I'll share it with you, but you got to tell me who you are."

"You have me confused with someone else."

"No, dude. I told you: Don't play that shit with me. I know who you are. Just a second." He slapped the steering wheel. "Gaddamit, I know who you are. You need to wash off some of that dust-makeup you're wearing."

"I need to go up north of Glendale, man. Can you help me out?"

"Man, we're buds. I'll take you to the fuckin' moon, but first you got to come clean with me."

"Great," Billy said. "But you're mistaken. I'm telling you: I'm nobody, really."

Pulling the shades down on his nose, Angeles Wilson peered over the top. "Tell the truth, dude. You was in

Billy Jack. You was his friend, the dude that got killed, right? You was Billy Jack's friend. That's it. Tell the truth now. I'll carry you all the way to Glendale, and I won't tell a soul where you live. You're him. Right?"

"Yeah, sure, man. Whatever."

They passed a sign that said 'Golden State Freeway,' but it meant nothing to Billy. He was lost.

"Billy Coker, huh?" he said. "So where's your ride at, Mista Billy Coker?"

This could be a deal breaker, but Billy couldn't lie. "I don't have one."

"Huh?"

Angeles turned to look at him. "Where you from, dude?"

If he said it, Billy realized he might scare him, but there was no choice other than to lie. He couldn't do that. "Raeford, Mississippi," he said.

Angeles Wilson's smile disappeared as if he had suddenly become aware that picking up hitchhikers was risky business.

"Mississippi?"

"Yeah, you know, like the river."

An unsettled look crossed his face and Angeles seemed apprehensive, fidgeting and looking first at the road then back at Billy. It was as if at any moment he expected Billy would pull out a white hood and rope.

"You ain't never been in no movie either, have you?" he said. It seemed almost an accusation that he had somehow been misled.

"I told you, I'm just trying to get up past Glendale to see my girlfriend."

Angeles glanced in the rear-view mirror then snatched the Volkswagen to the curb. "I sure wish I could help, but this is as far as I'm going."

Angeles Wilson was tossing him out like a used hamburger wrapper, and Billy wished he had kept his mouth shut, letting him think he was a celebrity. After all, this *was* the home of the professional schizophrenic, a place where everyone lived multiple personalities and it was considered normal. Instead, his instant friend had dumped his ass on the street and driven away.

Please, just take me to Glendale, Billy silently begged as he climbed in with another wanna-be wearing dark shades and a Wayne Newton hair-do. "Howdy. Where ya headed, partner?"

The driver spoke with a phony western drawl in a deep baritone voice, and he stared straight ahead, not so much to watch the road it seemed, but as if to demonstrate his absolute mastery of an overblown ego. A week on the road had Billy exhausted. He glanced over at this new character, no doubt a manly-man with a name like Bart or Roan to go with his ornate Rodeo Drive cowboy boots. He wore more gold chains than a New York mobster, and Billy wondered how this one would handle the high plains of Montana, mending fences and herding cattle.

"I'm headed up to Glendale," Billy said.

That apparently blew past Bart-Roan, as he explained that he was going up to Hollywood to see his agent. He began telling how he had already worked as an extra in several westerns.

"Yeah," he said. "There I was on the set with Robert Mitchum. God, Bob is so cool, and he said he couldn't believe I was only an extra."

Like the smog, a narcissistic psychosis seemed to permeate the air. Billy decided he was in a world of suspended reality, and it came as an epiphany of sorts as he also realized where the strategy for the Vietnam War had been born. It wasn't in the Oval office, or down at CIA headquarters in Langley, not even at the Pentagon. It had to have been created here in Los Angeles. Only here could they have incubated a strategy so far beyond the fringes of reality. It made sense. Like Vietnam, LA was another rabbit hole leading to Alice's Wonderland. The characters here were no less bizarre, and just as it had been in Nam, reality in LA was as fluid as Alice's dreams.

Bonnie Jo's place was in the San Gabriel Mountains above Glendale, but Billy's first rides had taken him on a circuitous route, ending near Hollywood. It reminded him of searching the mountain valleys in the Central Highlands. The hills and canyons around Hollywood weren't much different, but instead of villages with straw huts, there were the cul de sacs of the rich and famous. They held the same mesmerizing quality, perhaps not with the inherent threat that accompanies AK-47s and rocket propelled grenades, but with the same exotic perplexity.

Bart-Roan dropped him off on palm tree-lined Santa Monica Boulevard, and Billy continued thumbing his way past sprawling mansions with iron gates. He needed a cigarette, an unfiltered Camel or a Lucky Strike, something he could pull hard down into his lungs and hold for the steadying effect of a nicotine buzz. Darrell, the little prick, had kept his cigarettes and stolen his lighter. All Billy had was a book of matches from a truck plaza in Albuquerque. After making his way out of Hollywood, he found a convenience store.

"Give me a pack of Camels, please."

Billy dropped a wadded dollar bill on the counter, and the clerk, a young woman with dirty-blonde hair and dull gray eyes pulled the cigarettes from the overhead rack. She dropped the pack on the counter, probably as she had a hundred times a day, scarcely noticing him while punching the cash register buttons with slack-jawed indifference.

As she counted his change, there came a shudder, nothing of monumental proportion, but the unmistakable jolt of a tremor from deep within the earth's crust. A coffee can vibrated on a metal shelf and everything in the store quivered, but only for an instant. Their came a distant shout from outside the store, but then it was still.

It would have been nothing remarkable, except for a moment when his eyes met those of the cashier, Billy saw behind the young woman's facade of blissful domestication. He saw naked, adrenaline-driven fear in her eyes, that part of animal instinct that lies tenuously beneath the thin veneer of civilization. It was something he'd seen many times in its rawest form back in Vietnam.

He'd seen it in the eyes of villagers when the soldiers came into their huts in search of the enemy. He'd seen it in his buddies' eyes when they first stared the beast in the eye. He'd seen it in Curtis Teague's eyes the day Curtis carried him up to the firebase.

Taking the cigarettes, he started for the door. Behind him came the young woman's voice, still husky with fear. "You forgot your change."

Looking back, he paused. The mask had returned. She still seemed shaken, but her eyes had regained the soft focus of the terminally meek.

"Keep it," he said.

He hurried up the street, trying to escape the fear he saw in the woman's eyes. Billy remembered that night after the dance back in Atlanta. The past was again sucking him into its vortex. He tried to will it away, but he saw the face of a Vietnamese boy begging for a cigarette. Soft round cheeks, jet black hair, he wore shorts and sandals.

"GI have cigarette?"

The boy was probably ten or twelve years old, and he didn't have a man's voice as yet. He stared with big brown eyes. Billy wondered if he was an orphan.

"You're too young, kid. No cigarette."

The boy's face morphed to a hardened stare of resolve. Three days later after they ambushed an enemy patrol, Billy flipped one of the bodies while searching for papers. It was the boy. His AK-47 was still strapped across his back, his body riddled with 5.56mm rounds.

The past roiled before him, clouds of napalm billowing skyward as he sucked hard on the cigarette and squeezed his eyes shut, trying to will it away. It followed him, relentlessly reminding him that life would never be the same. His next ride passed in a daze, and it was late afternoon before the feelings subsided. Billy found himself standing at the end of a long winding driveway—Bonnie Jo's, he hoped.

An old Hispanic woman came down to get the mail and turned back toward the house. Billy caught up with her, but she backed away, wide-eyed and frightened.

"I'm a friend of Bonnie Jo's," he said.

She shook her head and glanced back up at the house. "You not a friend of Bonnie Jo's."

His ball cap had more grease on it than a truck-stop hamburger, and he had snagged his jeans, tearing them as he climbed from a truck near Amarillo. Blistered by the sun, dusty and generally looking like crap, Billy figured he was a member of the Manson Gang in her eyes.

"You go away," she said.

She turned toward the house and yelled something about a 'loco hombre.' A yardman appeared and came running down the driveway. Jabbing at Billy with the point of a garden spade, the old man backed him down the drive. Billy was about to give up when he saw her. It was Bonnie Jo trotting down the drive. She spoke to the old man and woman in Spanish then took Billy's hand. Despite her assurances, they continued eyeing him suspiciously as he walked with Bonnie Jo up to the house.

"You get better looking every time I see you," he said.

Her strawberry blond hair spilled from under a blue baseball cap, and her green eyes glistened behind wire-rimmed glasses. She was thinner than he'd ever seen her.

She smiled. "You might not look so bad yourself, if it weren't for that layer of grime. Where's your motorcycle?"

"How did you know I had a motorcycle?"

"Jackie told me about it when I called him."

"Why'd you call him?"

"I missed you. It's been six months. Why haven't you called?"

"I don't know. Reckon, I just needed some time to get my act together. And the motorcycle broke down on the way out here. I sold it."

They walked up the steps into a huge tiled foyer. The foyer opened into a larger room with pastel hues sparkling under skylights and walls of glass. The entire back wall was glass, and beyond was the panorama of the San Gabriel Mountains. A twentieth century California castle, the house was flooded with sunshine. Humbled by Bonnie Jo's home, words wouldn't come as Billy turned and looked about. A showplace designed to entertain the rich and famous, it had to be like living in a giant display case.

They stood in the great room, looking out at the mountains where hawks and eagles soared high against walls of sun-soaked nimbus. It seemed he should have been the one to speak, but Billy didn't know what to say. After nearly a minute, Bonnie Jo broke the impasse.

"Jackie told me you came home from Atlanta, walking without the cane and all muscled up. How do you feel?"

"Great," Billy said. "Better than I've felt in years."

"So, why did you come out here?"

"I wanted to see you."

"So, it's just a visit?"

"Well, yes, and I wanted to explain to you why I haven't called and—"

Billy froze.

"And?"

"And, well—hell, I don't know."

Her eyes remained locked on him.

"Bonnie Jo, you deserve more than I can ever give you. Hell, I'm just a bum. I don't have a job. I don't have anything."

"Is this a 'It's-me-not-you' brush off?" she asked.

"Hell, no, and you know it. I've told you before, I love you, and I meant it, but—well—"

"But-well what? If you love me, what else matters?"

Billy turned away. With his hands buried in his pockets, he stared out at the mountains. The plush carpet beneath his sore feet and the scent of the fresh flowers seemed almost surreal. Sunshine streaked the pastel walls with oranges and yellows, reflecting an inviting warmth.

"I need for you to explain," she said. "What's this 'but-well' business? Is there another girl?"

"*Hell*, no." He turned to face her. "Bonnie, I'm not sure I can explain."

"Just try," she said. "Do I mean anything to you?"

"You mean more to me than you'll ever know. Do you know what I used to sit and think about it in that damned jungle?"

She stared expectantly.

"It's weird, but I didn't think about the war or my buddies or the men who were getting killed, not even my family. It was a little fat girl with glasses that I didn't have time for back in high school, the one who gave me this." He held up his Saint Sebastian medal.

"What do you mean 'you didn't have time for'? You were my friend. You took time to know me, to hear my dreams and to care about me as a person. You talked to me, even when a lot of people made fun of you. You were sweet and kind."

"You think you know me, but you don't."

"I know you better than you know yourself, Billy Coker. You're a person with a heart, a person who knows how to love. Hardly a day goes by that I don't think of that last night when we danced there on your drive beside my daddy's car."

She wrapped her arm around his neck and gave him a sloppy kiss. Her eyes were moist, and it seemed no matter how he put it, she wouldn't understand.

"You keep that up, and we're going to end up the way we did that night," Billy said.

She smiled. "And it wouldn't be too soon."

"Maybe, I don't want to take advantage of you."

She cocked her head to one side and furrowed her brows. "What's that supposed to mean?"

"I need to know that it's you, 'Bonnie Jo,' that I love, and not the beautiful rock star."

"Dammit, Billy, that's just an excuse. Take advantage of me for god's sake. I want you to. I'll give up this rock star thing tomorrow if it bothers you that much. All I want is for us to be together."

Tears rimmed her eyes, but she quickly wiped them away.

"Maybe you're right," Billy said. "But let's slow down, and take it a step at a time, okay?"

She gave him a sad smile and turned to stare out at the mountains. After a few moments she turned again and pulled the tattered cap from his head. Holding it at arm's length between her thumb and index finger, she stepped back and sized him up.

"I think we better start with a hot shower," she said. "You smell like a goat, and a haircut wouldn't hurt either. You've gotten downright shaggy again."

"You mean a haircut like the one you gave me at the Peabody?"

291

She laughed. "Not this time. I'll take you down to Hollywood tomorrow, to the guy who does my hair. Let's get you cleaned up, and I'll get Mrs. Perez to make you a bed in one of the spare rooms. Then we'll eat. She's fixing real Mexican fajitas tonight."

21

BONNIE JO'S CALIFORNIA LIFE

S leeping until noon the next day, Billy awoke to the aroma of hot coffee served in his room by Mrs. Perez. The house was quiet, and she whispered that Bonnie Jo was outside on the poolside patio. It seemed surreal, as if he had been snatched from hell and mainlined to heaven. And he wondered for a moment if it really wasn't all just an illusion, an island paradise that could sink instantly into an ocean of reality. He found Bonnie Jo basking in the morning sunshine beside the pool, and she smiled.

"Come sit, Mr. Sleepyhead," she said. "Mrs. Perez is going to bring us some more coffee and something to eat."

Over a brunch of hot muffins and fresh cantaloupe Bonnie Jo told him about their planned trip to the barber and tour of Hollywood that afternoon. It was only a couple hours later when they pulled into the parking lot at the barbershop. Located off Wilshire Boulevard, the building was a pink and blue collage of marble with towering glass doors. There wasn't a Chevy or a Ford on the lot, and bold, gold script letters on the front corner of the building read "*Karl's*."

"Before we go inside, tell me more about this 'barber' named Karl, who works in this pink and blue building." Billy said.

"Out here we call those colors mauve and lavender, and Karl is referred to as a 'stylist'."

Their eyes met, and Bonnie Jo winked. "Don't worry. I call it 'California Shock'. I had it, too. These folks have a different way of thinking, but you'll get used to it after a while."

The cut-glass doors were trimmed in gold, and the twelve-foot high walls of the foyer were splashed with paisley swirls of gold metal-flake. A chandelier the size of a space ship hung sparkling with hundreds of crystal prisms, sending a shower of colors dancing along the walls. Billy's tennis shoes squeaked on the marble floor, but that quickly ceased as he stepped onto a plush rug that stretched all the way back to a receptionist's desk at the end of the hallway.

"Hello, Ms. Parker," the receptionist said. "Give me just a moment, please."

She picked up a phone and punched a button. "Karl, Ms. Parker is here. Sure." Hanging up, she glanced up at Bonnie Jo. "Sarah will be right up to escort you back."

Burying his fists deep in the pockets of his tattered jeans, Billy casually turned about on his heels as he took in the sheer lavishness of this palace barbershop. A few moments later, someone who looked like a cross between a mythical Amazon warrior and a Playboy bunny came out and greeted them. She raved about Bonnie Jo's latest release as they made their way back to a room that she described as 'Karl's private sitting room'.

The room fit the rest of the building with its jungle motif of potted tropical plants, wall-size prints of tigers lurking in cane thickets and a narcissistic orgy of mirrors hanging everywhere. On the periphery of the room were darkened alcoves with plush couches piled with pastel pillows, for what purpose, Billy could only imagine.

"Can I get something for you, a glass of wine perhaps?" the escort asked.

"Oh, no thanks," Bonnie Jo replied.

She turned to Billy. "You want anything?"

He looked at the woman in the itty-bitty skirt. "How about a double-shot of Wild Turkey on the rocks?"

The woman arched her eyebrows with a look of dismay. "I'm so sorry, but I don't believe we have anything like *that*."

Bonnie Jo shot him a covert scowl. "He's just kidding. A couple glasses of champagne will do just fine."

Billy shrugged and tried to look innocent. A few minutes later a little guy with shoulder-length tresses hurried into the room. Holding his arms wide, he ran with choppy little steps toward Bonnie Jo, greeting her with lavish hugs and kisses on both cheeks. After a moment he stepped back and fingered her hair on either side.

"Girl, I believe you're rushing this a little. You're hair looks fine."

"Oh, this isn't for me."

She turned and introduced Billy. A lengthy discussion ensued as Karl inquired with Bonnie Jo about the 'look' she wanted him to have. Billy sat quietly while Karl minced around, comb in hand, consulting with Bonnie Jo after each snip of the scissors. It was as if Karl was designing an evening gown, or perhaps, a boy-toy. He seemed like a nice guy, but Billy grew irritated that the little barber was conferring only with Bonnie.

"And, Jo, what do you think, dear, a little perm, perhaps? We could make this hunk of yours look like Adonis."

Billy cut his eyes over at her, and Bonnie Jo raised her eyebrows.

"Don't even think about it," he said.

Karl drew back, his mouth agape with an expression of mock-horror.

"You might look cute in curls," Bonnie Jo said.

"Yeah, if I worked for Ringling Brothers."

"Well now, Billy," Karl said, as he continued cutting. "You might be surprised how sexy curls make you look. You know that old saying about 'When in Rome', and this *is* Southern California."

"Thank god it's not Planet of the Apes."

Karl looked wide-eyed over at Bonnie Jo, but she laughed and said, "Oh, don't take him seriously, Karl. He's just trying to be an old stick in the mud."

"That's me," Billy said, "Just no fun at all. Hold the curls."

As he finished, Karl brushed, picked and teased Billy's hair into a state of California windblown chic that only a good shower and a comb could fix. And as they departed he called to the Amazon escort. "Olivia, dear, please tell Marla to make it seventy-five."

Billy stopped dead in his tracks. "Seventy-five?" He turned to Bonnie Jo. "Dollars?"

Karl overheard him. "Yes, since you're a friend of Jo's and it's your first time, I gave you a special discount, kind of a 'welcome to the club' thing, you know?"

Billy was incredulous, but before he could speak, Bonnie Jo smiled and yanked his arm. Looking back, she thanked Karl, and Billy decided to wait until they were in the car.

Outside, the California sun was still shining bright. "No wonder that guy has everything trimmed in gold. Seventy-five bucks for a freaking haircut?"

"Oh, Billy, quit being silly. He usually charges over a hundred dollars for men's haircuts. Everything is higher out here. Besides, Karl is one of the best stylists in LA. He makes average people look like movie stars."

"I don't care if he makes them look like French-fucking-poodles. I'll bet there's a barber shop some-where around here that gives haircuts for five bucks."

Bonnie Jo laughed. "You're such a tight-wad."

They spent the rest of the afternoon shopping, as Bonnie Jo outfitted him with khaki slacks, sports shirts and leather deck shoes. She led him by the hand through trendy shops and down sidewalks with potted trees as she pointed out the sights and an occasional celebrity. She was at home here, and it came to him that Bonnie Jo wore her designer jeans and white blouse with the same ease she'd worn her baggy sweatshirts back home in Mississippi.

They drove around LA taking in the sights until nightfall, when she suggested they go to a place with live music and dancing.

"I'm going to have to pass on the dancing," Billy said.

She gave him a puzzled look. "Why?"

"I don't know. I just don't want to."

"Is it because of your wounds?"

"I suppose you could say that," he said. "Let's just do something else, okay?"

She cocked her head for a moment, but then nodded. That was Bonnie Jo. She knew there was more, but she had the wherewithal to understand it was something Billy didn't want to discuss. This was one of the many things that made her so attractive. Bonnie Jo didn't push him. She knew when to give him his space and let him be.

They ended up having a late supper down near Marina del Rey, where the restaurant had menus on parchment with embossed leather covers. Their table, set with white linen and crystal wine goblets, was beside a huge window overlooking the Pacific. The ocean stretched away to the horizon, and the candlelight reflected in Bonnie Jo's green eyes. A pleasurable warmth rose inside of Billy. He loved her smile, and the way she still spoke with that soft southern accent reminded him of home. Despite the trappings of fame and beauty, she was the same girl he'd grown to care for in high school. Her every action was as natural as her beauty, and a bottle of Cabernet only served to intensify the feelings. He wanted her. He wanted to be a part of her, to hold and to love her.

Sometime after midnight they returned to the house, and as he sat beside her on the bed, the inhibitions created by their extended separation disappeared. He gazed into her eyes, and she smiled. Billy pulled his shirt over his head and tossed it aside, and Bonnie Jo gently touched the scars on his back, running her fingers carefully over them. He turned, kissing her softly as he began unbuttoning her blouse.

"Do they still hurt," she asked.

"Sometimes," he said, "but I'm sure the sight of a naked women will make the pain go away."

She laughed and they kissed again, this time with passion as he finished unbuttoning her blouse, then her pants. He touched and caressed her beneath the sheet, and she clutched him breathlessly as his lips found her neck, then her breasts. It seemed it would be everything he'd hoped for, and he sought to take her to the peak of passion before consummating their love, but a numbing realization began taking hold. He was going through the motions, but he had suddenly wilted.

It was the night at the Peabody all over again, but Billy refused to give up. When she realized what was happening, Bonnie Jo also tried. They both tried, almost desperately, but nothing happened. The arousal he'd felt earlier in the evening and which had grown so intense had inexplicably faded into a dull nothingness. He was limp, and after a while they both lay staring into the darkness.

Billy wasn't sure which of them was more affected. Bonnie Jo had to be confused and hurt, and another psychological tsunami had just rolled over him, pushing him to the bottom. He was both embarrassed and frightened. It had to be part of the same nervous tic that wouldn't let him dance. Here he was high atop a California mountain with an incredibly beautiful woman, poised for the kind of sexual bliss of which legends are made, and he couldn't get it up. He was in Camelot, but had just slammed head-on into a stone wall at the castle gates. The realization was that perhaps he wasn't in control. 'Crazy' and 'insane' were words beginning to slip around in the shadows of his mind. It was a growing fear. Was he? He'd seen it with others back at the VA.

Bonnie Jo sighed and punched a button on the console behind her head. As if by magic, the curtains on the far side of the room began retracting, revealing a breathtaking spectacle of sparkling lights in the valley far below. From her bedroom window above the front porch, miles and miles of metropolitan LA were visible, stretching away into the distance.

They were on top of the world, looking down at lights flowing along the freeways, rivers of diamonds and rubies sparkling in the night. Earlier they had been down there amongst them, but now they were detached observers. Another strange déjà vu took Billy back to the morning when he watched the people on the street below Jackie's apartment. The car lights in the valley represented that same hurried purpose that was so foreign to him since returning from Vietnam. Bonnie Jo was there beside him, hurting and not understanding, but he didn't understand what any of this meant.

"This is nice," he said.

"You aren't going to leave again, are you?"

It was as much a plea as a question. Billy turned and kissed her softly on the cheek. "No."

"It's a great life out here," she said. "You'll see. We can go to the beach or up to Tahoe, or almost anywhere you want. And Las Vegas is only a few hours away, too. There's so much to do. You'll love it."

But the days turned into weeks, and Billy was unable to make love to Bonnie Jo. Unnerved by his impotence, she began making excuses, saying how it must be his wounds, and given time, would get better. She said it, and neither of them believed it. Words were all they had to pacify the feelings of frustration, but the words were becoming increasingly difficult to find.

Desperate, they sent everyone home early one afternoon and took a lounger down near the wall in the backyard, and for a while it seemed it might work. Bonnie Jo said it reminded her of the swing in the oak tree back home, as Billy slowly undressed her, tossing her clothes in the grass. But as each garment settled onto the lawn he realized his libido was dead as ever, trapped in the depths of the past. Frustrated, embarrassed and feeling foolish, he lay there naked beside her in the backyard, limp as a rag and staring up at a cloudless California sky.

"Are you sure there's nothing I can do?" she asked.

The knot of anger again throbbed in his gut, but why at her? It wasn't Bonnie Jo's fault. He took a breath and looked over at her, quelling his anger the only way he knew how. "You can get me some suntan lotion, so my winky doesn't get sunburned."

She smiled, but her eyes were sad. "Please, don't kid around. Is it something about me?"

Billy sat up, snatching his jeans from the ground. "What do I have to say to convince you? It's got nothing to do with you."

For a mere moment the monster in his gut had shown itself, and perhaps it *was* because of Bonnie Jo. Perhaps it was because she was no longer the same girl he had fallen in love with in high school. Yes, the realization had been long coming, but somehow Billy came to understand that he *had* first fallen in love with her long ago. It was that night when they danced beside her father's car. He had not realized it then, nor did he for a long time, but he did now. It was that girl he wanted, the one who so needed him, the one he had let down. He wanted to go back and prove his love was genuine, but it was too late. He had betrayed her friendship, and he was no more worthy of this new Bonnie Jo than he was to be alive while Butch, Danny, Doc, Val and all the others were lying beneath headstones.

"Sorry," he said.

He helped her with her bra, and she reached for her blouse. Silence it seemed was the only salve that worked. They sat several minutes, and Billy was about to apologize further for snapping at her when she turned to him. There was a tear in her eye. He pulled her close, but he didn't know what to say.

Weeks passed as they pretended things were normal. She had Billy doing everything from publicist duties to scheduling and coordinating, but he was no more than a glorified gofer. The people who normally handled those tasks resented the confusion he created, and he began tactfully refraining from doing more than passing along her messages. Bonnie Jo was too busy to notice. Her work, rehearsals, recording sessions and all the other things that went with it tied her up for days at a time. This left Billy free to roam the Pacific Coast Highway, where he began hanging out with the surfers, smoking reefer and wondering what people in the real world were doing.

Bonnie Jo was on the road one weekend in June when he received a phone call from Curtis. Curtis had failed to make the final cut at the Falcon's training camp. He had returned home to Louisiana to find he'd lost his job at the refinery. All Billy's fancy talk about living the dream had put his friend in a fix, but before he got off the phone, Billy laid on the bullshit once again.

"Don't give up the dream," he said. "You can make it happen." What else could he tell him? Curtis had given up everything, because of what Billy had said. Now, he was back home, jobless, sitting on the porch again, and staring out at miles of saw grass swamps.

"But those younger boys seemed so much sharper," Curtis said. "I mean, I know I'm a better ballplayer than most of them, but it was like I had two left feet. I took a couple of sucker blocks and twisted my knee the first day. It was pretty much over after that. I just don't know. Maybe, I'm fooling myself. Maybe, I—"

"Hell, you never gave up that easy on anything. What we saw in Nam was a thousand times worse than anything those college punks can dish out. Stay in shape. You'll get another shot. Give up now, and you'll regret it the rest of your life."

Billy was watching his own life implode from inertia, yet he was feeding his closest friend a line of bullshit. It was something he'd learned from Bonnie Jo. No matter what happens, always show them the silver lining, except he wasn't certain how effective he was with Curtis. Perhaps Curtis was experiencing some of the same fears that plagued him, an unwillingness to trust life and the whims of fate.

Billy had once read a magazine article by a famous psychologist saying that many Vietnam vets were screwed up because they came home to an angry country. They felt "disenfranchised." After World War II there were VE and VJ day ticker-tape parades and a gleaming future. Television was invented and rock and roll music evolved as the 'Leave it to Beaver' lifestyle ruled the country. But after Nam, there were no celebrations, only congressional hearings and pissed-off people demonstrating in the streets.

Perhaps Kleingold's suspicions about potential violence had been right. Billy *was* 'pissed off' at the world, and now he was beginning to have second thoughts about living in this place where no one understood the real meaning of life. Perhaps coming to California had been a mistake. After all, he was sorely out of place around Bonnie Jo's friends. Their lives were about things that no longer mattered to him, singing, dancing, money. Problem was he no longer knew what *did* matter, or what was most important to him. He didn't know what he wanted, but life in California was pushing him closer to a darkened precipice.

22

WHERE HAVE ALL THE CHILDREN GONE?

Bonnie Jo's world was a dream, but it wasn't his. Billy had no dream. He wanted her. He wanted a normal life, but he couldn't make himself look ahead when there was so much wreckage behind him. His past remained unreconciled. Bonnie Jo cancelled business appointments to spend entire days with him, and her patience seemed unending. After they showered together that morning, Billy stood in front of the mirror combing his hair and toking a joint, while Bonnie Jo began telling him about Disney Land. If he had ten thousand years to think about it, it was the last place he wanted to go, but rather than hurt her feelings he nodded and tried to act like he really wanted to see Donald-fucking-Duck.

"What's wrong?" she asked. "I take time so we can be together, and you get in these blue funks and won't even talk."

The girl he loved was butting her head against a stone wall of his making, but he didn't know what to do about it.

"Nothing's wrong," he said. "I'm fine."

"Then why are you smoking a joint at nine o'clock in the morning? All you're doing is getting stoned again."

"I'm dressed."

"Thank god for that. The last time you got stoned I had to button your shirt for you, and that stuff doesn't help your sex problem, either." Her face flushed red. "I'm sorry. I shouldn't have said that."

Snuffing the joint, Billy left it in the ashtray and turned to walk out. "It's okay. You're right. I'm a worthless eunuch."

Her eyes flooded with tears, and she tried to hold him, but he pulled away. It was supposed to be a special day, but Billy was again hearing echoes from the past. The sound of helicopters in the back of his mind drawing closer each day, yet he still didn't understand their meaning. He wanted to make her understand, but it was impossible. He couldn't explain it himself.

"Let's go for a walk," she said.

Showered and ready to go with a clean shirt and khakis, he was supposed to spend the day with her at Disney Land, but they walked instead, down the hill to the brick wall in the backyard. The sun was shining, and except for the sound of the wind in the trees, an extraordinary silence blanketed the surrounding hills.

The San Gabriel Mountains could be good at times, giving him the peace he hadn't found elsewhere. The only sounds were occasional jets flying high overhead, or at night, the squeals of coyotes echoing through the canyons below, or when the wind was right, the distant whine of a Southern Pacific freight train hidden somewhere in a valley to the east.

"Tell me what's wrong, Billy." Her voice was soft and pleading as they held hands and walked down the hill.

"Hell, I don't know. Sometimes I feel like I'm getting closer to the nut house every day. I might go back to Memphis and see Kleingold, tell him how nothing makes sense anymore."

Billy climbed atop the wall and pulled Bonnie Jo up beside him. Facing the mountains, they sat gazing out at another spectacular California morning. A refreshing breeze stirred the trees as hawks rode the rising thermals high overhead. This was the one place that brought him some element of peace. Near the horizon, on a distant hillside, sunlight glinted from a car's windshield as it wound its way along a mountain highway. Turning to Bonnie Jo, Billy studied the worried look on her face. Another tear trickled down her cheek, but she quickly wiped it away.

Billy pulled a fresh joint from his shirt pocket, cupped his hands against the breeze, and lit it.

"Here," he said, handing it to her.

She took it, inhaled, and coughed.

"Easy," he said. "Don't rush it."

"This is the first time I've done this since you and Jackie introduced me to it back at the VA in Memphis."

She drew in again, this time holding the smoke in her lungs.

"Okay. Go ahead and let it out."

She did, then took a breath of fresh air.

"Worrying isn't going to help," he said. "This is something I have to work through myself."

She handed him the joint. "I still don't understand. Why can't you talk to me about it?"

"I'm the one who has to figure how to make it work."

"So what am I supposed to do, stand by and act like none of this is happening?"

"Look, it's mostly about Nam, and you wouldn't understand anyway."

Her jaw flexed.

"Here, take another hit on the joint," Billy said.

"You don't think I can understand Vietnam?" Bonnie Jo asked.

"It's not that you can't understand it, it's just that—" His mind went nowhere. "Oh, hell, maybe you're right. Talking might help, but part of the problem is I don't understand it myself."

"What is it that you don't understand?

"I suppose it has to do with life and what we're supposed to do with it. Nothing seems relevant anymore, and it's not simply my life and what I do. It's about everyone. Does anyone really know what the hell we're doing here on this earth? Since coming home, most of the things people do seems like a waste of time, futile endeavors to stay busy and forget about what they are really here for."

"So you're saying you no longer care about anything?"

He nodded.

"Does that include me?"

"No. I love you very much."

Bonnie Jo buried her face on his shoulder. Billy drew on what was left of the joint and handed it back to her.

"Finish it," he said.

She looked up at him instead. "You know, maybe you're right. Maybe you should go see a doctor. I'm sure there are some good ones in LA who can help."

Billy laughed.

"Why are you laughing?"

"An LA shrink? Now, there's an interesting prospect. Reality isn't something they see much, dealing with the druggies and fruitcakes in Hollywood. Besides, I can't even afford the barbers around here, much less a psychiatrist."

"The money isn't an obstacle. You know that, and you need to do something."

"Well, I'm not going to a shrink out here in California. That's for sure."

"You're a stubborn man, Billy Coker."

"I don't mind talking to someone, but it has to be someone who can relate to the things I've seen."

"Why don't you try telling me about it?" she said.

"Because you're not a shrink," he replied, "and it's not something you need to hear."

"Try me, Billy. I want to understand. Besides, who *are* you going to tell if you don't tell me?"

"Look, there are lots of guys who feel this way. I can work through it on my own. Making you go through it won't help."

"Dammit, Billy! I *am* going through it. I live it almost every day."

"Okay, calm down. I get your point."

"Then talk to me. Tell me about it. Is it Butch and Danny, your two buddies that got killed?"

"Butch and Danny?" he said. "Hell, they were just the first ones. Later there was Val, Doc Mazlosky, Tom Stoner, Reggie Washington, Sergeant Bentley. Then there were the new guys who got killed or wounded before we hardly knew them. Hell, I can't even remember their names any more, but why them? Why did they die and not me?"

Bonnie Jo remained silent, while Billy stumbled through a junk heap of wrecked memories.

"Everyone deals with this crap in his own way. I mean, I probably smoke too much dope and drink a little too much, but…."

Bonnie Jo stared at him without expression.

"I just want to know that life has some kind of meaning and all those guys dying counted for something. I think most men jump right back in, and no one around them has a clue about what they went through, so they try to act like it never happened. They don't think about it, because it's something they can't change. It happened and they have to live with it."

"Maybe that's the answer," Bonnie Jo said. "Maybe we should find something you want to do, as a way to forget the past."

Billy shook his head. "Maybe so, but first I want to understand why all this happened."

"What do you mean, 'why all this happened'?" she said. "Maybe, there is no reason."

Billy turned and lay back atop of the wall, staring up into a cloudless sky. Bonnie Jo sat at his feet.

"Don't you think people are crazy when they become workaholics or get engrossed in a hobby until it becomes an obsession?" he asked.

"Maybe, but not necessarily," she said. "I mean, you don't have to go to that extreme."

"No, I don't. And it's because the ones that do are gripping the loose edge of reality and trying to avoid their memories. They stay busy, because they know if they look back, they'll lose their grip and slide into the past."

"Do you feel that way?"

Billy wanted to stare into the sun until he was blind. What was he going to tell her: that there *was* this giant burned-out hole in his psyche, that he was already clawing at the ragged edge of sanity, and it was rapidly slipping through his fingers? He shook his head. "No, I can deal with the past. At least I'm trying, but I need more time. That's what Kleingold said."

"I'll be here when you're ready to talk, but I've been thinking about something else we can try. It's just an idea." She paused, her voice husky with emotion. "You've been through a bad time the last few years, and, like you said, you need to find a way to start over."

Billy shrugged. "Yeah?"

"My manager is planning a formal reception up here in August. A lot of people will be invited, my road crew, my producers and a number of well-known people from around Hollywood. I know it's not your style, but it might take your mind off things for a while, maybe even give you a different perspective. What do you think?"

"A reception?" he said.

"Well, yes. It's kind of a formal party. There'll be a band and dancing. I mean you don't have to dance, but what do you think?"

"I don't know," Billy replied.

She looked away. "You're probably right," she said. "It's a dumb idea. I shouldn't push you into something you're not comfortable doing. I just want you to re-engaged with life and enjoy being with me, but I don't know what to do."

Billy turned and looked into Bonnie Jo's eyes. She was trying her damnedest to help, and like she always said, he had to see the positive side of things. This party certainly wasn't his idea of good time, but it wouldn't hurt him either. Besides, a party with all those 'creative types' might be interesting.

"Actually, it doesn't sound so bad," Billy said. "Maybe, I can get to know some of your friends."

Billy sat up and looked out at the mountains lest his eyes give him away. He pulled her close.

"Do you really think it'll help?" she asked.

He pulled another joint from his shirt pocket and lit it. "It might. Here." He handed her the joint.

"I'm so hungry I could eat a horse," she said.

Billy smiled. "This shit does that to you."

23

THE RAGE OF THE PARTY

It was another cookie-cutter Southern California day with the sun shining overhead and a cool Pacific breeze drifting through the hills. They were sunning beside the pool, and Bonnie Jo was telling Billy about her plans for the up-coming party. He was rolling another joint and trying his best to seem interested when Ms. Perez came out of the house. She was carrying the telephone and pulling the cord behind her.

"It is a Señor Teague," she said.

Billy pressed the phone to his ear. "Curtis! Hey, Man!"

Curtis sounded a little down and out.

"It's great to hear your voice, again. So what's happening down your way?"

Billy cradled the phone on his shoulder while rubbing Bonnie Joe's back with a cocoa butter suntan oil. Curtis explained how he had given up on playing pro football. The refinery had rehired him, but he was starting over again at the bottom, cleaning the sludge pits. Bonnie Jo listened as they rehashed his tryout with the Falcons.

"Man, I wouldn't give up after only one try," Billy said. "You're too good, and there's got to be another team that'll give you a shot. Don't you have any contacts in the pros?"

"Why don't you tell him to give Raymond Hokes a call?" Bonnie Jo suggested.

Curtis overheard her. "You guys know Raymond Hokes?"

"Well, yeah," Billy said.

"You've got to be kidding. Sarge, man, you've been holding out on me. Do you really know *the* Raymond Hokes?"

Billy had heard a lot about Ray Hokes since graduation. He'd gone on, after flunking junior college, to play defensive lineman for Chicago. A two-time Pro-Bowler, they called him Dump-Truck Hokes. 'Dump-Truck' was a name he'd picked up in high school because of what he did to opposing teams' quarterbacks. Back home, Monroe County was notorious for its one-sided wrecks between the trucks and smaller automobiles.

"Yeah, I guess you could say we know him. He used to whip my scrawny little ass every day in high school."

"You mean, you went to school with him?"

"Yeah," Billy said. "Hell, maybe Bonnie Jo is right. I hadn't thought about him. Why not give him a call? Tell him who you are, and how we were in Nam together. Maybe he can pull some strings and get you a tryout."

"Hell, Sarge, this is the break I've been needin'. A word from him might be all it takes."

"Go for it," Billy said. "And good luck."

A mild Pacific breeze was blowing through the hills that afternoon, but it did little to relieve Billy's guilt. After hanging up, he pushed the phone away with his foot.

"What's the matter?" Bonnie Jo asked.

"Nothing," Billy said.

She rolled over, picked up her sunglasses and put them on. "You look like you just lost your best friend, so please, don't tell me nothing's wrong. What is it?"

"I just feel like I'm feeding him a line of bullshit, that's all."

Bonnie Jo sat up, straddling the lounger. She dropped her head and peered over the top of her sunglasses with those piercing but beautiful green eyes. "What you're doing is being a friend. You're giving him encouragement and hope."

Billy laughed. "Hope for what, a pipe dream?"

"It's a dream, but it's a real one he can achieve. You said yourself the pros were about to draft him out of college before the war. And what do any of us have but our dreams?"

Billy didn't answer, and Bonnie Jo always seemed to know when to drop a discussion. She said nothing more, and when Curtis called back a month later telling Billy how Chicago had signed him, she simply hugged his neck without a hint of "I told you so." It was the high-point of their summer.

By late July Bonnie Jo had finished putting together all the particulars for the big party. Billy realized it was going to be a regal affair when she took him down to Hollywood to buy a tux and had Karl cut his hair, again. He wanted her to be happy, but there was something about wearing a tux and bow tie that left him feeling like a charlatan. He was masquerading as something he wasn't.

By the night of the party, he'd slipped into another blue funk. Socializing with a bunch of Hollywood types was the last thing he wanted to do, but he had promised Bonnie Jo. Suiting-up, he put on his best smile, and paced the bedroom floor until he gained enough nerve to walk down the stairs. Trying to remain inconspicuous, Billy avoided eye-contact while quickly making his way across the room to one of the tables loaded with food.

It was a buffet set with sterling silver and white linen. Elegant white candles burned next to giant crystal vases overflowing with exotic flowers. The caterer had a dozen guys wearing burgundy monkey suits with black bow ties and little monogrammed towels draped over their arms. They were serving drinks and every kind of crab dip, caviar and party concoction imaginable. He opted for a couple of celery sticks and a glass of soda water.

Dropping back into a corner where he hoped to remain incognito, Billy surveyed the room. There were at least a hundred guests from every tier of Hollywood Society including several big name celebrities. Everyone wore a tux or an evening gown. There were also some of her road crew and a few brain-fried druggies sneaking around in the back rooms, probably hoping to score a quick hit of their favorite hallucinogenic. Billy was tempted to join them, but he'd promised Bonnie Jo a drug-free evening.

The house was filled with soft music, sparkling lights and the scent of flowers. The party-goers should have been enjoying themselves, and at first take it seemed so, but as Billy studied them, it became evident that their charm and gentility was simply another facade. Everyone was doing his or her best to seem carefree, but so desperately calculating every word to impress those standing nearby or some big-shot producer.

Gossip, chic jokes and skillful repartee filled the room, and they reminded him so much of the Lizards back at Raeford High. Each peacock spread his glorious feathers, each gorilla pounded his swelled chest, and each little bird trilled her best song as the menagerie worked the room for tidbits of approval. It was enough to make a person lose his cookies, and the longer Billy stayed, the more desperate he became. He had to escape.

Working his finger around the inside of his collar, he searched for relief, until he thought about the San Gabriel Mountains and the wall in the backyard. Crossing the room, he headed toward the door. He had to go down to his favorite spot atop the wall, get some air and suck down a quick cigarette. That was the plan, but an older guy with perfect hair hailed him as he crossed the room. The man had an abnormally dark tan and several gold chains substituting for his black bowtie.

"Hi, Billy. Art Schuster. How are you?" He had the voice of a radio announcer and shoved his hand at Billy, saying his name like Billy was supposed to know who he was.

"Okay, I reckon," Billy answered. "Have we met?"

He didn't want to seem rude, but he couldn't remember.

"Well, gosh darn, I hope so." The man's accent had suddenly changed to that of a down-home country boy. "My show, Magic Millions, you've seen it. Everyone has." Just as suddenly he had reverted to his game-show host voice.

"Oh, yeah, yeah. Hey, nice to meet you," Billy said.

Art Schuster raised his eyebrows and pursed his lips, giving Billy a sideways look as if he were a dumbass for not instantly recognizing him. Billy had seen the show once or twice back at the VA.

"I've seen you around town with BJ," Schuster said. "She seems quite infatuated with you."

"Oh?" Billy said, sipping his soda water.

"Yes, I would say you're a very fortunate young man."

Billy gave him a flat smile. "Kind of a 'fortunate son,' I reckon."

Schuster gave him a quizzical look. The remark had gone three feet over his head.

"So, Billy, how do you like it out here in California?" His voice rose above those around them, and he waved his drink flamboyantly about as if he were the sole creator of the glitz and glamour.

"It's nice," Billy said. "Kind of different."

"Different? My heavens, I should hope so. What did you do back in Mississippi?"

Billy began feeling as if he was being interviewed before the entire room. *'Well, Arty, I have a wonderfully sensitive wife who does the dishes and takes out the trash, two-point-five beautiful children who will someday be nuclear physicists and a golden retriever named....'* It was tempting to respond with sarcasm, but Billy fought the temptation.

"Nothing much," he said. "I haven't had the chance to get started in anything since leaving the service."

Billy could see it in his eyes as Schuster glanced around at the others standing nearby. This guy was sizing him up as a hick.

A waiter came by, and Schuster hailed him. "Another Chivas on the rocks, Sport."

The waiter nodded and turned to Billy. "May I get you something, sir?" Billy had promised Bonnie Jo he wouldn't drink.

"Sure, if you don't mind," he said. "Bourbon over ice."

"So, what kind of entertainment is there back in Mississippi?" Schuster asked.

Billy shrugged. "I reckon we do whatever we want. A lot of people hunt and fish."

"Damned," Schuster said. "Sounds exciting."

Billy came back with his best Gomer Pyle grin. It was his only defense for a sonofabitch doing his best to piss him off.

"So which do you do, hunt or fish?"

Despite his best effort, Billy felt his anger gaining the upper hand. "Aw, hell. If it gets too boring, we hunt us a colored boy to hang in a Magnolia tree, but mostly we just sit on the veranda and drink mint juleps all day."

Schuster's eyes narrowed, and he laughed. A flicker of discomfort showed in his eyes.

"Uh, sounds interesting," he said.

His inability to rule Billy like a game-show contestant left him ruffled. Finding sudden recognition of someone nearby, Schuster hailed them and walked away without a parting word. Billy grabbed another drink from the tray of a passing waiter and turned it up. It was time to get the hell out of Dodge. He made his way out the door, but half way down the side of the pool another person grasped his arm. It was a slight fellow with frizzy hair and the facial features of a rabbit, or perhaps it was a rat.

"Hi. Aren't you BJ's *Mississippi* boyfriend?" He said it loud enough to draw attention from several bystanders, and Billy didn't miss the emphasis on Mississippi. He was definitely a rat.

"Yeah," Billy said. "And I hope I'm her *only* boyfriend."

The man's handshake had the firmness of an over-ripe banana, and Billy was careful not to squeeze it too hard. The smaller man seemed charmed by his mindfulness.

"So, you're the big war hero we've heard so much about. I thought you'd be, well, so much more, I don't know, bigger than life, kind of like an action hero. Did you kill a lot of those mean old Vietnamese?"

The man turned and looked around at the people around them, and Billy felt the blood pounding in his temples. With this second cheap-shot artist standing in front of him, he began realizing Bonnie Jo's friends apparently spent a lot of time talking about him, and he wasn't incognito. He was the center-ring attraction and the hottest gossip item at the party. It also seemed they thought he held some sort of evil influence over Bonnie Jo.

"I'm not a hero," Billy said. "And I'd rather not discuss the war, if you don't mind."

He turned to walk away, but the little man's voice grew even louder. "No, I don't suppose you do want to talk about it. Have you ever told BJ what really went on over there in Vietnam? Does she know the real truth about all those innocent women and children you and your buddies killed?"

Billy paused with his back to the little man. *Maintain your composure*, he told himself. He swallowed hard, and forced a smile before slowly turning to face the man. "Look, I don't know who pissed in your corn flakes, but if you're looking for a fight, why don't you go over there and bitch at the other girls?"

"You fucking pig," the man said, "Sooner or later BJ will learn the truth about what you and your buddies did to those people."

Billy wanted to walk away, to detach himself from this mini-war protest happening before him. He wanted to do anything before his anger took over, but the man stepped forward, staring defiantly in his face.

Billy maintained a forced smile. "You know, you really don't have a clue what you're talking about," he said. "And I don't mind you voicing your opinion about me, but you should leave my buddies out it. Some of them can't be here to defend themselves, because they're dead."

The tone of Billy's voice, though low and calm, belied his smile. And only then did the man seem to notice his eyes. Billy could speak calmly. He could smile, but he couldn't hide his eyes, and his anger had again gained the upper hand.

The little man blinked and stepped back, then quickly turned to walk away, but it was too late. Billy didn't think. It simply happened. He caught him by the shoulder and spun him around. "Wait. Please," he said, "don't walk away."

"Get your filthy hands off of me," the man said.

Catching the front of his tux, Billy lifted him off the ground and held him with his arms flailing helplessly in the air. He wouldn't have hurt the little shit no matter how angry he became. He'd had enough fighting in Vietnam, but this pompous loudmouth needed to understand that freedom of speech came with certain risks. Gasps of astonishment surrounded them as guests looked on in wide-eyed horror. Billy held him there for what must have seemed the longest moment of the little man's life, dangling, and squirming like a bug in a bird's beak. And he could have hurt him, but Billy knew, or at least hoped, that despite his anger, he was still in control.

"Put him down!"

It was Bonnie Jo shouting from across the pool. The band stopped playing, and other than the gasps, everyone on the patio went totally silent.

"Put him down!" she yelled again.

Billy didn't look at her as he gazed up at his little friend, silhouetted against a star studded California sky. Yes, he would do as he was told, but not without leaving this little rat with something to think about. With a calm and deliberate motion, Billy tossed him into the pool where he landed, sputtering and thrashing the water to an indignant boil.

Billy looked back at Bonnie Jo, meeting her laser stare with one of his own. After several seconds, he shrugged and headed down to the wall. A few minutes later she showed up. The band was playing again back up at the house, and he invited her to climb atop the wall, but she stood with her fists balled on her hips. Her face was flush, and her lips were pressed firmly together. Her eyes narrowed until they were burning holes in him.

"Have you lost your mind?"

"That rat-faced little fucker was being a jerk, and I told him to run along, but he wouldn't."

"So you had to throw him into the pool? How do you think that's going to look in the papers?"

"Is that all you're worried about?" Billy asked. "What the newspapers will say?"

"You think I'm worried about *me*? Think about yourself."

"Myself?"

"I heard you told Art Schuster that we hang black people from Magnolia trees in Mississippi. Is that true?"

"You grew up there. Why would you think that's true?"

"Dammit Billy, don't mess with me," she shouted. "I'm serious, and I don't think you're cute. You know that kind of thing really did happened at one time, and now everyone here thinks you're some kind of white bigot. What do you think Curtis would think if he heard you say that?"

"He'd laugh his ass off, because he's not stupid like these people."

"These people are my friends, and I don't appreciate you saying they're stupid. Why do you hate them so much, Billy?"

"I don't hate them. Hell, I don't even dislike them. Don't you understand? As far as I'm concerned, if they leave me alone, I don't even know they exist. All this talk about who did what, who said such-and-such, and how so-and-so got his money—can't you see? It's all just a bunch of drivel. It doesn't mean anything. They talk crap because they aren't intelligent enough to discuss anything of real importance."

"That's not true. There are some very talented people here, and those are the kinds of things people discuss at parties. What is wrong with you, Billy?"

"God, you've got to be kidding. What's wrong with *me*? Have you looked around? I've never seen so many perfectly capped, whiter-than-white teeth, stretched faces and canned tans. If these idiots worked half as much on their minds as they did their bodies they might not be so compelled to judge people without all the facts. I've got to get out of here. That's all there is to it."

A tear rolled from her eye as she shook her head. "You're not the same person I knew in high school, Billy. You've changed."

"No shit?" he said. "That's an astute observation, but you better take a look at yourself, too, because I'm not the only one. You call these people your friends, but you've forgotten how the ones just like them back home fucked over you so bad. Maybe you should spend a little less money on this worthless shit, and use some of it to help people who really need it."

She glared at him, her bottom lip quivering and her face turning even redder. "Go!" She pointed toward the house. "Just leave. I can't stand this anymore. You're just a mean bastard who hates everyone."

At least she was up-front about it, but his was a cheap shot, and Billy saw it in her eyes. He'd hurt her, and now she was boiling mad. Jumping down from the wall, he walked past her to the house and went up to the bedroom where he began packing his bag. It was the excuse he'd been looking for. He could pretend that leaving was her idea.

24

A LONG LONESOME ROAD

A cold wind blew beneath a sodden sky, seeping in around the window frame. Billy's boxer shorts and flip-flops offered little warmth, and he found himself shivering. Having rented an apartment in Midtown Memphis, he tried to pull things together. The people on the street below raced madly about, and he wanted to jump back on the treadmill with them, to enjoy their mindless pursuits, but it wasn't happening. Late afternoon, when it grew quiet, thoughts of Bonnie Jo returned, and Billy was forced to look back at the wreckage-strewn path of his life.

They hadn't spoken in three months. She tried contacting him several times, but he didn't return her calls. He couldn't. What would he say? Turning away from the window, he went to the easy chair and fired up a joint. Another year was slipping away. His life had derailed entirely, a smoking train wreck of living off disability checks and hanging out at the trendy joints in the neighborhood. Only because pot was too expensive, he drank himself into a daily stupor. With hair to his shoulders and a full beard, he'd grown to look like the other derelicts in the neighborhood, but his new friends were lawyers and accountants who bought him drinks for war stories. They set drink after drink in front of him, while he obliged them.

His favorite hangout was a trendy joint called TJ's where the walls were decorated with the memorabilia of Memphis musicians like Elvis, BB King, Johnny Cash, The Boxtops, Booker T and the MGs and dozens of others. Billy sat at a large table with Bobby Raganti, a lawyer who was joined by several friends that afternoon. The liquor flowed, and by nightfall the place was crowded. Several mini-skirted women joined them at the table, while Bobby bought shots all around. The liquor freed him, and Billy obliged their curiosity with the unvarnished truth.

"Yeah, we'd humped up a mountain valley off the A Shau, lookin' for an NVA base camp. Hadn't found shit all week, so we pulled back and set up a perimeter to rest and re-supply. The enemy knew we were looking for them, so that night they looked us up. Within thirty minutes of the first trip-flares going off, they breeched the wire, and the machine-gunners melted the barrels on the M-60s. We ended up fighting them hand to hand."

"You mean you fought them with your bare hands?" a women asked.

Seals & Crofts were crooning "Summer Breeze" on the jukebox, and the aroma of prime-cut beef and hamburgers on the grill wafted in from the kitchen. These were good people, but they understood nothing about the reality of combat. Billy wanted them to know. They needed to peek behind that plastic curtain called 'civilization' and understand what their votes meant when some congressman whipped them into a fever-pitched frenzy of unbridled patriotism.

"Not exactly," he said. "We used whatever we had to fight with. Do you know what the stock of an M-16 rifle is filled with?"

They wagged their heads in unison.

"White stuff—like Styrofoam. I ran out of ammo and didn't have time to get to my bayonet, so I used my M-16 like a club. This gook lunged at me with a bayonet, but I side-stepped him and caught him square across the top of the head with my rifle—pretty much made mush out of his brains, but the stock of my rifle shattered, too. The only thing left of it was the white Styrofoam stuff and the buffer tube."

He didn't embellish, but their eyes revealed a hint of disbelief. It didn't matter. Other than giving them a small dose of reality, Billy's only purpose was to become totally inebriated. After finishing his last shooter of the evening, he stood wobbly legged and began walking toward the door, but someone at the bar reached out and grabbed his arm.

"You don't look like a war hero to me."

It was a young man sitting on a barstool. He wore dog tags and a black T-shirt that said 'U.S. Marine Corps'. No doubt a trainee from the Naval Air Station at Millington, he was crew-cut and muscled up like a young gorilla. Probably wasn't long out of Basic at Paris Island.

Billy eyed him up and down. Once upon a time his anger would have taken control, but even that too had faded into the nothingness that was now his life. He no longer cared. He saw the young Marine not as a threat, but as just another person who couldn't understand the pain he felt.

"Who said anything about being a hero?" Billy replied. "I was just there, that's all."

"I've been listening to your bullshit all night. If you were in all that shit, how come you never got wounded, and where are all your ribbons and medals?"

The barroom grew quiet as people stopped and stared. The juke box was between songs.

"You got any medals to show him?" Bobby asked.

Bobby had shown no skepticism toward his stories. A sudden coldness welled up deep inside as Billy thought of his medals and that day in Washington when he had thrown them over the White House fence. He thought of Butch and Danny, and the others, and took a deep breath, fighting back the emotions. He tried to hide his feelings with a fabricated nonchalance.

"I threw them over the fence at the White House," he said. "All but one."

"Yeah, right," the Marine replied. "Which one was that, the one the Wizard of Oz gave you?"

Mooning this asshole with the purple scars on his butt would give him what he deserved, but like his anger, Billy's humor, too, was now gone. He waved off the young marine and turned to walk out.

"You're a fucking phony," the Marine shouted.

Billy turned, and for a moment he wanted to be angry, but there simply wasn't anything there. "Were you over there?"

"No, but I'm not the one trying to make myself out like a big war hero."

Billy saw them there looking at him—Butch, Danny, Doc, Val, Reggie, Tom, all of them, watching him, smiling as if they wanted him to do something, to put this guy in his place, but he couldn't. They were the ones who deserved to be called heroes. "If it sounded like I was trying to be a hero, I apologize. The heroes are all dead."

"So, was all the stuff you've been telling us was lies?" Bobby asked.

Billy felt tears forming in his eyes, and turned to face him. "No, it's true. All of it."

"Then why don't you stand up to him?" a young woman asked.

Billy glanced at her. Sleek and beautiful, with dangling earrings and soft wet lips, she probably knew a lot about sex, but not a damned thing about war, fighting or death.

The Marine slid off his barstool. "Yeah, why don't you show me some of those hand-to-hand moves you put on the gooks?" He tugged playfully at his shaggy hair, but Billy pushed his hand away.

"Leave him alone," Bobby said. "He's harmless. Besides, it was good entertainment."

A bouncer was between them instantly. He held the Marine at bay, and turned to Billy. "I think it's time for you to go."

"Look at him," the Marine said. "The Hippie fucker is crying like a baby. You're nothing but a phony."

There was a riffle of nervous laughter. The marine was bigger, stronger and healthier, and Billy's unwillingness to meet his chest-beating challenge seemed to make the marine right in the eyes of the others. Nothing he could say really mattered. He turned and walked out the door.

The next afternoon, Billy awoke in his apartment. Standing in front of the window, he stared down at the street below. He shivered from the cold air seeping in around the sill. He had purchased an old Chevy Nova a few weeks back, and it was parked down on the street, covered with a dusting of new snow. Naked tree limbs outside his window swayed in the bitter winter wind. He lit a cigarette. The young marine had made him a laughing stock, and he could no longer face his friends in the bars. He was done with this place. He had to find some-where to go, a place where there was hope. If he stayed in Memphis, he would end up locked away at the VA. After fixing a cup of instant coffee, he found a pen and wrote a letter to Bonnie Jo.

> Dear Bonnie Jo,
>   I have been getting your letters, and I have read them all. They help me a lot, and I am sorry that I have never written back. I know I've made a mess of your life, and I am very sorry. I wish I could fix it, but I can't. You need to find someone who can give you the love you deserve. Stop waiting for me. I promise that if I ever get past all this, I will come back to see you someday, and maybe, if you want, we can still be friends. I am leaving as soon as the weather breaks and going to Florida. I hope the change of scenery will help.
> Love Always,
> Billy

He put the letter in an envelope and began packing his bags.

25

SAILIN' ON A SUMMER BREEZE

Florida was a place where dreams came true. It had to be. After forwarding his mail to Jackie's apartment, Billy hit the road. He was going where he never once imagined there could be a cemetery. They probably shipped the coffins somewhere far away or else buried them at sea. As a kid, he had seen the magazine photos of palm trees, white sand and lithesome women in sundresses. He saw himself on a catamaran skipping across the waves, living life where Nielson sang about the sun shining through the pouring rain. Florida had to be that place, a place to start over.

Driving all night, he ended up somewhere south of Panama City, and after a roadside nap, he continued southward along the coast. The sparkling green waters of the Gulf broke in a gentle froth on sugar white beaches, and green palm trees lined the roadway. Florida was just as he had dreamed, a place of life and beauty.

He crossed the Sunshine Skyway, and as the sun again dropped down on the horizon that evening he walked out on a long wooden pier south of Venice. Passing the fishermen and the remaining tourists, he walked to the very end and sat on the railing, looking out beyond the mouth of the bay. There was new life stirring in the warm gulf breeze as seagulls soared and pirouetted above the water. He inhaled the salty air through his nostrils. A magnificent flaming orange sun scattered its glow amongst the clouds as it slowly disappeared far out in the Gulf.

This was his opportunity for a new start. Even Rat Rizzo never made it this far. He died on the bus, but Billy was here, free and with no strings attached. He didn't have to answer to anyone. This was where he would start life again, and surely he could find meaning and equilibrium in a world with such beauty.

Taking advantage of the elixir of sunshine, Billy became a deckhand on a charter boat. At night he did some bartending, and between jobs he roamed south to Key West and back up to Tampa Bay. He drank, got sunburned and purged his mind by avoiding television and newspapers. After all, who needed them when there was so much to do? Summer time in Florida was glorious. The smell of salt, ocean breezes and broiled seafood filled his nostrils while sleek fishing boats plowed foamy white wakes and bronzed women strutted about in bikinis, all under blue skies.

When the fishing season ended and the weather changed most of the tourists disappeared. Billy was forced to head north to the pan handle to find work, but there were only construction jobs available. He began working with a crew pouring concrete. A physically demanding job, it drained him as he fought to maintain the pace with the rest of the men. Each night he rubbed his scarred muscles with liniment, but each morning they remained knotted and sore. A white helmeted supervisor stood with arms folded, watching him, as he struggled with a load of steel rebar. Billy knew he wasn't carrying his load. He received his severance notice the first week after New Year's and headed back south toward Venice.

The first warm days of spring came again, along with the tourists and the young women in their bikinis. This new summer once again brought relief, except it didn't quite match the previous one. Tending bar again, Billy began drinking. It wasn't long before he was fired again, and he went back as a deckhand on a charter boat called The Nora Lea. It provided little more than drinking money, and the ghosts of his past returned. Billy found no escape from their torment.

The charter boat captain idled the engines while one of the fishermen, sweating and red-faced, fought a large Amberjack alongside the boat. The fish, silver and gray, lunged back down into the deep green water, bending the fisherman's rod in a powerful arc. The reel's drag squealed, but the tiring fish had made its last lunge for life. The moment didn't escape Billy as he reached into the churn of white bubbles and snatched the gaff into the Jack's gills. He hoisted it onboard, and it lay bleeding on the deck while the fishermen slapped high-fives and cheered.

Billy gazed out beyond the ripples created by the boat, to where the ocean lay perfectly flat all the way to the horizon. There was hardly a breath of air stirring. The Gulf was a beautiful place, but two years had come and gone. He had sold his car somewhere along the way, and he had been living out of his suitcase for the last several months. It was time to do something different. He was finished.

The evening was a quiet one with a gentle on-shore breeze as Billy made his way back to the same wooden pier he had first visited two years earlier. From somewhere far up the coast came the rhythmic thump of choppers, probably from one of the military bases. Back in Nam, the sound of choppers approaching always meant fire support was coming, or reinforcements, or they brought medical evacuation, but that was then. Now, they brought only memories—bad ones. The wooden pier was gritty with sand, but warm beneath his bare feet as he walked out toward another blazing sunset. He had the last of his deck-hand earnings in a pocket, thirty-something dollars, but he had abandoned his shirt and shoes back in the sea oats on the beach. The swim out into the Gulf would be easier without them.

A couple of old fishermen, diehards still waiting for a fish to strike in the waning moments of the day, leaned against a nearby rail. Billy reached the end of the pier and gazed down into the emerald green water, now quickly fading to a nighttime gray. The beautiful Gulf waters were calling him home. Pushing his hair and beard back with both hands, he sucked in a deep breath and waited. The fishermen would soon leave. That was when he would be free once and for all.

The old man nearest him, probably a retired sailor, chewed a soggy cigar and eyed him curiously. If he jumped from the pier now, the man would probably call the cops. There'd be boats and helicopters following him out to sea. He'd probably be caught before he reached the mouth of the bay and end up locked away in another VA hospital. He waited, but the old men clung tenaciously to their fishing rods, hoping for that last strike before dusk gave way to nightfall.

Billy gazed up at the first stars appearing above, sparkling little diamonds set against a deepening purple night sky. Somewhere beyond the jetties seagulls squawked, and the crashing surf was a siren's call, but the old men refused to leave. Back in the bay, moored along the docks, there were fishing boats, and the reflection of lights from a bar sparkled and shimmered across the water. A gold and white Miller High Life sign glowed under an open veranda as the sounds of an old Righteous Brothers melody floated across the bay. A few drinks might help him muster the courage he needed, while he waited for the fishermen to leave. He walked back down the pier.

There was a sign above the gray wooden door, "CAPTAIN J's", and from inside came the tinkling of bottles, along with the gentle murmur of voices. A genuinely rustic place, the bar held an authenticity that the tourist joints lacked. Billy sat on a barstool, and fished the greasy wad of bills from his pocket. Mounted Swordfish, Red Snapper and Jack Caravel lined the weathered wooden walls, along with an assortment of bleached shark jaws, old rope, nets and glass floats. The place smelled of crab boil, liquor and sea salt.

"What'll it be?" the bartender asked.

"A Miller Highlife and a couple of tequila shooters with a lemon," Billy said.

The bartender reached into an icebox beneath the bar, popped the cap from a bottle and set it in front of him. "Be right back with the shooters."

The bartender's arms looked as if they'd been burned and peeled a thousand times over the last fifty years. A shaggy beard made it difficult to guess his age. On his right forearm was a faded tattoo. It might have been an anchor with a cross made of stars.

"Here you go." He placed two shot glasses in front of Billy, along with several slices of lemon and a jigger of salt. Carefully, he filled the glasses with Cuervo.

"Anything else?" he asked.

"This'll do for now," Billy said.

He shoved the wad of money across the bar. Picking through it, the bartender took what he needed and pushed the rest back. Afterward, he walked to a cash register at the end of the bar, put the money inside and began wiping a tray of glasses. Four shooters and two beers later, Billy motioned toward the man's arm. "You a sailor?"

The man glanced down at his arm. "That's the Southern Cross, and no, I don't do much sailing any more. I was in the navy for twenty-five years, but I'm retired now, just helping out around here to make a buck."

He pointed to a black and white photo on the wall. There was another bearded man standing in front of a charter boat.

"That's Captain J," the bartender said. "He's my younger brother. I help him out, running the bar, working on the boats or whatever is needed."

There was another photo of a much younger man in a flight suit, clean-cut and wearing gold aviator sunglasses. He was standing in front of a Navy Sikorsky helicopter.

"Is that you?" Billy asked.

The bartender grimaced. "That was our baby brother, Lieutenant Commander John Staples. He was a naval aviator. Got killed in Vietnam."

Billy drew a deep breath and nodded. "Yeah, I got a good dose of Nam, myself."

The bartender extended his hand across the bar. "Tom Staples is my name."

"Billy Coker."

They shook hands.

"Marine?" Staples asked.

"No, I was an Army grunt."

Staples nodded. "So what brings you around here, Coker?"

"Looking for work, I reckon."

Staples motioned with his chin toward the boats moored outside along the dock. "You can make pocket money working the boats as a deckhand. We use mostly high school kids during the summer, but J's always looking for people the rest of the year. You interested?"

"Doesn't sound bad," Billy said.

"Have you done any deck-hand work before?"

"Quite a bit out of Charlotte Harbor."

"Check back tomorrow. I'll ask him if he can use another hand."

26

EVERYONE'S WAR

Awaking to another world-class hangover, Billy shuffled back down to the bay the next morning. The sun cut his eyes like broken glass. Having passed out in the dunes behind a motel parking lot, he'd missed his midnight swim, but now, he was ready. Folding his shirt on top of his shoes, he left them sitting on his suitcase and again walked out to the end of the pier.

It was a brilliant blue day with a brisk breeze white-capping the water into a foamy spectacle of glittering sunlight. The seagulls dove into the flotsam at the mouth of the bay, and a catamaran skipped across the swells far out in the gulf. It reminded Billy of the day he was wounded. It was a brilliant, beautiful day, a good day to die. Problem this time was a kid sitting at the end of the pier, a little girl with a plastic bucket full of blue crabs.

The little pixie held a yellow rope attached to a crab net. She gazed steadily down into the blue green water swirling beneath the pier. Her flip-flops lay beside her along with a couple of bloody fish heads, no doubt bait for the crab net. She looked up at him from beneath a straw hat and smiled. Her freckled cheeks and dimples reminded him of Bonnie Jo. Mustering what he could of an acknowledgement, Billy nodded, but the little girl quickly turned her attention back to the crab net.

"Having any luck?" he asked.

She glanced at the pile of crabs in the bucket, then up at him. Raising her eyebrows, she smiled again, but this time it was as if to tell him he was a dumbass for asking. Kind of reminded him again of Bonnie Jo.

"Yeah, right," he said. "Stupid question."

"Oh, certainly not," she answered.

Mature beyond her years, hers were the articulate words of a child who'd probably been hanging around adults. Billy sat down beside her and dangled his feet over the end of the pier. Far out in the gulf, a huge gray ghost of a ship inched across the horizon, and he wondered if he could make it that far before going down. The little pixie eyed him carefully.

"Going for a swim?" she asked.

"I was thinking about it,"

She leaned back, bracing herself with one arm as she stared up at him.

"You look like a fuzzy bear. Are you a hippie?"

There was something about her that pierced his black mood with the tiniest pinhole of light. It shone in the darkness of his clouded mind on some phantom of thought deep within, one that reminded him of something good. He couldn't quite grasp what it was he felt, but he realized he was going to have to wait, again. Watching him swim out into the ocean and commit suicide wasn't something this little girl needed to experience.

"I never considered myself a hippie," Billy said. "I just have a beard and long hair."

He leaned through the rail of the pier and gazed down into the water. Schools of brightly colored fish, mostly yellow with black stripes, swirled in the crystal water around the barnacle encrusted pilings. The little girl continued leaning backward, studying him carefully.

"What happened to your back?" she asked.

She'd seen the deep purple scars, extending above the top of his britches. Billy reached back and pulled up his pants.

"I got wounded."

She stared in tightlipped silence for several seconds. "Did it hurt?"

"Yeah."

She nodded and stared at him with intense green eyes. "Were you in a war?"

"Yeah, in Vietnam, but I was lucky. A lot of my friends didn't come back from over there."

"I know," the little girl said.

Billy looked down at her as she adjusted her straw hat. She had deep green eyes like Bonnie Jo's, but there was a grim look on her face. It kind of reminded him of a Shirley Temple character acting like she really knew something about war and death. He gave her a patronizing smile. "You do, huh?"

"Yes. My daddy got killed in Vee-ette-naum."

She said the word very carefully, with a sense of awe and respect, and it caught him off guard. For the first time he saw a deep wisdom lurking there in those clear green eyes. She *did* know something about war, and even if she wasn't fully aware of its entire meaning, she was privy to one of its hardest lessons.

"He was a pilot in the Navy. His helicopter got shot down."

Billy reached down and softly patted her back, wanting to say something meaningful, but he was stunned by his own selfish stupidity. He hadn't considered this child as anything more than another spoiled kid out for day of fun in the sun.

"When did it happen, baby?"

"I'm not a baby. My name is Emily, and it happened when I was five."

She was clear-eyed and direct.

"How old are you, now, Emily?"

"I'm six, but my birthday is in October, and I'll be seven."

They sat in silence for a while watching the sparkling waves at the mouth of the bay. The little girl had reversed roles with him, and he suddenly wanted to help her, or at least make her understand that he truly felt her loss.

"Where's your mama, Emily?"

"She works over there at Captain J's."

She pointed back toward the docks, and it all came together. He had seen a woman there the evening before, working behind the bar. She'd been all business as she counted the day's receipts from the cash register. Billy knew now that it was because she was still grieving over the loss of her husband, who he also figured was the man in the photo, Lieutenant Commander John Staples.

"Do you want to see his picture?" the little girl asked.

Her intuition was spooky.

"Sure," Billy said.

Wordlessly, she stood and began retrieving the crab net hand-over-hand. A large blue crab was in the net.

"Here," he said. "Let me help you."

Billy tried to catch the crab from behind, but it latched onto his finger.

"Dammit," he said as he shook it loose.

"Not that way, dummy," the little girl said.

Carefully turning the net upside down over the pail, she shook it, and the crab landed amongst its comrades, clicking and rattling. After giving him the tightlipped look of a scolding teacher, she slid her feet into her flip-flops.

"You obviously have never crabbed before," she said.

Handing him the bucket, she took Billy's hand and led him down the pier. The door at Captain J's was propped open with a chair, and her mom greeted Billy with a stare of suspicion as they walked inside. Coming around the end of the bar, she eyed him carefully, while taking Emily by the hand.

"Hello," Billy said.

"Hi."

There was an unmasked chill in her voice.

"He's my friend," Emily said.

Billy gave Emily the bucket of crabs.

"Take those back to the kitchen," her mother said. "Then wait for me in Uncle J's office. I'll be back there in a minute."

The little girl smiled and rolled her fingers in a good-bye wave as she disappeared through a door behind the bar.

"What can I do for you?" the woman asked.

"I suppose you could get me a beer," Billy answered.

She uncapped a bottle, and set it up on the bar.

"That'll be a buck-fifty," she said.

Her voice sounded like it was made to grind rocks. Taking the money, she dropped it in the register and disappeared through the back door. A few minutes later she reappeared. Eyeing him carefully, she walked down to where Billy sat.

"You ready for another beer?" This time her voice was noticeably softer.

"Yeah, and bring me a tequila shooter too, please, with a slice of lemon."

She set another beer and a shot-glass on the bar. As she poured the tequila, she looked him up and down. "Emily tells me you were wounded in Vietnam. Is that true?"

Billy licked the salt, killed the shot of tequila and bit the lemon. "Yeah, it's true."

While he turned up the beer, she busied herself wiping the bar with a wet rag. Several seconds passed before she spoke again. "Strong, silent type, huh?"

"What's there to say?" he replied. "I got my ass sliced, diced and shredded by a rocket propelled grenade. That's about all there is to it."

"Were you a Marine?" she asked.

"No. Army, Hundred and First Airborne."

She continued wiping the bar, almost desperately it seemed, then re-aligning the bottles on the wall, anything it seemed, to stay busy. Or was it to stay close-by?

"Did she tell you about her daddy?"

"Yeah. Sorry."

"Me, too."

"Did she really know him?"

"Yes. We were stationed up at Pensacola for eighteen months before he shipped out. Emily still thinks her daddy hung the moon."

"I take it his wife feels the same way."

She didn't answer, but turned and walked to the far end of the bar, where she began wiping glasses. A few minutes later Tom Staples, the bartender from the night before, showed up. They talked quietly down near the cash register. Afterward, she disappeared through the back door. Staples walked over and set another beer on the bar in front of Billy.

"I talked with J, and he doesn't need any deckhands right now, but you can help around here some. It pays five bucks an hour plus tips, but the tips aren't all that good. Biggest crowd comes in when the boats get back in the afternoon. After that, most of the tourists cut a trail for the franchised joints up on the strip. Might need to comb your hair a little, maybe trim your beard, but you don't have to do much. You can tell by mine that J isn't real particular."

Something was happening that Billy couldn't explain, but he decided to help wait tables and bartend with Tom and Emily's mother, Liz. A few days later, they realized he was living in the dunes, and Tom came to him. He had been paying Billy by the day. Billy was sitting at a table drinking up his meager wages. Tom brought a beer and sat across from him.

"Billy, I have an offer for you, but it comes with some strings attached. You interested?"

He shrugged. "I don't know. What is it?"

"Look, I'm not trying to get into your business, but Liz and Emily like you a lot. Liz thinks you need a chance to—well, maybe to get your feet back on the ground. Anyway, we thought—"

"Tom, I don't want to sound unappreciative, but I'm not asking for anything."

"Why don't you hear me out?"

He reached into his shirt pocket and pulled out a pack of cigarettes. The pack was flat and bent, and he carefully fished out a couple of unfiltered Camels. Giving one to Billy, he flipped the top on his Zippo and struck a flame. Billy bent forward, the cigarette quivering in his lips as Tom lit it. The ceiling fan caused the flame to dance precariously close to Billy's beard.

Tom laughed. "Don't worry. I'm not going to torch you."

After lighting his own, he propped his elbows on the table and leaned forward. "Look, we need a night watchman of sorts. I was wondering if you'd be interested, but the straight and skinny of it is you're going to have to cut back on your drinking."

He glanced at the bottle of beer Billy was rolling between his thumb and fingers.

"We've got a spare two-room apartment in the back. It's not much, but it comes free with the job, and we'll pay you something. Not sure what we can afford, but we can talk about it."

The 'bullshit' alarms were going off in Billy's head. These people didn't know him from shit.

"How do you know I'm not going to pack up everything I can carry out of here some night and burn the place down behind me?"

Tom drew hard on his cigarette and looked out at the bay. "Because people who have been awarded the Distinguished Service Cross, the Silver Star, the Bronze

Star and a Purple Heart and the other medals you have don't do things like that."

Puzzled and pissed-off at the same moment, Billy was caught off guard as he stared across the table at Tom.

"I was in the Navy for twenty-five years," he said, "and I have more connections than a stockbroker. Yeah, I had you checked out."

"Look, Tom, I—"

"This isn't just about you, Billy. Yeah, you need a place to stay, but I think, maybe, if you talk with Liz some it might help her. You were over there, and I'm sure you must have worked with some of the chopper pilots. You saw it all. I just want you to consider the offer. Okay? The only string is the one about the drinking. You've got to cut back. What do you say?"

Billy nodded, and his bottle of Miller was still half full when he dropped the cigarette butt into it. "I reckon it beats the hell out of sleeping with the sand crabs. Got another cigarette?"

Billy trimmed his beard, and Liz used a razor to shape his hair into something that no longer resembled a zombie on a Tesla coil. They were gathered around a table one night after closing when Billy first talked about Vietnam. Tom claimed it was for Liz's benefit, but both seemed starved for the words that would explain John Staple's death, words that would perhaps fill the void, something that might heal the gut-sick feeling of loss their hearts held.

"You know," Billy said, "there's nothing like the thump of rotors when your ass is in a bind. Whether it was a dust-off, a gunship or just a re-supply chopper, those pilots never blinked, even when the shit got tight. And if our asses were on the line, they came down into the treetops with us. That took more guts than I ever had. They were some brave bastards."

Tom and Liz nodded as their eyes developed that inward focus, and Billy knew what they were thinking. "You know," he said, "I'm here today because of a chopper pilot. I'm not talking about the one that medevac'd me after I was wounded. It was before that. Our company was patrolling in the mountains west of Hue. We were in triple-canopy jungle on the side of a ridge when the NVA ambushed us from the opposite hillside. They had us pinned down. Thank God the choppers were on station, because the enemy was hosing us down good and we were steadily taking casualties. Our platoon leader was down, and I was layin' flat on my back with his RTO. We were both hugging a log the size of a pencil.

"I grabbed the radio handset and a chopper pilot comes on the net saying 'I'm on you,' and I'm wondering what the hell he means, but the trees started swirling and then, I know. He's right above us, and he cuts loose with his Vulcans.

"I'm yelling at my guys to fire back, you know, gain fire superiority? But then something hot hit me on the neck and chest and I thought that was it. I was hit and fixing to die. I panicked, jumped up and stumbled down the hill clawing at the burning sensation inside my flak jacket. My men saw me and thought we were gonna rush the enemy. They all jumped up and went charging down the hill and up the ridge at the NVA.

"Turns out it was just hot brass falling through the trees from the chopper's machine guns. A couple pieces landed on my neck and went inside my flak jacket. I was still dancing around, trying to get that hot shit out, while my guys overran the enemy. The CO said we saved the entire company that day. Said we were heroes. We all got Oak Leaf clusters with "V's" for valor on our Bronze Stars for that one. But that chopper pilot, he's the one who really saved our asses that day."

"Now, that's funny," Liz said.

She choked up and tried to smile, but bowed her head. Tom put his arm across her shoulders.

"I know what you're thinking," Billy said, "and you're right. John Staples was like that. I know, because I saw his Navy Cross back there in Tom's office."

Unlike the people at the bar in Memphis, Tom's interest wasn't focused on the war stories and the fighting, but more on the soldiers and Billy's friendships with people like Butch, Danny and the others. The more Billy talked about it, the less frequently it intruded into his conscious thoughts. The feeling of loss that had once flowed through his veins like the blood itself, began slowly and irrevocably becoming something more bearable.

Liz acted as if she loved and hated him at the same moment, and Billy understood. He had felt the same way with Bonnie Jo. Liz wanted something from him, but she didn't know what it was. That same feeling had eaten away at him when he was with Bonnie Jo. He wanted to embrace her, to hold her and to feel her love, but for some reason he couldn't. So, he pushed her away. He ran.

Billy wasn't sure what Liz could learn from their conversations, but Tom was certain it was making a difference. For once in his life, Billy hoped he was helping someone else, someone who truly needed him. And since he was no longer feeling particularly suicidal, there was plenty of time to wait and see.

Another quiet evening of good food, good drink and good company was coming to an end. The fishermen and most of the late evening crowd had come and gone. Tom and Jay had gone up to Tampa Bay to look at a boat, and Billy was left with Liz to close up that night. After fastening the shutters around the outside, he uncapped a Miller and sat on a barstool. No longer compelled to drink himself into a nightly stupor, Billy nevertheless enjoyed a few beers on occasion. On the other side of the bar, Liz was counting the night's receipts.

Looking up, she smiled. "We can't go on meeting like this, you know?"

Billy laughed. "Yeah, right."

Seemingly embarrassed by her own joke, she gave him a self-conscious smile and continued thumbing the bills into stacks by denomination.

"What's the matter, Liz?" he asked.

She stopped counting and looked up at him. "Nothing. What makes you think something's wrong?"

"You seem so serious all the time, like you're afraid to enjoy life."

Her eyes hardened. "I'm serious most of the time, Billy, because I have a kid to raise and no husband."

Liz liked to drink pineapple juice and rum. Billy walked behind the bar and poured her one with a dash of coconut crème. "Here," he said. "Drink this. It'll take the edge off."

"I'll take the drink, but I don't need to take the edge off of anything."

Her jaw was set, and she was trying her damnedest to play the hardass. Billy looked off to one side and sipped his beer. After a few minutes she finished counting, and looked up at him with a tight-lipped smile. "So, there. All done."

"How long are you going to run from it?"

Her smile turned to a tooth-grinding grimace. "I'm not running from a damned thing, and if you haven't had a person you loved get killed in that fucked up war, you need to mind your own business."

Billy tried his damnedest to give her a smile, but it didn't quite work.

"Well, hell," he said. "I reckon I *am* qualified, because I've had several of them killed in that fucked up war. You know all those guys I've mentioned whenever we talked about Vietnam? Well, they all got killed—every damned last one of them. Which one do you want me to tell you about? How about Doc Mazlosky? Now, there was an interesting guy. Bobby Mazlosky was our company medic, and the crazy sonofabitch saved so many men until we thought he was God's own first cousin. I mean, he never, and I *do* mean never, hesitated to go out and try to save somebody when they got hit. Bullets, artillery, nothing stopped him. After a while we didn't think anything could hurt him. At least until—"

Billy couldn't go on. He paused, sucking down a deep breath.

"Okay," Liz said. "I'm sorry. I mean—"

"Don't be sorry, Liz. Hear me out. You want to know how I ended up down here, working for beer money?" Billy didn't wait for her to answer. "Probably the same way you did—just one too many deaths. So if I ask you what's bothering you, or try to talk to you, don't get your panties in a wad and tell me I don't know what it's like. I damned well know. I know several times over what it's like to lose friends—friends that were closer to me than my own brother."

Liz walked around the bar to where he was sitting. Billy stared straight ahead as she came up behind him. Putting her arm across his back, she let her head fall against his shoulder and let out a sob.

"I'm sorry, Billy. I didn't mean to be that way."

He turned to face her. Tears streamed down her cheeks, and he pulled her close. He held her, wanting to shelter her from the terrible feelings that ruled her every thought. After a long while she raised her head and gave him one of those fabricated smiles that are more difficult to make than a house of cards.

"I better put the money in the safe and lock up for the night," she said.

"Sorry," Billy said. "I didn't mean to ruin your night."

Tightlipped, and with her eyes still red and moist, she nodded. He may have frightened her, but he was certain they had broken new ground.

"No apologies needed," she said. "I probably needed to hear that."

27

EMILY

Sitting in a ladder-back chair at a table on the veranda, Emily was stringing a seashell necklace one day when Tom asked Billy to go to the supermarket to pick up supplies. Liz had problems getting a sitter for Emily when school was out, and she occasionally let her hang around the docks or out at the pier. Emily overheard, and before he could leave, the sweet little thing was pitching a tantrum.

"I want to go to the grocery store with Billy," she wailed.

In desperation, Liz finally relented.

"I'll take care of her," Billy said.

Liz looked at him with the guarded eyes of a mother who didn't want to trust anyone.

"I promise," he said.

Liz gave him a little hug. "I know you will, Billy. Just watch her. She's a handful."

Billy buckled her into the seat, and they headed for Delchamps. Driving up the highway, he gazed out at the gulf beaches along the way. He wondered if Bonnie Jo had finally given up on him. Lost in his thoughts, he was surprised when Emily looked over at him and frowned.

"What was that about?" he asked.

"You know my mama is very sad about my daddy? That's why she didn't want me to go to the grocery with you. She did the same thing to Michael until he went away."

Billy glanced down at her. Perhaps, her little hissy fit wasn't so spontaneous after all.

"Who is Michael?" he asked.

"He was a man. He was a pilot like daddy, and he liked me and Mama a lot. He took care of us until Mama made him go away. I liked him, too."

Although Billy felt no attraction for Liz, they had grown close enough for him to feel her fear and distrust for life. It was probably that same inescapable depression that had caused her to push this man, Michael, away. She was lost the same way Billy had been since Vietnam.

"You've got to understand, Emily. Your mama is still missing your daddy a whole lot. It hasn't been two years, yet, and she needs more time."

Emily said nothing more as Billy pulled into the parking lot and got out, but he could tell she was mulling it over. She had a lot of awareness for a six-year-old, and actually seemed to think things through. Wearing her favorite chartreuse flip-flops and straw hat, she walked with him as he led her by the hand into the store.

They cruised the black and white checkered floors, up and down the aisles, until the grocery cart was nearly full. It was fun, letting Emily play the role of the proprietress shopping for her restaurant as Billy inquired about the different purchases—at least until they passed the magazine rack. Billy jerked the cart to a stop and stood dumbfounded. It was Bonnie Jo on the cover of the Rolling Stone.

Other than a passing TV news blurb, this was the first he'd seen, and it was too much to resist. Emily watched with studied curiosity as he snatched up the paper and read the headline. Billy glanced down at her, but she remained silent.

"Do you know who this is?" he asked, flipping the cover around to where she could see it. He didn't wait for her answer. "She's a friend of mine, and it says here she's sponsoring a big rock concert at the Astrodome in Houston."

According to the paper, Bonnie Jo was helping organize the Great Mid-Western Charity Rock Concert in Houston, Texas. There was a list of rock and roll greats, and she was at the top. It was a benefit for disabled veterans and billed as the greatest rock festival since Woodstock.

"That's BJ Parker," Emily said. "My mama has all her records."

"We used to be good friends," Billy said.

"Is she your girlfriend?" Emily asked.

"She used to be."

"Why aren't you her friend anymore?"

Emily had him fixed with another honest and open stare. Billy stared back at her, but there was no answer that seemed appropriate.

"We need to get these groceries back down to Captain J's." He began pushing the basket but paused again as he continued reading the story. Emily poked her finger at his side, but he pulled away.

"Just a minute, I want to finish this."

Bonnie Jo was the organizer, and she had gathered an impressive list of musicians and rock groups, all for the benefit of disabled veterans. When he finished reading the article, Billy looked down for Emily. She was gone. Probably wandered over to the next aisle, or wherever kids go when they run around in a grocery store. He pushed the grocery cart around to the next aisle. No Emily. Strange, but okay. Kids do this kind of thing he told himself. He quickly cruised across the front of the store, looking down the aisles as he went.

By the time Billy reached the other end of the store and looked down the produce aisle he was in a borderline panic—no Emily. Looking past neat rows of celery, piles of red bell peppers and bags of potatoes, he searched toward the back of the store. This was insane. She couldn't simply disappear. With his heart thumping in his ears, Billy left the cart behind and sprinted down the produce aisle, across the back of the store, then back to the front. She was nowhere in sight.

"Emily!" he shouted.

People all around stopped and stared. With his long hair and beard, he was sure they were frightened by his shout.

"I've lost a little girl," he said.

No one said anything as he sprinted across the front of the check-out lines to the front door. There he stood searching the parking lot. A black pickup with tinted windows cruised slowly past, and an old couple further out in the lot loaded their groceries into the trunk of a Cadillac.

"Sir?"

He wheeled about. "What!?"

A woman standing behind him in a green jacket drew back.

"I'm sorry," he said. "I can't find Emily."

"It's okay, sir. I'm the manager. We'll help you."

"She was standing beside me just a minute ago," he said.

"What does she look like?" the woman asked.

One of the cashiers called out. "Is this her?"

Billy ran her way and stretched to look over the counter. A little girl in jeans and a tube top looked up at him, startled.

"No, she's wearing a straw hat and green flip-flops. She's about—"

He saw her. Emily was sauntering up the frozen food aisle, running her finger through the condensation on the glass doors. Vaulting through the row of baskets in the checkout line, Billy ran down the aisle. Emily stopped and looked up, bug-eyed as he ran toward her. Sweeping her from her feet, Billy pulled her close.

"Where have you been?"

"Ouch. You're squishing me, Billy."

He unclamped his arms, letting her drop to waist level.

"Sorry," he said.

"What's wrong with you?" she asked. "Why do you look so scared?"

"You just disappeared."

She pursed her lips and gave him her usual heavy-browed look of disdain. "Billy, don't you know, ladies have things to do sometimes. I didn't want to tell everybody. Besides, you were reading."

"You were in the restroom?"

"Billy," she pleaded. "You're embarrassing me."

His heart began slowly dropping back into his chest. "Sorry. I didn't mean to embarrass you."

As Billy caught his breath, the adrenaline-driven fear subsided, and they walked back to the produce aisle to retrieve the grocery cart. This time, with Emily safely at his side, he pushed the groceries up to the checkout-line. At the cash register, Emily pulled his hand and pointed to a rack of tabloids. There were the usual "Woman Conceives Baby From Space Alien" headlines, but one paper was different.

"There she is again," Emily said. "But she doesn't look very happy in that picture."

The paper had a front-page photo of Bonnie Jo, and she looked like shit. Sunken-eyed and with matted hair, she had obviously gained weight. The headline read: ROCK STAR SUFFERS BREAKDOWN. Billy snatched it up and tossed it on the counter with the other newspaper and the groceries. He cast an embarrassed glance at the cashier, who had begun ringing up the groceries. He had freaked out in front of everyone when Emily disappeared, and right in the middle of it there was this strange life force again pushing Bonnie Jo back into the present.

As they walked out of the store, he pulled the paper from the grocery bag and looked again at the photo of Bonnie Jo. Her eyes, ringed with dark circles, appeared tired and sad. When he reached the car, Billy stopped again and began reading. Emily waited patiently. It couldn't be true.

The paper said Bonnie Jo had been hospitalized and cancelled several concerts. The article accredited it to 'an emotional breakdown' after she began using prescription drugs. The paper further explained how unnamed sources claimed she was longing for a mysterious lover. He quickly turned the page as the writer speculated on a number of celebrities and sports stars as well as a long lost high school sweetheart. That's when he saw the picture.

There he was, his senior photo from the high school yearbook, the one with the dorky crewcut and Mona Lisa smile. Beneath it was the caption: 'Have you seen this man?' Quickly closing the paper, he glanced down at Emily to see if she'd made the connection. With his long hair and beard she apparently hadn't. She looked up and smiled.

Billy remembered the day the photographer in Tupelo put him in the fancy black coat and clip-on bow tie, while he sat there in cut-off jeans and muddy running shoes. The irony of the illusion had always stuck with him. He often wondered who he was and who he could have been. Billy opened the car door and helped Emily inside. As she slid across the seat, he sat down beside her and opened the paper again. Rereading the article, he gleaned it for more information.

Despite the warm sunshine, he began trembling. There was no way it could be true. Bonnie Jo would never let drugs ruin her life, and she certainly wouldn't be waiting for him after all this time, but the paper said she went from the most eligible bachelorette in the country to a drug ridden recluse.

"What's the matter, Billy?" Emily asked. "Is BJ sad?"

"Yes."

"I know how she feels. She misses you, like I miss my daddy and Michael."

Billy looked down at her. How could this little gnome see so clearly into his deepest thoughts?

She fixed him with a steadfast glare. "You shouldn't make her feel that way, just because you're sad."

After pulling back out on the highway, he turned and looked at her. "I think you're right, Emily."

It would have been less painful had she answered, but talkative little Emily suddenly clammed up as they headed back to the pier. Billy stewed in his thoughts as he drove almost catatonically down the highway. He had been so self-centered that his fear of having a relationship with anyone had driven him to the brink of oblivion, but he had done the same thing to Bonnie Jo. He'd never truly considered what their relationship meant to her.

Back at the bar, he unloaded the groceries, and for a while he tried to carry on business as usual, but he couldn't concentrate. He couldn't count change, he couldn't do anything, except think about Bonnie Jo. Pulling the newspaper from his pocket, he read it again. Again he heard Emily's voice in the back of his mind, the innocent words of a child, but words so damned obvious when he looked beyond himself. It was the simple truth without all the complexities and entanglements adults weave into their lives.

The years had disappeared, to where, God only knew, and maybe all the crap in the paper about Bonnie Jo longing for a long-lost lover was just tabloid sensationalism. The claim of her drug-use seemed far-fetched as well. She was always the reluctant one, who he first encouraged to smoke pot. If drugs were about to destroy her, it was his fault. He had to do something, but he had to first know if it was true.

For several hours he paced back and forth, fighting the compulsion to act quickly. It would be stupid to run back to Bonnie Jo without first getting the facts from someone who knew her. He had to know the truth, but he needed to do something before it was too late. If she needed him, he intended to be there for her.

The hours passed, and the afternoon sun was peeking in under the veranda when Billy decided to talk with Liz. Together they had found a growing peace with their pasts. Liz was behind the bar. Emily was outside at one of the dockside tables, stringing more seashell necklaces, and Tom was busy somewhere in the back. When he could no longer stand it, Billy walked up to the bar and sat across from Liz.

She looked up. "What's up?"

"I want to talk with you for a minute or two while Emily is preoccupied."

Liz nodded, and gave him a flat smile. "I noticed you seemed upset when you got back this morning. She didn't throw another temper-tantrum at the store, did she?"

"No, as a matter of fact, she was very well behaved. We even had a long conversation, and that's what I want to talk about."

"Oh, and what did you two talk about?" She wiped a wet spot from the bar then gave Billy her undivided attention.

"A lot of things," Billy said. "She talked about her daddy, and a friend of yours named Michael. We also talked about a friend of mine."

Liz looked at him. Her face tightened as her brown eyes moistened. Billy felt her pain as much from his own perspective as he did hers. He paused, but to say nothing was to leave his debt to Liz and Tom unpaid.

"You know, sometimes kids see the true nature of things a lot better than us adults. I was telling Emily about an old friend I haven't seen in a long time, and she said some things that made me see matters in a totally different way. It's funny, but when she talked about her feelings concerning her father, and your friend Michael, and about you, it made me see my own problems from a different perspective, one that wasn't so much about me. She depends on the things she's learned from each of you to give her perspective on life. And I think she is still hoping for someone to come fill the void you both have from the loss of John."

Billy felt himself trembling inside and took a deep breath to calm himself.

"You see, I've had these same kinds of problems for a long time. I ran away at first. Then I pushed away the only person I truly cared about, and the more Emily talked, the more I saw my friend in her and I saw myself in you. Anyway, before I leave I want to thank you guys for all your help. I'd probably be dead by now if it weren't for you and Tom. You guys have given me a second chance to get it right."

"Where are you going?" she asked.

"I'm going back to where I came from to try to find a girl who means everything to me, and hopefully, make amends. Regardless, I'm in a better place, now, only because of you."

Billy slid off the barstool as Liz stared back at him in silence. He turned to walk away, but paused and looked back at her. "Have you ever sat down and really discussed with Emily your feelings about your husband's death and Michael, and asked her how she feels about it?"

Liz's eyes widened, looking confused and guarded at the same moment. She glanced at the door behind her as if Tom might suddenly appear and rescue her.

"Well, yes, plenty of times." Her voice carried the tremulous edge of someone fighting fiercely to hold down a welling emotion. "I mean, how much can you tell a six-year-old?"

"She may be a six-year-old, but she sees things very clearly."

Billy fearing he'd said too much, turned again to walk out.

"Wait," she said. Looking down, she fidgeted with the cloth she had used to clean the bar. "What did she tell you?"

"Nothing, really, and everything. They were simple things, but she made me realize how much you and I are alike. As a matter of fact, just working with you these last few months has taught me a lot about myself. We're both living in a vacuum of sorts, stuck in an emotional time warp where our feelings of loss rule our lives."

Billy shook his head. "I don't know, maybe, I've said too much, but I think you need to talk with her, maybe more like she's a little sister, I mean just this once. Look,

I've probably stuck my nose in where it doesn't belong, so let's leave it at that, okay?"

With that he went to his room and began packing his bags. It was time to go, and he couldn't wait a moment longer. Despite their pleas to stay the night, Billy said good-bye to Tom and Liz and caught the first bus to Memphis. He had wasted so many years, it now seemed he had to hurry. He had to save what pieces of his and Bonnie Jo's lives that remained salvageable.

28

SEARCHING FOR ANSWERS

In Vietnam it was difficult to differentiate the innocent villager from the guerrilla who wanted to nail your ass to a tree. And that was only one of the many things Billy had to learn when he first got there. There was the terrain, the weather and so much that was never mentioned in combat training. One jungle trail seemed no different from the next, but if the squad took the wrong one they walked into an ambush or a nest of booby-traps. It was only because of men like Danny and Butch that he had learned to survive.

The problem now was much the same. He needed to find some old friends who could advise him. He had to know if the tabloid article about Bonnie Jo was true. He had to know if she was really waiting for him. Jackie and Curtis would be the ones most likely to know.

Billy arrived in Memphis only to discover a stranger living in Jackie's old apartment. Jackie had moved away, and his number wasn't listed in the phone book. The bank would probably have the new address on Billy's account, but he decided to call Curtis first. After a couple of false leads, the information operator found Curtis Teague's number in Chicago, and he answered the phone.

"Man, Sarge, we thought you had gone off and died somewhere. Where the hell are you?"

"I'm back in Memphis. So, you're still with the Bears?"

"Yeah, married a little gal from down home, and got me a pretty baby girl. So, where have you been?"

"Down in Florida. How about I come up for a visit?"

"Heck yeah. When are you coming?"

"I can catch a bus out of here in the morning, and be up there sometime tomorrow."

They arranged to meet at a tavern down near the stadium the next evening. One of those old places without all the trendy crap, it had a huge mahogany bar with mirrors and oaken booths with high backs. It was relatively quiet as they ordered beer and hot sandwiches. Billy, not wanting to appear too much like a psycho, began talking about Florida and how he had worked the charter boats. He skipped the part about dressing the fish for tips, scrubbing decks and making minimum wage. Curtis was a linebacker for the vaunted Bears defense, anchored by none other than Raymond Hokes.

Curtis talked about his little girl and life in the wintry north, but after a couple beers Billy could wait no longer. "I need your help with something."

"What's that?"

"You know, I haven't seen Bonnie Jo for a long time, and, well, I was hoping you might have seen her or talked with her recently."

Curtis fixed Billy with a questioning stare.

"We had a rough time, and I walked out on her. It's been a long time."

Billy omitted the part about his impotence, but covered most everything else, including living in California and his reaction to her friends. He explained the psychological problems that had plagued him, and how he wanted to make amends, but wasn't sure how to proceed. When he finished, he sipped his beer and waited, but Curtis said nothing. There was only uncomfortable silence while Curtis continued eating his sandwich.

"Like I said, before I try to find her, I was hoping maybe you might have heard from her."

Curtis raised his brows. "So, exactly what is it you want to know, Sarge?"

"Have you talked with her? If so, what did she say?"

Curtis stared back at him with a blank expression, then shrugged. "She called me a time or two last year and the year before looking for you, but other than that, she didn't say much."

"Look, maybe I just need some advice," Billy said, "but first I'd like to know what she said."

A grin slowly spread across Curtis's face. "Damn Sarge, I can't believe *you* of all people are asking *me* for advice about a woman."

His sarcasm scraped Billy like a dull razor. "And asking you for help is something you think is funny?"

"No, no, it's not that. It's just that you were always the man. Everybody in the platoon thought you were Cool Hand Luke with the ladies. I just never figured you to have woman trouble. That's all."

A throbbing filled Billy's ears. "Sorry to tarnish my playboy image. But chasing whores in Vietnam has nothing to do with finding someone you love. Just forget it."

"Aw, hell, Sarge, don't go getting pissed off. Let me try to help." He paused, rolling his beer bottle between his palms. "Look, first of all, I don't think you're asking the right questions."

Billy was feeling like a bigger fool by the moment. "So what the hell do you think I should be asking?"

Curtis shrugged. "Well, you're asking me what this lady is thinking, except you got to understand, there really ain't no way of knowing. And even if you think you know, you can't apply logic to it, 'cause there ain't nobody really understands women and love. That's like understanding physics or religion, except those things are a whole lot easier."

Billy shook his head. "That's not the problem. I've known Bonnie Jo since high school."

"Hell, Sarge, that's my whole point. Regardless of what you think you know, you really don't know shit. What you're *really* saying is you don't know yourself."

"Huh?"

"Yeah. You've got to understand yourself first." Curtis grinned. "You know what I think?"

"What?"

"I think that shit we went through in Nam still has your head fucked-up. You're still thinking about that, instead of living."

"So, no shit, genius!" Billy's temper blew apart like a cheap watch in a fist fight. "Some people have to think about things like that, and I'm one of them. You should try it sometime."

Curtis stared back at him, his teeth clenched, jaw muscles flexing. Several seconds passed in silence as he picked up his beer and drank what was left. When he was done, he took a deep breath. "You know, Sarge, you aren't the only person who ever went through this. When I got back from Nam, I had it, too."

His eyes became ringed with moisture. "I didn't know anything, except I was thinking about puttin' a .45 to my head. You know, me and Reggie, we was tight before he got killed. I used to take so much of that boy's money playing knock rummy, hell I sent his mama a check when I got the job at the refinery and a letter explaining how we were friends. But I kept wondering what I could have done to keep boys like him, Doc and them others from dying. It got real bad before I almost gave up. That's when I sent another letter to a buddy of mine. This buddy, he came down to see me, and he talked me into getting off my ass and going out to do something. It wasn't easy, but if it hadn't been for him and my Uncle Sookey, I'd probably have ended up drinking myself to death or else blowing my brains out. At the least, I'd still be sitting on that porch down yonder in Terrebonne Parish wondering where the hell my life went."

Curtis's eyes reddened, and the ringing in Billy's ears grew louder. Curtis looked away.

"But, when I came down there to see you, you told me you'd never had it so good. I remember. You said the people around there treated vets right."

Curtis turned and looked Billy in the eyes. "I know what I said, Sarge, but knowing what you went though, maybe I didn't want to put my troubles on you, you know? Yeah, I went through it, too, and I learned one thing." Curtis paused and cleared his throat. His eyes had grown bloodshot. "Billy, you gotta stop thinking about the past, and quit trying to piece it all back together. I tried that, and it didn't work. God knows, there ain't no answers for the things that happened over there."

Somewhere outside a commuter train rumbled past, and the faint sounds of automobile traffic penetrated the walls. The bartender brought two more bottles of beer while they sat in silence. Curtis was right. Billy realized he had been trying to piece the past back together—a past so shattered it was impossible to reassemble. Every little decision in his life had become a monumental task, and he was totally paranoid of what the simplest choice might bring.

They talked into the wee hours of the morning as Curtis made him see there were no clear-cut answers and no way to right a thousand wrongs. He needed to go find Bonnie Jo, but first he needed to go find Jackie. He was the one person most likely to have heard from her. Hopefully, Jackie could help him.

When he got back to Memphis, Billy went to the bank to find his disability checks were still being deposited each month. The only difference was Jackie's new address and phone number. He dialed the number, and a woman answered. She called Jackie to the phone, but he wasn't very talkative. He gave Billy directions, and said it was okay to come by.

Billy paid the cabby and walked up the drive to the front door of Jackie's house that Saturday afternoon. He rang the doorbell and gazed about. The houses all looked similar, and the yards were neat and trimmed. He admired the serenity of suburbia the way one admires a great-aunt's floral-print dress. Suburbs were perhaps good for Jackie, but Billy found a certain discomfort with the entire arrangement. The door swung open, and he found himself staring at Margaret Riker. His chin must have bounced off his chest a couple of times, but Riker ignored it.

"It's good to see you again, Billy."

"Yeah," he said. "It's, uuhh, good to see you, too."

Riker showed him inside, but he must have looked like he'd seen a ghost, because she stopped and looked back at him. "You okay?"

"Yeah, I guess so."

"He's in there watching the ballgame."

Billy glanced back at her as they walked through the foyer. *Surely not*, he thought.

"You really look good," she said.

Since his return to Memphis, Billy had shaved and gotten a haircut, even bought some new jeans.

"Yeah," he said. "You, uh, look good, too."

"Through that door there. And you two try to behave."

He flashed back to the days when he knew her as Nurse Riker, the domineering ward nurse from hell. She left the door ajar and disappeared. Jackie sat in his easy chair, but he didn't look up as he greeted him. "Billy-Boy, how are you?" Despite the greeting, his eyes remained riveted on the TV. "I heard you out there trying to flirt with Peggy. Pull up a chair, and make yourself comfortable."

Jackie finally glanced over at him, while Billy stared back at the doorway where he'd last seen Riker. "Yeah, me and Riker got hitched a couple years back."

He handed Billy a can of beer, but seemed nonplussed by his arrival. A big Braves fan, Jackie didn't even look up—Atlanta was at bat in the bottom of the ninth. Trailing by two runs, they had the bases loaded with their best batter coming to the plate. Billy pulled a chair up beside him.

"How much is riding on the game?" he asked.

"If they pull it out, it'll put them in first place. Why?"

"Just wondering."

Jackie glanced at him, then turned off the TV. "Okay. So what's going on?"

"Nothing. You didn't have to turn the game off."

"I laid up there in that damned hospital with you for over six months. I can tell when something's wrong. Besides, you finally drop out of the sky after all this time, so I guess I'll try to act interested. What happened?"

"Nothing happened," Billy said. "I just came by to shoot the breeze."

"Yeah, right. Do I look stupid or what?"

Billy pulled the two newspaper articles from his pocket and tossed them on Jackie's lap. After a quick glance, Jackie handed them back.

"Old news," he said. "I've already seen them both."

Billy held the articles in his hand, not quite sure what to say next.

"What's the matter?"

"Well, what do you think about them?"

"What do you mean?"

"I guess I want to know if that stuff about Bonnie Jo using drugs is true."

Jackie stared at the blank TV screen.

"Look, I'm sorry I didn't call or come around. It's been a bad time for me, but I'm not going to cry on your shoulder. I came here to see if you've talked to Bonnie Jo recently, because I want to go see her."

Jackie turned to gaze out the window. "Peggy and Bonnie Jo have stayed in touch the last few years. Matter of fact, they've become pretty good friends. At first she told Peggy how she was ready to wait for you, no matter how long it took, which by the way, I thought was a really stupid idea. I'd've written your ass off a long time ago, but you know how women are. They still believe in Santa Clause and the Easter Bunny.

"Anyway, Peggy and I have been helping Bonnie Jo for the last year with the VA connections for that benefit concert down in Texas. Bonnie Jo said you were the one who made her see she needed to do it, but then you fell off the face of the earth. She wanted to do it to make you happy, and she waited a long time for you to come back, but she decided to go ahead with it this year. I guess she figured she'd waited long enough.

"We're helping her with some of the details involving the VA. Matter of fact, we're taking a group from the hospital and flying them down to Houston next week for the show. Bonnie Jo is paying for it all. She sent us VIP passes, and we're going out with her after the concert."

For a moment Billy felt the isolation of knowing that life had gone on without him, much as it had while he was away in Nam.

"And I wish I could tell you that newspaper article wasn't true, but I can't. I mean, it's partially true. She's been worried sick over you for years. She held out for a long time, hoping you'd come back, but I think she started giving up. She began having trouble sleeping and took some prescription medicine, and later it got a little out of hand. Seems, *someone* also got her started smoking pot. She's started putting on a little weight."

Jackie shot him a sideways glance.

"Peggy and I talked with her, and she didn't want to admit it at first, but I think we got through to her. She's been doing better, but she's not out of the woods yet. We still haven't been able to get her to date other guys. The one big plus is that she's still one of the hottest things going in the music business, if she doesn't kill herself with the drugs."

Billy turned up his beer and drank, long and hard.

"What the hell is your hang-up, Billy?"

"All I know, now, is I want to see her."

Jackie slowly shook his head. "Is that it, you just want to see her? I thought you told me a long time ago that you loved her"

"I do, and I want to see if she will still have me."

Jackie paused and searched Billy's eyes. After a few moments, he nodded. "I guarantee you she will, if you stop acting like a flake and running away."

"I'm done running, but we've got some things to work out between us."

"What kind of things?"

"Let me ask you a question, first," Billy said. "I never imagined you and Riker would, you know, get interested in one another. How did you—?"

"It was the time he took you up to Washington DC, Billy." Riker was standing in the doorway behind him. "I realized then that Jackie had something a lot of people don't have. Not that it wasn't a *really* stupid thing to do. You two never were the brightest bulbs on the string, but it was a very unselfish thing, and he told me how he was sure it would help you, and how he carried you into that bus station restroom, and how it scared him when he thought you were going to die."

Red-faced, Jackie turned to look out the window. Riker walked into the room and sat in his lap, hugging his neck. She was definitely not the same straight-razor-toting-bitch he'd known back at the VA. Always bordering on petite, she now looked entirely different without starched whites and a clipboard. Her hair was down, and she was wearing faded jeans with a royal blue Memphis State sweatshirt. She was actually quite attractive.

"That's it?" he asked. "That's how you decided you loved him?"

Riker laughed. "No, Billy. That was just the start, but let me ask you something. I heard the TV go off a couple of minutes ago. For Jackie Harmon to do that with the bases loaded in the bottom of the ninth, you guys must have been discussing a life and death matter. Right?"

Jackie laughed, "Everything with Coker is life and death."

He reached to turn on the television.

"Don't even think about it, Harmon," Riker said. "I'll break your arm."

She made a playful karate chop at his forearm, then bent forward and kissed him on the cheek.

"He did that because he loves and respects you. That's what I find special about him. He cares about other people."

Jackie rolled his eyes.

"Stop," Peggy said.

She turned to Billy. "I think you and Bonnie Jo can share that same kind of love. You were made for one another, but you've been afraid to live again."

Billy stood in dumbfounded silence.

"That girl has waited for you all these years. She needs you."

Billy went back to his hotel room that afternoon, and for the first time in years he didn't drink so much as a beer. He spent a restless night walking the floor, staring at the clock and wondering what ghosts from his past remained. He also wondered if Jackie and Peggy were right about Bonnie Jo taking him back.

The next morning, he returned, and the three of them sat at the kitchen table near a big picture window, sipping coffee. Outside, the morning sun sparkled on the dew covered grass, as a squirrel ran along the top of the back yard fence. Peggy poured him a second cup.

"Look, Billy, if you're afraid to tell her how you feel—"

"I'm not afraid," Billy said, worn out with their efforts to develop a plan for his reunion with Bonnie Jo. "It's just that I want to make sure I..."

Billy shook his head and stopped again. He *was* afraid. He was afraid of screwing it all up again. He was afraid the impotence thing would happen again. He was afraid the war would again rise up and steal his soul as it had for the last several years.

The "Nurse-Riker-look" came over Peggy's face, and Billy could see why Jackie had let her carry the conversation. "You just want to make sure of what, Billy? You say you aren't afraid to talk to her, to tell her that you love her, right?"

Billy shrugged.

"Just answer my question. Can you look Bonnie Jo in the eyes and tell her you love her?"

"Of course I can."

She slapped the table with her hand. "Then tell me when and where you want to do it!" she shouted. "I've suggested everything I can think of, but you—" She stopped, took a deep breath then gazed out the window. After a few moments she turned back to Billy.

"Sorry," she said. "I didn't mean to lose it. Look, I've got an idea. What if I set up a meeting between you two, one where she won't know it's you until you show up? It won't exactly be a surprise, because she'll know she's meeting with someone important. If I can pull it off, are you willing to follow through, to tell her that you love her?"

"Just like that?" he said. "You arrange a meeting, and I'm supposed to walk in and tell her I love her?"

She nodded. "I've got a great idea how to make it work. Trust me on this, big boy. I got you through the VA, didn't I?"

It seemed overly simplified, but Billy nodded anyway.

"That's right," she said. "Now, I want you to make plans to go with us to Houston. We've got a charter flight with a couple seats still available. Can you do that?"

Billy imagined seeing Bonnie Jo again. He wanted so much to see her, but there remained the impotence problem. What if they reconciled, and…

"Helloooo, Earth calling, Billy. Are you still with me?"

She snapped her fingers in front of his face.

"Yeah, yeah, whatever you say, Rike—I mean, Peg."

"We leave Saturday morning," she said. "I'll get you on the charter. Just have your bags packed."

Peggy smiled, and for the first time Billy saw the real woman behind the no-nonsense nurse, one with a heart as big as Bonnie Jo's.

29

ANOTHER MOUNTAIN

The Astrodome dominated the horizon, its white hulk rising from the Houston landscape, gleaming in the afternoon sunshine. Billy rode in the lead van with Jackie and Peggy, as a special police escort cleared the way for the caravan of vehicles carrying the disabled vets from the airport. They were getting VIP treatment, including blaring sirens and cops saluting at every major intersection. When the motorcade finally rolled to a stop, the motorcycle policemen dismounted and stood at rigid attention. Billy's stomach crawled as he stepped from the van. He had reached the base of another mountain.

While they helped the vets from the vans, Billy stood staring up at the building called the 'Eighth Wonder of the World'. The flags along the walkway popped in the Texas breeze as the shear immensity of the structure held him mesmerized. His senses were suddenly razor keen with the same adrenaline rush he had so often experienced in Nam. It was because somewhere inside was Bonnie Jo, and at that moment, Hill 918, with all its fog-shrouded mystique, could not have been more intimidating.

"It's time to lock and load," Jackie said.

Managing a feeble smile, Billy followed the line of wheelchairs down the walkway. It was intermission as they were ushered through a special entrance. The first acts in this huge charity concert had begun at noon, and the VIP seats on the main floor were full by the time the disabled vets were rolled in.

"Let's go up there," Jackie said, pointing to a second-tier balcony.

As the evening show began the ushers seemed unconcerned with the haze of smoke swirling high above the over-flow crowd. Tiers of gigantic black speakers on scaffolding pulsed with a beat that vibrated in his chest as Billy climbed the stairs to the next level. He heard an usher say this crowd was bigger than any concert crowd they'd ever had.

Making their way to a railed balcony, Billy, Jackie and Peggy found standing room with a clear view. Below, the musicians on stage were silhouetted by backlights in the darkened stadium as they played a steadily increasing beat of drums and electric guitars. When the crescendo reached its peak a shower of swirling lights splashed across the stage, and a deep voice thundered from the speakers, "Ladies and gentleman, please welcome, BJ Parker!"

And then she was there, skipping across the stage, Billy's love and his nemesis, Bonnie Jo, still a knockout with her flowing strawberry-blond hair. She wore faded jeans and a sequined red, white and blue blouse, and perhaps it would have made a difference to the old Billy, but it didn't now—she had regained some of the old form from her high school days. It didn't matter to the fans, either. With her blouse glittering beneath the lights, Bonnie Jo twirled and joined the music with her voice. The crowd roared.

After a few minutes her first song ended, and she was breathless as she spoke. "Thank you. Thank you. It's great to see you all here tonight."

All across the stadium, another huge roar swelled from the crowd.

"I want to express my thanks for the support you've shown for this event, and to the musicians and production people for their time and efforts. We appreciate all of you. As you know, this is a charity benefit for disabled veterans—"

Somewhere in the cavernous stadium someone let out a "boo," but Bonnie Jo didn't miss a beat.

"And I know we all have mixed feelings about the issues that surround the war in Vietnam, but this is not about the war. This is not about politics. This is about young men who did what they believed was their duty.

This is about men who were wounded in action, young men who, regardless of their politics, felt compelled to do what was required of them by their country. We have come together to thank them for their service and their sacrifice, and we're going to have a good time doing it. So let's hear it for our vets."

Bonnie Jo promised to return, and there came another thunderous roar of applause as she introduced the next group. Their electric guitars blasted out the first chords, and Peggy nudged Billy. He looked down at her. It had been several days since they last discussed their plan.

Now, as she looked up at him, Billy realized Peggy was talking, but the music was so loud her lips moved soundlessly. He bent closer and strained to hear, but there was nothing, except the thunder of rock music.

"Try again," he shouted.

She pressed her mouth against his ear. "Have you thought about what you're going to say to her?" she shouted.

"Yes," Billy replied.

"And?"

He hesitated as the music pounded in his temples. Peggy grabbed his hand. "Let's go out to the concourse," she shouted.

This was it. Peggy was taking him to Bonnie Jo. Jackie started to follow, but Peggy turned and waved him off. He looked at Billy with a big grin and gave him a thumbs-up. Billy figured he was about to get another

Nurse Riker lecture on the way, probably something about not acting a fool or hurting Bonnie Jo's feelings. As they walked out onto the concourse, the reduction in decibels came as a relief.

"So how is he going to find us after the show?" Billy asked.

"I told him if we got separated, to meet us back-stage."

They walked casually down the long corridor, but Peggy remained silent for several minutes. Vendors hawked T-shirts and programs, while an army of security guards prowled the concourse. Billy stopped and bought a couple of Cokes, and they continued their walk. After an eternity Peggy broke her silence.

"So, are you ready?"

"I guess so," he replied.

There was the slightest twitch at the corner of her mouth as she stared down the concourse. It was apparently the wrong answer.

"'I *guess* so' doesn't quite show the enthusiasm I hoped for." Her words had the metered cadence of a ward nurse. "I'm concerned you're making this more difficult than it has to be."

Billy laughed. "Don't pull your Nurse-Riker act on me, Peg."

Her head snapped around as she glared at him.

He smiled. "That shit doesn't work anymore. I found out you have a heart."

Billy winked, and Peggy's face softened, giving way to a smile.

"Okay," she said. "But you and Jackie made me be this way. Without my bluff, you two would have owned that hospital."

Billy put his arm around her shoulders and gave her a hug. "Sorry I gave you such a hard time."

"That's okay. I accept your apology, but right now time is running out. You've got to make up your mind. I'm going to put you in front of her, and at the right moment, you have to say the right words. You ready?"

"That's the whole reason I came here."

"Okay. You're ready?"

Billy laughed. "What do I need to say to convince you?"

She smiled, "It's just knowing your past, I think I have good reason to be worried. Don't you?"

"Okay. Sure. Given my past, you probably do, but the way I see it, this is my last chance."

"You can do it, Billy."

He heard his own words to Curtis Teague, and looked down at Peggy. Her encouragement was genuine. He only hoped he could do this thing without some psycho event occurring. After all, the realities of the past few years weren't that far gone.

"So, are we going to meet her now?"

"Not right now," Peggy said.

"Does Bonnie Jo have a clue I'm here?"

"No, but leave it to me. She will. I have a plan, and when the time is right, I'll tell you. I just want you to be ready, to tell her that you love her."

"I hate surprises," Billy said.

Peggy stopped and turned to face him with her fist on her hip. "Look, Mister, you don't have a choice. When I tell you to do it, you tell her you're here for her and that you love her. Got it?"

"Got it," he said with a salute.

Continuing their walk, they circled the building. More than anything, he wanted to make Bonnie Jo understand he was a changed man. His mind wandered, and they ambled down the long concourse until Peggy suddenly glanced at her watch.

"Oh, my gosh! It's almost time for Bonnie Jo to come on again. We have to hurry."

As they ran up the concourse, Peggy talked breathlessly. "Okay, Bonnie Jo told me about her plans for this next set. After several songs, she's going to talk briefly about one song in particular, and you've got to follow my lead. No hesitation. Are you with me?"

"Sure," he said.

Rushing back down the aisle, they spotted Jackie still standing near the rail. The smoky beams of the floodlights slashed across the huge stadium, punctuated by flashing strobes near the stage. Billy looked out over the spectacle below. This was the stratosphere, and he could barely make out the expression on Bonnie Jo's face as she skipped back onto the stage, but she was smiling, and the crowd rocked with her through the next several songs.

She had been on stage for nearly twenty minutes when she announced a change of pace.

"Now, I want to slow it down a bit," she said, breathing heavily.

The stage lights dimmed, and the band began playing a soft prelude to her next song, something vaguely familiar. Billy recognized it as the crowd applauded anew. It was the one Bonnie Jo had hummed for him that Sunday afternoon, so long ago, while they were sitting on the bus bench outside the VA, the one she had written for him before leaving for California. He felt a lump in his throat. She had never forgotten.

Peggy nudged him. "You ready?"

The lump disappeared as he stared back at Peggy. "What?"

Bonnie Jo continued talking on stage as she related her visits to the Veterans Hospital in Memphis and how she had helped a friend with physical therapy while he recovered from his wounds.

"Are you ready to tell her that you love her?"

"Now?"

"When I tell you, I want you to shout it as loud as you can," Peggy said.

"You mean, I'm supposed to yell it out from up here?"

Billy had envisioned tearful hugs, perhaps even a surprise entry into her dressing room, but nothing like this.

"Sure," Peggy said. "She's going to dedicate this next song to you, so be ready."

Billy turned and looked back at Bonnie Jo standing on the stage. The crowd was spellbound in silence as the band played softly. It seemed a half-mile separated them, as Bonnie Jo stood, a solitary figure in the beam of a spotlight. It was the Bonnie Jo he had watched that night at the Raeford High talent show, the one who had treasured his words of encouragement.

"This was my first big hit," she said, "and I want to dedicate it to my friend, Billy, a Vietnam veteran. It's called *Islands in the Sky*. This is for you, Billy-boy, wherever you are tonight."

Peggy nudged Billy. "Now," she hissed. "Yell it. Tell her you're here and you love her."

Billy hesitated.

"Now!" she said again.

The crowd remained as silent as a church at midnight, and Bonnie Jo was swaying gently with the music as Billy leaned on the rail and cupped his hands around his mouth.

"I'm right here, Bonnie Jo, and I love you!"

People turned to look his way. Billy stepped back from the rail, feeling stupid and embarrassed. Down on the stage, Bonnie Jo stopped swaying and cupped her hand above her eyes. Squinting, almost desperately it seemed, she tried to peer past the stage lights into the darkened stadium. A hesitant smile crossed her face, and she missed her first cue. The band stopped playing, and an unsettling silence hung over the huge stadium.

"Billy?" she said into the microphone.

Her voice, soft and quavering, echoed through the speakers, as a barrage of imitators began shouting "I love you, Bonnie Jo," drowning out the possibility of him saying anything more. The band began playing, again.

"We better make our way down there," Jackie said. "I think Bonnie Jo is going to be looking for you when she leaves the stage."

Bonnie Jo began singing *Islands in the Sky* as the three of them walked up the aisle to the exit. When they reached the outer concourse, Peggy grabbed Billy by the collar. Pulling him down, she kissed his cheek.

"I knew you could do it," she said. "Now, let's go down there and get that girl."

With that they began making their way through the crowd. Even with their VIP passes, Peg was forced to use her Riker-act again to get past the security guard. By the time she finished with him, the wide-eyed guard was apologizing profusely.

"It's okay, bud," Billy said as he passed. "She has that effect on men."

They made their way into a corridor leading to the dressing rooms. Hurrying through a crowd of technicians and performers, Peggy led the way as she caught up with another guy in a gray suit.

"Where's BJ?" she asked.

"Her dressing room is right over there." He pointed at a door.

Looking at Billy, she nodded toward door. "Be my guest. We'll wait here."

Billy walked over and knocked lightly at the door. Nothing happened. He knocked again, but another guy in a suit walked up, a bouncer-type the size of a truck.

His voice boomed like the Wizard's at the Emerald Palace. "Can I help you?"

"I'm looking for Bonnie Jo," Billy said.

"For who?"

"Bonnie….uh, BJ, BJ Parker."

"And who are you?"

Billy began feeling like the cowardly lion, as this hulk of a man confronted him.

"A friend," he said.

"Well, *friend*, she's not in there right now. What do you want with her?"

This guy was as big as Raymond Hokes, and Billy flashed back to that day when Ray pinned him to the restroom wall, but Peggy was suddenly there beside him. She had her hands on her hips and that "Margaret Riker" look in her eyes.

"Miss Parker is expecting him," she said. "We need to know where she is. Now, either help us or get the hell out of our way."

Nearly two feet taller, he towered over her, but there was that special something about Peggy. She could stop a charging Rottweiler dead in its tracks, making it turn tail and run. Peggy stood her ground, and the man took a step back.

"Miss Parker is out there," he said, pointing down the walkway. "She's standing below the left side of the stage."

They took off, and when Billy rounded the corner she was there in the shadows with her back to him. Gazing out at the crowd from the darkened alcove, Bonnie Jo was searching for him, he was certain of it. Peggy stopped and pulled Jackie back. Billy continued walking. He eased up behind her. Bonnie Jo's perfume filled his senses, and he stood close for several long seconds before whispering in her ear.

"I'm back here."

Bonnie Jo spun around. Her eyes were filled with tears, anger and innocence all at once, and her lip quivered. Billy bowed his head in shame, but she reached out for him.

"Oh, Billy—Billy. I—I've been so worried. I..."

Her voice was husky with emotion. Billy stepped forward and gently thumbed a teardrop from her cheek, but more tears overflowed onto her cheeks and she stifled a sob. He pulled her close, and their lips met. After a moment she pushed him back at arm's length. Her jaw was set, and her eyes glared wide with anger.

"Billy, I can't go through any more of this. If you don't mean to stay, stop now." Her voice quivered with every word. "I can't. I just can't. I've waited and waited for you, and I can't—" She broke into sobs.

"I was hoping we could go somewhere after the show," he said, "and talk about spending the rest of our lives together."

He pulled her close, and she looked up at him. "You've got to promise me no matter what happens, you'll never leave again."

"Bonnie Jo, I've been pretty screwed up all these years, and I've put you through hell, but I want to spend the rest of my life with you."

She drew another trembling breath. "We can make it work. I know we can."

Billy held her close, and Bonnie Jo didn't look up as she spoke. "Oh, Billy. You were right about the people I called friends back in LA, and look at me, now. I've gotten fat again, are you sure?"

"I fell in love with you back in high school, so why would you think I have any doubts now?"

She looked up at him. "You loved me when we were in high school?"

"It took me a long time to realize it, but it was you that got me through Vietnam."

Their lips met again as they embraced, holding one another tightly until Billy became aware of someone standing behind him. It was Jackie and Peggy. Jackie put his arm around Billy's neck, and Peggy gave Bonnie Jo a hug.

"Can you do your closing set?" Peggy asked.

She dabbed at Bonnie Jo's face with a handkerchief.

"I don't know, but I've got to try," Bonnie Jo said. She sucked down another quivering breath then clutched him again. "Oh, Billy, I love you. I love you. I love you."

"Go on back out there," he said. "I'll be waiting here for you."

Bonnie Jo turned to Peggy. "Don't let him out of your sight until I get back, okay?"

"You've got it," Peggy answered.

30

MY ONE TRUE LOVE

That night after the concert they talked into the early morning hours. Billy and Bonnie Jo decided to move slowly as they brought their lives back together. Bonnie Jo had a few weeks off, and Billy suggested they take a trip together, a vacation of sorts. She wanted to see where he had been for the last several years, so they flew down to Tampa and rented a car.

Making their way down the coast, they ended up sitting on the veranda at Captain J's, watching the fishing boats come into dock. It was late afternoon, and while the charter boat crews hung their fish and photographed the fishermen with their catches, Bonnie Jo and Billy talked about the past. Cameras flashed and the fishermen smiled as they held their fishing rods in front of their catches of red snapper, amber jack and grouper.

Billy and Bonnie Joe talked randomly about the years they'd been apart, sharing mostly stories about the good times. The conversation went well until she surprised him with news of the upcoming class reunion at Raeford High. She seemed almost excited about a special invitation she'd received.

"I don't understand," Billy said. "Why in hell are they having a class reunion after only five years?"

"My understanding is that Raeford is starting a new annual Blackberry Festival, and some of the cheerleaders and football players thought it would be a convenient time to have one."

"Are you seriously thinking about going?"

Tilting her head to one side, she gave him a quizzical look. "Of course I am. Why wouldn't I?"

"You actually want to see that bunch of jackals again?"

She grinned, closing her eyes for a moment as she understood his point.

"You're way too cynical, Billy. Sure, some of them were mean, but there were some really nice people, too. Besides, that was a long time ago. Don't you want to see them?"

"Not really."

She paused, then shook her head. "You're not getting off that easy. I need a date, so you're going."

He laughed. "A date for a class reunion?"

Her eyes suddenly grew cold as Arctic ice. "Okay. What do you want me to say—that maybe I really *don't* want to go back either?"

"Sorry," Billy said. "I didn't mean to piss you off."

He flagged the bartender. "Two more shots of tequila and some more lemons, please. Oh, and if you don't mind, a dozen more oysters."

"Look, Billy, I'm going. Just say you'll go with me, please?"

"Okay, okay. I'll go with you. Are you happy?"

She wrapped her arms around his neck. "As long as I have you, Billy Boy, I'll always be happy."

"So, be happy," he said. "And when we get there I'll act happy too."

Across the bay the sun was sinking behind the sand dunes as the last of the fishing boats cleared the jetties, returning to port.

The bartender set four shots of tequila in front of them, and Billy glanced at his watch.

"I thought happy hour was over," he said.

"The extra shots are on the house," he answered. "I finally figured out who this lady is. You're BJ Parker, aren't you?"

She smiled and nodded. Looking across at Billy, Bonnie Jo raised her eyebrows as if to ask if he was going to reveal himself. Since he'd been there last, his hair had been cut close and his beard was gone. He was also wearing dark sunglasses and a baseball cap. Tom Staples was so focused on Bonnie Jo he still hadn't recognized Billy.

"Problem is," Tom said, "you seem familiar, too. Do I know you?"

Tom stared intently as Billy obligingly removed his cap and sunglasses.

"Billy?" he said.

Bonnie Jo autographed a coaster for him as Tom and Billy hashed over the latest news.

"Where's Liz hanging out these days?" Billy asked.

"Man, it was the damnedest thing ever, but the next night after you left, she went to the phone and called this old friend of hers. He was a pilot who had a big crush on her, kind of looked after her and Emily for a long time after Johnny got killed. They split up, but like I said, she called him, packed up the following Monday and moved up to Pensacola. He's an instructor up there, and they're engaged to be married."

"Next time you hear from her," Billy said, "give her my regards, Emily, too."

"I sure will. They'll be tickled to hear from you. You know they think the world of you? Tom paused, pressing his lips together. "I suppose we all do."

Luckily, no one overheard them, and except for the murmur of low conversations the bar remained quiet. Beyond the moored fishing boats a couple of gulls winged their way across the bay toward their evening roost. Tom went to the back to help the cook fill orders.

"If we go to the reunion," Billy said, "I don't want to say something stupid, something that might embarrass you. You know?"

"Like what?"

"I don't know. I'm just afraid they'll ask personal questions about us."

"You can't worry about things like that."

Bonnie Jo sipped from her shot-glass. Billy downed his.

"Do you remember the nick-name Barbara Barnes called me?" he asked.

"I remember she called you 'Weird Billy' once."

"Yeah, that was it. Do you know why?"

Bonnie Jo shook her head.

"She said it was because I hung around with geeks and freaks."

Bonnie Jo picked up a shot glass and handed another to Billy. "Well, here's a toast to us geeks and freaks, Billy Boy. We're going back to Raeford and show them they're forgiven, aren't we? We're going to have a great time, right?"

Billy nodded as they clinked glasses then killed the shots of tequila. Bonnie Jo set her glass aside and grabbed him behind the neck, knocking his cap askew as she kissed him passionately.

"You know, I've always heard oysters have that effect on women."

It was Tom, who had returned with the second order of oysters. Billy shrugged and Bonnie Jo simply smiled. When Tom was gone, they sat in silence for a long while. That was one of the things Billy liked most about Bonnie Jo. She never seemed prone to fill voids of silence with mindless blather. Looking across the table he saw the highlights of the evening sun glowing in her eyes, and after a while it sank below the horizon, leaving a deep purple sky and an intense orange afterglow burning just above the water.

As the day faded, the first cool breeze of evening wafted across the pier. The boats along the docks became black silhouettes, stark and lonely, as if life had passed from them. They were monuments to a sunny day now gone, and Billy thought about Butch, Danny and the others. Their memories would always be there, but for the first time in years he realized they didn't prevent him from seeing the future.

Billy looked into Bonnie Jo's eyes, and he wanted to take her by the hand and return to the hotel at that very moment, but she had said she wanted to move slowly. This was only their second night together. Perhaps it was for the best, but his body was on fire. Then looking into her eyes, he thought he saw something there as well, the same burning desire to fulfill the physical ache that had been denied so many times before. He wondered if he was reading her correctly.

Later that evening when they returned to the hotel room, Billy tossed the keys on the nightstand and turned on the TV. He had taken advantage of her one time. It was up to Bonnie Jo this time. She fell back on one of the two queen beds in the room and smiled. "Those shooters made me a little tipsy."

Billy sat on the other queen bed. "Do you need to get some fresh air? We can take a blanket and go for a walk on the beach."

Bonnie Jo sat up quickly and grabbed the extra blanket from the bed. "Let's go."

Leaving their shoes behind, they walked far out beyond the lights, down the beach to where the tourists seldom ventured. The night surf thundered as it brought in the evening tide, and they wandered back into the dunes. A trillion stars shone overhead, and a warm breeze stirred the sea oats.

Finding a secluded spot, Billy spread the blanket on the sand, and they lay side-by-side gazing up at the stars in the night sky. Only the sound of the surf and the call of an occasional sea gull joined their solitude as Bonnie Jo rested her head in the crook of his arm. Billy softly kissed her forehead. She looked up at him and smiled.

"I need you, Billy Boy."

His fingers trail across her lips, then her chin and neck, and eventually to the top button of her blouse. The blouse opened almost effortlessly. Carefully Billy traced a line with his fingers down the center of her abdomen, then across to the top of her jeans. She rolled toward him and pulled his head toward hers.

Never had her mouth tasted so sweet, and her body burned with an almost feverish intensity. Pushing her bra upward, Billy freed her breasts and pushed his tongue hard against her glowing nipple. It was an almost frantic and sudden reaction. Nothing mattered, except that he be a part of her, to pull her close and push himself deep inside her.

Bonnie Jo joined him as they hurriedly, almost desperately, shed their remaining clothes. And with the last stitch flung into the sand, Billy pulled her beneath him. They came together as he felt the certainty of his rigid fullness pushing gently into her loins. The heat of her body enveloped him, and she moaned. He pushed his tongue deep into her mouth and she met his pressure, grabbing his buttocks and pulling him all the way inside.

Their love found an easy rhythm as natural as the incoming tide, and the sound of the crashing surf matched the intensity of their passion. Bonnie Jo arched her back, and when it seemed it could get no better, she suddenly shuddered and buried her face against his neck as they found freedom from the tensions that had tormented them, body and soul, all those years.

They lay in one another's bodies for a very long time before Billy gently rolled onto his back and stared up into the universe. The Milky Way was a white veil of diamonds painted across the night sky. He was finally free of the past. He had found life again, and it was here beside Bonnie Jo. He drifted into a peaceful trance.

After a while he rolled on his side and looked at her. Her eyes were closed, and contentment filled her face. She lay there as the ocean breeze feathered through her hair. Bonnie Jo's breasts glowed soft and round in the starlight, rising and falling with each breath. Billy felt it again, a growing warmth in his groin and he drew the blanket around them, pulling her close.

"Again?" she said in a hoarse whisper.

"We've got to make up for a lot of lost time."

And he pushed deep inside her with the certainty that they would be one forever.

31

RAEFORD'S MVP

Billy and Bonnie Jo had been reunited for nearly two months when they flew into Memphis for the Raeford class reunion. Social gatherings were never his forte, and this reunion was going to require Billy's best efforts. He remembered being about as enthusiastic when the army told him he was going to Fort Polk for AIT, but Bonnie Jo was excited and he didn't want to disappoint her. She had purchased a new dress, and he gazed over her shoulder into the mirror as he buttoned up the back.

"Yea, though I walk unto the valley of the shadow of the Lizard-crowd, I shall fear no evil, because BJ Parker is my shepherd, and she leadeth me down the kudzu path."

"Boy, you are so silly."

He grinned at her reflection in the mirror. "Damn, you look good tonight."

She smiled. "You look pretty handsome yourself."

The sun had set by the time they drove into Raeford that evening, and Bonnie Jo seemed totally relaxed, but Billy was nervous. He wanted only to get through the evening without saying something that embarrassed Bonnie Jo. As he turned into the school parking lot, she pulled down the sun visor and used the mirror on the back to freshen her lipstick.

Raeford was never a place for fancy formal wear, but it had stepped up a notch for this night. The invitation read, "Strictly Formal." There was even a footnote describing formal-wear as a coat and tie or an evening dress, a message Billy figured wasn't entirely unwarranted in Raeford. The intent was respectable, but as he opened the car door 'formal' took its first setback when he caught a whiff of cattle manure from the pasture behind the school.

Wrangler Jeans and Lynyrd Skynyrd T-shirts were probably more appropriate, except he was on his best behavior. He was wearing a suit and tie Bonnie Jo had suggested for him, and he had to admit, he did look pretty sharp, but Bonnie Jo was a knockout. She wore a sparkling evening gown and dangling diamond earrings, and her million-dollar smile completed the perfect ensemble. With her natural beauty and poise, she made 'formal' look easy and comfortable.

Several people recognized Billy as soon as he and Bonnie Jo walked into the school gymnasium, but no one seemed to recognize her until she signed in and filled out her nametag. Word spread like a wave through the crowd.

"BJ Parker is here."

"BJ Parker is here."

"BJ Parker is here."

The class president, several jocks and some of the cheerleaders arrived inside of a minute, clustering around her. Her new entourage failed to make the connection between Bonnie Jo and Billy, and he was brushed aside as they led her away. She glanced back at him, but he winked and put his finger across his lips. Incognito worked for him.

Billy wandered over to the makeshift bar at the old concession stand and ordered up a double-shot of Wild Turkey on ice.

"No Turkey," the bartender said, "but we have plenty of Coke and some lemonade punch."

It was destined to be a long night. Billy turned and looked about for someone he might know. Several faces were familiar, but he was suffering mental gridlock with most of their names until he spotted two he remembered. It was Cindy and Judy, his two visitors back at the VA hospital. They were standing across the gym with several more of the old cheerleaders casting furtive glances his way. They had already spotted him.

Billy smiled and gave them a coy wave, but their body language quickly became stilted as they looked away. Poor things. He felt bad for them. They were probably still pissed about the ass-chewing Jackie had given them.

The first thing to come off was the fancy suit coat. He tossed it over the back of a metal folding chair and loosened his tie. The gym still had the musty odor of sweating basketball players and phys-ed classes from years past. As people crossed the hardwood floor, their footsteps and voices echoed up into the steel support beams high overhead. Somewhere beyond the lights, in the shadows of his memory, Billy could still hear that old pervert Roper yelling as they ran endless laps.

The band was playing songs from the sixties, and a mild nostalgia ate at him as he sipped his lemonade punch. That's when he heard a soft female voice behind him.

"Hey, Billy."

It was Sissy, the girl who had given him his masters in female anatomy. She was wearing her trademark double-coating of cosmetics, but looked as good, or maybe better than he remembered. He reached to shake her hand, but she brushed his arm aside and embraced him with a hug and a kiss. As she pressed her hot breast against his chest, he thought for a moment she intended on picking up where they'd left off years ago.

And when she finally let go, Billy felt himself blushing as he looked around to see if Bonnie Jo had noticed.

Thank god, she was still surrounded by her newfound groupies. Sissy wrapped her arm around Billy's waist, and turned to the man standing behind her.

"This is my husband, Doctor John Williams," she said.

"Nice to meet you, sir," Billy said, extending his hand.

"Please, call me John," he said.

Nice fellow, Billy thought. It was a wonder he hadn't punched his lights out after the hug he got from Sissy.

"Medical doctor?" Billy asked.

"Ugh, yes."

"What's your specialty?"

"Gynecology."

Maintaining his best poker-face, Billy nodded, and Sissy squinched up her lips at her husband as if he'd committed some major faux pas. The good doctor shrugged, and Billy sensed the broken promise that had just occurred. Sissy turned and looked away, as a crimson blush crept from beneath her makeup, down her neck. Sissy Conroy and a gynecologist went together like a hand in a sterile latex glove, but who was he to judge? She didn't do it alone, and he could have ended up with her as easily as he had with Bonnie Jo. His younger years were lived with a reckless abandonment of rational thought. No, he couldn't judge her from the promontory where his shattered glass house stood.

"So where do you guys live?" he asked.

"Alexandria, Virginia," Sissy said. "John graduated from Georgetown."

"Oh," he said. "Georgetown, that's, uh, good. I mean, it's a good school."

"Are you married?" Sissy asked.

Billy grinned stupidly. He had to look stupid because he felt that way. "No, not yet."

"I can't believe that. The biggest Romeo in the class, and you're still single. Did you bring a date?"

"Yeah, she's over there." He pointed to the crowd surrounding Bonnie Jo.

"Oh, she must be a BJ Parker fan. Can you believe we have a famous rock and roll star in our class, and the strangest part is I can't even remember her?"

"Really?" Billy said.

"I looked her up in the yearbook." Sissy's voice dropped to a mock whisper. "You should see her picture back then. She was a fat little thing with glasses. She's really changed."

Billy nodded. "Yea, but she's still the same sweet girl, don't you think?"

"God, Billy! No way. She's BJ Parker, now. You know?"

He smiled. "Yeah, I suppose you're right."

"So, which one is your date?" Sissy asked.

Before Billy could answer, there came a squeal of glee and his name being called by another female voice. He turned to see Barbara Barnes running across the gym floor with arms spread wide. His high school female archenemy actually seemed overjoyed to see him, as she ran up and hugged his neck. It was like they'd been best buds all their lives. He was beginning to have pangs of guilt. Perhaps he was the only one childish enough to carry around the baggage of adolescence.

After another minute or two of small talk, Sissy asked again. "So, which one is your date?" She motioned toward the crowd surrounding Bonnie Jo.

"Bonnie Jo," Billy said.

Her brows dipped. "Who?"

"Her stage name is BJ Parker, but Bonnie Jo is her real name."

"Sure thing, Billy," Barbara said with a sideways smirk. "And I'm here with Jake Tupperman."

Jake was Mr. Football the year they graduated, and it must have still seemed like something great to Barbara.

Sissy turned to her husband. "You have to take him with a grain of salt. Billy always did like to kid around."

Barbara took up the cause. "Seriously, which girl are you *really* with?"

"I am serious," he said. "I'm with Bonnie Jo."

An incredulous smile froze on Barbara's face as she cut her eyes toward Bonnie's mob.

"I don't get it," she said.

"Don't get what?"

"The connection. How did *you* get a date with *her*?" She caught herself. "I mean, how did you two meet or whatever?"

"We went to high school together," Billy said.

Barbara fought her catty nature as she maintained a facade of politeness around her shameless curiosity.

"I know that, dummy, but you always dated girls like Sissy here. Did you *really* know BJ back then?"

"Yeah," he said. "You might say she was one of my *weird* friends."

Barbara didn't miss the jab, but seemed too over-whelmed by the moment.

"Would you like to go over and meet her?" Billy asked.

She didn't answer as she continued staring out of the corner of her eye at the crowd surrounding Bonnie Jo.

"Barbara?"

She snapped out of her trance. "Huh? Oh, yeah, sure!"

Billy excused himself from Sissy and her husband, and walked with Barbara over to the center-court circle where Bonnie Jo's group was gathered. Painted on the gym floor was a wildcat, eyes ablaze and fangs dripping in crazed anger. The Raeford Wildcat had never looked up the skirts of any finer crowd than it did tonight. Of this Billy was certain. The puzzled smile of incredulity re-mained frozen on Barbara's face as they crossed the gym floor.

"Yeah, I suppose you could say Bonnie Jo was a late bloomer," Billy said.

"I'll bet some of those cheerleaders just hate her," Barbara answered.

The remark was vintage "Barbara."

"Why would you say something like that?"

"Well, just look at her, and look at them. If she's a late bloomer, well, some of these early bloomers have already lost a few of their petals, if you know what I mean. Do you know Cassie Andrews already has three kids? And look at her. I'll bet she's gained twenty pounds since we graduated."

"I suppose it happens to us all, if we live long enough," Billy replied. "Bonnie Jo isn't as slim as she was for a long time."

"God," Barbara said, "She doesn't need to be skinny. She's a freaking superstar."

It was tempting to remind her of the abuse she and the others had heaped on Bonnie Jo, but he'd promised to be on his best behavior. Billy made his way through the crowd, and introduced Barbara. Within seconds she was dominating the conversation, reminiscing about imaginary events she had shared with Bonnie Jo. Bonnie Jo cast a knowing glance at Billy, and he smiled as he backed from the crowd. That's when he felt a firm hand on his shoulder. He turned to face none other than Jake Tupperman.

"Man, I'm surprised to see you here tonight," Jake said.

He didn't bother with a "hello", "wassup" or anything resembling a greeting, but Billy wouldn't have expected as much from Jake.

"Hey, Jake, how are you?"

"I take it you haven't heard the news about Marty Macklin?"

"Reckon not," Billy said.

Jake gave him a flat smile. "He's coming up from Starkville tonight, and he said, if you were here, he was going to stomp your ass just for old time's sake."

Assuming it was a joke, Billy laughed.

"Don't laugh," Jake said. "I'm serious."

He looked Billy up and down with the glare of a dueler's second.

"You're not the hundred and sixty-five pound light-weight you were in high school, are you? How much do you weigh, now?"

"Two-oh-five," Billy answered, "but you can't be serious."

"Hey, I'm just passing on what Marty said on the phone."

"Well, we're adults now, and I'm not interested in fighting. I had enough of that in the military."

"Military, huh? Were you in Vietnam?"

"Yeah, for a while."

"Hey, that's totally cool. Did you get into any of the actual fighting?"

Jake was a dumbass, but who else would think going to Vietnam was cool?

"I saw a little action, but it's not worth talking about."

"Oh." Jake looked disappointed. No doubt, he wanted to hear a war story.

"So, what'd you do drive a jeep or something?" A knowing grin crossed his face, and he poked Billy in the chest. "You were a cook, weren't you?"

"I suppose you could say that. I cooked C-rations nearly every day. How the heck did you know?"

"Oh, you just fit the part," Jake said. "I remember how you squealed on Coach Roper. Besides, I know a couple of the old football players, Hardy Miller and Bubba Lykes who went into the National Guard when we graduated. They told me a lot about the Army. The Green Berets and the Marines did most of the fighting in Vietnam. You know?"

"Really?" Billy said.

"Yeah, you should know that." Jake gave him a sideways look. "Are you sure you were really in the military?"

Billy nodded. "Yeah, I was, but I really don't like talking about it."

Jake laughed. "I guess you ain't got much to talk about. You know, I thought about being a Green Beret myself, but I never got around to joining."

"I'm sure you'd have made a good one."

Jake hooked his thumbs inside his belt, and winked at Billy. "Yeah, only a few of us can make the first string."

Billy wanted to knee him in the balls, but decided instead to give Jake one of his vintage Gomer Pyle smiles. The dumbass wasn't worth the squeeze it would take to get an ounce of sense from his pea brain. Billy hoped the Marty Macklin thing was simply more of Jake's mindless blubbering.

There came a commotion from near the gymnasium entrance as a huge man stood framed in the doorway, his head barely clearing the top of the door.

"I'll be damned," Jake said. "It's Raymond Hokes."

Without a parting word, he turned and charged across the gym floor toward Ray, who was immediately mobbed by most of the jocks. Ray was big as a house, and so was the woman with him. She also looked vaguely familiar, and Billy tried to recall where he'd seen her before. She reminded him of someone in particular, but it was too improbable.

Later, after the initial orgy of mini-reunions, Billy found a seat beside Bonnie Jo, and dinner was catered by a local restaurant. Billy mixed his peas with the potatoes and sliced the chicken breast. Bonnie Jo hardly touched hers as people continued coming by the table to talk. Afterward Jake Tupperman walked up on the stage and stood behind the podium.

Jake, by some unknown proxy, had been chosen emcee, and other than Bonnie Jo and Ray, he was the star attraction for the night. Having played junior college football before going on to Ole Miss where he played intermittently for two more years, Jake was the object of envy for most of the jocks and cheerleaders. The bellwether of the Lizards, he grinned and waved as they went berserk with cheers and applause.

"Hey, Hey!" he began. That was the sum of his greeting as he grinned and pointed to some of his old buddies sitting at the tables.

"I guess I've sort of been elected master of ceremonies this evening. That means I get to introduce everybody. First, though, I'm supposed to give a speech."

There was another round of applause.

"Man, are we good or what?" Jake said. "College ball-players, pro ballplayers, we've got it all. Heck, we even got us a rock star in the class. Too bad she couldn't sing country, but we'll take what we can get."

He shot an over-animated wink down at Bonnie Jo.

"It's really great to be back here in the old home town. I guess you guys know I live down in Jackson now, Madison, actually. It's a little nicer place. Got a pretty good insurance business down there. Hey, if you ever need insurance, just give me a call. I've got it all, home, auto, life, and I'm licensed in all of Mississippi. I can take care of *you*.

"Yeah, I had a really great four years playing college ball, especially at Itawamba, and I would have played more at Ole Miss, but I got injured. Just the same, I think I made a good showing for old Raeford High. I got honorable mention most valuable player my second year down at Itawamba, which ain't too shabby, even if I *do* say so myself. I mean we had three other guys on the team that went on to play Division I ball."

There was another burst of applause and hoots of approval from the jocks. Jake held up his hands as if to restrain the already dissipated applause.

"I wasn't the only star. Now, I want to introduce the man who *really* made it big, Raeford's own professional football star, Mister Raymond Hokes."

Billy cringed at the thought of Ray giving a speech, but he opened with a greeting of the class members, their spouses and the faculty. Sounding like a cross between

Vince Lombardi and Junior Samples, his speech was ten times better than Jake's and not near as self-centered. The cultured life in Chicago must have had a positive influence on him. Ray returned to his table and Billy actually found himself nodding in approval.

More class VIPs were introduced, including some of the old teachers, class officers and various other jocks. They also introduced some of the cheerleaders. There was the usual reminiscing, and then it was Bonnie Jo's turn. She was supposed to be the last speaker for the evening, and it was one of the first times Billy ever saw her looking nervous. As she made her way to the podium, the crowd grew silent. She stepped tentatively to the microphone.

"This is indeed flattering and a real honor," she began. "It is very special to be recognized by your peers for your achievements, and I want to thank you all. As you probably know, I've been fortunate, having lived in California and having traveled all over the United States and Europe, but I can still say, like Dorothy in the Wizard of Oz, there's no place like home. Coming back to Mississippi and seeing my friends and neighbors from so long ago has been a truly wonderful experience, and I want to express my sincerest thanks from the bottom of my heart. Thank you, for having me here tonight."

Applause burst forth, echoing around the gym, before slowly dissipating.

"I'm not given to long speeches, so I'd like to take this opportunity to share my time up here with some others who were not mentioned tonight. I feel we often place too much emphasis on celebrity status and not enough on the real contributors to our community and society. How many of you knew we had a rocket scientist in the class?"

There was a ripple of laughter.

"Well, he's not exactly a rocket scientist, but I'm not kidding. He works for NASA and is involved in the space program doing scientific research, research which has resulted in several astounding breakthroughs in the field of aerospace engineering."

A buzz ran through the gym as people began looking around.

"He graduated from MIT with honors, and now works with the space program in Huntsville, Alabama. He has already been recognized nationally for his outstanding accomplishments."

Billy hadn't seen him, but there was no doubt who Bonnie Jo was talking about.

"Ladies and gentlemen, I would like to re-introduce to you our fellow classmate, Melvin Henderson."

Melvin stood up at a table as Bonnie Jo motioned for him to come up on the stage. There he was, old Melvin, looking goofier than ever as he stumbled over his chair and damned near pulled the white linen tablecloth off as he made his way to the podium. He gave a heart-warming and intelligent speech that was followed by a polite round of applause.

In your face, Marty, Billy thought. Old Melvin has more on the ball than you ever will. Although Marty wasn't there to squirm in his guilt, Billy noticed some of the jocks averting their eyes as Melvin returned to his table. Bonnie Jo moved back to the podium.

"I have one other person I want to introduce this evening," she said. "This man has probably given more for the well-being of his community and his country than anyone I know."

She looked directly at him, and Billy felt his face flush. He shook his head in desperation as he mouthed a silent "No."

She winked.

"This person, our fellow classmate, was a paratrooper with the One Hundred and First Airborne Division and a non-commissioned officer who served in combat in Vietnam. He received several of our nation's highest military decorations, including the Bronze Star with an Oak Leaf Cluster and V for valor, the Silver Star, the Purple Heart, as well as the nation's second highest award for heroism, the Distinguished Service Cross. Yes, he was wounded in action while saving one of his men, and he spent over a year recovering from his wounds. Ladies and gentleman, I would like to re-introduce to you my choice for Raeford's Most Valuable Player from the Class of 1968, my personal friend and a *real* hero, our fellow classmate, Billy Coker."

Bonnie Jo met him halfway and gave him a hug. "Knock 'em dead, boy," she whispered.

Bonnie Jo took her seat back at the table below as Billy stepped up to the podium. His mother had always said if you couldn't say something nice, it was better to say nothing at all, and for once that seemed totally achievable. The applause faded into an uncomfortable silence as Billy stood frozen, looking out over the audience. Scores of expectant faces from the past were upturned, waiting for him to speak. His head buzzed, and someone cleared his throat as Billy's eyes sought out Bonnie Jo.

He expected to see her smiling, but her eyes were fixed on him with burning intensity. She had twisted her napkin into a tight roll, and was unconsciously gripping it as if were a lifeline. The gymnasium was quieter than a church at midnight. This speech was going to mean a lot to her, more than it could ever mean to him. He couldn't let her down, but he wasn't going to let himself down, either.

Billy noticed a head turn. It was Jake whispering to Hank Bowers. Jake looked back at Billy, and their eyes met. Billy held his gaze, until Jake looked down at the table and fidgeted with his fork. He flipped it over, then picked it up and stabbed at some imaginary target on the table.

Hank Bowers acted squirrelly, too, as he glanced sideways at nothing in particular. It was showing in their eyes as the Lizards became sheep, growing ill at ease and milling in nervous anticipation. For once, Billy felt not disdain, but pity for these disaffected souls.

"Ladies and gentlemen, distinguished guests, faculty and fellow classmates, I am indeed fortunate and honored to have the opportunity to speak here tonight."

Billy paused as he looked down at Bonnie Jo. She had stopped twisting the napkin, and her face seemed to relax as she smiled up at him. More than anything, it was her look of relief that told him she was happy he hadn't greeted them as jocks, jackals and judgmental jerks. Now, he had to follow through.

"I suppose it has been my long journey back here tonight that has rewarded me with the understanding of the things I learned while here at Raeford High. Perhaps many of you have achieved that same understanding. These events we call 'class reunions' enable us to look back through the filter of so many years, as we come together to revisit the experiences we shared. We have returned to this place, where we spent time learning and growing together, to rekindle old acquaintances and reminisce about old times. And as trivial as they may now seem, those relationships and events were an important part of who we have become as adults.

"If I could say anything meaningful tonight, I suppose it would be how human nature lets us forget the bad times and leads us to think about the good things in our lives. Yes, Raeford High provided me a learning experience in many ways. It was here that I learned the most about myself. Many of you may believe the lessons we learned from our textbooks were the most important things, but I believe it was the things we learned from one another about human nature. These weren't always the most pleasant experiences, but they were the ones that best prepared us for the adult world.

"If the year I spent in Vietnam was comparable to a doctorate on human nature, I can honestly say that I would never have understood, or perhaps even survived, had it not been for what I learned here at Raeford High. And it was because of many of you here tonight that I was prepared for that experience. With that said, I want to express my heartfelt thanks and appreciation to each and every one of you, faculty and students, for the experiences we shared so many years ago. Never had I imagined how useful those lessons would become once I stepped into the adult world. After the challenges here at Raeford High, I was well prepared for Vietnam."

Thanking Bonnie Jo and the crowd, Billy told them how he had always known they would someday be a star-studded group. As he turned to go back to his seat, there was a light ripple of applause, and Bonnie Jo came up to meet him. They walked together from the podium, but there came a sudden commotion. Ray Hokes had stood up amongst the tables. His massive form loomed in the candlelight as he began applauding.

Slowly at first, his huge hands came together, making a ponderous thudding that echoed throughout the gymnasium. He continued for several seconds before Melvin Henderson stood and joined him, and before long the rest of the crowd followed. Even the Lizards began standing out of embarrassment as the entire gymnasium echoed with whistles and applause.

"Not bad for such a short speech," Bonnie Jo whispered in his ear. "They're giving you a standing ovation. Now, wave at them."

As they walked back to their seats, Billy turned and gave his best Rose Bowl Parade wave. When the applause settled, the band began playing God Bless America, and it wasn't half-bad, even on electric guitars. As they finished, Raymond Hokes appeared. He was pulling the big woman behind him, but Billy still wasn't quite sure who she was.

"Billy Coker," he said. "By damned, I can't believe it's already been this long since I saw you."

The sonofabitch was even bigger than he'd been in high school. They shook hands, and Ray's grip made a sheet metal press seem like child's play, but Billy held his own.

"You're the man who changed my whole life, and I want to thank you," Ray said. "If it hadn't been for you, I'd have never hooked up with my little Roberta Ann here."

It *was* her, Roberta Ann Hoefstra, not as ugly as he remembered, but definitely as big. She grinned shyly, but Billy wasn't fooled for a minute. This was a woman who could knock a buffalo to its knees with her bare knuckles.

"We got married and got us two big ol' boys, and we're happier than a family of coons in a persimmon tree."

Billy felt the grin stretching across his face as his teeth clenched tightly. He glanced back at Bonnie Jo. Her smile was relaxed, and she was cool and calm as ever. She always seemed better able to accept these things, but Billy was about to bust a gut—a family of coons in a persimmon tree? Ray and Roberta Ann had to be the life of the party in Chicago.

"And you a war hero, why it don't get no better than that," Ray said. "Curtis told me how you carried him down off that mountain. Look man, I just want to tell you something. If there is ever anything, I mean anything at all that I can do, you just call me. Okay? I mean it. You just let me know."

As the conversation tapered off, Billy realized the night had turned out better than he could have imagined. Bonnie Jo had danced with a dozen different guys, but she sat out the slow dances with him at the table, waiting, since he'd promised her at least one slow dance. As each song began she would ask if he was ready, but each time he said, "Not yet." Time was running out.

Around ten-forty-five, Billy noticed one of the women sitting near the doorway pointing his way. She was directing a guy in jeans and a black cowboy hat. The band had taken a break, and Billy and Bonnie Jo stood talking with some other folks when the man came toward them across the gym floor. As he drew closer, Billy recognized him. It was Marty Macklin.

Billy had convinced himself that Jake really was joking. No one in his right mind would actually do something that stupid at a class reunion. A buzz rolled through the crowd, and the room grew noticeably quieter as Macklin stood facing Billy. Apparently, the rumor had spread.

Marty looked smaller than he had in high school but a little broader in the shoulders and still hard as rock. Someone had said he was a farm manager for a corporate cattle operation down near Starkville. Marty looked the part, with snakeskin cowboy boots, a black plaid western shirt and a large silver belt buckle. Turning, he tossed his big black Stetson on the floor.

Billy held out his hand to greet him, "Hey Marty, how's it going?"

Marty glared at Billy's hand as he locked his thumbs behind his belt.

"I reckon we got some unfinished business, Coker."

His eyes were blood-shot, probably from an afternoon spent getting soused. Loaded with liquid courage, he was ready to fight. Bonnie Jo tried to step forward, but Billy held his arm across her chest.

"No, Bonnie. Stay back."

Ray Hokes was coming their way, as well, but Billy held up his hand and signaled for him to stop. It seemed the gymnasium itself was holding its breath as Macklin stood there in front of Billy still wanting to be the high school bully. Billy wanted to turn and walk away. There would be no loss of face, but he was afraid Macklin would interpret it as weakness and jump him.

"Let's go," Bonnie Jo begged.

Marty displayed his trademarked leer, with his mouth upturned at one corner. Drunk and unpredictable, his eyes were narrow and hard.

"Marty has a decision to make," Billy said.

"You want to try to sucker-punch me again?" Marty asked.

"Marty, I regret that I had to do that, but to answer your question, no, I don't want to punch you again. I made up my mind a few years ago when I got back from Vietnam, to never again fight for something that wasn't worth dying for. So you're out of luck, but I won't let you walk on me, either."

Jake stepped from the crowd and began whispering in Marty's ear. Marty's eyes remained locked on Billy as Jake put his arm across Marty's shoulders. After a few seconds, Jake finished and stepped back, motioning for Marty to follow. The gymnasium was so quiet Billy could hear the big trucks passing by on the highway out front. No one in the gymnasium spoke, and the silence echoed stark and empty in the rafters high above.

The corner of Marty's mouth twitched slightly, and he blinked. Billy breathed a sigh of relief. Marty had seen the light at the end of the tunnel. He had seen it shining brightly and suddenly realized that it wasn't the freedom of daylight at the other end, but a locomotive coming his way.

Jake motioned again for Marty to join him, but Marty held up his hand as a smile slowly filled his face.

"I can't believe you fell for that, Coker. Can't you take a joke?"

With that he held out his hand. Billy leaned forward and shook it cautiously as the crowd gave a communal sigh of relief. There came a commotion as some of the idiot cheerleaders began cheering and clapping, but their applause quickly tittered into silence. It was over. Marty turned, picked up his hat and walked away. He joined Jake and the rest of the Lizards in their corner of the gymnasium.

A few minutes later Marty slipped quietly out a side door. Several cheerleaders and Jake waved him goodbye, and Billy sensed the epiphany the Biff Lomans of the class had just experienced. They had come to realize they were no longer, or perhaps, never were the center of the universe.

The band announced the last song of the night, and Billy turned to Bonnie Jo. It was do-or-die time, one last hurdle. He had to dance for the first time in years. She grasped Billy's arm as the bandleader talked into the microphone.

"This is a special request from BJ Parker. I'm not sure that we have the talent to do it justice, but our keyboard and fiddle players say they do. So, for Miss BJ Parker, my fellow band members and I present this song just for you, Floyd Cramer's *Last Date*."

She turned and raised her face to Billy's. A slight film of moisture gathered in her eyes as the music began.

"You women come up with some of the sappiest ideas," he said.

She wrapped her arms around him. "Oh Billy Boy, I love you. I've loved you ever since that night, and I'll always love you."

A tear hung precariously at the bottom of her eye, and he carefully pushed it away with his thumb.

"Well," he said. "That being the case, I suppose we should make it official. What do you think?"

"Official?"

She seemed dazed as Billy took her by the hand and led her to the center of the gym floor.

"Yes, official," he said.

She wiped a tear from her cheek and cocked her head quizzically to one side.

"Will you marry me, Bonnie Jo?"

Her eyes widened, and filled with more tears as he pulled her close. She buried her head against his chest. "Billy, oh Billy."

"I'll take that as a 'yes,' and until we find a ring to put on your finger, you can hang on to this for collateral."

He took the Saint Sebastian medal from around his neck and put it around Bonnie Jo's. Holding her close, they danced, and for the first time in years Billy saw the future and felt the music in his heart.

EPILOGUE

Billy turned the rental car into the long driveway, and Bonnie Jo studied the old swing as they drove past. It had been a week since the reunion, and they had made another two hour drive down to Raeford from Memphis. As if celebrating the beautiful autumn day, the giant oaks in the front yard were ablaze with their red and yellow leaves fluttering in a mild breeze.

"It looks like someone might have been expecting us," Bonnie Jo said. "The swing has a new coat of paint."

"I just hope the owner goes along with this."

Bonnie Jo smiled. "Don't worry. If she's a woman, she'll understand."

Billy parked the car and reached into the back seat to get the record album.

"Here's your bribe gift. Want me to go with you to the door?"

"Sure."

A few moments later, they stood in anticipation as the door clicked and opened. A woman, perhaps forty-ish, pushed her hair back with one hand.

"Yes?"

"Hi. I'm sorry to bother you, ma'am, but we didn't have a phone number to call ahead. My name is Bonnie Jo. I lived here when I was a little girl, and I was hoping—"

"You're BJ Parker. They told us you lived here when you were a child." The woman put her hand over her mouth. "Oh, my."

Bonnie Jo clutched Billy's hand. "This is my fiancée, Billy Coker, and I was hoping you would let us sit out there on the swing under the oak tree. I mean, just for a little while. You see—"

"Of course you can."

"We used to sit out there when we were in high school, and we just wanted to do it again, you know?"

"Yes. Yes. Of course, but can I go get my daughter first? Please? She's up in her room, and she just loves your music."

The woman quickly returned with the girl. An obviously self-conscious early-teen, the girl stood wide-eyed beside her mother.

Bonnie Jo extended her hand. "Hello, I'm Bonnie Jo Parker, and I brought something for you. What's your name?"

The girl extended her hand but seemed fixated as she remained silent.

"Her name is Amy, and I think she's a little awestruck at the moment," the mother said.

Billy gave Bonnie Jo the marker, and she autographed the record album. "Here you go."

She handed the girl the album. "Billy and I are going out there to sit on your swing for a while. After that we're going into town to get a hamburger at the Dairy Queen. If your mom says it's okay, perhaps you can go with us."

The girl grabbed her mother's arm. "Oh, please, please mama, can I? We can go to the mall later. Please?"

After the meeting, Billy led Bonnie Jo by the hand down to the swing where they sat in silence. Neither seemed willing to be the first to speak, but after a while Bonnie Jo turned and looked expectantly at him. He reached into his pocket and retrieved the small white box. Opening it, he removed the ring, a large blue diamond solitaire. He took her hand and gently slid the ring onto her finger then looked up into her eyes. They had grown moist.

"You're not going to cry again are you?"

"I can't help it, Billy Boy." She looked upward where cottony wisp of clouds floated in a brilliant azure sky. "I was always hopeful, but I was never quite sure. Now I know. There really are islands in the sky."

The End

A FINAL NOTE TO THE READER

If you enjoyed this story, your written review of *Raeford's MVP* will be greatly appreciated. By posting your comments on the retail site where you purchased the book and on Goodreads.com, you can tell others what you liked about this book. This is the best way to spread the word to other readers. Also, feel free to share your comments with your friends on Facebook, and check out other books by Rick DeStefanis, including *Melody Hill* and the award winning novel, *The Gomorrah Principle* at *http://amzn.to/1QE6tfP.*

ABOUT THE AUTHOR

Writer, photographer, and avid outdoorsman Rick DeStefanis lives in northern Mississippi with his wife of forty years, Janet. While his nonfiction writing, such as *The Philosophy of Big Buck Hunting*, focuses on his outdoor excursions, it is his military expertise that informs his novels. His works, *Raeford's MVP*, *Melody Hill*, and the award-winning novel *The Gomorrah Principle*, all draw from his experiences as a paratrooper and infantry light weapons specialist serving from 1970 to 1972 with the 82nd Airborne Division. Learn more about DeStefanis and his books at http://www.rickdestefanis.com/, or you can visit Rick on Facebook at *Rick DeStefanis, Books and Photography*

GLOSSARY

AFVN: Armed Forces Vietnam Radio Network

Airborne: The United States Army's designation for its paratroops

AK-47: Russian-made assault rifle, standard weapon used by North Vietnamese

Claymore: American made mine that could be directionally aimed and wire detonated

CO: Commanding Officer

CP: Command Post, field location where the commander is located

C-Rations: Combat field rations for individual use (US military)

Chopper: Military slang for a helicopter

DEROS: Date of Estimated Return from Overseas Service

F-4 Phantom: American fighter bomber jet often used in close support for ground troops

HE: High Explosive, usually refers to artillery rounds

Kit Carson: Vietnamese Scouts employed by American Forces

LRRP: Long Range Reconnaissance Patrol, often referred to as "Lurps."

LT: Slang for Lieutenant

LZ: Landing Zone, a place usually designated for landing helicopters

M-16: US Military Assault Rifle

M-60: US Military .762 mm machine gun often referred to as "The Sixty"

Mini-Gun: Essentially a multi-barrel Gatling style weapon with an extreme rate of fire

MOS: Military Occupational Specialty

NCO: Non-Commissioned officer (The sergeants)

NVA: North Vietnamese Army, referencing the well-trained regular enemy troops

OCS: Officer Candidate School

PRC-25: The standard US portable field radio carried by ground troops in Vietnam

Puff The Magic Dragon: Either a C-47 or C-130 aircraft armed with infrared detection capabilities and multiple weapons systems used for ground support, normally around firebases

RPG: Rocket Propelled Grenade, used extensively with lethal results by enemy ground forces in Vietnam

R&R: Rest and Recuperation, refers to leave granted for this purpose

RTO: Radio Telephone Operator, the guy who carried the radio, usually a PRC-25

TAC: Tactical Air Cover, often referred to as "Tac-air" by ground troops

VC: Vietcong, civilian communist insurgents in Vietnam

Willy Peter: Military slang for the White Phosphorous Grenade, often used to assist enemy combatants in vacating tunnel complexes

Made in the USA
Las Vegas, NV
09 February 2024